J. Robert Lennon lives in New Y_____ t of *Falling Stars*, *The Funnies* and C_____ nta Books.

'A recent favourite of mine. A phantasmagoria of American paranoia and self-loathing in the person of a deranged but somehow good-hearted middle-aged mail carrier in steep decline, the voice of the book hums with a kind of chipper angst as the character careens from one humiliation to the next. The book felt like a compulsive bad dream, impossible to shake' Jonathan Lethem, *Daily Telegraph*

'Lennon's language is kinetic and unpretentious, bulging with mimetic enthusiasm . . . his casual, slapped-on metaphors are often funny. A generous novel with some outstanding and funny individual scenes. It is also a grand achievement in terms of narrative organization. Lennon develops an intricate pattern of overlapping themes: communication and voyeurism, isolation and responsibility' *London Review of Books*

'What does get the pulse racing is the sheer quality of the writing and the depth of the message . . . written in the clearest prose and with a maniacal energy throbbing in the background . . . Lennon leads us from tragedy to black comedy and back again . . . it is here that Lennon shows the depth of his talent. Triumphantly, in the end, he is the mailman with a message for all of us' *Herald (Glasgow)*

'At his best, Lennon puts you in mind of John Updike's Harry Angstrom visiting Ben Jonson's *Bartholomew Fair*' *Guardian*

'An excellent and highly readable novel . . . J. Robert Lennon has written a moving and gently celebratory book' *Times Literary Supplement*

'Although I felt depressed when I finished *Mailman*, I recognized this was because Lennon had done his job well, revealing the endless sadness of everyday life' Matt Thorne, *Independent*

'One of the finest writers in the USA . . . *Mailman* zips along with great brio and black wit' *GQ*

'What better way to depict small-town America than through the eyes and odd actions of a mad mailman? While it's amazing that it hasn't been done before, Lennon manages to pull it off hilariously' *Esquire*

J. Robert Lennon

MAILMAN

Granta Books
London

Granta Publications, 2/3 Hanover Yard, Noel Road, London N1 8BE

First published in Great Britain by Granta Books 2003
This edition published by Granta Books 2004
First published in the US by W. W. Norton & Company, Inc 2003

A CIP catalogue record for this book is available from the British Library.

3 5 7 9 10 8 6 4 2

Printed and bound in Great Britain by Mackays of Chatham PLC

To all my dear mailmen,
I thank you.

He goes off whistling, loving the weather.

Photons beat on his broad chest,

neutrinos penetrate black leather and swamp his toenails.

There is a secret to life, but he hasn't delivered it yet.

—John Updike, "The Mailman"

CONTENTS

—

MAILMAN

PART ONE

—

ONE

An American Mailman

———

So God, the story goes, made the earth. There was nothing much to it, at first: the firmament steaming gray, with maybe a smear of slime upon its featureless face. A blank canvas. God looked it over, decided it would do, and went ahead with the detail work. He had to grip it with one hand—those huge sweaty digits—while the other daubed and dotted; and as this second hand applied the final touches—to the Amazon, the Himalayas, the great forests and seas, the plains and the steppes, the lowlands and snowcaps—the first one, forgotten, worked itself into the land, heaving up knobbled muddy hills in the soft rock, gouging dank trenches. And when the Creator was through admiring His work, He flipped over this virgin world and noticed what His giant mitt had done, and figured, well, this might look all right, if I filled it with water. And in this manner the Finger Lakes were born.

But if the Finger Lakes are the handprint of the Creator (never mind, for now, the implications of a seven-fingered God), then this one, Onteo Lake, the longest and deepest, is the middle finger: an unwitting message from earth's inhabitants to intelligent life every-where: the largest bird-whipping in the known universe. Or maybe it is God's message to us, His signal that He has moved on to greener pastures. Maybe this was a practice world, hastily executed and tossed into the galaxy's backyard, like a houseplant left for dead. Maybe it wasn't supposed to take root, to filthily flourish. Maybe when springtime arrives in the universe, the Creator will notice it, quietly chuckle, and put it out of its misery.

At any rate, if the lakes are God's fingers, then this town—Nestor, New York—is the imprint of His big reeking palm, these crisscrossing streets its loops and whorls, this highway—Route 13—its heart line, which seems so strong, so clear and broad, but which finds its sudden terminus a couple towns away, as if Nestor were the outer limits of His love, a shabby outpost of divine oversight.

If so, Mailman considers, it's a fitting myth for Nestor, a town convinced that it is both the center of the universe and its armpit, depending on whom you talk to and when. A town both arrogant and self-loathing, dumpy and glorious. A college town, a working class town. Fingers of God, indeed. At least the perp left prints.

It's morning, the first Friday in June, the year 2000. That's what they say, "the year 2000," dignifying the digits with an article, as if the year is a killer, a tyrant, as in "The Impaler," or "The Terrible." Mailman is driving north, uphill, on 13, that doomed arterial, with the lake spread out like a slug on the left, a forested crag of crumbling shale rising on his right. He drives a small car, a Ford Escort hatchback from the days when Ford was a joke, maybe the worst car ever made, this little blue hedgehog half made of plastic, with an engine that pants and whines as it climbs. But it is not his real car: his real car is his mail truck, parked at the new main P.O., which is four miles from here, on the edge of town. He experiences a brief *frisson* thinking about the truck, about slipping into its duct-tape-mended leather bucket seat and sliding his hands over its oversized steering wheel; he imagines the letters he'll fill it with and the secrets they harbor, and his mood lifts accordingly.

The Escort will make it, but at half the speed limit. Giant jeeps and pickups barrel by, dwarfing their single occupants, men in neckties heading for Syracuse or out past the city limits to their drone jobs in the tech industry. What's a lone man need with a giant machine like that? The Escort stinks but it is proportionally correct, built on a human scale. I control my car, Mailman thinks; not the other way around. As if in agreement, the car downshifts, shudders; in the back seat, his pile of broken office supplies rearranges itself with an amiable clatter. To drown out the racket he switches on the radio. Stock reports: Nikkei, Hang Seng, FTSE. What difference does it make if some fatcat in Yokohama is dumping salmon futures? None at all, unless it gets put on the radio. People care about what they're told to care about.

Now a chipper announcement: Get your NestorFest button today! It's the annual self-congratulatory citywide jerkoff, starting this afternoon: City Square full of longhairs hawking their cheesy doodads out of plywood booths, restaurateurs setting up greasepits on the sidewalk, experimental theater groups emoting in intersections, tiedyed shirts and wormy local fruits and everywhere a plague of little kids. The Chinese students bumbling around like junebugs. The stumpy carrothead mayor and his annual address: "It's all about community." Well, leave me out of it. Give me a quiet orderly town, students away for the summer, no lines at the coffee shops, low volume in the mailbags, cloudy days when the swelter gives way to thunder and in an hour all's clear and cool and the yards are covered with dead branches and old birdnests blown out of trees. Regular life. No parades, no block parties, no event tents or boat races or Taste of Nestor or Rhododendron Daze. Leave well enough alone.

The road levels out, the Escort accelerates. Mailman hazards another glance at the lake, ablaze now with sunlight. Not bad: maybe God knew what He was doing. Down at the pier they're stringing bunting for the sailrace, all the way up Onteo Lake to Reevesport and back; the finish is sometime on Sunday. Last year the winner got in at two a.m. and was disqualified because nobody was around to confirm it. Poor sucker. Not that he feels bad for the lake-house dock-rat crowd. They love it here in the summer with the boats and the horses, but as soon as the first snow comes, when the first temperature inversion traps the pulpmill stink in the valley, they're off to Vail for their ski vacation or Bermuda for a couple of weeks in the sun. Or they live elsewhere in winter, the academics doing double duty at NYTech (the Ivy League's Geek Annex) and the University of, say, Hawaii. They call it "dividing their time." "I divide my time between Nestor"—or since they all live north of here in Willard where the property tax is lower, they say *the Nestor area*—"and Southern California." Or: "We love the Nestor area but we *winter* on the South Carolina coast." Winter is only a verb if you're rich.

Radio says *Tech Minute*. Radio says *smart toaster*, says *wearable computing*.

Up ahead, past the airport Radisson Suites, past the billboard for the defunct BBQ Chop Stop ("A place for families. A place for you," he has read daily for five years), is the turn for the P.O. The traffic lights are fitted with flashers, as on broadcast towers; this intersection is the highest point in Onteo County. Mailman pulls onto the Wayne Road extension, passes the UPS and FedEx offices, whips them both the finger. Well, maybe not FedEx: those guys are all right, they're sullen and ugly and don't give a shit what you think of them. They've got the quasi-governmental name and the national colors, so there's that quality of bureaucratic slovenliness, except without any of the oversight of the USPS. But UPS is another story. All those handsome craggy wiry-haired men, not a one of them over 35, hopping up on your porch in their smirks and brown suits and handing you the forty-pound computer to sign your name on. Smug bastards! And the women!, these busty blonde hiker types with the fine hairs on their arms and legs, the ponytails and just the slightest sheen of sweat on their brows, the way they pant while you sign, and the manly "thanks" they leave you with, their butts bunching under the plain-wrapper slacks as they sprint back to the truck and throw it in gear. God help me, just leave it on the stoop!

Nobody would blame you for mistaking the new P.O. for a high school gymnasium. Painted cinder blocks in back, industrial stucco in front, the Letter Carrier's Motto spelled out above the door, already decimated by weather: RAIN NOR H AT NOR OOM OF NIGH . . . It's ten to seven now. Mailman parks in the rear, as far from the building as possible: he needs the exercise. He takes note of the other cars, who's here and who isn't yet. The carrier supervisor, Len Ronk, is not. Big head, big face, big glasses, skinny little body, always says "your basic." "This is your basic arch-supported shoe here, go out and get yourself a few pairs." Punch clock switches on at seven, but Ronk doesn't come in until seven-thirty. Why? Because he doesn't have to. Why not? Because he's in charge.

Mailman hops up onto the loading dock where the mail trays are stacked. He's late-ish so most of the good rigid plastic ones are taken, only the corrugated kind left, but he tends to stash a few of the good ones behind the lousy ones, and they're here this morning, right where he left them, wedged in next to the orange support beam. He carries them through the bay door and is nearly flattened by a mail handler clearing wheeled cages out of the way.

"Whoop. Sorry, Albert."

"No harm," says Mailman. Public menace, that one.

The carriers are clustered around the clock as always, waiting for it to make the plasticky thud it makes when it turns on. They're all holding punch cards and styrofoam cups of coffee and talking a mile a minute, cattle waiting for their turn at the bolt. The building looks like a gym on the inside too, with the letter lines spread out over the floor where the carriers sort, and an enclosed catwalk extending along the walls above them and across the middle, just over their heads. The catwalk belongs to the postal inspectors, the Postal Service's cabal of regulatory enforcers: every six feet there's a one-way window where they can peer out. You never know when they're in there; you never see them. Sometimes you hear their slow footsteps, if you happen to be under the catwalk when they pass overhead. Like a goose on your grave.

Are they there as a matter of course, or only when someone's suspected of something? Nobody knows. What do they wear? Suits? Uniforms? Do they carry weapons? Uncertain. Those who have seen them have only seen them for a few seconds, and remember little: a sideburn, a mole. They can come out anytime and flash their badges and cuff you and drive you to Elmira and interrogate you until you break. They can imprison you. That is, if you've done anything wrong. Like what?

Stealing mail. Opening mail. Destroying mail.

You hear stories. Entrapment. Blackmail. A janitor nailed for keeping a postcard he found in the trash. A gay postmaster, framed in a coin-stealing scheme, shamed and run out of town. Carriers strong-armed and made to confess. Rejects from the CIA, the FBI, would-be agents too blunt, too dumb, too impulsive for those august bodies, they come to the Postal Service, where their short tempers are given long leashes, for the purpose of spooking the rank and file.

The punch clock turns on. The cards are punched, a regular rhythm, a march. Howdies all around. Mailman heads for his cubby, where the raw mail awaits. He's got the same setup as everybody else: shelves on three sides with slots for each address; street and number printed clearly underneath, his route in miniature all around him. He sorts with fast hands, watching the day take shape underneath them, taking note of stuff he might want to read later. Light mail this time of year, no holidays (Father's Day coming but the dad volume is a drop in the bucket compared to the mom volume); summer catalogs were a couple weeks back. And most of the students are gone, they've stopped shipping their junk home. The population has dropped by half. These kids are worth a king's ransom to Nestor, of course; their generation has no sense of restraint or taste and they buy whatever they can get their hands on and need a whole new wardrobe every three weeks—but everyone agrees, it's nice to see them go. Back to Long Island, back to Connecticut, back to Park Avenue. Korea, Malaysia, Bhutan. Singapore.

Every year one or two of them cracks. Most of them from NYTech, where the pressure is high; a few from Nestor College, on the opposite hill (most popular majors: television production, recreation management, undecided/general). Somebody goes missing—pals say he never showed up at the party, or went off by himself, or sounded funny on the phone yesterday—and the parents are summoned, and they come to Nestor for the search. Search: because in this feel-good burg of crashing waterfalls and majestic gorges, the way to do yourself in is to jump. And when they jump—usually in midspring, after the midterms and heavy rains—they land on the rocks and are washed away, to nestle in a bramble or beach on an outcrop or plunge into the murky lake. For nights afterward you can hear the shouts of searchers, the rescue choppers buzzing the creeks, and you read in the paper quote after quote about how it makes no *sense*, he was so *happy* all the time, there's no *way* she would kill herself, such a kind person, such a giving person, so loving. But of course nice people off themselves too.

Mailman's thoughts have generated a toxic cloud that passes between him and this sunny day. He is reminded of a woman he knew; his sorting hands are frozen. But enough: it's Festival time! Lighten up!

At least he's off the Collegeville route. Collegeville generally goes to the PTFs—Part Time Floaters, or, more accurately, People They Fuck. On call at all hours, nastiest routes, filling in for other people's vacations. But they're kids, young guys (or women, more of them these days, which Mailman has powerfully mixed feelings about), they can handle it. No, Mailman works downtown, mixed-race, mixed-use, high-density. Gets to walk almost the whole way, with only a few quick truck trips. He's got something the other carriers lack, something he's saved and maintained from the old days: his cart: a handy little three-wheeled jobber with pouches the size of trash bags on either side, which he can literally stuff with mail. He can finish his route by eleven-thirty, on a good day, depending on how much time he spends poring over the mail he borrows from his customers.

He finishes sorting. Clock says eight. He lays out his trays, bands and tucks, stacks them up, grabs a wheeled cage, loads it and heads for the parking lot.

It's a hell of a nice morning. The Festival freaks are going to have a blast. Blue sky still pink at the edges, with fluffy little white clouds more decorative than meteorological chugging across it. His truck is parked next to the light pole which more than once he's grazed returning in the afternoon. Nothing a little white paint wouldn't fix: the first time, he told Ronk about it and let himself get shouted at; they sent a temp out there with a piece of sandpaper and a paintbrush. Second time he figured out where the paint was kept and did the job himself. Passed inspection a couple months later, and why not? It was better work than the kid had done the first time. He loads the truck and climbs in (ahhh!) and his hair stands on end as he revs the engine and squeaks out of his spot. Sometimes on mornings like this he thinks that, if he had it all to do again, he'd actually choose to deliver the goddam mail for a living. Generally he recovers his senses by ten o'clock.

It's a different trip down North Hill: better wheels, better vista. He grabs the inside lane and overtakes Volvos and Subarus as the whole of the town comes into view below: the lake crowded now with boats, NYTech on North Hill's far end, Nestor College on South, the prison on West. Clumped around the lake and mossing its way up the banks is civilization, the poor and hip in the valley, rich and entrenched on the mountainsides, institutional on the summits. He sinks into it with the truck rumbling around him. On the radio is Mad Lester's AM morning show. *Mornin', everybody, it's another WNYT Fab Friday comin' at ya!* Lester's talking to Saul Bean, reviver, maintainer, and tireless booster of NestorFest—

. . . and we're hoping to see everybody out there today, Lester, there's an expanded food court this year, and there'll be music from the Singers With Attitude and the Cornucopia of Crafts and face-painting and mask-making for the kids, and tonight the fire

*department's going to set the old Chapin-Caldwell house on fire
and put it out again, as a demonstration . . .*

—so quick Lester can't stop him, his voice bright and desperate as a
parakeet's.

Mailman knows Saul Bean's desperation all too well: he has delivered Bean's love letters to Minna Combs, a twig-skinny anti-development liberal on City Council who used to meet Mailman in the yard to
intercept the mail before her husband could get a look at it. Poor
woman, home for lunch from her job at the law office, disheveled and
sweating through her dress from a long morning of pro-bono
bailouts, and just about every day for a month there was a shakily ball-
pointed letter from Saul Bean. She tore them open and read them
right there in the yard. After a while she started having Mailman
stamp them RETURN TO SENDER, a true blessing: this made it much easier for Mailman to read them himself. Oh, they were juicy ones, for
sure; it was tragic when Bean finally gave up. *I remember your whatsis
on my thingy . . . that night when you suchandsuched my youknowwhat . .
. you must tell your husband that we whatchacalled, then we can be
together . . .* One night they screwed, it seemed, one lonely night after
a zoning hearing at which he was trying to get a temporary variance
for that year's 'Fest; she fought on his side; he approached her afterward; she bought him a drink and one thing led to another. Mailman
sees her now and again, walking on the Square (she's a Square loyal-
ist, never goes to the mall or the shopping strip on the highway) with
the husband and kids, husband good-looking enough but very, very
(you can see it in his face) uptight, and the kids, perpetually adoles-
cent, blankeyed, underfed. Probably vegans, the lot of them. Poor
Minna Combs. Does she ever think about that one explosive night
with crazy Saul? Does she wish he were less crazy or she less married? Or has she banished him from her thoughts? Mailman will
never know; she never wrote back.

He misses the Bean letters—they were classics, among the jewels of his archive of xeroxed mail. He fears that he'll never see their equal. He's no fool, he knows the end is near, that penmanship is dead and e-mail is king. Damn the powers that be and their manifest destinies!: but that's a lament for another day.

Don't forget, says Mad Lester, *to play the scrambled quiz at ten, winner gets a free scrambled egg plate at Pop's Deli and a chance to win a thirty-five-millimeter camera.* Yes, yes, Mailman tells himself: another reason to live! Glances at his watch. Plenty of time.

He's in the city now, neat row houses sheathed with flowering shrubs, big sycamores and square privet hedges; he cruises Schuyler Street, which bisects his delivery zone, his sphere of influence. He zooms underneath the NestorFest banner, makes a right on Taft, and pulls over between North and Sage, his favorite block for parking, in the shade of huge old silver maples that let some of the light through, so that when he returns the truck will be cool but not clammy. He climbs in back, into the half-dark, and performs the daily ritual of separating out those letters in whose company he will spend his evening. The work progresses with the speed of twenty—sheesh, almost thirty!—years' experience. A personal letter, half-sealed. Another with the flap tucked in, the adhesive unlicked. A manila envelope lined with bubble plastic, stapled shut without any tape. It amazes and infuriates him to discover how haphazard people are about their mail: don't they realize their privacy is at stake, their credit card numbers, their secrets, their nude or partially nude photographs? Don't they have any self-respect? Besides, a reader of other people's mail wants a challenge. He wants to make use of the mountain of photocopied interlibrary-loan books and comb-bound self-published spy manuals and not-quite-legal mail-ordered instructional videos and adhesive-dissolving solvents and solvent-hardening adhesives and forgery guides and paper catalogs and stolen rubber cancel stamps he has stockpiled in the master bedroom. He wants the thrill of unwrapping without destroying, of removing without offending, of seeing without being seen. He wants the conquest as well as the content.

And so there is something infuriating about easy days, which this one is shaping up to be. Something depressing: as if his secret life is a secret not worth keeping, a secret nobody would pay to find out. To compensate, he sets aside a few extra letters: customers whose lives are usually too boring to bother with, or whose problems, interesting as they might once have been, have become dull through repetition. How many unplanned pregnancies, for instance, have to befall Jodie M. Steiner of 325 Creekedge Lane before she stops sleeping with her parents' seventy-year-old neighbor (Thomas Effening of 327 Creekedge, professor emeritus of sociology and boinker of several other neighborhood nymphets of the past—a reliably interesting let-ter-writer, to be sure)? For how many years is Mark Poll of 830 North Sage Avenue, Apartment 5A, going to get drunk and vandalize cars in the middle of the night before he finds some other way to deny life's emptiness? But you never know, you never know—it's worth his while to check from time to time. He sets aside nine letters. A diverting night.

The way he sees it, his job is to deliver the mail, to bring it from the P.O. to his customers and from his customers to the P.O. This task he reliably accomplishes each day. What happens to the mail in the interim is nobody's beeswax but his own.

He opens the back door and pulls out his cart, unfolds it, sets it on the pavement. Two trays' worth of mail go into each bag. Cart stuffed, he begins to walk. Around his truck, down the street, up a newpaved driveway reeking of tar and onto the heaved and weedy sidewalk, cart wheels clicking in the cracks. He has memorized the terrain, every impeding root-raised slab that must be wheelied over, every crumbling Sakrete patch, each handprint and initial scratched in wet con-crete (X.V. IS COOL, K ❤ D) by the past's children, children now in college or married and moved away, a few still in the houses the side-walk girds. East he walks toward the cliffedge, where trees grow out at an angle before facing the sun or stand stunted from bare rock and bad access to water. Hellos to squinting housewives, idling academics in the drive washing their Volvos. Hellos to children (why aren't they in school?) and wide berths around cats, writhing on sunpatched pavements with gravel and leafcrumbs adhering to their bellies.

On the porch at 310 Coolidge: chessboard, set up for play. Mailman climbs the steps and contemplates his move. An old man lives here, Martin Hostetter, retired thirty years from NYTech materials science, now in his late eighties. Used to play chess with his old carrier, a long time ago. Now he plays with Mailman, one move per day, six days a week. Mailman hates chess, hates games of strategy that evolve and change, where tactics lose power with repetition; he prefers a static situation for which a single approach can be developed, perfected, absorbed, rendered invisible, such as a mail route. But Hostetter insists, even though he always wins. Sometimes the old man tries to throw the game by making some bonehead move which a better player than Mailman could exploit for a win, but Mailman's responses are always undone by the middle of the next week. The old man must sit out here afternoons and plot out all the permutations, he must take time to study the board. Whereas Mailman gets five-six seconds per move, he has work to do after all, so what's fair about that? Nothing. Yet he plays.

He makes his move (Nc3, Bb4) and drops the mail in the box. "Afternoon, Mr. Hostetter!" Is he in there? No telling. Mailman's never laid eyes on him.

Today he's humping: NYSEG bills. Fleet Bank credit card bills. Flyer about the school budget vote, once turned down, minimally revised, up for referendum again this Tuesday ("Don't forget to vote! Your children's future depends on it!!"). *Newsweek* (cover story: THE WAR OVER NAPSTER: people with no taste stealing from people with no talent). The *Nestor Investor,* a free ad rag full of classifieds (*For Sale Nautalas* (sic) *Machine! Desperately Need Animal Cages! Custom Built Cedar Dog Homes!*). Pottery Barn catalogs and J. Crew catalogs and Land's End catalogs (models inside frolicking, beckoning, sipping beverages, enjoying breezes); Hold Everything catalogs and Sharper Image catalogs and Brookstone catalogs (the products labor-saving, class-enhancing, boss-impressing). He drops the mail into the mailboxes with a clang, thud, clunk (depending on the mailbox), knows there are lonely people inside waiting—it's the best part of their day— for all this garbage, people who smile and weep and chuckle at twenty-year-olds on beaches flying kites in identical seventy-dollar shirts, they seem like friends, those models, lost friends you might once have known, looking awfully familiar as they tumble past on their way to someplace fun, joking, elbowing, shouting, laughing, and you wonder what would happen if you joined them, would they clap your back and invite you along, to pile into the jeep and hit the road, go camping, go to the city, anything? *That world*, you tell yourself, *I'll go there!* But it costs too much to go there, or you're too tired, or you're too depressed, or you don't have anybody to push your wheelchair, or your wife left you, or your head hurts, and so you stay home. You stay home and hope something good comes in the mail. You read the catalogs. You order the clothes and wait for them to arrive.

The mail privileges, it compels. It can make or ruin your day.

It's nine-thirty. He can do the houses along the creek and still get back to the truck in time for the scrambled quiz. With a tray's worth of mail in his cart he scoots down the street proper, skipping the sidewalk entirely, which is older here and in greater disrepair than elsewhere. Must be the wet ground. Delivers to 325 and 327, homes respectively of Jodie and Tom, May-December lovers. He has Jodie's latest letter from her pen pal Amanda in the truck, awaiting perusal. He passes the section of creek where the footbridge collapsed in 1983 in a rainstorm and wasn't replaced; a gas main runs across instead, which neighborhood children walk over as if it's a footbridge. Farther down here a child once fell in and drowned. It was August, hardly any water, but the kid hit his head on a rock and lay facedown with his mouth and nose submerged. Police went to inform his mother and found the house crawling with roaches and rats, month-old dinners under the couch, family cat dead and half-skeletal in the boy's room, years of unopened mail. They jailed her for neglect and took her four-year-old daughter away. A developer bought the lot and tore down the place, put up grad student apartments. Unopened mail! A sure sign you've gone around the bend.

He's back in the truck by ten till ten, plenty of time. He pulls out, drives to the corner of Sage and Hoover, where there's a pay phone he can use. The streets are lousy with Festival-goers, cars full of teenagers, sidewalks clogged with families walking four, five, six abreast. He parks on the yellow, in front of a hydrant, and switches the radio on. News again. Do we really need it every twenty minutes? Can we concentrate instead on, say, not running red lights? On not alienating our spouses? On our personal hygiene? Instead we're being asked to attend to this distant election, Bush grinning like a dimwitted grocery clerk, Gore as stiff as Clinton's wanker. Come on, Lester, get to the contest.

All right! Now it's time for today's scrambled quiz, sponsored by Pop's Deli, Deli the Way Dad Liked It. Winners receive a coupon good for one scrambled egg breakfast with the purchase of any other breakfast of equal or greater value.

Ha! Making you buy to get it. And then they'll ask you if you want drinks. That's where the money is. OJ concentrate and instant coffee, buck-fifty or two bucks a pop. Pure profit, you can hardly blame them. He gets his pencil and paper ready.

Today's scramble is "tree cable." That's T-R-E-E-C-A-B-L-E. And today's hint: the answer is something a lot of Nestorians will be doing today. All right, the tenth caller at 271-WNYT will receive a coupon for a free breakfast, and will be eligible for this month's drawing to win a thirty-five-millimeter camera from Camera Obscura, on the Square, and we'll be doing that drawing today at eleven. Tenth caller, unscramble "tree cable." That's 271-WNYT.

Mailman's got the letters arranged in a circle, that's a good way of seeing what should go next to what. "Creet bale"? Almost got "Laertes" except for the s, but he can't remember who that was . . . "Beat leer C"? How about "erectable"? Erectable means electable! As opposed to "celibate." Wait: "celebrate"! What Nestorians are doing!

Ah! Ah! He leaps out of the truck, remembers he needs change, reaches in to take some off the dash, runs to the phone.

Somebody's using it. Shit!

"Excuse me, I really need to use the phone."

It's a woman, fortyish, nice bod, pretty face. Short. Hair straight with some gray, the gray suits her. No wedding ring. She looks up blearily, like she's just waking. Kind of sexy, actually. "Just a second," she says to the phone, and to Mailman, "Excuse me?"

"I need the phone. Really. It's a matter of life and death."

She squints, grimaces. "Oh!" she says. "Um . . ."

"Well, nobody'll die, but it can't wait, I need it now." He begins to bounce on his toes, but that'll get him sweating, so he stops. Sweats anyway.

"Okay, well, I'll just— just a second."

"Please. I'll give you—" He looks at the change in his hand and counts it. "I'll give you forty-two cents if you get off and let me make a call. Please. It'll just be a minute and then you can have the phone back."

"It's a mailman," she's saying now, holding up a finger. "He wants the phone."

"It's a contest, a radio contest, I have to be the tenth caller . . ."

". . . I don't know, he's just a mailman, he just parked here and . . ."

"Oh God, oh God," Mailman is saying, hardly knowing he's saying it, surely everybody in Nestor has solved the scramble by now, someone may at this very moment be winning. The woman's hand is still on the receiver where she's replaced it and she is looking at Mailman and smiling, in a wary, not 100% friendly way, and says, "I think you owe me forty-two cents."

Deal's a deal. He hands over the change. She holds it in her out-stretched palm a moment as if to let it cool, then pockets it, turns and walks toward the Square. Thank God! He picks up the receiver and puts in his quarter and dials and it rings once and Lester himself comes on the line.

"Sorry, you're the eighth caller." Line goes dead.

Oh. He puts the phone down, picks it up again. His money is gone. He jiggles the metal tongue, looks in the change return. There's somebody else waiting to use the phone now, young guy, goatee, holding a skateboard with a picture of a skull on it. "Wait," says Mailman, "wait a second, would you? I need the phone again. Just wait."

"Whatever."

He starts to look around on the ground, in the gutter, in the grass for a glimmer of money. He pats his pockets, looks in the change return again. He says, "Wait, okay? Don't use the phone. Please. Just wait."

"Whatever."

He runs down the block and catches up to the gray-haired woman. Her look of surprise is extremely attractive. But no time for that! "Please. I'm sorry, I need that money back, I know I said you could have it but I lost my only quarter."

She shakes her head. "Look, would you just leave me—"

"Please!" he says, shouts practically, thinking, Why am I making such a big deal of this? it's only a couple of scrambled eggs, but it isn't the eggs, it's the principle of the thing. He reaches out and grabs the woman's arm. Oops.

"Jesus *Christ*," says the woman, pulling away.

"I'm sorry, I didn't—"

She reaches in her pocket (tight denim shorts, fills them out very nicely, now stop that), pulls out the change and *flings* it at him. It chimes on the sidewalk. "Here, take it!"

"Thank you, I'm sorry, thank you," he's saying, "thank you . . ." Picks up only the quarter and turns to find the skateboarder reaching for the receiver.

"No! No!" Mailman sprints the half block and the kid jumps back, lets the receiver fall, he's holding up his hands, "All right, all right, take it easy," and Mailman grabs the receiver and pushes in the quarter and dials the number and Lester says:

"Hello, caller number ten! You're on the air! Have you got today's scramble?"

For a moment he cannot speak.

"Caller number ten?"

"Celebrate! Celebrate! Celebrate!" he's shouting.

"Sounds like you're celebrating yourself, caller ten—and you should be, you've solved today's scramble! What's your name?"

"Albert Lippincott!"

"Well, Albert Lippincott, *you're a winner*! Where are you calling from?"

"Corner of Sage and Hoover!"

"Albert, are you having a blast at NestorFest?"

Oh, for Chrissake. "No. I'm working." Lester's voice, so exaggerated, so toylike: bizarre to be having a conversation with it. His own voice sounds comically drab.

"And what do you do for a living, Albert?"

"I'm employed by the United States Postal Service."

"All hail the men in blue! Well, you know what, Mailman Al? *You've! won!* a coupon for a scrambled egg breakfast at Pop's Deli, Deli the Way Dad Liked It, free with purchase of any breakfast entrée of equal or greater value, and *you are eligible!* for this morning's eleven a.m. drawing to receive a thirty-five-millimeter camera from Camera Obscura, on the Square!"

"Great!"

"Congratulations, Albert Lippincott, caller number ten!" He hears a click. "Jussec, Al," says Mad Lester. A fumbling, a clanging. - Mumbled conversation. "Still there, Al?" The voice deeper now, uninflected.

"Yes."

"Gimme your address and I'll send you the coupon."

He considers. Give your address to a radio station, what happens to it then? Probably they send it to corporate, it's the whole reason they have these contests, to get the names and addresses and phone numbers of listeners, pretty soon he'll start getting catalogs of "golden oldie" tapes, Greatest Radio Highlights of All Time, 100 Years of

Radio, Best of Radio Bloopers. Forget that. He says, "I'll just come to the studio."

"Ah, well, it's a lot easier if I send it. I can pop it in the mail today."

Ha! Pop it! Pop's Deli! "No, I'll come. What's your address?"

Mad Lester sighs, gives him the address. Mailman hangs up. The skateboarder muscles in and grabs the receiver. Mailman stands a moment catching his breath, watching cars and people pass, thinking, Was that really worth getting all worked up over? What was the point? So I get to have a free breakfast, big deal. He doesn't even like Pop's Deli, the brown carpet waitress-worn, the wallpaper tacky with airborne grease. And he isn't going to eat two breakfasts by himself, he'll need a date. The woman with the change, the Gray Fox: now, her he'd like to have breakfast with.

He climbs back in the truck and starts it up. He could always find her, apologize for grabbing her arm. "Let me make it up to you and buy you some breakfast. Pop's Deli?" Or, "Hey, everybody's gotta eat, right?" Or, "Most important meal of the day, you know." Her expression, guarded at first, would soften and with some prodding he could get her number. Wait a few days, then: "Hi, remember me? The mailman? How about that breakfast?" But a coupon, on a first date? Save it for later, when they know each other better: "Say, want to go back to Pop's, site of our first date?" He'd pull out the crumpled coupon: "Remember when we met? When you threw that change at me? Well, that phone call won me this coupon!" They'd have a good laugh about it, and he'd take her home and they'd do it on his cot.

All right: baby steps, baby steps.

He sets off to finish his route. Parks, unloads, delivers, whispering as he walks, a kind of chant: *Breakfast is free / Get your hand off me / How about a date? / That would be great.* This is his favorite neighborhood in Nestor: working-class people, academics, professionals; some law and doctor offices and a café, people always on the streets, they say hello to him as he passes, glad to note his speed and agility with the cart, that's their mail, after all. He likes the gardens here, cluttered yet cultivated. The mail practically delivers itself. When he gets back in the truck, it's 10:48, almost time for the weekly drawing. Not that he wants the camera. He's never had one, it makes people uncomfortable, whatever moment you want to capture is ruined. "Wait, hold that, lemme take your picture." Fiddling with the buttons and dials while everybody's waiting to start having fun again. As a result he doesn't have any pictures of Lenore. It seems strange, they were married so many years, yet no pictures, except maybe the wedding album, which is probably still in the house somewhere. Well, he can't look at that. It's all right, he's got his memories. Also he sees her all the time, she lives down the street.

He turns the key and switches the radio on and fishes in the glovebox for something to eat. Granola bar, Tic Tacs, graham crackers, prunes. His mouth still tastes funny from this (and every) morning's ritual: he wakes up without opening his eyes (a trick he learned from a Vietnam vet, Chuck Balling, who used to live on his route; *Always assume the enemy is watching*, the guy used to say), chews twenty grains of raw brown rice, and absolves himself of all the previous day's mistakes. *Then* he can open his eyes. Some mornings, like today, take longer than others.

He'll try the prunes and granola bar: health food. Want to look good for the Gray Fox, ha-ha. News update: list of top-grossing movies. How's that news? Rich people getting richer, big whoop. People panic if they haven't seen the most popular movie. Nothing to talk about at work then. Also in the news: stock market, trade bill, corporate merger. More money. Just giving the people what they want. Well, someday things will change and they'll get theirs, oh will they ever.

A cloud passes over the sun and Mailman feels a chill. He rolls up the window six inches. Three children bicycle by. He feels a longing. For what? To be young, to ride a bicycle? Or to have children? Not that he ever wanted any. Too many children in the world already. He wouldn't have been a good father, the same way he wasn't a good child. He couldn't figure out how it was done. Never was carefree, never played well in a group, never learned what to do with the unstructured hours of the day. Liked science, liked to look under rocks and find out the names of things: bugs, trees, weeds, clouds; but somehow it was always stressful, always there was the understanding of how much there was left to learn, how there would never be enough time to know it all. On his fourth birthday his father gave him a watch. He was supposed to make a chart showing where in the sky the sun was at various times throughout the day, and at the end of the summer the two of them would analyze the data. But he was four! He couldn't remember to do all that! He filled out the chart wrong—a beautiful chart made of rolled paper carefully columned—and he slept with it a couple of times and creased and tore it. "Well, Albert," his father said, more puzzled than angry, "I thought you could do better than that." He remembers lying in his bed crying, telling his sister Gillian, "Daddy doesn't like me." And Gillian slapping her brow with the back of her hand, sighing deeply. "Albert, you will learn, Father is a tragic man." And taking him into her arms.

Dow up, NASDAQ down. Markets are the new weather. Now it's community calendar time: a seniors' meeting (retirement age is dropping, probably they'll make him quit, but what the hell is he going to do at home all day? Goddam the AARP! with their capital gains income, making sure everybody of a certain age walks in step—well, count Mailman out), quilting, victims' support group (whatever that means: everybody's a victim, storm victims, harassment victims, victims of the patriarchy, of your mother, tonsillitis survivors, flu endurers. Get the whole town into the Women's Community Center for Chrissake, they can all have a big pity party), master composting class. And now, at last, the drawing. Lester brings on a little kid, the nine-year-old who won the Onteo County Spelling Bee.

"Brittany, what did you spell to win?"

"Ontogeny, O-N-T-O-G-E-N-Y. Ontogeny."

"Huh! What's that one mean, Brittany?"

"The development or course of development of an individual

organism. I beat a girl who didn't know how to spell medieval. M-E-D-I-E-V-A-L."

"Super job! Okay, can you pick a name out of the hat?"

"Yes."

"And who's our winner?"

Mailman's lost for a moment, marveling at this insufferable little girl, curse the parents raising her: what could be less useful than a spelling bee? So you can spell: big effing deal. Memorize the entire dictionary and you still can't write *King Lear*. Not that he could tell you anything about *King Lear*; he read it maybe once in high school—is that the one about the island? No, that's *The Tempest*. Lear was the old man, he had daughters, what'd they do: have sex, go nuts, get killed?

When he hears his own name he mistakes it at first for the voice of his English teacher during his final year of high school, a prematurely gray man of forty or so, posture as stiff as the spine of an old book, always ducked out to the toilet and sometimes wet himself. But nobody mocked him, they all liked him, they didn't want to know that kind of thing could happen to him but there it was, the small round stain encircling his fly. Always he excused himself and came back in five minutes wearing new pants, no comment or apology. These days he'd have diapers, there wouldn't be any leakage but he'd make a crinkling sound when he walked and people would call him piss-pants. Wonders if it's better this way or not. A good man, his voice reedy and faintly English, *Albert Lippincott*, the voice dignified the name.

"Albert Lippincott."

"How about that!" Lester shouts. "It's this morning's scramble winner, postal worker Albert Lippincott. Mr. Lippincott, you've won a thirty-five-millimeter camera from Camera Obscura on the Square, so come on up and get it! Starting Monday, unscramblers will be competing for a genuine leather catcher's mitt from Be A Sport at the Triangle Mall. Now it's time for a high school sports update and call-in therapy with Doctor Phil Gumm."

He doesn't know whether to be elated or horrified. Everybody at the P.O. is going to give him the business. Hates that crap, the "joking around," the "gentle ribbing," the "just fooling." Everything's got to be a joke, they can't just say "David, congratulations on your marriage, I know you'll be very happy together," instead it has to be something like "Now you're legal," or "Cow's on your side of the fence now, Davy-boy," some such trash. Right now they're plotting their one-liners. "Gonna take some dirty pictures, Al?" "Here, photograph this," pantomiming a giant penis. Always sexual. That's all people think about, so that's all they joke about. Couple of guys walking down the street, if they pass a woman with big breasts there's sure to be some laughter, elbowing, huh-huh-huh, desire is a big farce to them, then when they actually convince a woman to sleep with them it's quick, bang-bang, see you later, my work here is done. Not that that has anything to do with anything.

He pulls out into traffic. Guy in a pickup comes up close behind, his way of showing Mailman who's boss, letting him know he isn't going to slow down for any goddam mail truck driven by any goddam mail-delivering prick. Mailman taps the brakes. Pickup lurches dangerously close, reels back, honks. Middle finger is pressed against the truck windshield, plexiglas sign at the end of the hood reads ROCK AND STEEL. Stays right on Mailman's tail for three blocks, then turns off with a squeal and another honk and a shout out the window.

Sage Street leads to the Square, downtown's pedestrian mall, looking a bit shabby these days from competition against the Triangle Mall and the new development on Route 13: giant boxy retail stores with two-hundred-foot parking setbacks. All undercutting the tchotchke-based downtown economy. There used to be a newsstand, an ice cream parlor, a barbershop. Now it's all lumpy pottery and CVS. Things improve at Festival time and in December; the empty store-fronts open with unnamed fly-by-night operations selling sandals or hemp products or handmade jewelry, and the Square looks nice, busy, thriving. But most of the time it looks half-dead.

He can't find a space on Sage so he parks on the yellow again and loads his cart. He skirts the 'Fest, delivering to the customers outside the Square, where the crowds are smaller. On the south side, Carpet Emporium is as silent and imposing as ever. When he began this route he once made the mistake of hand-delivering its mail: the chipped black door had been slightly ajar so he ignored the BY APPOINTMENT ONLY sign and went in. There were maybe ten rolls of carpet in the warehouse, a cavernous corrugated-metal room with a cement floor; instead the space was dominated by gleaming motorcycles and electronic equipment sitting on aluminum shelves. Four men in suits (no neckties) sat on folding chairs playing cards at a folding table, giving the impression that they too could be calmly folded up and made to vanish within a matter of seconds. They frowned as Mailman approached. "Morning!" he said. One of the men nodded; another rose, took Mailman by the elbow (a hard grip just a notch below painful, a few notches below injurious) and walked him to the door. Out on the sidewalk he pointed to the sign, glared at Mailman, took the mail from his hand, stuffed it into the small black unmarked mailbox, glared a second time, then took the mail out again and disappeared with it behind the door. Today the door's closed. He drops the mail into the black box and hurries on.

He passes where they're building the new library. Used to be Woolworth's before Woolworth's tanked. He used to snack at the lunch counter; this was pre-espresso, pre-croissant, pre-baguette, pre-scone, when all you could get downtown for lunch (aside from the vegetarian restaurant, which was staffed by hippies in the days before hippies liked money) was a tuna melt and a cup of Sanka, brought to you by old women in cafeteria hats. Lousy eating but without the pretensions. All kinds ate there, down-and-outs waiting for the bus, drunks waiting for the bars to open, children, the mayor (a real mayor then: fat and sweaty, he didn't give a flying fig what you thought, unlike the present pipsqueak and his opinion polls). Always a good conversation you could listen to or participate in. People just don't talk the same anymore, nobody listens, it's just a couple of unconnected monologues. Once he was sitting at the lunch counter and heard some kind of missionary pitching God to a total stranger. "I want you to look deeply into your soul, Lisa." Took maybe fifteen minutes to convert her. Those were the days! Anyhow, the library's moving out of its old building come fall, though it's hard to believe they're going to finish in time, especially since they decided to put solar panels on the roof. He hopes they'll let him in.

Circles around through the parking garage, delivers to the apartments east of the Square. He reaches 200 Keuka, a drab brick building of twenty or so units, and he feels a twinge of guilt. He has unfinished business here. There is a certain letter he has at home, among his borrowed missives. He can't deliver this letter yet, because he has failed, so far, to repair the damage he has done to it while steaming it open. He has had this letter for a week. It is addressed to Jared Sprain of apartment 20, and it reads:

Box 5
Rangers Station
Clearwater Natl Forest
Idaho USA

Hey J-Man

Dude I don't know what your thinking when you wrote me that letter but I gotta tell you that it fricked me out mightyly, me being up here in the fire tower with no phone to call you and tell you what a fucken loony you are and you better shape up. So heres this letter whichll have to do the same thing. Your a fucken loony!!!!! No seriously I wish I knew why you feel that way becuase it doesnt make sense what with your amazing talents as a painter and sculpter too man—at the acad. we were always hanging out talking about how your gonna kick our asses someday, every body thought so, it was tottaly obvious you were some kind of fucken genius. So you owe it to us to go out there and be a genius and do your amazing paintings and sculptures and not to sit around telling people how your life is meaningless and everything, which I think you know deep down is tottal bullshit. Your an IMPORTANT PERSON *and everybody knows it. Zofie was up here over the weekend and I showed her your letter and she tottaly agrees with me, theres no reason for you to feel fucken suicidal or anything. So I just want to say snap out of it man! and alls well up here tho boring as shit. I only brought pencils and paper figguring Im going to work on my drawing all summer but what a mistake! At least I have my guitar.* WRITE AGAIN! CHILLOUT FRIEND!

Hopper

Jared Sprain is some kind of artist all right, always getting supplies from Chicago which Mailman delivers with a knock to his door (Sprain is always home; he has no job other than art and collects a monthly check from the government for reasons that are unclear but that Mailman suspects have something to do with mental health). He's maybe thirty, thin and dark and unshaved, looks like he's been in the desert; and in fact he has gone to the desert, his mail is held for two weeks every year during his "therapeutic outing," which is a wandering tour of the barrenest corner of Utah. How he affords it Mailman doesn't know, judging from the checks. Probably family money: Mom and Dad's letters have the stink of the upper middle class, the smugness of tone, pride of social place, e.g., *Your sister is going out with a Yale Man,* the kind of thing people who have never had money think people who have money are always thinking about. Whenever Mailman knocks, Sprain answers, calls him Man, Mailman calls him Hey. Mailman's never crossed the threshold into apartment 20—Jared seems afraid to admit him or anyone else for that matter—but it is easy to see inside the place: a single room, white walls, paintings hanging or leaning here and there: big swirly abstracts, giant clay sculptures of vortexes and whirlwinds, tornadoes the color of blood with hands and eyes sticking out of them, hanging mobiles of strange bent-wing birds drooping and oily with varnish. Mailman doesn't know anything about art, but those images have stuck in his mind, and whenever a package comes (twice a month) he looks forward to delivering it and makes some excuse for hanging around in the doorway talking. And Sprain is always willing to talk. Hey, Man, thanks a lot, he might say, in a voice like air being let out of a balloon, so what's up with you? And Mailman chats while he looks over Sprain's shoulder at the paintings and sculptures.

He feels bad about the undelivered letter. There have been others like it, cheer-up letters, in response to Sprain's meticulous, formulaic expressions of misery. *On days like today, with the wind beating against my windows, I feel that all of man and nature are against me, and see all I do and hear all I think and judge me to be worthless, and worse a faker, a cheat, and I feel that life's end would only be a mercy.* Sometimes he sends the same letter off to several people—Sprain has a lot of correspondents, spread all over the world—and a few weeks later the reassuring responses (much like the one in Mailman's out box) come pouring in. But the letter-writers seem to be reading from a script, just as they seem to know Sprain is too; and though they are far away from one another and don't know one another, the responses are strangely similar, as if there are only a few possible reactions to the kind of letters Sprain writes. But still Mailman feels bad, because there is something honest in these predictable responses, and he really ought to hurry up with the one sitting at home.

The problem is the envelope: the ruined envelope: it's been painted with pale watercolors that smeared and bled under the teakettle's steam. What can he say: he thought the colors were printed on, because who hand-paints an envelope? And when the colors ran, Mailman panicked, and in his panic he tore the paper. At least it's a regular envelope, the cheap kind, he's got a thousand of them here, but the trick will be to reproduce the painting. It wasn't much of a painting but Mailman's never painted anything in his life, he doesn't even own any paints. That's why he hasn't delivered the letter.

200 Keuka is silent at this hour. People are out at work if they work or still asleep if they don't. The mailbox row is bent and rusted, like a relic. Unlatches his keyring: it's easy to find the right one because it's the size of a cigar, a big skeleton-type thing, you could probably open the boxes with a screwdriver. Not very secure. He's told the landlord: it's not secure, and it sticks to boot. You're making it hard for me to do my job. But the landlord doesn't want to hear it, he just shrugs, plumps up his lips and half-turns away. Jerk.

Mailman inserts the key and twists it every which way, gets his fingers under the metal lip and tries to pull. Sticks, as usual. He rattles the key and whacks the boxes with the flat of his palm, trying to dislodge whatever tongue of metal's jamming the lock. "Come on." Gets his hands in at both ends, pulls: the ends of the row bow out comically, but it won't give. "Son of a bitch!" Pounds with his fist. Ouch. Wait: take the key out and try again. But the key's wedged in there now, won't turn or slide out, seems kind of crooked in the slot as if it's been bent. Jiggles it. Nothing. He rams his shoulder against the boxes, a thunderous crash. "Goddammit!" Outgoing mail resting on the ledge above is dislodged and flutters down around his feet. Shit, shit, shit. Panting, he picks up the fallen letters and holds them in one hand while he uses the other to pummel and pull and shake the boxrow. There's a humming in his throat: he's growling, growling at the mailboxes. The sonsabitches! Open! Open! Shoves the outgoing mail into his pocket, slams his palms against the boxrow, bam! bam! bam!, "Open the goddam hell up!" Finally he steps back and takes a breather. After a moment he notices somebody's there, behind the heavy entrance door, peering through the plexiglas window: a girl of twenty or so, dull straight hair, expression of horror. "Hey," he says. She smiles weakly. "Complain to your landlord about these mailboxes, would you? I can't get him to replace them." He's trying to sound reasonable but his voice is quavery and hoarse. He's gasping and shaking. Grins at her. To show he's not insane he turns back to the boxes and tries the key and he knows the second he touches it that the boxes are going to open. Just like that. Something came loose in there at last. Looks at the girl, her expression hasn't changed. "Got it!" he says. She turns and goes back into her apartment.

Most of the boxes are empty, three of them still full of yesterday's mail. That's not unusual, people go away on long weekends and a few don't care about getting the mail, they'll leave it in there days on end, completely forgetting it's come. One of the full boxes is Jared Sprain's. That gives him an ominous feeling. Why? Doesn't mean anything, could be he's on his retreat, but it would have been nice to find the box empty, suggesting that everything is just fine. Which it is. Everything. Fine. He fills the boxes with the day's mail. A couple of parcels are too large, so he brings them into the building: clothes for No. 6, clothes for No. 8. Nothing for the top floor but he's already inside, no harm in going up and seeing for sure if old Jared's away.

He climbs the stairs. On the landing between two and three there's something funny: black and white cat, backed into the corner, hair on end, quietly keening. Looks afraid. Is there another cat up here somewhere? He pauses and glances up the steps. Sees, hears nothing unusual. He takes three steps: now his head's above floor level and he can look up and down the hall. All clear. Looks back at the cat. "No big deal, kitty." Cat shakes itself and runs off down the stairs.

He walks to the end of the hallway, to the door marked 20. Listens. No sound from inside. He knocks. "Hey." Waits. Nothing. But still he waits, listens. Checks to see if anyone's watching then gets down on his knees and peers under the crack. No motion, only sunlight on the floorboards. Okay. If he's away, he isn't missing the letter I didn't deliver. He'll get it tomorrow. Swear? I swear.

Back out to his cart: he supposes he left it for a bit too long, but nothing's amiss. It's easy to steal mail but people never do, not from him. He finishes his loop, returns to the truck. Loads in the outgoing and loads out the incoming; cart full, he heads for the Square and the Festival now in full swing. The food vendors are set up on Center Street in front of the bank: it's lunchtime, it's crowded. He stays close to the building, passes beneath awnings. Can't leave mail outside, not in this mob, so he pushes the bank doors open with his back (eschewing the big blue button with the wheelchair on it), pulls the cart in by the handle, then spins it around and drops the mail at the desk.

From Center he moves into the Square proper and is forced to slow down; pedestrians shuttle between shops without looking. He noses through the crowd and into each door, his cart like an icebreaker, revelers parting before him, couples and families breaking up and rejoining behind. At the west end of the Square a string band is playing, banjos and fiddles, trombone and bass, children dancing and people clapping and having a good time. He doesn't much like the music, a nostalgia trip, the notes played with ironic detachment, but it's better than a goddam DJ. He reaches Sage and doubles back. Kids play on the monkey bars: dangerous as hell, they could crack their heads open! In the amphitheater: women dancing in white jumpsuits with leather fringes, woolen legwarmers, white scarves in their hands that look like toilet paper. Music from a boombox: Latvian? He has no idea what Latvian music sounds like, but if somebody were to say "Oh, yes, that's the folk music of Latvia," he would have no trouble at all believing it. An awkward dance: lots of balancing on one foot and frowning at the sky. Wherever it's from, dancing there is not a form of recreation. And here's the craft fair: fake Indian stuff, drink coasters made of varnished slices of treetrunk, birdhouses and feeders, birchbark lampshades, organic dog biscuits, handmade furniture.

By the time he's back to Center Street he's hungry so he gets in line with his cart at the Thai stand. Long line, but he wants what he wants: a spring roll with sweet chili sauce. While he's waiting he checks out the sleepy-eyed high school babes behind the steam table scooping up noodles and panang curry. Ah, hell. Last thing he needs to think about. And then he sees her, ahead of him in line: the woman from earlier, the Gray Fox. She's with another woman, this one tall and skinny like a man, no hips, sunglasses hanging around her neck and her hair bunched under a ballcap. He leans to the left and right, making himself conspicuous back here: they're separated by five-six people, all sweating in the heat. Hello! Hello! Line moves up, the women order, they get their aluminum pans of food and sprinkle peanuts and cilantro on top. They're coming this way: they'll pass him.

"Hey!"

They look up. Tall woman says, "Hey."

"Do you remember me? The phone booth? Or not booth rather, public phone by the park? You were on and I had to get on and I gave you forty-two cents, and then you threw it at me?"

"Oh," says Fox.

"Yes, so, ah. I wanted to say sorry I was so, ah, insistent and grabbed your arm by which I didn't mean anything untoward." *Untoward!* What a dork! "I mean, the problem was I was in a terrible jam, I had to call up the radio. And win a contest."

The tall woman's grinning a little, looking back and forth between Mailman and her friend, trying to figure this out. But Fox has no expression, her face is twisted by aversion to sun, as she isn't wearing hat or glasses. Tall says, "Do you two know each other?"

"That's what I'm saying," Mailman says, "we don't. Didn't. But now we sort of do. I had to make a call and I paid her to hang up, and then I called but I needed to call again, so I said— I asked for my money back. But, ah, see—here's what I'm trying to tell you, it was a contest, on the radio, and I won!, that is, I got a free breakfast at Pop's. Deli. And then a camera. Although that was later."

"We have to go," says Fox.

"But see, see," stopping them as they begin to move away, "the problem is I can't get the free breakfast"—and he realizes oh shit, he wasn't going to tell her about the coupon, now it sounds like he just needs somebody to eat with so he can cash it in, which is kind of true but of course that's not the *main* reason he's asking her—"unless I buy another, ah, breakfast. Which is why I wanted to find you, to make it up to you for my grabbing your arm, by buying you a breakfast at Pop's. Not just because of the coupon. The coupon only gave me the idea. In fact we can save the coupon for another date."

"Date?"

"That I'm asking you on."

Guy behind him in line pokes him, says, "Are you in line? Move up."

"Okay," he says to the guy and moves up. But the women don't move with him, they're several feet behind him now and when he turns to continue asking out the Gray Fox she's walking away, looking over her shoulder at him, talking to her friend. No doubt explaining about the lunatic mailman who grabbed her arm. Goddammit, he blew it.

Guy behind him again says "Move up." Again he moves up. After a minute—Mailman is going over every second of the exchange, wondering how he could have made it work—the guy behind him says, "Tough break. She's hot."

"Yes."

"I think they're lesbians, though."

Mailman turns. "Really?" That would explain a lot: with that in mind it's amazing they were so polite. Probably they thought he was all right, just a little overexcited, if things were different Fox would have found him funny and charming. *Breakfast? Okay, why not?* Well—lesbians. Embarrassing misunderstanding, is all.

Guy says, "Nah, probably not, now that I think about it."

In a couple of minutes he's got his lunch and he sits under the trees eating it. He was lucky to find a free bench. It's past noon. The Nestor types walk by: tall shaggies in natural fibers with babies on their chests or backs or shoulders but never in strollers or carriages with all the accoutrements; stout blondes (these the native upstaters) without chins, fed on potatoes and cheese and barbecued chicken; the Asians from NYTech with incomprehensible English slogans on their tee shirts (FRIENDLY AMAZING!, GO FOR IT STYLE); the monied and not very smart Nestor College kids, girls with big boobs, boys with long too-neat necks; the skinny old professors; the limpers and ticcers; the narrow-nosed mustached (but never bearded) greasy-capped tiny-eyed day laborers: he wonders if it's all in his head or do people really fall into types? If you were to make a three-dimensional chart, along three axes (say, body shape, facial features, and coloring), and place a point for every person in Nestor, would the distribution be random? Or would clusters appear, as in a three-dimensional map of the universe, clusters that look like taffy or cotton candy, types adhering to similar types and reproducing more of the same? Amazing (friendly amazing!) the way shapes and statistics and equations reflect other shapes and statistics and equations in nature, as in those photographs of the birth of a star, the bulging plumes that resemble thunderheads which in turn resemble the collision of different-colored, different-temperatured fluids in a glass.

He catches himself: this is the kind of hokey handclasping everyday-science professed by Maurice Renault, world-famous scientist-citizen of NYTech, who Mailman studied under during his ill-fated tenure as a student of physics. Not something he likes much to think about, neither the ideas he had nor the hubris which convinced him they were good, nor the unfortunate series of events that ended his academic career before it began (nor the long recovery in-hospital under the care of Lenore Inness, the nurse who would later marry and divorce him). Unfortunately, it's hard to miss Renault, Nestor's only celebrity. Always hanging around downtown, showing himself off, appears at the lectures and concerts where he is photographed nodding in the audience with his chin on his fist, he's the guy National Public Radio calls up whenever something happens in the world of science that requires a smug self-aggrandizing comment. Creepily handsome at seventy: the lined face, the goldrimmed glasses, the white coif swept as if by the winds of creation. The jeans and chamois shirts. His legacy downtown is a set of sculptures, models of the planets rendered in stainless steel and balanced on four-foot pyramidal spires. The sun's the size of a basketball and the planets are laid out across town according to their relative distance to the sun, so that you can walk two-three miles to the end of the solar system. Except all the planets are out of scale, they've been enlarged "to show detail," so that Mercury looks about half the size of the sun, which it ain't, and about the same size as Earth, which it also ain't. Plaques at the base of each read MAURICE RENAULT'S PLANET WALK. He cut the ribbon in '98. Walked all the way to Pluto with a bunch of ethnically mixed schoolchildren (Pluto used to stand next to the Children's Science Museum, which last year ran out of money; weeds have grown up around the sculpture and it's covered with spraypainted gang tags: like the real Pluto, a chilly ball in a howling wasteland). Nestor made it onto the *Today* show. "A tiny hamlet nestled against beautiful Onteo Lake, home to world-renowned New York Technical Institute and its Center for Advanced Astrophysics." Tiny hamlet, my ass! It's a small city, as the Chamber of Commerce fondly says, "of twenty-five thousand souls." As if other towns, though more populous, might have fewer "souls." As if Nestor will be empty after the Rapture. *As if!*, as the kids say.

Spring roll dispatched, he crumples up the basketweave-imprinted paper tub and lobs it into the trash can standing next to the sun. He pushes his cart through the throng to his truck and gets in. It's hot, but he rolls up the window. Ah: the half-silence of the inside of a vehicle, when all around is chaos. Sounds are muffled and deepened by the truck's metal shell. Relaxing enough to put him to sleep. But he has to pick up his breakfast coupon. And his camera! He pinches himself several times on each cheek and checks the WNYT address where he wrote it on the back of a yellow package slip.

Vista Road. Out behind NYTech—quickest way there is through campus. He follows Euripides Street, the steepest in town, under the big stone arch visitors are led through to impress them. All the buildings have been expanded over the past ten years, the hundred-year-old physics building and humanities building and biology building; historic preservationists wouldn't let them add on in the same style so they did these po-mo cartoon annexes that look like a schoolchild's drawing of the original. He turns onto Tower Road and speeds past the space sciences center, past the shedlike stone cottage that leads down into the particle accelerator (fourth largest in the country, as if that meant anything). Tower peters off into the county highway which leads him up the hill, onto Vista and past the observatory. About a mile beyond there's a little windowed shoebox of a building; the antenna tower rises up in a pasture nearby. No number, but this must be it. He pulls into the lot, hops out, tugs on the painted steel door, which is locked. A sad place: weeds grow everywhere, reclaiming the parking lot, cracking the pavement; stunted juniper bushes filled around with white gravel founder in the clayey hilltop soil. He thumps on the door with the flat of his fist. "Hey!" Soon enough it opens and there's a receptionist peeking at him through the crack.

"CanIhelpyou?"

"I'm Albert Lippincott, I won the camera and breakfast this morning."

Frowns. "Who?"

"I won the scramble and the drawing."

"For what station?"

Mailman doesn't understand the question. She rolls her eyes, says, "This is three stations. WCHY Christian music, WCHT Christian talk, WNYT college talk."

"WNYT. I won their contest. I want to see Lester."

He's led to the "waiting area," which is three plastic paintspattered contour chairs and a card table covered with five-month-old issues of *Time*. The receptionist leaves, comes back, opens a package of Andy Capp's Pub Fries and begins alternately to crunch the fries and sip from a bottle of Evian water. He stares at her incessantly for ten minutes and she looks up not once. The phone doesn't ring. Pretty soon Lester emerges.

"So here's the famous mailman, goo-ood morning!" He's a grizzly, three hundred pounds if an ounce, with a big gray beard and a thin gold chain around his neck.

"Yes."

Lester holds out a cardboard box and a slip of paper. "Congratulations, scramble champ! Remember you won't be eligible to win again for six weeks!" He points over his shoulder. "Sorry, friend, I got to get back before the PSAs are finished."

"All right."

"Sayonara!" says Mad Lester and strides away on chicken legs.

Mailman gets in the truck, checks out the coupon, opens the box. The camera is cheap black plastic, no flash. Instructions xeroxed on a single piece of folded paper: INSTRUCTIONS FOR YOU YOUR NEW CAMERA USAGE. Stupid hunk of junk. There's film in it though. He points it out the window and snaps a picture of the radio station. Not much fun. He tosses the camera on the seat and drives off. To think he was excited about winning—what a sucker! He'll never play the scramble again. He rumbles down North Hill in a fever, swerving around squirrels and errant stones with curses on his lips. He reaches downtown in minutes—he never was far from civilization—and is about to head for the highway and P.O. when he happens to glance down Keuka and sees the flashing lights of several cop cars, a fire engine and an ambulance.

He pulls over by the parking garage and speedwalks toward the scene. People are clustered in the street; a cop directs two lanes of traffic into one. Mailman slows his pace, afraid to come too close too fast. But there's no avoiding it: he finds himself standing in front of 200 Keuka. He hears the ambulance doors slam shut. Beside it are a couple of longhaired guys in shorts and rock band tee shirts with tears streaming down their faces. One of them's holding a frisbee. Mailman has a terrible feeling.

"What is it?" he asks them.

"Our friend," is all the frisbee kid can get out.

The EMTs are in no hurry. They're smoking cigarettes. "McGwire's spent, man. He'll never hit like that again."

"Like hell he won't."

"He'll put on thirty pounds in a year."

"Like freaking hell."

The frisbee boys are loosely embracing, like old trees weighted with snow and ice. There is no police line tape, not yet, but nobody seems to want to get any closer. Now there's a cop looking at Mailman, eyes narrowed, and he comes up and stands before him, glaring down from the several inches he's got over him. "No pictures," he says.

"What?"

Cop reaches down and plucks from Mailman's hand the camera. Holds it in front of his face. "No pictures."

Mailman wants to explain, tell the cop he wasn't taking pictures, he was just standing here, but he can't speak, his eyes are fixed on the camera in the cop's hand, this object he didn't own until a few minutes ago and doesn't remember bringing with him: it is as if the camera simply *occurred* to him, like a bad idea. And then he remembers the worst idea he ever had.

He was twenty, a junior, a would-be physicist. He was at the library, researching a paper. It was late, he was alone at a someone's carrel, reading; the sounds of the pages turning, of his own breaths, mingled with the footsteps of distant students, their coughs and scratches, their whispers, and these noises settled in around him, a cloak of not-quite-aloneness. He was comfortable, absorbed in the work.

Then it struck him: the idea. *The* idea. His body shook with it, his ears rung. His paper, the one he came here to work on, was meaningless, forgotten. He dropped his pencil. He stood up, banging his thighs on the desk. Sweat broke out thrillingly under his arms and on his forehead and neck and in his crotch. He began to pace, to think. He chuckled. He shook. He stalked through the stacks for hours, muttering to himself. Frightened students pressed themselves against the shelves as he passed. They were all parts of his theory—they were, and the books they clutched to their chests, the change in their pockets, the glasses on their noses—and so for that matter were Kennedy, Khrushchev, the Yankees and Nancy Sinatra.

Hadn't this been coming? Hadn't he felt a pressure building, a largeness confined in him, compressed there, crowding out all other parts of himself? Sure he had: and now, here it was! Hello!, he thought. Welcome! The theory (as far as he can remember now) was that everything *small* was a mirror of something *large* and everything *large* a mirror of something *small*, that the world that could not be seen because it was *tiny* was the same as the world that could not be seen for its *hugeness*: and human beings were the fulcrum of the scale of the universe; *before* civilization they were far enough away from the large and the small to render each invisible, but with the *dawn* of civilization *exactly close enough to the large and small to make both out*. From Mailman's point in time and space (the physics library at NYTech in September of 1963) the future stretched infinitely *forward* and the past infinitely *back*, and Mailman (just under a year away from delivering his first piece of mail) was at the *very center*, he was *point zero*, the very thing that would *divide the age of incomprehension from the age of understanding*. This was not about him, he was merely at the right place and time, when man and his world and his universe were about to make the giant leap out of ignorance. His theory would answer every question. There was no astral body it couldn't describe and explain, no social phenomenon it couldn't foresee, no form of life or energy or spatial temporal mental emotional reality it could not embrace. That which could be imagined could be realized *and in fact already existed somewhere*, for there was no line between the imagined and the real. His head was filled not with equations or images, sounds or sensations: but a previously unconceived amalgam, as if some extradimensional vessel had broken open and its contents flowed *into him*. And now *he* was the *vessel*. He ran from the library, his clothes heavy with sweat; he jumped, rolled in the dewy grass and the dirt, he climbed trees and shook their branches, skidded fearlessly into Teeter Gorge and let the water carry him over rocks that bruised and scraped his skin; but he was *invincible*, physical matter could not break him, he was the *receptacle*, molded out of the stuff of eternity. *I am the vessel!* At dawn he was running, shouting in a half-reclaimed farm field beyond campus (where the vet school now stands) and in the light of day his theory (and you could hardly call it a *theory*; it was no *theory* but a *genuine actual-size infinitely dimensional map of all realities of this universe and all others*) seemed not *less* true but *more*: its very *conception* had made it true and the longer it lived the stronger it grew, and now the sun had made it *eternal*. By noon he was standing, scraped blood-ied wealed bugbitten and bageyed on the proscenium in the middle of Renault's Basic Astrophysics survey course, two hundred students tit-tering, mumbling about this slight and manic man who had just slammed in through the back doors and run to the stage screaming (Mailman does not remember all this but he'll take the witnesses at their word) as he grabbed Renault by the shoulders—

"I have it! I have it! I have it! I have it!"

—intending to open his mouth wide and let the *answers* stream out and enter the older man's head *through his eyes*, which Mailman recognized for what they *really were*, not primitive instruments of sight but *portals into an everything not yet unlocked in the human mind*. Later Renault would tell Mailman's doctors that his former student *had tried to eat him*, in point of fact *had attempted to bite his*, Maurice Renault's, *eyes out*. Of this account Mailman still has serious doubts. He suspects Renault overreacted just a little bit. Renault after all was angry. Whatever: the point is that by the following morning Mailman had been apprehended and placed under the care of Lenore and the helpful doctors of the university hospital's seventh floor, where he resided for some two months afterward. He'd never noticed the place before, it was just another gray rectangle of recent vintage on some unimportant corner of campus, he could never have imagined what would go on there, what would be done to him. It was Lenore who would later suggest he take the civil service exam, while he waited to rematriculate. (In those gentle days the Postal Service didn't ask you if you were nuts.) He would do so, he would become a mailman. Temporarily, he believed. Until his wits were fully about him.

As for his theory, it was like that serendipitous arrangement of moss and fallen branches that seen from a distance resembles a face. Never would he be able to step back far enough to see it again. Yet he remembers knowing it. Nothing has ever felt so true, a kind of unattainable truth impossible to describe. He still feels like this truth was taken from him. Renault, the doctors, the drugs: they took it, they shut it off. It was his and they stole it.

Now, bathed in the pulsing light of the emergency vehicles, he is again filled with the fear and anger of those miserable days; so he grabs the camera from the cop and runs: runs off toward the Square and the crowd he can melt into. Stupid, he's thinking, the best way to get a cop to chase you is to run: but behind him no footsteps are sounding and no voice is calling out to him to stop. He runs until he reaches his truck, then sits in it gasping, heart racing, a familiar feeling.

At home he changes his clothes, fills a bowl with water, then settles himself in the mail room. Its windows are a bit larger than in the other rooms and let in better air, the air off the garden. These windows are draped over now with a thick brocade. Since the old days, when it was their bedroom, Mailman has junked the big king bed and set up a five-foot collapsible buffet table with a fake woodgrain finish, on which he's put a single-coil hot plate and teakettle, and a reading lamp, and a wooden box filled with glues and inks and solvents, pens and pencils and erasers, mailordered or borrowed from the post office; underneath are three corrugated plastic mail bins full of envelopes and writing paper. Across the room, taking up much of the far wall, are stacks of milk crates pinched from the loading dock of Value Dairy. They contain every piece of mail (excepting catalogs and flyers and political leaflets and ad circulars and credit card solicitations and animal rights brochures) he's ever gotten, every letter, every business transaction, every postcard, beginning with (in 1944, when

Mailman was too young to appreciate it, let alone read it) a handwritten letter from London, where his father had gone with the army. Next to the crates stands a photocopier he bought from the P.O. when they got a new one; he has learned how to service the thing himself, and has gotten so good at it, and has been good at it for so long, that it rarely breaks down at all now. Under the windows stand four black three-drawer filing cabinets (also salvaged from the P.O.) which contain photocopies of all the letters he has illicitly opened and read over the past twenty years.

And here, on the table, lies Jared Sprain's painted letter. No recognizable image, just some swirlies, clockwise eddies that flow into counterclockwise eddies and seem to set them in motion, as on the surface of Jupiter or Saturn. Maybe Sprain's friend had that in mind, motion creating motion on the surface of things, the tiniest movement here determining the next over there, like the famous beating butterfly's wings that cause a hurricane halfway around the world.

But what about human life? Is it susceptible to the beating of wings? Can a single stupid letter full of misspellings erase a lifetime of depression and near-madness? Can a Sprain be soothed by words? Remember, there were other letters, more articulate, more sincere than this one, that failed to do the job. Then again, maybe they succeeded: maybe he would have killed himself a long time ago if not for those letters.

Because that's certainly what has happened, Jared Sprain has killed himself. There is no other explanation for the idle EMTs, the speechless frisbee dudes. Jared Sprain is dead, he did himself in.

But the letters: how often did they come? Every month, let's say. If every decent letter helped him survive a month, how long would a rotten letter like this one have held Sprain off? A week? Let's give Hopper a week: if the letters were at all meaningful (and he isn't saying they are; this is *for the sake of argument*), Mailman hasn't actually *killed* Jared Sprain, only taken *one week off* his life. Not that it would have been a great week: maybe it would have been dreadful. Painful.

You might then say that it was a shame he didn't check out earlier and save himself the misery. You might say this of all the letters: that his pain had been *unnecessarily prolonged* by his well-meaning but ultimately destructive friends. Maybe Jared Sprain was *not meant* for this world. The point is that the entire situation is ambiguous beyond any identification of blame. Even if Mailman is responsible for Sprain's death *falling on this particular day,* Friday, June 2, 2000, he is in no way responsible *for the death itself,* the true responsibility for which must either be shared by everyone who ever knew or spoke to or even so much as looked at him (every butterfly whose wings ever agitated his airspace), or must be assigned to Sprain himself. Or, alternately, to no one. Maybe that's it, maybe no one is to blame.

And who knows, maybe it isn't Sprain who's dead. Maybe it's somebody else.

He picks up the crumpled and torn letter. After a moment's thought, he admits it to himself: he'll have to use a damaged mail sack. He rummages in a box under the table and pulls one out. It's plastic, resealable, with text printed on it:

Dear Postal Customer:

The enclosed has been damaged in handling by the Postal Service.

We are fully aware that the mail you receive is important to you. Realizing this, each employee in the Postal Service is making every effort to expeditiously handle, without damage, each piece of mail with which USPS is entrusted. Nevertheless, an occasional mishap will occur.

The Postal Service handles approximately 177 billion pieces of mail each year. It is necessary, therefore, that highly sophisticated mechanical/ electrical systems be utilized by the Postal Service to insure our customers prompt delivery of their mail. At times a malfunction will occur, the result of which is a damaged piece of mail.

We are constantly working to improve our processing methods so that
these incidences will be eliminated. You can help us greatly in our effort
if you will continue to properly prepare and address each letter or parcel
that you enter into the mail stream.

We appreciate your cooperation and understanding and sincerely regret
any inconvenience you have experienced.

Your Postmaster

Mailman uses these about three times a year, whenever a piece of borrowed mail is damaged beyond repair. Nobody's ever complained:
people accept the idea that their mail may be damaged. He is again
reminded of the complacency of human beings and weathers a wave
of disappointment.

He looks up, out the window. Sun's behind the far hill on the
other side of the lake, it's evening. He's hungry. He pops Jared
Sprain's letter into the plastic sack and, without thinking, sticks it in
his shirt pocket. He takes the camera too, and drops it in the pocket of
his shorts: its weight there is a comfort. He's tired as hell so he drives
the Escort.

The Square is still crowded, people pressing and jostling, kids trying to ride skateboards between them; dogs everywhere, darting and
snuffling. He gets himself a chicken sandwich on a kaiser roll. All the
benches are taken, but there's a space on the low concrete wall next to
the chessboards. He settles down and sinks wearily into his sandwich.

"Howdy, Albert."

He turns. It's his carrier supervisor, Len Ronk, sitting with his
wife, pigeons on a phone line. Mailman manages a smile. "Oh, hi."

"Don't you remember me, Albert?" Darla says brightly. Like Len,
she is nondescript, heavy yet insubstantial. "I met you at the post
office picnic last year."

"We've known each other for three years."

Len is giving him the elbow. "Your basic chicken sand," he says and holds up a sandwich just like Mailman's. "Except mine's got cheese on to it."

"I don't like cheese."

"What are you, whaddya call those people, vegan?"

Jesus Christ! It's a chicken sandwich, for crying out loud! "No, I just don't like cheese." It's true, cheese seems to him a byproduct, the worst thing about milk removed and isolated, like weapons-grade plutonium.

"No cheese! That can't be any fun for the kids!"

Darla agrees: "Kids and cheese just go together."

"If I had any I'd let them eat it."

There is a silence. The Ronks sit close, holding hands with the hands they're not holding their dinners with. Ah, love. With Lenore it always seemed like more and more talking was necessary; they talked in bed when they woke, and more at breakfast; through dinner and the evening, and toward the end even on his lunch breaks which he used to spend alone: all in the service of improving (and later "saving") their marriage. Seems to Mailman they were trying to save it from the moment they began it. The week they married they sat down and Lenore took his hands and told him they would have to have some ground rules. Ground rules? Sure, who does what around the house, who makes the food, washes the dishes, the laundry: they were a modern couple, both professionals, they had better get things straight. Mailman never minded doing his share but he didn't see why they couldn't just wing it, do what had to be done when it needed doing, by whomever was available to do it at the time: probably him actually, since her hours were long and odd and she was mostly asleep when home. Somehow she knew they weren't meant to stay married, elaborate precautions would need to be taken to keep them together. It always felt that way, precarious. Always she thought he was about to have another breakdown: every time he got angry or frustrated with himself (which was many times daily) or "in a funk" she would make him lie down and breathe deeply and tell her what he was feeling, and maybe it was time to go back on his medication and he couldn't just do whatever he wanted anymore, he had to do what was good for the marriage. And he would say what's good for the marriage is leaving me alone for thirty minutes, okay?, and she would say that attitude is no way to handle their problems, and he would say it wasn't her problem it was his, and he could handle it by himself, and she would say if that's the way you want it fine. But then again. Then again whenever he said "Where's my watch?" she said "On top of the coffeemaker." Whenever he said "I can't take it anymore" she said "Yes you can." Whenever she came home he felt, however irritated he was with her, that things were in order, things would fall into place. She had that effect. She still does, though mostly, he supposes, on her present husband.

Ronk is staring at Mailman now, his little eyes focused on a corner of shiny plastic, emblazoned with a blue Postal Service eagle, that juts out of Mailman's shirt pocket. Mailman clears his throat, pushes the damaged mail sack out of sight. The chicken sandwich has left a bad taste in his mouth, like lighter fluid. He starts picking apart the roll and tossing the pieces in the bush behind him, and sparrows swoop down out of nowhere to scavenge them.

"I'd best be going," he says.

"Off to the big fire?" Ronk asks, still eyeing the suspicious pocket.

"Big fire?"

"They're torching that old house," Darla says, "you know the one."

Right: the old mansion on the lake. Used to be owned by Nestor's first mayor, Richard Chapin; designed by Robert Caldwell, guy who built the town. After Chapin a series of rich people lived there, they used to make movies in Nestor in the twenties and the house was used for exterior shots. Then the stock market crashed and the owner croaked and nobody would buy the house: by the war it was dilapidated, and since then there'd been any number of attempts to grass-roots it back into shape. But the foundation was cracked and the boards were rotten and any kind of restoration would basically mean knocking the thing down and building it again from scratch. So finally it's history: they'll put up a snack bar, restrooms, a new lifeguard stand and restore swimming to the southern laketip.

"Right," he says, "that's where I'm going," and gets up to leave.

"Wanna join us on the shuttle bus, Al?" says Ronk.

"I'll walk."

And so he walks, his camera in his pocket bumping his leg, wearing a sore spot into the flesh. But it's better than having the camera around his neck: can't stand that, the proud alert photographer look, ready at any moment to snap a picture; those awful people wearing complicated vests and ballcaps with the names of battleships on them and roving eyes that say *I will record this moment for posterity* as if we should all be grateful. He'll take the sore leg over that any day. He heads northwest toward the lake and inlet, the 'Fest fades behind him and he's in the lousiest part of downtown, empty storefronts with their busted windows, a former nightclub-cum-church (GOD LOVING CHURCH ALL WELCOME!); shoe repair shop that tried and failed to branch out into tobacco, cigars and loafers still moldering in the display window four years later. An old man doing tax prep in a basement office. A lot of bars with Irish themes, McNally's Irish Pub, Nestor Irish Bar and Grill, Shaughnessey's. Child of about eight in dirty pants sits on a stacking chair outside McNally's, waiting for Mom or Dad. The fire station: lone truck inside, one man leaning against a pole reading the *Nestor News*. The rest of the department's down at the lake. Hope to hell there's no fire on South Hill tonight. Mailman waves to the fireman and the fireman waves to him. Now he's got to cross Route 13: four lanes one way and four the other. A recorded voice announces: *You may now begin crossing Route 13. You may now finish crossing Route 13. If you have not yet begun crossing, do not begin to cross Route 13.* He passes three car dealerships and the lumberyard and at last reaches the inlet. It's almost dark. On the canal path he is passed from behind by young boys eager to see the fire. They'll be disappointed: it's better in the movies, with explosions to boot.

By the time he arrives the building's already in flames and a crowd of hundreds cheers wildly. Fire engines are parked on the sandy ground, under the giant willow. Firefighters wait in full gear, yellow coats and hats, faceguards and giant boots. Their hoses are at the ready, attached to the park hydrants. Mailman stands at the back of the crowd; heat buffets his face. In a few minutes the fire is good and raging and a siren wails, and the firefighters heave themselves toward the burning house. The cheers intensify. The hoses open, water sprays, soon the exterior is smoking and smoldering. The firefighters stagger through the door, the water splashes and shisses against the interior, steam and spray pour from the windows. A second wave of firemen prop a ladder against the blackened siding; one man climbs, aims his hose at an upstairs window. Beautiful house. Damned shame nobody could save it. Protesters pleaded with the town but there's no sign of them here. Mailman scans the crowd for a familiar face, but it might as well be residents of another town trucked in for the spectacle. He begins to grow lonely. The flames are dying now, the windows more gray than orange. Out of his pocket he pulls the camera. There: make the fire stand still: something we were never supposed to see. They took pictures of the nuclear tests; some thought the pictures would reveal the face of Satan, or God. In a way they were right. Nukes are why he got interested in physics, the power of science, he couldn't imagine anything else worth doing. Another photo: water in stasis: he could describe the stream with equations: the pressure, the shape and size of the hose, its motion relative to the water's flow. These days they can make computer simulations that look like the real thing. It can all be predicted.

Then there's an accident. He sees it only through the viewfinder: the fireman on the ladder loses his balance; the hose goes wild, water shooting through the house and out the window on the other side, where another man's knocked off his ladder and falls fifteen-twenty feet, landing on his back in the sand. Through the camera's frame Mailman watches: firemen rush to the fallen man's side, the crowd surrounds him. Nothing now can be seen. Paramedics arrive, the man is carried off on a gurney. Yellow-coated arm rises, thumbs-up for the crowd. Wild cheering.

Mailman doesn't cheer. The scene has depressed him, he feels responsible. Decides it's time to go. Then he remembers: his car is near the Square, twelve blocks away. The thought of walking that distance makes him want to cry. Come on, you just did it a few minutes ago, it's a short walk: you walk ten times that every morning! But it seems a terrible distance, he can't imagine ever reaching his car.

It takes forever. The air is clammy as a filthy palm. He puts one foot in front of the other, breathing in time with the steps, his head down, his hands in his pockets. *Gonna make it, piece-of-cake-it, gonna make it, piece-of-steak-it.* When he gets to the Square he heads south and follows West End Avenue past the new library. At night you can see inside, all the girders and beams exposed, lit by bare bulbs. Skeletal, like a burning building. He turns left onto Keuka and there is 200. It's quiet. Doesn't look like a place where someone killed himself, but what place would? Rat-and-roach-infested tenement? Abandoned house? Empty lot by the train tracks? Everyplace is a place where you can kill yourself, if you want. He climbs the steps. The row of mailboxes looks different at night, a yellow bulb lights the vestibule, the old brass just as tarnished but warmed somehow, like the salty instruments of an old sea captain. He slides his fingers under the lip of metal at the far end of the boxrow and pulls. C'mon, c'mon. He can see down into Sprain's mailbox, still full, dead men read no mail. "C'mon, dammit," he mutters. He pulls a little harder, and the whole assembly begins to separate from the wall. Enough room now. Grunting, he reaches into his pocket with his free hand and takes out the baggie'd letter. Has to bend it a little to get it in, but it drops. Thank God. He releases the boxes and they slam into place.

When he turns he sees her through the door: the girl from apartment 1, the one who saw him this morning. Suddenly he remembers her name. He's read it on her mail. Kelly V-something, Vanelli, Virelli, Valhalli, something. She's wearing a robe, clutching it closed. Sleepy.

"Hi," he says. "How are you?"

His voice sounds strange here, echoing off the tiles, as in a men's room.

"What the fuck . . . are you *doing*?" she says. Voice has the flat, cigarette-roughened timbre of a much older woman.

"I'm the mailman. Forgot a letter this morning." Smiles.

She doesn't. "Uh-huh. I saw."

"Yes, lucky thing, couldn't get them open all the way, they stick."

She's looking at him with a kind of ravenous detachment, like a lizard, something that watches its prey with preternatural calm. Or is it just that her eyes are unfocused from sleep? Whatever the case, the gaze deepens, he licks his lips and blinks, and she says, "What's your name?"

"Len Ronk."

She smiles in a not kindly manner. "Nice to meet you, Len." And she vanishes behind her apartment door.

Alone in the vestibule he pats his shirt pocket and is surprised to find it empty. A moment of panic. No, no!—the letter's delivered, it's all right now. But the panic persists, intensifies. His heart is thudding like a trapped man. *I am the vessel!*, he remembers remembering: but no, the mailbox is the vessel, he is just the mailman. Just the mailman. Stepping onto the sidewalk he flinches at the pavement's density, its lethal weight. Cars pass, their lights raking across his back. Above him bats circle in the streetlight, sending their robotic signals. He covers his head with his hands. Yikes! For the second time today, he begins to run. Spasmodically, involuntarily. His arms flap at his sides like ribbons and his feet slap the pavement. It doesn't feel good, it doesn't relieve this awful pressure under his ribs; instead he feels like a toy, winding up. And then, finally, something comes unsprung, he's cracked open, he can feel his heart tearing from his chest. He screams, of course, but what a relief! He darts into and around traffic, dodging drunks and vagrants and students on the sidewalks, his heart howling after him, a few feet behind. Every man and woman is a cartoon of fluttering hands, every streetlamp a nova of light and heat. He sees his car, alone on a once-packed street, and makes a break for it. Shouting wordlessly he unlocks the door with trembling fingers. He dives in, slams the door behind him, locking his terrible heart outside! There's an old army blanket on the back seat, hairy with paper scraps and crumbs and coffee stains, and he pulls it over himself. Do I cry now? Do I? Yes: he sobs and sobs. Please help me, his lips are saying, but there is nothing here to help, there is only his heart, pulsing like an alien outside the window, trying to break in, to find the bloody hole it came out of.

TWO

Five Cats and Three Women

When he wakes it's very late, which is to say early: two forty-five in the morning and 72 degrees Fahrenheit according to the rotating clock at the bank, the only thing visible from his vantage point on the floor of his car. Takes a minute to remember what happened. Running? Chased? His heart: an hallucination. Okay, sure. Had a little breakdown there. His left side throbs under the arm.

He sits up. It's unusually bright out: stars, moon arrayed across the sky with a brisk, chipper anality; the streetlights coldly glowing. Saturday already: already Saturday. He wedges himself between the seats and opens the glovebox, where there's a bottle of aspirin. Likes it better than the other pain relievers: acetaminophen and ibuprofen were designed, developed; their effects, however efficient, have the taint of artificiality, like a Twinkie. Aspirin is the original, a mystery to science, a beautiful accident: its bitterness, its excellent structural cohesion that gives under exactly the right amount of pressure from the teeth. And after the initial rush, the instant cessation of the ache, comes the ache's temporary return, soon to be enveloped and suffocated as the drug enters the bloodstream. There's a rhythm to it. He doesn't get that feeling from acetaminophen and ibuprofen, that's for damn sure. Opens the bottle, shakes out the aspirin, crunches them. Has those feelings. Excellent. Hoists himself onto the beautifully pre-served back seat upholstery (he bought the car new and only rarely has anyone ridden in back), clears away the junk and reclines until the pain in his chest retreats, fading into unfamiliarity then superfi-ciality then obscurity then oblivion. Then he climbs over the emer-gency brake and belts himself into the driver's seat and drives home.

Soon as he gets in he takes a long hot shower and dons his jam-mers. Cats rush to the bathroom to lick the steaming tub. He eats a bowl of cornflakes and washes it down with carrot juice. Ought to be making the juice himself—most people don't realize that the vitamin potency of fruit and vegetable juice vanishes mere minutes after its extraction—but the juicer is too damned hard to clean and all he feels he needs is the flavor of the juice anyway, to convince his body it's ingesting something that's good for it. When he's finished he leans against the kitchen counter eyes closed and the day rushes back to him. Christ: he'll have to set the alarm for early so there'll be time to mull over the day's mistakes. He goes to the bathroom, pees, brushes his teeth. In his bedroom he lies on the cot, eyes wide open. Looks at the digital clock on the floor across the room with the phone next to it. Gets up, resets the alarm for half an hour earlier. Ought to go back to bed but instead he sits crosslegged on the carpet staring at the lumi-nous numbers: brings the clock up close to his face until he can see individual cells, each light-emitting diode, can hear their hum as they struggle to remain lit. He feels that way himself. There is the barest hint of soreness as his chest expands and contracts with breaths. Puts the clock down. The cats are rustling about the house: her cats. Semma's. His dead lover's. No, don't think of her that way. His lover who has moved on to the next world. His lover who has passed. Cats led him to her, cats bore her away.

He never wanted cats, never dreamed he would have them until the day Lenore brought him one; she'd gotten it from the biomed lab, where they'd planned to euthanize it. A kitten. Lenore had long since dumped him and took up with her GP: but the doctor was allergic, and the cat was a longhair, and Lenore asked Mailman could he please keep the thing for a while, those bastards wanted to murder it, she'd come by now and then to make sure everything was all right, and meanwhile she would find it a permanent home. And by the way she had named it McChesney. He could have said no, he was well within his rights, but he didn't want to seem like a bad sport (something about the doctor, a fraternal kind of conviviality, this unspoken understanding that though he was an important man who saved people's lives he would nonetheless treat you like an equal, inspired in Mailman this hideous cringing cowardice) and anyway, how hard could it be, cats take care of themselves, right? But he had not considered the emotional toll. It—or rather *she* but Mailman thought of her as an *it*, a kind of mobile knickknack, a shitting bauble—took and took and took from him but never gave, it had no loyalty, no moral organ, no sense of personal responsibility. The best you could say for the cat was that it was well groomed, cleaning itself often, even compulsively, especially in the summer, which is also when it liked to stalk chipmunks in the grass, to bring them inside and torture them in a secluded spot until the life went out of them. He kept that cat for something like twelve years, living alone with it in the house he used to share with Lenore, until last fall, when he'd finally had enough.

A guy might reasonably expect a cat of this advanced age to mellow out, quit sprinting from the room every time he sat in a chair, stop sniffing its food bowl for ten minutes before even the first tentative bite of kibble. But no. Instead, like a human being, the cat grew entrenched in its bad habits and developed ones that, though entirely new, were absolutely true to form, for example *refusing to use its litter box*, instead demanding to be let outside so that it could relieve itself in somebody's garden (as if that were somehow cleaner), and the cat did this many times each night, to the point that Mailman didn't bother going back to bed once the cycle of opening and closing the front door got under way. At the height of this routine he was getting perhaps (like last night!) three hours of sleep daily which could best be described as fitful; his dreams were full of monstrously distorted cat sounds and he half-woke on several occasions during those hours to respond to door-opening requests that proved to be false alarms.

So, on his day off one week, Mailman went down to the hardware store and bought himself a heavy-duty molded-plastic pet portal. He pulled the basement door off its hinges and jigsawed the appropriate-sized hole, then screwed in the pet portal and spent much of the next several days directing the mewling McChesney through it: a thankless task, as the cat extended its claws when picked up and coiled itself into a ball of the greatest possible diameter, so that Mailman was forced to wedge it through the opening, suffering multiple bleeding wounds on his hands and arms in the process. But in the end the project was a success: the cat seemed to relish its newfound independence; apparently it had enjoyed the summoning of Mailman no more than Mailman had enjoyed opening and closing the front door for it; and a blissful peace fell over the house and lasted for the better part of two weeks.

Two weeks! Oh how he longs for those days, he and the cat living their own separate lives, having no physical contact, neither needing to acknowledge the other, with only the food and water bowls to fill and the cat box to occasionally glance into, just in case. It wouldn't be a stretch to say that these were two of the best weeks of his post-wife life.

Then they ended. It was two in the morning and quite black inside and out of the house; the moon was new, the stars obscured by August clouds. The cat was asleep on the other side of the bedroom, as it tended to be, apparently preferring Mailman's unconscious company to his actual living presence, which was fine by Mailman. The night was still and restful and unseasonably cool. The occasional passing car served only to deepen the silence that surrounded it, and to deepen Mailman's sleep.

What woke him then? The click of toenails on the kitchen linoleum? The scent of a foreign beast? A sixth sense? Whatever it

was, Mailman was awake. In the dim light filtering down the hall
from the streetlamp that shone into the kitchen, he could see its low
silhouette in the bedroom doorway: another cat. Mailman groaned,
and then McChesney was awake, hackled like a stegosaur, and the
cats began to screech and hiss and back into corners. Mailman
switched on the light and saw it: fat and black and tailless by accident,
not breed, it had the bony haunches of a male, and as Mailman
watched, it lifted its leg and sprayed the corner of his bed. Of his *bed*!
He threw his pillow at it—"Out! Out!"—and it bounded through the
door and scuttled away down the hall. McChesney was arched and
puffed, growling like a terrier under its nimbus of fur. Now he could
smell the spray—piss! Cat piss in his house!—and when he went to
retrieve his pillow it too had been sprayed, and suddenly the whole
room smelled of it, like an unwashed dry underarm, like a stairwell in
a parking garage. He leapt out of bed (scaring the living shit out of
McChesney, who exited the room as if yanked by crook), gathered the
pillow and sheets and blanket and mattress pad into his arms and
shoved them, along with an excessive amount of detergent and
bleach, into the laundry; then from the kitchen he grabbed a bucket
and squirted dish detergent and water into it, and with a sponge
scrubbed the wall and carpet and floor and the frame of his bed, the
smell of the foreign cat filling his entire head, his entire *being*, no
that's not right, how can something fill one's being? But that's what it
was like: once his head was full, the smell (on his hands now and on
the sponge and in the soapy gray slop in the bucket) seeped down and
infiltrated wherever it was in him the essential purest ore of the self
was kept, and made *that* smell like cat piss too. All this from one goddam cat. He cleaned for a good half hour and still he could smell it, so
he threw the sponge and bucket into the backyard and slept on the living room floor.

Next night he blocked the cat door with a cardboard box full of old
clothes. McChesney mewled to go out in intervals that seemed flaw-
lessly spaced to interrupt the final stages of wakefulness before they

were engulfed by sleep, and in his half-dreams as he drifted, Mailman was reaching, swiping, grasping for some unrecognizable thing that looked close enough to touch but in fact was impossibly distant. He woke mostly dead and it took him nine hours to deliver the day's mail. That night he took away the clothes box and the intruder cat came back and howled again and ate all of McChesney's food and *shat in Mailman's left shoe, and* sprayed, this time on the sofa, and so he blocked the door again. This went on for several weeks, until most of his ruined furniture stood in the yard and some neighbor (if he found out which one he would burn his/her house down to the *fucking foundation*) called the cops on him about it. And so the furniture was hauled away (274-HAUL) by a goateed fatty with a twenty-year-old pickup, who charged him forty dollars. But it was all right, the furniture had been Lenore's and he'd wanted to get rid of it for a long time, even if it meant there was no place to sit or eat breakfast.

One night, instead of reporting to bed, he went to the cellar, arranged a folding chair beside the cat door, and sat down. He resolved to stay all night, if necessary, however long it took. When at last the offending cat hopped suavely in, carrying itself with all the blithe confidence of a mall cop, Mailman grabbed it by the scruff and pressed it to his lap. The claws came out and dug into his legs and the lips curled back revealing pitiful fangs. But Mailman was oblivious to pain or threat. Giggling, he fumbled with the collar until the tags came into view and he memorized the address: it's on his own block, for Chrissake, isn't that the place with the kids who throw eggs at his house on Halloween and also on the nights leading up to and following it? The place with the motorcycle and the dead rosebushes? The place that caught fire and they put it out but never repaired anything, so there's plastic over the burnt-out window and smoke damage on the peeling clapboards? Oh, man. Oh, man. He thrust the cat into the clothes box (emptied earlier of clothes) and folded down the flaps and marched out the front door intending to put a stop to this nonsense once and for all—he would tell those people a thing or two, how the hell they ended up in this perfectly good neighborhood he'd never know, there ought to be some kind of law keeping people like that out, a law against cigarette-stained mustaches and garments with the Buffalo Bills logo on them and rusted-out American cars with no mufflers and mullet haircuts and distended lard-fed bellies with dirty tee shirts stretched over them and children's toys sitting out in the grass with tall weeds grown around them and twisted filthy air-hardened rags caught in the hedge.

But when he got to the address it wasn't them—*they* were asleep behind their curtained windows, the Harley stowed somewhere out of sight. Instead it was the house next door, a trim brick bungalow with flowering plants in boxes on the porch and a spotless moonlit Mercedes parked perfectly straight in the newly asphalted drive. The house was uncurtained and a lamp burned at the rear of a large open livingroom (a marble sculpture resting on a baby grand piano, abstract oil paintings on the walls), where a thin grayhaired man, outlined by the blue glow of a laptop computer, could be seen bent over a small desk. The sight of this man gave Mailman pause. He stood on the sidewalk with the cat scratching and keening in the box under his arm and considered leaving the man alone, he looked so beautifully content, so *seasoned,* with his trim neck and square shoulders, working on whatever it was he was at work on on his computer: look: there by his elbow was a steaming mug of coffee, he was burning the midnight oil, probably didn't even know his cat had left the house, might as well give the old fella the benefit of the doubt. But in the end he thought he ought to let the guy know, as a kind of neighborly service, what his cat was up to, the poor thing might get some disease or hit by a car or tortured and killed by the people next door: so he climbed the tidy stone steps and crossed the porch and lightly knocked. He could hear the grayhaired man's approach; the porchlight went on and a face appeared in the door's small window: thin nose, narrow mouth, piercing eyes, around sixty-five, looked like some kind of genius, probably a professor of something-or-other. "Yes?" Mailman held up the box and the two men listened for a moment to the sound of the cat exerting itself. "I suppose you've found Dissy."

"Dissy?"

"Short for Odysseus. He is, of course, a wanderer. I tremble"—an eye roll—"as I inquire where you found him."

"In my bedroom."

"Oh, dear. Do come in." Door opened wide and Mailman entered, he could smell a recently blown out candle, freshly ground coffee (and there also was the blurb of the coffeemaker in the last moments of its brew cycle), something else he couldn't quite identify, a smell of human effort. Immaculately clean if lived-in house, not a cat hair in evidence, carved mahogany coffee table scattered with magazines, a wine bottle and other junk, blankets wadded on the sofa, a couple of fancy old chairs bearing embroidered pillows, but all around them dustless corners and art hanging at right angles. "Yes," the man said quietly, "I'm afraid I haven't had time to straighten up." He took from Mailman's arms the shuddering box.

"That's okay. I just wanted to return your cat. He sprayed my house, I have to tell you, I've had to get rid of a lot of furniture, and I was hoping I could convince you to, if it's not too much trouble, to either keep him inside at night or have him fixed or—"

"Beg pardon," the man said, "Mister . . ."

"Lippincott."

"Mister Lippincott, I shall not have my cat quote-unquote fixed as you put it when there is nothing per se *wrong* with him. Nor will I prevent his egress. He must seek lady cats to fuck."

Mailman's eyes were drawn to the piano, where the marble sculpture he'd noticed from outside was beginning to resolve itself into the figure of a man, seated upon a stylized tree stump, his head thrown back, his arms behind him, supporting his backward lean. And the stump—it seemed strange—it sort of extended around and obscured the man's knees—

"How would you like it, Mister Lippincott, if you were visiting a lady friend at her residence, and at the very height of your passion you were interrupted, seized by giant rough hands, imprisoned in a box and delivered to some white-coated Mengele who unscabbarded a knife and cut your testicles off? No, there shall be no 'fixing,' sir."

—no, wait, that isn't the stump, it's—it's—

"I regret I could not be of assistance, Mister Lippincott, good night."

—it was form of a woman, a kneeling woman, kneeling in front of the man, and she appeared—that is, she seemed to be—could it be?—*fellating* the man? Could that be right? Could his neighbor actually have a marble statue of a *blow job* on his piano? So that when he played, say, a Chopin polonaise, he could peer over the score and be inspired by the sculpted image of *oral sex*? Where, he wondered as he was ushered out the door, would a person *get* such a thing? For months now Mailman has walked past this house, and the statue is still there, indecipherable from the street, exerting its influence over his perception of the entire block and the people who inhabit it: the children on their bikes and the little old ladies and the avuncular priests on their way to mass: poor slobs, infected now with the subtle, subliminal germ of perversion. But then, on that night, he was left only with a lingering distaste and without a solution to his cat problem.

And so he closed up the cat door for good, and it came to pass that he couldn't stand it anymore and had to get rid of McChesney at any cost. So one night he got out of bed and shoved the cat into the pet carrier and got into his car and drove about fifteen miles out to the rural edge of the county and dumped his cat in a field. It was easy. Somebody would find it, he surmised, somebody would feed it and take it in and get along with it just fine. Next time Lenore came by he'd tell her McChesney ran away and he'd put up posters in the neighborhood, for her sake, but of course it wouldn't make any difference, by then the cat would be with some loving country family and would live in a barn and chase mice all day long, which is what cats are supposed to do.

The next morning he woke feeling great, said hello and howareya to everyone at the post office, drank the weak office coffee out of a styrofoam cup, heard two jokes and told one (the one about the priest, the rabbi, and Bill Clinton), walked his route whistling and gave rubber bands to children and ate a fine lunch on the Square and returned home, where he was greeted by a ringing phone.

"Hi, is your cat lost?"

A chill of absolute horror. Impossible! Somebody must have seen his car, written down the license plate number, called a buddy at the police station who was able to look up the registration info ("Ordinarily we don't do that kind of thing but if this joker was abandoning his cat I'm willing to bend the rules") and gave the caller his name and phone number: and now they were just playing with him, pretending it's all innocent and that the police aren't on the way to his place right now to haul him in on cruelty-to-animals charges. Oh, God, what have I done?

"Hello? Do I have the right number? I found McChesney, is she your cat?"

He later realized he could have gotten out of it, there were dozens of ways, "Oh, I just got this number, I don't know who had it before" or "We used to have a cat but its name was Walter," something, *anything*, and the caller would have just said sorry and hung up and probably brought the cat to the SPCA.

But no. He said, "Where did you find it?"

"She was wandering in the weeds along Bird Sanctuary Road. I stopped to pick some goldenrod, and there the poor dear was. Where do you live? I'll walk over with her."

"Um, I live downtown." Thinking: how did she *know*?

Long pause. "Downtown *Nestor*?"

"Yes."

"Heavens! That's ten miles! How long's she been lost?"

"Couple of days."

"Oh, what a tale she must have to tell! Thank goodness she had tags or she might have been lost to this life."

Tags? The cat had *tags*? Of course: the clinking when it eats out of its bowl. He never thought to check. Idiot! The woman was asking him should she bring the cat over and he said sure, bring it over, and she said "All right then" in a tone indicating she didn't approve of the "it." In other words, a cat person.

Mailman slumped on the livingroom floor (he hadn't yet replaced the furniture) with his head in his hands and briefly mourned the past something like fifteen flawless hours of normal human life without the burden of a pet. Why did people saddle themselves with animals? He could hear himself debating it with an animal lover: "But man and the animals have been in partnerships of some kind for millennia" (this animal lover might say, his loosely curly hair framing a tanned bespectacled face, his chambray work shirt reeking slightly of woodsmoke and dog) "and there's no reason this shouldn't continue today." "But you see," (Mailman would reply) "in antiquity man employed the animals in useful tasks such as the plowing of fields and the guarding of property, and the animals lived outside, not in the house, which is clearly not the place for them." "Oh, but many dogs serve as sentries in modern times, and they are quite happy living in the house." "You say happy, but you can't know; in fact I'd argue there can be no happiness without self-determination, and a dog depends heavily on his so-called master for the necessities of life." "Are you saying that thousands of years—oh! Did you hear that? That was the call of the ruby-crested weed thrush—that thousands of years of domestication, which have bred into these animals an intense affinity for man, have been a mistake? Because I would argue that the domestication of animals is what made civilization possible. Imagine, if you will, how agriculture could have gotten started without oxen to—" "Yes, yes, okay, you've made your point, but what about the cat?, which is what we're talking about here, the cat was never very useful, wild cats aren't social like wolves are—" "Some of the big cats are social." "—okay, whatever, but domesticated cats sure aren't, they're simply self-interested and don't really want to be with us, and for that matter I don't think dogs really want us either, they only like us because we happen to be there, happen to feed them and let them crap." "If you're looking for my approval, Albert, for this cat-dumping plan of yours" (because that's what Mailman had decided to do, to cut off McChesney's collar and try again tonight, this time several dozen miles farther down the road) "you aren't going to get it. Your little McChesney will be devoured by coyotes." "Survival of the fittest. Don't you enviro types believe in that?" "I believe," the animal lover said, getting up from his giant natural-fiber-upholstered down-filled cushion, "in tenderness." Well, screw tenderness, Mailman was going to do it, his brief life since McChesney was simply too good, too *normal*, and he couldn't live with the damned thing another second. As soon as this woman, this cat person, had come and gone, he was going to get into his car and redeliver the cat unto its destiny.

It couldn't have been more than twenty minutes before she showed, she must have hung up the phone and jumped right in the car. She was holding the cat in her arms, not in any kind of carrier or cage, and walked slowly into Mailman's house stroking its head while gently kind of *squeezing*, the hand soft and deliberate and *practiced*, and this would have turned him on mightily if not for the look of smug satisfaction on the cat's face, those dark little lips slightly parted and the pointy teeth exposed. The woman was in fact rather sexy: though her face looked older than its years (he guessed she was around fifty but the face wouldn't have been out of place on a sixty-year-old, with its slight grayness and deepish wrinkles and a certain crooked looseness, as if the skin had come free of a few of its moorings but not in a symmetrical way, and the nose splotched and spotted and the eyes deep in the head: but for all that not a bad face, in fact a cute and friendly one), her body looked far younger, sheathed in a kind of clinging linen caftan: stocky yet smooth, muscular, her rear holding up beautifully, her wide round strong hips and legs and really nice-looking breasts (even with a cat pressed against them), large without seeming heavy; the overall effect was one of extraordinary fecundity and longevity, as if she were going to live forever. Immediately he began looking around the place in a panic to find her a chair, but there weren't any, so he had to go to the kitchen and grab a couple of gray metal folding chairs and set them up. But of course, "Actually, maybe I should leave these in the kitchen in case you want to sit down and have a coffee or tea or something," he said, and she, still holding and stroking the cat and smiling with what seemed slight though genuine amusement, replied "Yes, that would be delightful," and he returned the chairs to the kitchen.

They sat down. He made tea. She cooed at and petted the cat, which efforts were irritating him far more than turning him on, though they were still turning him on. This was Semma ("That's right, Semma, S-E-M-M-A"): married once, two adult kids, divorced ("He didn't wish to receive what it was I had to give him") for five years, lived today with three kitties and a roommate named Lily who owned a loom ("That's right, a loom"). He told her his story and she asked him what he liked most about cats, and he said, "Oh, I don't know, I guess just the essential, you know, a thing about them that, it's just that certain quality, they seem so possessed of this, and I respect and admire a thing that has this thing, and knows it has this thing and seems to say 'I am the thing I am and this is mine and that's that,' and it's really nice to have that kind of presence in your life." She told him she knew exactly what he meant and said, "What I love about cats is their angel-like ability to receive pleasure." He thought to say "*Angel-like?*" but did not, instead, "You like that they receive pleasure, I see." "Yes, they take such pleasure in pleasure." "So what about them gives *you* pleasure?" "I take pleasure in pleasing them. That is the source of my pleasure." He said, "That's very wonderful of you," and she laughed and said, "Yes, it is a wonderful thing." Before she left she said, "Here, take my phone number, if you ever need to get away and would like McChesney to have a sitter, you can call me, she loved Bitsy and Wrinkles and Huck." She handed him the number written on an ATM receipt. He noted that her balance was in the high four figures.

That afternoon he cut off McChesney's collar with a scissors and drove out to the Onteo Lake Motor Park to dump her. It was the middle of a gray day and hardly anyone was around. He parked by the woods and tossed the cat out and it ran right into the trees as if content, even eager, to go. He never saw the damned thing again.

The next day he called Semma and said, "Hi, it's Albert Lippincott, you brought me my cat, and I had such a good time talking with you, and maybe we could see each other, what do you think of dinner?" She said, "I would be very pleased to see you, shall we dine in or out?" "Oh, in, out, I dunno, how about," he said, thinking sex, "in?" "Let me receive you at my house at eight tonight." "Great," he said, "thanks." "What are your dietary needs?" "No cheese, otherwise I eat it all, are you a vegetarian?" To his surprise she said she wasn't, she loved meat, "I love everything about animals, including the flavor of their flesh, which I think the gods made for other beasts to consume, even human flesh which the fiercest animals are meant to eat," and Mailman did not question her about the word "gods." She said "You should bring McChesney," and he said, "I think I should tell you that McChesney is actually sick, dying in fact, which is probably why it, or rather she, strayed so far, she's a little demented, I think she's looking for a place to die, so I've sealed up her cat door. Don't worry, it's not catching." "Good heavens, I'm sorry, what on earth is wrong?" He said, thinking of the lab the cat came from, "Cancer." She said, "Of what, she seemed so healthy." He said, "It's everywhere, it's what do they say, metastasized? Some days are better than others, she gets painkillers." "Oh, I feel pain for her." "No need, it isn't your fault, I've come to terms with it really, I prefer not to talk about it." "You poor man, I'll show my sympathy by making good nourishing food."

He arrived right on time, met the roommate (a longhaired distracted woman of about forty who seemed already to have eaten and who subsequently spent the whole night in her room making fabric), and sat at the table, where cats (also longhaired) repeatedly jumped onto his lap, and he repeatedly pretended to like it. "Are they bothering you?" Semma asked over their giant filets mignons. "It's just they remind me of my own cat and her illness." So Semma got up and put the cats out for the night.

They had dinner and drinks. They spent some time ogling each other while she named each tree and bird that could be found in the vicinity of the house. She said, "I've been delighted by your company." He said, "You're delighting too. Ful." She said, "Would you like a tour of my home?" "Please." She showed him around, led him to the bedroom. "This mattress is made entirely of organic and unbleached fiber. Here," she said, taking his hand and leading him to the bed, "smell it, it is utterly unadulterated by inorganic chemicals." He leaned over, sniffed the bed. It smelled like her, like sex. "Sure, smells great, here, come smell it with me." They sprawled across the mattress, stroking the comforter. "I too am made entirely of organic materials," she said. "Funny, so am I, we ought to get along fine." They sniffed one another like dogs and then took all their clothes off. He was right, her body was terrifically smooth and firm, if he squinted she could pass for a husky thirty, but he barely got to touch her: she really worked him over, feeling him everywhere and saying "Mmm, mmm" as if she were the one being touched, and then when they finally had sex (Semma on top, synchronizing the rhythm of her efforts perhaps unconsciously to the jingling thump of the pedals of Lily's loom behind the all-too-thin wall) she made the exact same sound as the pigeons that had roosted on the balcony outside his college dorm room, this at a time when he absolutely did not want to be thinking about pigeons. And even then, with her shoulders heaving and breasts sloshing above him, when he tried to put his hands on any part of her besides her knees, she pushed him away and instead ran her fingers through his hair and over his chest and even reached behind her to massage his legs, never pausing in her dovey humming or her methodical pinioning upon him. In the end he just gripped the knees and rode it out. Afterward she lay on her stomach (rendering inaccessible most of the interesting stuff) and blindly massaged his hip and arm and ribs with strong fingers and said, "Was that pleasurable for you?" He said, "It was great, all that touching you do, I would love to give you that kind of pleasure, what do you say?" "Oh, but I felt pleasure, very intense pleasure." "Sure, me too, I don't mean that, I mean giving you the kind of pleasure you gave me, wow, it was amazing the way you did all that, I mean how about I do that same thing to you?" "Nothing is more pleasurable to me than pleasing the man I'm with, I hope you mean it when you say you're pleased." "Oh, of course, very pleased." "Then I'm pleased too." They slept awhile and he figured he could give it another shot, so he woke her and they again went at it, this time him on top, except when he put his hands on her breasts she took them off and began kissing and sucking on his fingers, and never once let go of his wrists. Afterward she said "Did you feel pleasure?" and he said "Yes, I'm very pleased" and left it at that.

They saw each other for about a month. After the first few days he realized McChesney's absence was going to be a problem, so he called her one night (late, to give the impression that he was all torn up over it) and told her the cat had died. She said, "I'll be right over, we'll have a burial ceremony." "No, that's a bad idea, I feel like— I think basically that this is something I must do alone." "You say that because you don't want to be embarrassed in front of me, but you need a friend, I'll be there shortly, we'll find a good spot." "Well," he said, "all right, sure, that's fine." He hung up, shouted, "Shit!" Went down in the basement and found a wooden box with latches and a rope handle that some wine had come in; he stuffed it with old clothes and nailed it shut. It had the approximate heft of a dead cat wasted away from multiple cancers. By the time he finished she had arrived. They took the box out to the bird sanctuary ("She loved birds," Semma said, though how could she have known that? and was it even true? and if it was, wasn't it true of all cats?) and buried it in a clearing near a pond. Then she embraced him and sobbed exactly once and said "Poor Albert, let me please you," and she undressed him but not herself and did her hand thing for a while, then stripped off her undies and straddled him on the weedy ground with her dress still on, and pleased him. Then he thanked her and they went to his place and slept, and ate cold cereal for breakfast, over which they exchanged occasional slightly shy (though there was no reason to be shy, really, it seemed like the shyness was all an act that one of them had started and the other picked up on and gone along with, but he couldn't think of who was who) grins.

Thinking about it now (as he sits unsleepily on the bedroom floor) he finds himself knitting his hands together, weaving the fingers (as if upon Lily's loom), and thinks: I think I'll call my sister. Thinks: why do I always call my sister when I'm thinking about sex and/or death? Thinks: that doesn't bear thinking about. He picks up the phone. He calls her.

She's home and awake. He figured as much: she's an actress, mostly of the stage but occasionally the screen (on a TV cop show she once played the mother of a rape-and-murder victim who learns from the show's dark-eyed hunk star that her daughter is dead: Gillian had no lines, only stage directions: trembled, mouthed the word *no*, raised her hands to her face, collapsed against the actor portraying her character's husband, buried her head in his chest and wept as he intoned, *It can't be, she was just here a few hours ago.* Mailman doesn't have a TV so he went to a bar to watch it when it aired—he had to buy a couple of lawyers double bourbons to get them to change the channel—and wept at the sight of his sister weeping). When she's in a play she gets back to her apartment around two or three and usually has some people over and a few drinks and doesn't go to bed until daybreak, then sleeps until about one in the afternoon. "Gillian," he says and his guts rearrange themselves the way they do when he is about to hear her voice, which usually necessitates his at some point having to call her back so he can go sit on the toilet.

"Albert!"

He can hear glasses clinking and jazz playing and people laughing and talking in emphatic voices, and the sound of a blender intermittently turning on and off as if someone is hitting the PULSE button, checking the results, hitting the button again. "Can you talk? I mean are you busy?"

"Well, the house is full of people, darling, but I've always time for you."

"Did the play go well tonight? How'd you do?"

She laughs, *HEEheeheeheeheeheehee, OOHhoohoohoohoohoo.* "I did *fine*, Albert. You sound exactly like Father."

Father and Mother: that's what she calls them. "No, I don't."

"You do, dear, that pointed *question*, betraying his complete ignorance of what I actually *do* for a living. It isn't a multiple-choice exam, Albert dear, it's a *performance*, it is an *artistic endeavor*. It cannot be quantified. I cannot say to you 'Albert, I scored a ninety-one on a scale of one to a hundred,' or 'Albert, I was judged as excellent in three categories and very good in two.' I can tell you that I am *satisfied* with my performance tonight, though as always there is room for improvement. Is that an acceptable answer?"

"Yes."

She is sixty to his fifty-seven. Never was a looker but onstage (when she was young) always played the seductress: mistresses, adulterers; women who cheat, maim, kill to satisfy passions. She had a buxomness, an appealing solidity. Drove him crazy to watch. In one play, way off-Broadway in 1974, another woman (as the cheated-upon wife or thrown-over girlfriend or whatever) reached out nightly and tore Gillian's shirt off revealing bare breasts which she quickly threw her crossed arms over. Mailman went to see it intending to surprise her afterward but left during intermission and drove four hours straight back to Nestor. Never told her he came: maybe in New York that kind of thing is not shocking or embarrassing but to him it was both. He has never understood why she always has to play the object of men's desire (and occasionally women's), she seems to like these roles, even seeks them out and has become known for them. Now that she's older she tends to play the spent sexual object, the vain woman clinging desperately to her physical attractiveness (à la Norma Desmond in *Sunset Boulevard*, which Gillian went to see six times even though she was only ten, having told their parents that she was going in for repeat viewings of *Harvey*), which Mailman doesn't think suits her. Though what does he know, it's been three years or so since he's even seen her in person and at least a year since he's seen her on television, where nobody looks like they do in real life anyhow.

Friday's prunes and granola bar turn over in Saturday morning's stomach. He quietly belches.

"Well, brother dear, to what do I owe the unexpected pleasure of this call?"

"I was just thinking of you."

"Mmmm," fake sexy yumyum sounds accompanied by the slip and smack of the licking of lips, "well I'm certainly glad to hear that, in what *context* exactly were you thinking of me?"

"I just wanted . . . I had, it was like, uh, a sort of an episode? I had a . . . fantasy?"

"Ooo!"

"Well, an hallucination."

"This is America, Albert, we have *a* hallucination here."

"Yes. Well, it was— I had this hallucination."

"How fascinating! But *please*, Albert, *stop*, you're over*whelming* me with details."

"Yes, uh. Well, I sort of—I seemed to think that—"

"Spit it out, dear."

"—that my heart had come out of my chest, and . . . and was chasing me down the street."

Her response is a long high screaming laugh that proves to have been a reaction not to what he has said (as he first assumes, as anyone would) but to some pinch or ass-grab in the kitchen ("Bernard, go off and do that to *yourself,* if you please!"). At any rate, in the wake of the laugh he no longer wants to talk about what happened, and hopes that while she's laughing she'll forget what he said. But she says, "I'm sorry Albert, you were telling me about *an* hallucination you had, your *British* hallucination as it were? Did you fantasize you were fucking the Queen, ha ha?"

"No, nothing like that, it's nothing," he says, thinking, Ah, shove it, asshole, forget I ever called, "I just felt weird earlier and couldn't, or rather can't, ah, sleep. Tell me what's doing, or I mean going on, with you?"

"Well, did I tell you that I was in Florida last month?"

Florida: home to their parents, still alive and idly kicking. "Really? Did you see Mom and Dad?"

"Darling, I *stayed* with them for nearly a *week*."

"You stayed in their house?"

"Oh my, no. I stayed in an hotel. Ah! Now you've got me doing it. *A* hotel. I stayed in *a* hotel and drove my lovely little rental car to their bungalow each morning at ten, and ate brunch if you could call it that at the IHOP down the street—which they *drove* to, Albert, though it was mere blocks away!—and then sat around the house while Mother retired to her boudoir to spend several hours freshening up, by which I mean drinking gin, and Father retired for an equal deadly long time to his little workshop to nearly kill himself with his chemicals and burners and metals and what-have-you, while I sat on the afghan'd sofa reading back issues of this science magazine *Science* which I'm sure you're *intimately* familiar with. By the time we regrouped it would be suppertime, which is to say four o'clock, which is when *everyone* eats in that land of the living dead, and we'd go out to one or another fried seafood restaurant and Father would say to the waitress, who *invariably* had gigantic tan tits, 'This is my daughter, the actress,' as if some little beach whore would care that an old lady she has never before in her life seen has been on television once or twice. Then we'd eat, and Mother, already mostly drunk, would drink more still, and start talking about how she used to sing in a joint like this—she actually used that word, *joint*—in her heyday—she said the word *heyday*—and would start *singing*, my God, very quietly at first and then louder and louder. And Father would talk about how wonderful those days were when as we both know those days were not at all wonderful. And by the time we were finished with all the eating and drinking it would seem like midnight, but it was only seven-thirty or eight, and we'd go back to the house and Mother would again *retire to the boudoir* and pass out, and Father would again retreat into the 'workshop,' and I would walk the flesh-strewn beach, until the sun set over the water, which of course reminded me of L.A. and Richard, and I would burst into tears."

"Richard?"

"*Richard*, Albert, my once-fiancé, who died of an overdose of *blow*, Albert." This angrily, she's very upset he forgot. But how in God's name could he remember, everything that happens to her comes to him in exactly the same "theatrical" manner, it's impossible to tell what's really important to her from what's just practice.

"I'm sorry. Of course."

"Of *course*. Well. I just burst into tears nightly. Then I would visit an awful bar in a nearby resort hotel and try to get men to buy me drinks. Or rather should I say *succeed* in getting men to buy me drinks, for nothing in the world could be more easy, though none of said men could have been a day under seventy-five. And then it was back to my own hotel, having turned down offers of whatever, marriage, cunnilingus, the foxtrot, to collapse before the free cable TV and watch each night the same awful science fiction movie about the asteroid destroying earth."

"I saw that one. Weren't you in it?"

She seems taken by surprise. "As a matter of fact I was. As a matter of fact I was part of a subplot about a grandmother whose grandchildren are visiting, and we all had to huddle in the basement as the small chunks of asteroid, because you see the big rock broke up in the atmosphere and rained death, as they say, to earth in tiny pieces, as the chunks struck things like the *power station*, causing it to explode and start a huge forest fire."

"It was a departure for you."

"It was a piece of shit I did for *money*, Albert, the *departure* was that I got *paid*. 'The pay's the thing,' as Shakespeare might have said, ha ha. So. That's how Mother and Father are getting on. Now tell me how you are."

"How I are. Am. Well, I think I told you, I had that sort of episode, and— can I call you right back? Sorry, I have to— it'll just be a minute—"

"Go, go, be sure to light a match when you're done."

He hangs up, runs to the toilet, flings down his pajama pants and relieves himself mightily into the bowl. He's done in seconds—that's how it is with him, he probably spends less time on the toilet than almost anyone else on earth, especially anyone his age or older. Yet even finished he lingers, reluctant to call Gillian back. Doesn't like what she said about the asteroid movie, a person shouldn't so baldly admit she feels that way about something she did that is important or moving or powerful to other people. Not that the asteroid movie was actually good—as with most of the movies he goes to he left it feeling angry at its hackneyed pandering to American themes and types (e.g., the crass yet muscled and handsome outsider who proves to have great integrity and gives his own life so that others may live, which is to say a Christ figure; the idea that Americans of every stripe set aside their differences and work together when the chips are down; the self-ish entrepreneur who capitalizes on others' misfortune, who is unwaveringly portrayed as evil even though his life philosophy comes closer to matching that of your average American than any other Hollywood character type, and who is dispatched by the movie's end in some sickly comic way, in this case by a little tiny asteroid fragment penetrating his asteroid-proofed bunker and drilling itself into his forehead while he's trying to get it on—"The world's going to end, you know. Don't you want to do it while you still can?"—with the until-now-innocent daughter of a sympathetic aeronautics engineer;

the idea that random disasters can be averted with a little "American know-how" and a lot of good old American "attitude"; the idea that death is optional except for martyrs, bad guys, and a small percentage of faceless innocents who when it's all over will be mourned in candlelight vigils and starkly minimalist museums and grave miniseries and will prove an inspiration to us all as we recover and take up the yoke of business as usual). But there's something about this kind of movie that is important; this kind of movie is not intended to be good, but to serve as a ritual, a shared experience of a sort that probably used to exist when humans lived in little roving bands of a hundred or so and spent all their time killing the things they ate and turning the things' fur into clothing, but no longer exists in any natural or organic way, and so has to be created by giant multinational corporations. That is, it's shallow to downplay one's role in the creation of such a spectacle. So maybe he won't call her back. But as he is cinching the drawstring on his jammers, the phone rings.

"While you were pooping I started worrying about you," she says, and the background is quiet now; he assumes she's moved into the bedroom and shut the door against her party. "I don't like this little break*down*let of yours. I wonder if you might be working too hard."

"It wasn't a breakdown. And I'm not working too hard."

"I think of the postal carriers"—he is strangely gratified that she uses the current term for the Postal Service's delivery personnel, even though he himself prefers the extremely literal if not quite as descriptive and certainly not as gender-neutral *mailman*—"who have shall we say *lost touch with reality* and gunned down people at work. You're not moving in that direction, are you, Albert?"

"No."

"Well, good. That's very good, I can say with *considerable* relief. But if not work, then what? I hope you haven't had your heart broken recently?"

"No," he says uncertainly, which uncertainty Gillian either misses or pretends to miss.

"Well then I hope you're at least having your rocks off now and then." The trilling stage laugh, *TEEheeheeheeheehee*. "I'd hate to think of you having to service yourself nightly, my dear, surely there is a woman in your life I don't know about." And then, more quietly, not for his ears, "Not yet, Bernard."

Deep embarrassment. Mild abdominal cramping. "I do not service myself nightly." This at least is completely true.

"Oh, I'm sorry, brother dear, did I embarrass you? I forget about what a *monster* this city has turned me into! But back to you, Albert: what do you think this episode of yours signifies? Perhaps we ought to do a little analysis right here, over the phone—why not?, I say. I've had a few run-ins with head shrinkers, I've more or less memorized the patter, we can pick apart the various elements of your hallucination and try to interpret them."

"I don't think that's a very good idea."

"Come, now—it'll be just like old times!"

"No," he says, "it won't. Actually, it's getting late here"—actually, it's the same time here as in New York, but what he means is that three-thirty in the morning is indeed very late in Nestor whereas three-thirty in the morning in New York is just three-thirty in the morning; and she seems to agree implicitly that this is so because she doesn't object to his formulation—"and I have to get up in two hours," he lies, "and get ready to go to work."

"Well, when you're ready"—she sounds disappointed and for a moment he wants to stay on with her, it's the first time he's had any kind of power in the conversation—"to talk, I'm ready to talk. Oh, Albert."

"Oh, what?"

"Nothing, no, never mind. You're a good boy, Albert, take care of yourself."

They hang up. Just like old times, indeed. He switches off the light, lies back on the pillow, closes his eyes. There was a game they used to play, or rather Gillian played the game, Mailman simply lay there: this was in their old broken-backed family cottage outside Princeton, New Jersey, where their father taught chemistry: the one that was full of the apparently pointless projects their father always engaged himself in and their mother so despised: rerouting all the heating ducts or plastering over a doorway and opening up a new one two feet to the left or creating a doorbell that caused a red light to blink inside the house instead of a chime to sound. There Mailman shared a room with Gillian. He had his own bed but often slept with her, she arranged him on her pillow with her dolls and called him Jessyboo and before they went to sleep covered him from head to toe with kisses. She would sing "Sweet little Jessyboo, don't you know that I love you?" and took all his clothes off and dressed him in her doll clothes (this was the game), which were too small, or her own clothes, which were too large. If he can be said to have an earliest memory, that's it: the feeling of being naked between his sister's undressing and then dressing of him. This went on until he was nearly five and she nearly eight; given the kind of person their mother was and is, it's likely that Gillian at least sensed, if not understood, something of what sexual attraction was, though certainly not its implications, or not all of them anyway. Maybe that's why she stopped the game, one night when he lay limp as he did when he wanted to play and she pouted dimply at him—"Albert, grow *up*"—and turned her back to work at arranging her things in the dresser. The comment drew their mother into the room, where she found Gillian placidly folding clothes and Mailman writhing nakedly on the bed. She emitted a wordless shout and strode to the bed and slapped him. "Put on your clothes! Put on your clothes! You sick little sonofabitch, you are going to turn your sister into some kind of little *whore!*"

After that they stopped sleeping in the same bed. Albert's own bed felt stiff and strange to him and seemed to result in stiff and strange dreams, usually involving his parents or Gillian or one of his new acquaintances in kindergarten reacting to his overtures, pleas, confessions, etc., with a frozen, inhumanly emotionless expression, and running away. He wanted desperately to unburden himself of the dreams, but at the time Gillian would not have him, and in fact had focused her attention elsewhere, to the fads and inspirations and girlish allegiances of life in school and among children her age.

And then they moved to a new house: a four-bedroom Victorian in Princeton filled with light and echoes and mice. Their parents at last had managed to seek out, agree upon and arrange the purchase of this place, and though their father would take an absurdly long time to accustom himself to it, to their mother it was perfect, the realization of her dream of a respectable façade behind which she could indulge her ambition to become a sultry nightclub singer. She would have to leave town to do it, because Princeton was dry and contained no nightclubs: but the house did provide an entire room just for her, which she promptly decorated with red velvet curtains and a giant vanity featuring a thousand little drawers and cubbies and a mirror surrounded by lightbulbs, and she hung framed magazine clippings of famous singers and bought a special private record player from which the sounds of her own private unborrowable Edith Piaf records could perpetually be heard. And of course now Gillian and Mailman would have their own separate rooms as well.

His was ten by ten with a single window that no matter how wide it was opened would admit no fresh air. The room's ambient smell was of insecticide and feathers and rancid furniture oil, and as such it wasn't so bad: the smells weren't those of human beings, whom Mailman regarded as the source of all foul odor. But quickly—in a matter of hours—this stagnant cube of space began to fill with his own smells, like that of his feet, a smell akin to the one he could not get off his right hand the day, when he was four, that he fell asleep on the back porch clutching in it a slice of deli cheese. And the smell of his underarms, still immature (unlike his mother's heated stink when she emerged from her dressing room and whatever it was she did in there) yet characteristic of his diet (white bread cold-cut sandwiches) and level of activity (low). Odors came from uneaten food he left in the room, from the underwear in his laundry hamper, from his *hair*. Now and then his father would come in when Mailman was reading or drawing and would lean against the wall in a carefully posed facsimile of casualness and ask him how it was going or what he was up to, and pretend to listen to Mailman's reply while nodding, and then at last he would begin his highly technical and obsessively detailed description of what *he* was up to down in the basement ("Trying to figure out how to process titanium without contaminating it. We've had to melt it in a vacuum. Makes it hard to do on a large scale. Maybe reacting titanium tetrachloride with magnesium. Gives you magnesium tetrachloride and a kind of spongy titanium. Also possibly reacting it with sodium, with continuous thermal decomposition of the iodide and arc dissociation of halides. Or possibly electrolytically, that seems promising. Electrolyzing molten-salt electrolyte we can recover some deposits pure enough to melt into ductile metal. I dunno. It's exciting"), while wearing an expression of distant longing not dissimilar to the expression on the watercolored face of Guinivere, in a storybook Mailman'd gotten for his sixth birthday, as she watches Lancelot riding away on his horse. And swirling around his father was always the smell of the lab, of powdered metal and acid and the injudicious use of electricity, and these smells lingered in Mailman's room long after his father had left. And so his bedroom—which had seemed such a grandly generous gift—quickly became a kind of living hell, to which he never felt compelled to escape whenever a fight broke out between his parents, as was wont to happen. Instead he hid in his sister's better-ventilated room, under her bed, unless she was there at the time, which she usually was: so he would have to leave the house completely.

One day not long after they moved in, he came home from school (having been humiliated on the playground over his inability to hit a ball with a bat), entered his sister's room, lay under the bed and fell asleep. Gillian tended to come home later, after fooling around with her girlfriends, and on this day, when she flung the door open and slammed it behind her and threw herself onto the bed, Mailman woke quietly (not unlike, he considers now, the waking trick Chuck Balling would later teach him) and decided to stay, stealthily, and spy on her. On the bed she rolled and sighed and made wordless vocalizations with the tenor of various emotions: anxiety, surprise, misery, and finally something low and animal he couldn't put his finger on but that gave him a sudden and unrelievable chill. This sound was repeated a few dozen times over five minutes or so and was accompanied by slow languid rolls across the bed. Then she hopped off and went to her vanity, an unlit miniature of their mother's, and stared at her face (an unlined miniature of their mother's) in the mirror. Mailman watched through the embroidered eyelets of the soiled pink dust-ruffle that enclosed the space beneath the bed, as Gillian pressed the thumb and pointer and middle fingers of one hand together and gently touched the resulting three-lobed bud to her face, to her cheeks and nose and chin and neck. She distended her lips into a parodic kiss and made kissing sounds; she took one hand in the other and stroked it, cooing softly and gazing into her reflection's eyes. Then she unbuttoned her blouse and removed it and folded it and set it next to her on the bench, and touched her fingers to her bare chest where no breasts had yet formed.

Mailman was growing uncomfortably hot under the bed, his head was beginning to tremble from the effort of peering through the eyelets and sweat was trickling down his neck, falling from his throat and pooling on the dusty floorboards below him: yet he felt that he was witnessing something of extreme importance, something that would vastly expand his understanding of what was possible in the world, and he concentrated as deeply as he could on maintaining his posture. Gillian continued to palpate herself, her shoulders and belly and arms, but the fingers always returned to the chest, her nipples already different from Mailman's, elevated ever-so-slightly on smooth, gradual, nearly conical layers of pale flesh. And then—it was involuntary, spasmodic—Mailman's neck gave up the fight and his head dropped nearly to the floor. It did not hit: he caught it in time. Yet he grunted with the effort and when he heaved his head back up and looked again through the eyelets, her reflection in the mirror was gazing directly at him. He waited, breath held, but nothing happened. She continued to stare, her fingers covering her nipples. And then, extraordinarily, she turned her back to him and continued what she had been doing, now with renewed vigor, pouting and kissing herself and swiveling on the seat without regard for Mailman's presence. This went on for some minutes, while Mailman sought for and discovered an acceptable position, balancing his chin on his two stacked fists, and when he was at last comfortable his sister stood up from her seat and shucked off her skirt and panties.

He had not in the least expected this. Naked, she pirouetted and leapt, her bare feet thudding against the floor, in a dance that seemed to mix ballet with calisthenics, a performance both graceful and athletic. Mailman had developed an erection, though it seemed to him more the result of discomfort (the circumstance usually responsible for it) than anything else. *This is something people do,* he thought. He watched his sister dance for some time—in memory it seems like an hour at least, but corrected for the temporal elasticity of childhood it comes out to more like five minutes—before she suddenly grew bored, or self-conscious, or both, and turned her back to him and put her clothes on and ran out of the room. In a moment he heard the bathroom door click shut and the faucet turn on. When he climbed out from under the bed, it was into another world: the air cool and sweet, a pleasant breeze blowing through Gillian's two windows. Outside the leaves were beginning to turn, a jay screamed, a squirrel corkscrewed haltingly up a maple tree. A car passed. From his mother's room, music. He wanted to go outside and play, and so he bypassed his own room and went down the stairs and out the back door and wandered through the neighborhood's backyards, trying unobtrusively to look in people's windows.

It seemed that there was life everywhere. He had never noticed.

Things trembled and tossed and made sounds. The sweat evaporated from his forehead. He walked for miles through backyards, circling the college from a distance of several blocks, never walking for long on sidewalks or public streets, taking note of people's gardens and the things that stood in their windows. He suddenly liked everyone, even the boys who had mocked him that day: especially them. He imagined they lived in these houses (and maybe they did), imagined their parents scolding them for their transgressions, imagined the boys feeling guilty and angry and sad. He felt like he knew them: like he could approach them tomorrow and make some gesture, some overture, and they would be surprised and pleased and apologize for what they had done. The more he considered it the more plausible this scenario seemed, until at last (his throat and lungs and blood purged of all taint) he knew it to be inevitable. They would apologize and welcome him into their fold. They were boys, after all, like him.

At some point Mailman falls asleep, or nearly so. He notes his own surprise as he sinks into unconsciousness. Sleep has never come easy. Waking life intrudes into sleeping, sleeping life into waking, the borders noisy with rumbling tanks and popping gunfire. Entering into sleep, for him, is like entering into the homes of his customers: those lonely people in their cold mazy domains, dangerous solitudes lurking around every corner. But now more than ever he needs it, to purge the events of last night: that bitter flavor of madness rising in the back of the throat. So it is with gratitude that he allows sleep to take him, with the first pleasure he has felt in hours.

Then he feels something brush against his leg, and then against his arm, and he hears a terrible feral howl, and his head explodes into a skull-splitting ache.

"God damn! God damn!" He's clutching his head and shouting into the still-gloomy depths of his bedroom, and the cats—it was the fucking cats, the sick little fucks, I'll kill 'em all! I'll skin 'em alive!—

who have been fighting on the floor beside him part and scatter and are gone from the room in an instant. He turns to the clockface and witnesses it switching from 5:59 to 6:00. What's that, three hours' sleep? He knows with sinking certainty that he isn't going to get any more than that: might as well get up and prepare for the inevitable shitty day. Stupid cats: he never should have taken them. He should have turned that woman away at the door.

It was about eleven, a warm night, probably the last of the year. He hadn't heard from Semma, not in a couple of days; he was thinking of calling her. He was thinking that she was all right, that Semma; a little loopy, sure, but full of life: life that, frankly, Mailman could use a bit of himself. But it was late. Too late to call your . . . girlfriend? Was that was he was about to think? So be it, then: girlfriend. I'll call my girlfriend tomorrow! Then the phone rang. He'd been in the back room reading his, or rather other people's, mail, and he got up and went to the kitchen and picked it up and heard a woman's voice, tone-less, midwestern, a voice trying to make itself heard between wrack-ing sobs, saying, "Albert? Is this Albert?" and Mailman said "Yes, hello, who's this?" and the voice said "Lily Gallagher," and he said "Sorry, I don't think I know any Lily Gallagher," and then he remem-bered: sitting and having a cup of tea in Semma's kitchen and spying on the table a letter addressed to Lily Gallagher, that is to say Semma's boarder, the amateur weaver, and thinking that it was a nice-sounding name, good rhythm, a variety of sounds pinned into place by the l's, like water rushing through a garden hose wrapped around a row of saplings, Lily Gallagher.

"Semma's roommate Lily, okay?" the voice managed to say, seem-ing to calm itself by speaking its name. And Mailman said, "Lily, yes, sorry, the last name threw me, is everything okay?," knowing things were obviously not okay, otherwise why would she be calling him at all, let alone while crying? And she said "Nah, it's not okay," and began to sob again, and he said "What is it, Lily, is it Semma, is some-thing wrong with Semma?," thinking what a stupid question, who else is there going to be something wrong with, and she said, or rather sort of screamed, "She's dead! She's dead!"

"What!"

"Dead!"

Mailman managed to get out of Lily that Semma had been picking wildflowers by the side of Bird Sanctuary Road in the dark (he thought: Picking flowers in the dark? What the hell for? And then it occurred to him that they might be for him, she might have been going to invite him over for the night and thought he might like some fresh flowers around, and he thought Don't!, don't bother!) when a family of four pulled off to the side so that one of the kids could pee, and at that particular point the shoulder was narrow and the driver, who was not familiar with the area and did not realize this, overshot said shoulder and plowed into the weeds behind which Semma was standing, and her back was broken and an artery severed, and she was paralyzed and lost a lot of blood, and by the time they got her to the hospital she was dead.

"So she's dead now?" he asked, not understanding why this seemed so difficult to believe.

"Yah, right, dead! Sorry! Gotta go!"

Mailman said all right, he thanked her and she hung up and immediately he thought: What do I do now? What's expected of me? What am I: the boyfriend, probably one of many for a good-looking divorced woman her age, never met her family, ex-husband or children (though he heard the voice of the youngest, a student somewhere in California, once when Semma was chopping vegetables in the kitchen and he was sitting at the table and the phone rang and she said "Pick that up for me, will you Albert?" and he picked it up and said hello, and the voice said "Lemme talk to my Mom, please," and Semma ended up arguing with the kid for half an hour); he didn't even know if she had living parents or siblings. There would be a funeral, wouldn't there? He would have to go: but for whom? For himself? Did he need proof that she was actually dead? No, he would go for the friends, the family: but he didn't know them, he only knew Lily, and so slightly that he didn't even know if he would recognize her if he saw her on the street, or the grocery store, or the park, anywhere except at Semma's house scampering into her bedroom to weave. And what if he didn't go? Only Lily would notice (or maybe not, she might never have noticed him except for his generalized male Semma's-boyfriend presence), and even if she would resent him not going, even hate him, that hatred could only manifest itself, what?, five times for the rest of his life, the grand total of times their paths might happen to cross in town, a generous estimate given that before Semma, he'd never even laid eyes on Lily. No, he wouldn't bother going, it would only make people miserable when they asked him who he was and he told them he'd been "going out" with Semma or "involved" with her, which they would inevitably and correctly interpret as meaning they were regularly having sex in the days before her death. Forget it, he'd stay home. And now he got a sudden, awful image of Semma wrapped in rags, wedged into a cheap box, like his fake burial of Mc-Chesney, and for a moment he felt responsible: she was killed, wasn't she, picking flowers at the spot where she'd found his cat? And now he thought, what about her cats, those irritating longhairs, will they be put to sleep?, and while he didn't mind (not much anyway) being responsible for the death of one cat, his cat, he did not feel good shouldering the death of four cats. And one woman. His girlfriend.

That night, lying in bed, he missed her and found her desire (or rather, it could safely be said, *need*) to please him not annoying or disturbing or sexually offputting, as he had considered it in the past, but charming, generous, and exciting: and he realized that he had been *taking* his pleasure from her all along, he hadn't allowed her to *give* him anything, he had resisted her generosity and allowed himself pleasure only in the physical sensation of sex and never, as she had wished, the emotional sensation of caring enough about somebody to let her give a thing to you without strings attached. And thinking of this he began to weep, and then to sob; and the understanding that he was sobbing not for Semma but for himself, for what a terrible man he was and how greedy and selfish and cold, only made him sob harder, so much so that when he finally slept he kept waking up from the involuntary hitching of his chest, and rose the next morning feeling like he hadn't slept at all. And then he started to miss McChesney. That was unexpected: he hadn't thought about the cat in days, the cat was unimportant: but as the morning wore on, he felt more and more distant from the thoughts he'd had the night before about Semma— felt more and more that she was, in fact, weird and screwed up—and came to feel more and more miserable about the dumping of McChesney, who, as the imaginary animal lover had pointed out, had by now probably been shredded and eaten by coyotes. Now, *that* was unjust: somehow more unjust than Semma's death, which after all was the result of crouching invisibly in the weeds by the side of a busy narrow-shouldered country road. But McChesney's end was impossible to regard as anything but a colossal gyp. He'd killed her. All that day he delivered the mail in a funk, and when he got off work he drove out to the woods in the motor park and stumbled among the trees calling her name. But it was beyond futile: what cat came when you called? Not McChesney, anyway. That night he sobbed again, this time for the cat he'd killed, for all the terrible selfish things he'd done in his life, for the feelings he withheld from the people who loved him, for all the sadness and anger and shame he'd caused: he curled himself on the floor of his empty living room and sobbed, and called out "McChesney, come back!" until the hour grew late and he slept.

A few days later Lily showed up. She was wearing a sort of baggy hooded sweatshirt that he was willing to bet she'd weaved herself: a kind of amazing pattern, colored stripes without clear borders so that each seemed to fade into the next. In her arms was a large cardboard box. It contained three longhaired neutered male cats. "These're fer you," she moaned, "Semma always felt bad your cat croaked."

"Oh! I don't— I couldn't—"

"Nah, it's all right, her brother and kids and ex don't want 'em and

I gotta move 'cause they're selling the house." And she put down the box on the stoop and burst into tears.

"Oh—no, wait, it's all right, I just— Is there anything— Here, why don't you—" he said and led her into the house and sat her down in the kitchen and made her a cup of coffee while the cats sniffed around, exploring their new home.

She sipped the coffee and at last opened her mouth, only to say, "The poop trays're in the car."

"All right."

And then she began again to cry: and so Mailman went to her, held her, patted her coarse gray hair and her narrow bony back, and in about ten minutes they were rolling around naked on the living room rug. He doesn't quite know how it happened, it just did. He supposes she grabbed his shoulders and then sort of stroked them and then felt his chest, and he felt hers. Or something. It's hard to remember now, he remembers only the screwing. Compared to Semma she was so skinny, so quick, her arms and legs first here, then there, then somewhere he couldn't reach; and together they tumbled over and over and gasped and growled. Somewhere in the middle of it he felt tears coming on—What the hell! he thought, is this crap never going to end?—and to keep them in check he shouted: "Come!" he shouted, "Come! Come back! Come back! Come back!"

He never saw her again. How many men, the heartless bastards, would like to say that about a woman they spent a single night with? He tried to call her later that day, but she was gone: she'd been on her way out of town when she came to him, and she had left no forwarding address (he checked at the P.O. too). He could always find her over the Internet; how many Lily Gallaghers could there be? But there'd be no point. She isn't Semma. She's probably in California, which is where he guesses women with looms go to live, and he doubts she'd be pleased to hear from her dead ex-landlady's boyfriend whom she boinked a couple days after her funeral. Who'd want to be reminded of that?

As he always does when he's spent time lying in bed and thinking about Semma, he rises reluctantly and with a sense of predestined defeat. Why does thinking about Semma make him think about Gillian? Why did he have to call Gillian and be reminded of how much more fun she has than he does, of how much better she knows him than he does himself? Wakened by the cats, he's got half an hour to kill before he can go out to the coffee shop, which is where he intends to waste the better part of his morning. Saturday. Ordinarily he'd be working but he had vacation time to kill and wasn't planning on going anywhere this year (not that he goes anywhere any year, save for that abortive stint in the Peace Corps), so he agreed to have a PTF fill in for him each summer Saturday. Except he's left with the problem of what to do with the morning hours, once exclusively a Sunday problem but now and for the next several months doubled. Figures: shouldn't make coffee, since I'm going to have to drink a hell of a lot to stay at the coffee shop for as long as I want to, and I shouldn't read the paper either, because then I'll have nothing to do there. So he decides to take a shower. Immediately it seems like a great idea. It's already three after six (thinks: Christ, have I been standing here thinking about women and cats for three entire minutes?). Once he gets in the shower and washes and gets out and dresses and walks six blocks it'll be six-thirty easy, if not later. So he undresses and gets in the shower.

It feels terrific. A while ago he got sick of his energy-crunch-era shower head and its pins-and-needles headache-inducing deadly-fog-style output and had somebody install one of those giant shower heads the size of a dinner plate with about a thousand large holes in it, like the heads on the emergency showers that used to be (and probably still are) in every high school chemistry classroom. Wonderful. Lathers up his hands and cups the soap in the right. Washes in the following order: belly (still not much of one even at his age: though the skin is hanging a little bit heavy there, if he lifts up his arms he can make it look like the belly of a man of twenty), chest, shoulders, arms, armpits (a little stiff under the left there, a little sore), sides, right buttock, asscrack, left buttock, right thigh, left thigh, right knee and calf and ankle, left knee and calf and ankle, right foot left foot, back, face, ears, hair. Doesn't use shampoo: it's the same stuff that's in soap and costs ten to fifteen times more, not that he can't afford it, but on principle he refuses to be ripped off. Doesn't wash his crotch: just lets it sort of rinse. He steps out of the shower and pats himself dry with a gigantic fluffy towel. Thinks about a girl he knew in college, an Orthodox Jew, who told him once that she wasn't supposed to *rub* herself dry after a shower but instead had to *pat* herself dry, because the patting was supposed to be less erotically stimulating than the rubbing. She told him this as if it were a kind of mild joke but admitted that she adhered to it anyway, from force of habit and faith. This all part of a large midnight rendezvous in a notorious campus forest glade in which everyone said embarrassingly candid things while a couple of them drank beer and a couple of them smoked pot or felt each other up and the others gazed in astonishment and envy at the ones drinking and smoking and feeling. At any rate, from then on (and today still) he could not and cannot take a shower or bath without thinking of this girl (remembers her clearly but his clear memory is probably a fabrication, her face has likely changed in his mind over years, but the changed face, anyway, is always clear) and imagining watching her pat herself dry, or watching her *watch him* watching her pat herself dry, or taking the towel and patting her dry himself, generally as part of a scenario in which he is on his way to the men's showers and, lost in thought, takes a wrong turn and ends up walking into the women's showers (in this scenario they live in a co-ed dorm, which didn't exist at NYTech in those days, but whatever), or in which he is returning something to her that he borrowed, a book perhaps, and is admitted to the women's dorm and wanders the halls looking for her and asks a girl where she is and is told "third door on the left," which turns out to be the women's showers, and in any case is stunned by her sudden naked emergence from behind the shower curtain, and she screams and he covers his eyes and says "Oh, I'm so sorry," and she says rather angrily, her hands over her pubic hair and breasts, "Would you hand me my towel, please?" and he opens his eyes and obliges, and she sort of sighs as the towel touches her, and he sort of doesn't let go of the towel, instead begins to pat her with it, and she reaches out (she is within reach of the shower room door) and locks the shower room door, and he continues to pat her body with, and soon without, the towel, and the two of them return to the shower together and have sex, which of course a girl dedicated enough to her religious faith to follow such a peculiar edict would never in a million years have had with him. So inevitably this passes through his head as he pats himself dry in his own bathroom with his excessively fluffy towel, drying in *the exact reverse order of body parts* that he washed himself, again ignoring his crotch, which remains damp but not uncomfortably so.

In the bedroom he switches on the radio and gets dressed: shorts and a white tee shirt, gray socks and brown shoes. He is never quite comfortable out of uniform: civilian clothes make him feel like he is *wearing another man,* someone irresponsible and uninterested in the affairs of the world, someone soft and pliable from years of desk work with some whey-faced middle manager glancing periodically over his shoulder. On the news Texas governor G. W. Bush is issuing a stay of execution. Well, good for you, Sheriff! What a swell guy! That makes up for everything!

Dressed, he opens the front door and picks up the paper from the stoop. Paperboy always rubberbands the paper tightly, which on one hand makes a nice neat package for him, the paperboy, to fling at the door, and on the second hand also makes a nice neat package for Mailman to carry to the coffee shop, but on the third hand makes the paper very difficult to actually open without breaking the rubber band or having to snap it off violently, which action tends to result in a nasty sting on the hand (the fourth hand?) or arm. Hefts the paper: heavy today, for the *Nestor News* anyway, a terrible paper if there ever was one, most of the articles AP wire stories about celebrities or which consumer products are better than which other consumer products (but never taking into consideration the possibility that *not buying any consumer products* is an option); only the local news is written in-house, and badly at that, riddled with misspellings and usage errors, often in the headlines themselves (LOCAL FARMERS SEE CRAP INCREASE); and at least once a week an article ends in mid-sentence, the result of some kind of computer layout mistake. In the old days that would never happen: the missing letters would be *lying right there on the floor,* each letter was an actual physical object placed carefully by an actual physical human being, a man probably with a soiled apron and inky fingers and very thick eyeglasses. Words, letters used to matter: which ones you chose to print or say. Not anymore: everybody sounds like everybody else, they're all using the same vocabulary they got from television advertising: *I need to make the choice that's right for me. I never settle for anything less than the very best.* Same thing with bumper stickers (which he hates): people choose to voice only those opinions that can be summed up in a four-by-sixteen-inch space and cannot be refuted or debated, since they are being announced on the back of a moving car: *Guns don't kill people, people kill people! Pro-choice, pro-child! Save Mother Earth! Get your laws out of my body! Kill the liberals!*

Or his favorite, *Religion is destroying the third world!* How can you put that on a bumper sticker (he thinks, as he lunges off the porch and onto the sidewalk)? He saw that one on a beat-up Toyota in Collegeville that parallel-parked beside him as he was walking down the street. A couple of students got out and he said, "Hey! What's with the bumper sticker?" And the driver, tall blond woman in a cocktail dress, said "Excuse me?" as if he were some kind of nut. "That sticker, 'Religion is destroying the third world,' what's that supposed to mean?" The driver scowled, looked at her friend, shrugged, "It just means what it means." "You actually believe it?" "Yeah, I'm an atheist, I'm not some, like, robot doing what some white male priest is telling me to do." He said, "But how can you put that on a bumper sticker, it's complicated, you'd need a whole car! I mean what about Mother Teresa, and all those martyrs and saints, Augustine, that other guy, what about Martin Luther

King? How about whatshisname, the plant guy? How about the Dalai Lama, aren't you people supposed to like him? You're just dismissing those people with a bumper sticker? How about all those people who need religion when somebody dies or something? How about some-body whose baby gets a disease and dies and they want to kill them-selves but there's this whole thing, this belief thing, that makes them think no, that's wrong, I have a purpose on earth?" "Hey," the girl's friend said, "quit harassing us, this is harassment." "But it's you who's harassing me with this bumper sticker, shouting out this stupid opin-ion and running away!," even though when you got right down to it he agreed with the sticker. He was shouting and sweating now, the air was cool and his face was steaming like a pie. And the driver of the car said, "Well you know what? It's none of your business, asshole, so up yours." None of his business! None of his business! That's the problem with this country, people like her who want to be protected from hear-ing, even having to look at, other people who aren't like them, but at the same time want to "assert their individuality," want to "be them-selves," want to wear beliefs like a pair of baggy painter pants and dump them the second they go out of style. They shout their opinions into a void *because they're afraid somebody will hear them*. And this news-paper—the goddam *Nestor News*—is the mouthpiece of this very ethos. This godforsaken pulpy turd of a rumor sheet, that once printed an ed-itorial that *actually contained the sentence* "If you can't say something nice, don't say anything at all": this is the newspaper he's going to spend the morning reading.

He takes his time walking along the creek, because the rushing water sounds nice and the shrubs along the sides are teeming with sparrows and goldfinches, and the houses that face the creek are quiet except for the occasional strain of television or the clunking of a piano badly played or somebody singing, presumably in the shower. This town does not rise early, save for postal workers and bakers and espresso jocks and trashmen, and the streets have an imminent qual-ity (soaked as they are in diffused morning light before the sun has had a chance to climb up the far side of North Hill) that reminds him of the moments before an experiment was to take place: before the particles collided and the results clattered out of the printer, and the theory (which could change everything but probably wouldn't) was proven or disproven. It was the hour when ideas seemed ready to crack open and reveal themselves, naked and deformed and ugly. Life, preparing to happen.

More Coffee! is wedged into a narrow brick storefront and run by a tall, droopy, tired-looking man named Graham whose freakishly narrow head complements the building: his small mouth always hangs slightly open, as if forced that way by whatever invisible vise has got him. The shop is licensed only to sell coffee to go, but the tiny room (formerly an appliance store, an ice cream parlor, a head shop, a used clothing store that changed ownership and name every six months, another head shop, and a chiropractor's office) contains a few mismatched tables and chairs which Graham has put price tags on (Mailman's favorite table, a sort of wheeled instrument tray that he presumes used to belong to the chiropractor, is marked $1,423.78) in order to slip under the zoning radar. There's a line at the counter, so Mailman quickly claims a seat by dropping his keys loudly onto a tabletop and unwrapping the newspaper (rubber band breaks, stinging his *goddam hand*) beside it. The headline reads—

GRADUATE STUDENT FOUND DEAD
Foul Play Not Suspected

—and as he reads it Mailman remembers the events of the day before and immediately his left side begins to ache again, just behind the ribs underneath his armpit. He gets in line and rubs the spot. That makes it ache more. He closes his eyes and wills the pain away and to his surprise it does in fact slightly fade. When he gets to the front Graham says "Oh, it's you," and Mailman says, "Hi, Graham, may I have a coffee?"

Graham fills a cup and hands it to Mailman. "Business stinks, in case you were wondering. Last month the law offices a couple blocks down moved to the new office park. Now all these guys who used to buy coffee here are stopping at the *Starbucks* on the *strip*. Where there's *parking*."

"Oh."

"What else do you want?"

Mailman isn't hungry, but he's just heard this sob story and thinks it'd be cruel to eschew pastry at this particular moment: so he orders a bear claw, immediately regretting the choice, as now he's noticed some almond croissants, a snack he vastly prefers, and there are only two of them left, and both are sure to sell in the next ten minutes. But he doesn't want to change his order, Graham's already slid the bear claw onto a plate, so he holds his tongue and accepts the plate with a sigh.

"What? Something wrong?"

"No, nothing." Gives him a five.

"The bear claw's a little beat up, is that it? Well, I gave it to you on purpose because you're a regular and I figured, one crummy-looking pastry isn't going to keep a regular away. But that was stupid, *stupid* of me. Times like these, when I make an obvious mistake, I feel like I should never have gotten into food service." As he talks he slides the broken pastry—Mailman had not noticed its condition—into the trash and replaces it with an intact one. He hands Mailman his change. "Here's four singles, I charged you for the coffee but the pastry's free, don't argue." And he hands over the coffee and bear claw.

This has the exact opposite of the desired effect: instead of sending a little extra money Graham's way, Mailman has caused him to *give away* two pastries, a loss that the purchase of coffee does not make up for. So he says "Thanks, hey, maybe I could have one of those croissants, too," and hands over two of the singles he's just been handed by Graham. And Graham says, "Oh. I was thinking I'd eat those with my wife for breakfast, that's her at that table over there. But

it's okay, we can just eat chocolate ones. Though I'm mildly allergic."
He again makes change, which Mailman dumps into the tip glass.
"What the hell are you doing?" Graham says. "I don't deserve that."

"Sure you do."

"Well, you're a good man. A better man than I."

They shake hands and Graham disappears in the back, and there
is a thunderous crash, as if an entire shelf of pots and pans has fallen
onto a tile floor.

Sits down, opens the paper. Ignores for the moment the top headline and examines the others: FESTIVAL FUN FOR ALL, MAN ARRESTED FOR
STABBING, LIBRARY ROBBED. Reads the last. Somebody ripped off the
fines box in the middle of the day yesterday. Serves them right. Never
been to a library so persnickety about fines, they won't let you take out
a single book unless you're all paid up, even if you've got a solid
responsible history, even if it's only fifty cents. And then when you
show up at the counter to actually pay the fine there's nobody there
and you have to wait, or whoever's there says "I can't take that now,
the computer's down" or "You'll have to come back tomorrow, we've
already counted up the fines for the day and can't accept any more."
That's what probably happened, somebody came to pay their fine and
nobody was at the counter, and he got so fed up he went back there to
put his money in the fine box and suddenly thought, No, I'll take the
fine box, I deserve it as much as anybody else. Well, bully for him.

He makes his way through the coffee cup without touching the
pastries. The problem: he wants to save the one he most wants—the
croissant—for last, but if he eats the bear claw first he won't be hungry
enough to really enjoy the croissant. Yet if he eats the croissant first, he
won't enjoy the bear claw at all, and if he doesn't eat the bear claw, Graham will try to give him more money back. Why must breakfast always
be so damned complicated? In the end he decides to eat what he wants
to eat, to hell with Graham's feelings, if he has to throw out the bear
claw he can do it surreptitiously, when Graham's not around.

It's about seven-thirty when a familiar girl walks in and asks

Graham to make a fancy drink. Graham makes a face then busies himself brewing and steaming over in his coffee corner. The girl leans back against the counter and takes a look around. She examines the paintings on the walls, mostly black acrylics with vague geometric designs floating around in them. Then she checks out Graham's wife, a woman as puffy and soft as Graham is pinched; she is wearing a stiff shiny hairdo and a sweatshirt that will soon be uncomfortably hot, and is reading a pamphlet of some kind. Finally the girl looks at Mailman. Brow wrinkles, jaw sets. Mailman smiles. "Hi." Good-looking, somewhat Asiatic features though she's obviously white, nice light brown clean hair, no bra, as is the style these days. He's about to ask her if he knows her from somewhere, obviously this would just be a courtesy, God knows he wouldn't be trying to pick her up, she's of course far too young for him or rather he's far too old for her: but you never know. That is, it's nice to be nice, it's proper, but if a side effect of being nice is the creation of sexual attraction, then so be it. It happens to people!: May-December (à la the intergenerational entanglement of Jodie Steiner and Tom Effening). Or in this case more like April-October, which doesn't sound half as bad, both months being blustery and cool. But before he even finishes saying hi she turns away and pretends to look once again at the paintings, which they both know are awful. All right, he says to her in his head, be that way. And he's beginning to doubt his having recognized her in the first place, and so puts her out of his head and turns to the paper.

No getting around it, he'll have to read the article.

GRADUATE STUDENT FOUND DEAD
Foul Play Not Suspected

A Nestor man was found dead in his Keuka Street apartment Friday. No coroner's report has been issued, but police believe the death was a suicide.

The victim, unidentified by police, was said by

bystanders to be in his early thirties. His body was discovered by friends who had come to ask him to play frisbee.

The victim was said by some neighbors to have been a graduate student. Others described him as unemployed. One friend said that he was an artist.

Police say they have contacted the next of kin but will not yet release the victim's name. Detective Nathan Light says that foul play is not suspected. "The posture of the victim suggests suicide," he says.

A bystander reports that the victim was found to have hung himself.

No other details were available at press time.

Mailman's never been a trembler—he's prone instead to sudden jumps, jerks, knocking things over, lurching backward and banging his head—but sure enough, when he lifts his coffee to his lips, his hand is trembling.

Now, stop that!

He is embarrassed for himself, at the very idea that his own lapse, his failure to deliver the letter, could have hastened Sprain's death—who does he think he is, anyway? Mister mover-of-mountains? Mister radiator-of-power? Mister nexus-of-cause-and-effect? As if his little illicit postal-interception hobby could exert more influence on Jared Sprain than, say, abusive parents, or chemical imbalance, or disappointment in love, or whatever makes people off themselves! How ridiculous! He no more killed Sprain than he sent Semma into the weeds for flowers. He lowers his coffee cup to the table, he steadies his hand. He draws and releases deep breaths.

But then again . . .

As if in response to the pathetic trembling of his coffee-clutching arm, his newspaper-smoothing arm jerks, sweeping newspaper and bear claw (yet untouched) to the floor with a tremendous crumple and clatter. Everyone turns. Graham, who's been sitting across from his dispirited spouse holding both her hands and making hopeful google-eyes, leaps up and replaces free of charge the fallen pastry. "No, please, don't, it's my fault this time—" "No arguments." "No, please, I had a little spasm, I'm fine—" "Do you need a doctor? Is it your heart?" "No, no, it isn't my heart." And he looks up grinning and shaking his head and sees at the table next to his the young woman with the sort of Asiatic features staring at him and he knows who she is.

"Oh, hello, I don't know what happened, I just—"

She gets up from her seat and takes the one across from him and says, "I saw you. Last. Night," the voice breathy and labored and filled with unnatural pauses.

It's her, it's the girl from 200 Keuka who was standing in her robe watching him wrestle with the mailboxes yesterday afternoon and then again that night. Didn't notice at first that it was the same girl: she looks a little different in the daytime, seedier, tireder, sadder. She's staring at him with an intent and unforgiving expression that does not seem entirely *there*, that seems aimed not simply at him but at something he unwittingly represents. It's almost erotic, she's down deep in his eyes rooting around inside him, he blinks and leans back in his chair. She waits for him to reply.

"Last night? Where?" Across the room Graham can be heard to mutter and shake; when Mailman hazards a glance he sees Mrs. Graham reassuringly patting her husband's arm.

"You *know . . . where.*"

He coughs. Says, "I think I recognize you from my route, I'm a mailman, I probably know your name actually because it's on all the mail I deliver to you but I can't always match the faces to the names, especially when you live in a large apartment building where I don't actually come in contact with—"

"See? You know. I . . . *saw* you. I live behind the mailboxes. I hear you every day, screaming. And swearing. And . . . banging."

Of course this is an accurate description of his antics at the boxrow, but from the mouth of this girl the words seem false, exaggerated. "Look, I don't know that I do those things exactly, the boxes are always sticking, you can blame your landlord for that—and anyway who—what—"

"I want you to know . . . I reported your *behavior*. To your *superiors*. You're going to be in *big trouble*."

He can't help but laugh. It isn't funny, what she's saying, it's really very serious, she could do far more damage to him than he could ever manage to do to the boxrow at 200 Keuka, but the laughter is surprised out of him. More of a bark, really. He quickly coughs, in a ridiculous attempt to obscure the bark.

"There isn't anything. *Funny* about this."

"No, I didn't mean, I mean—"

"I want you. To tell me," she says, leaning over the table a little and her tanktop falls forward revealing her breasts which he can't help looking at, which looking she notices and does nothing about and even maybe smiles, seeing that she is right about him, he's not only a loose wheel, a hothead, a live wire, but is also a sexual predator who takes every opportunity he can to look down girls' shirts—which is true! He does, he looks! But he's no predator! He does not in any way connect his aggressive (yes!), violent (it's true!) feelings against the mailboxes at 200 Keuka to the really-very-nice-to-look-at breasts of this very angry girl or the girl herself of which the breasts are a part! Sex and violence are not in any way joined in his worldview!—and she wants him to tell her, she says, "what you were doing . . . in Jared Sprain's mailbox. *After midnight*."

"Me? In— yes, I was there, it— I put in, it was a letter, like I told you."

"A *letter*." As if there could be no unlikelier thing.

"Yeah, it was— see, I forgot earlier that day to deliver it and I put it— I had it— it was, and this happens all the time you can ask any mailman at all, it was lying on the floor of my truck when I got back to the P.O. and so I took it home with me personally and delivered it when I was off, strictly speaking, off duty. And I knew I had tomorrow, or rather I mean today off, so I knew I wouldn't otherwise have gotten to it until Monday. And as for midnight, I took it— it was, I had it with me when I went out to the Festival, and I watched the fire, and then was walking and remembered, ah, here it's in my pocket!, and I just dropped it right off."

The girl smiles. Is he off the hook? She says, while reaching down next to her chair for something, "But you knew he was . . . dead."

"Me? No. Or rather— I know now, owing to the paper."

"You knew. I saw you. In the afternoon. You were there. You knew. Why'd you bring a letter . . . to a *dead man*?" He can see it all reflected in her eyes, a swirl of conspiracy, of unexplained actions, shady dealings, mysterious outcomes. He watches her reach into the satchel beside her and pull out . . . a plastic zip-lock bag. A USPS damaged-mail bag. Containing Jared Sprain's letter. He's pretty surprised to see it. Jerks, jumps, grips his chair to keep it from toppling. Sputtering, he tries to speak: fails: the girl grins.

"You— you can't— that's illegal! That's, you stole the mail of another! Person! Postal customer!"

"So . . . report me."

"I— I will! That's! You can't!"

She delivers what seems to be a carefully planned speech. "You won't. You did something . . . bad. You're *doing* something bad. I know you. You're a *bad man*. I know your *real name*. I know the name of your . . . *superior*. I know . . . *something's* going on." And she starts getting up.

"Wait, I— I won't do anything, but listen— you don't understand that—"

And it's the sight of her leaving, the sight of her narrow bony back passing through the doorway and catching fire in the bright daylight, that makes him remember about her: her name, Kelly Vireo, and her handwriting, tiny and crooked like the gears of a wristwatch, and her life story: her birth to a single mother, the impoverished small-town childhood, the rebellion, the drinking and drugs, the wising-up, the confrontation with mom, the search in San Francisco for the father which culminated in discovering him: a half-Korean quarter-Latino quarter-German male prostitute living in a condemned warehouse building (no plumbing, only the trickle of rainwater into plastic five-gallon paint buckets and an unenclosed corner where everyone pissed and shat) with a ravaged collection of insane, dying or otherwise dis-enfranchised middle-aged men; the demanding to know why he left her mother, the learning that he had picked her mother up in a bar and had sex with her in an effort (spearheaded by his parents and their clergyman) to cure himself of being gay. The hearing this father say, "You asked for it, you got it. Now get out." The returning to Moravia, New York, only to tell her mother she would never talk to her again. The not having talked to her since. All this Mailman remem-bers, and knows, and can do nothing about: can't tell her he under-stands (though he sort of does, or is trying to) and is sorry (and he is, sorry to have read what he read about her, sorry to feel the pity he feels for her which, because it was illegally obtained, cannot be put to use vis-à-vis comforting words, overtures of friendship, etc.) and that there are no hard feelings. There are hard feelings. It must have been her, her complaints, that put him on probation, that sent him to the USPS-appointed anger-management shrink. He ought to resent her for it—God, he hated those shrink sessions!—but it's hard to muster up the proper emotions. He considers, and then like a good child picks up his bear claw and eats it.

THREE

Teachers

——

The shrink, he remembers (as the bear claw, stale and flavorless as an old library book, congeals in his mouth) was named Gary Garrity. Gregarious Gary Garrity. "Nice to meet you, Albert, you may call me Gary." Thanks, asshole! I was going to call you Mister Doctor Sir! They met in a little booklined study in Garrity's house, and while they talked (or, rather, endured long stretches of not talking) Mailman could hear Mrs. Gary Garrity screaming at the screaming Garrity children. *Do you want a slap in the face? Because that's what you're asking for, a slap in the face! Is that what you want? Is that what you want?*

Mister Doctor Gary Garrity, for his part, pretended that nothing whatsoever was amiss, that, as he'd suggested to Mailman, "this room is an *inner sanctum*, while we are here nothing else exists, I am focused *entirely* on you and your problem, Albert." But this amazing poise in the face of his hotheaded wife and unruly brat kids was, in Mailman's view, not sane: a sane person would shake his head and say, "Jesus Christ, sorry about all that, the damn kids are nuts these days." A sane person would occasionally roll his eyes or raise his eyebrows to assure his patient that, although he was aware of and annoyed by the commotion, he would nonetheless dedicate as much attention and energy as was possible under the circumstances to the problem at hand. But no: instead there was this clearly irrational imaginary obliviousness, presented in a manner which seemed to suggest that Mailman should follow suit—and further that, if Mailman failed to follow suit, it would indicate even deeper psychological abnormalities than the ones they were currently addressing. And so Mailman followed suit.

He had been assigned to Garrity for three anger-management sessions, which was the number of anger-management sessions he was required to attend in order to keep his job with the Postal Service. This was a couple years back, before Semma, before the cats. In the wake of the complaints (Kelly Vireo's, he now knows) he was brought to the windowless office and dressed down; he was told he had "a problem"; he was offered "assistance." He was encouraged ("we strongly recommend") to continue the sessions above and beyond the required three, but the sessions were only *making him angrier,* so he quit. "I quit," he would tell Ronk. "Up to you," was the smug reply.

What'd they talk about? Mailman's problem "with authority." At their first session, Gary Garrity wanted to discuss Mailman's father. So Mailman talked about his father: the reclusive Edgar Lippincott and his secret lab. Mailman was no idiot, he knew where Gregarious Gary was trying to go, but if he wanted to talk about Mailman's problem with authority they ought to have been talking about his mother. Garrity never asked about her, though, and Mailman never brought her up. Instead, conversation led to his teachers. Maurice Renault, of course (and at the mention of the great astrophysicist, Gary G. smiled and nodded and said, "Ah, Maurice Renault"), and Jim Gorman, his English teacher during the third year of high school. And his kindergarten teacher, Rhonda Petrash.

That was 1948. The Truman administration. Mailman was a squirt, a squib, a good old skinny American kid; in the class picture, in the ranks of the plump and cheerful, he looks like a Dust Bowl waif, transplanted in time, hair slicked back and eyes too wide. On sunny days, he told Garrity, during recess, when the class was sent to play in the schoolyard, he always stayed in. On rainy days, of course, all the children stayed inside, and he was forced to stay with them, and so his solitude within the crowd, on such days, was the product of ostracization from the group, and not of personal choice. But on sunny days he sat alone, permitted (for the only time during the day) to fondle and examine and smell the contents of his desk: his pencil and pad and chalkboard and chalk, and (if recess on this day was before lunch) his lunch. And once he was finished doing that, he would move to the play area, where there were blocks and books and a terrarium containing a turtle, and an aquarium full of fish and aquatic plants, and an ant farm. For a while he would simply sit by the open window, and listen to the other children shouting outside, and enjoy having the play area all to himself. And then, slowly, he would pull out the box of blocks and tentatively remove one and then another and another, and place these blocks on the carpet and arrange them in a satisfying pattern, and then he would place more blocks on top of these, always sure to get it right, because according to his personal set of rules he could not again move a block once he had let go of it. It would take him most of recess to perform this task, and when he heard the whistle summoning the children back into the school he would take one final look at what he'd made and bring his small fists down upon it, so that the blocks flew all over the play area, sometimes rolling right off the carpet and clanging against the metal legs of somebody's chair.

Of course he wasn't really alone: he was under the supervision of Miss Petrash, the teacher, the only woman Mailman knew with long, straight hair. Long, straight, black hair with bangs, and large black eyes, and a small nose and mouth; and a tiny chin no bigger than a marble beneath the mouth, but prominent owing to its distinctive roundness and the smallness of her face. People, adults, considered her peculiar: in this triumphant America, this perfect America that had won the war, this scrubbed-clean America, why would anyone want to go around looking like that, like some hideous flapper? The children simply feared her, told stories about her: that she was divorced, that she was living with a man, that the man was really an ape-man, that they ate kids. But the Miss Petrash of solitary indoor recess was different; when alone with Mailman she said nothing, did nothing, only watched him with the beginnings (never the middles or endings) of a smile tempting her face, and it was this secret pocket of his teacher's personality that Mailman loved best of all, that more than anything else kept him indoors during recess. This Miss Petrash had his respect and even love, while the other one, the one in evidence when all the children were present, was a figure only of distaste and terror.

But why? It wasn't like she struck them or even raised her voice, it wasn't as if she could be regarded as having *abused* them. But they sensed her dislike, her hatred even, which manifested itself in petty humiliations, seemingly random punishments, the apparently intentional sentencing of innocent children for classroom crimes clearly committed by others: she seemed to regard them as a kind of hive, a single entity of generalized ability, personality and disobedience. A paper airplane, for instance, thrown at her from one side of the room would, without fail, direct her attention to the opposite side, where a student would be chosen without hesitation and directed to stand in the corner while wearing what she called the "swell hat." It was in fact her own hat, a kind of velveteen beret with a little puffball on top, which she proudly wore year-round regardless of the temperature, but she told the class that on any of their heads it looked *really swell*, and when a student was punished she would make a great show of placing the swell hat on the student's head, tugging the sides down over the student's ears and fluffing up the ball on top, until the rest of the class giggled in spite of itself, even as it knew anyone at all could be the next victim. And she would say "Boy, you look *swell* now, you look *really swell*," and she would lead the student to the corner and order him to remain perfectly still until he cried. That was the rule:

the student *had to cry*. Most of the girls were willing to cry almost immediately, whether or not the tears were the result of genuine emotion, and so female penitents could quickly return to their desks. But the boys had greater trouble forcing themselves to cry, and a few times a boy stood in the corner, wearing the swell hat, for the better part of an hour before cracking. Mailman himself cracked quickly, earning the respect of neither the boys nor the girls, though possibly earning the affection of Miss Petrash, who nonetheless did not speak to him when they were alone.

She did have a single alternate state of mind, something that might be described today, by someone like Gary Garrity, as a manic phase. It materialized only three times that Mailman can remember, each time with the announcement of some kind of huge project, something daring and ambitious and impossible to pull off, which the kindergarteners were expected to put together and present to the rest of the school. In the fall it was to be a play, written, rehearsed, designed, and staged by the children. In the winter the project was to turn the woods behind the school building into an active bird sanctuary. And in the spring the class was to compose a "symphony" ("It is like," Miss Petrash explained, "a very long, beautiful, sometimes shocking and violent, song"), which they were to perform on the last day of school, using instruments they would have to acquire and learn on their own time. Miss Petrash announced each project with a grandiose flourish, gesturing wildly in front of the chalkboard, making diagrams and describing the lavish preparations required in order to execute it, and by the end of the day the class would have complete confidence in their ability to succeed at the project, and each student would go home with a specific task to accomplish, the completion of which, said Miss Petrash, was utterly imperative if they wanted the project to work.

But of course none of it ever worked. The play, which was to be a war story about a soldier who returns from battle to find that nobody recognizes him, was denounced by the parents and principal as unpatriotic, communist even, and promptly scuttled; the land Miss Petrash had hoped to use for the bird sanctuary was cleared, paved, and turned into the new school parking lot. ("Heathens," Miss Petrash was heard to mutter as she watched the bulldozers rumble over the woods.)

But it was the symphony project that failed most spectacularly. Despite Mailman's father's prestigious job at the university, the village they lived in at the time was predominantly working class. Children were going home from school convinced they could expect to learn to play, say, the bassoon, only to be told that there was no way their respective families could afford music lessons, let alone musical instruments. They returned to class dispirited, empty-handed, humiliated. In the end, Miss Petrash railed against the entire class, waving her finger and reproving them for what she perceived as their "chronic misbehavior and ignorance," whatever that meant, and told them they had simply gone too far and as punishment would not be allowed to perform their "precious stupid symphony."

And so they were surprised the next day to find that their desks had been cleared from a large area in the center of the room and a movie projector had been set up: a monstrous, monolithic metal block of a thing with giant spools of film attached, a sort of Brobdignagian cousin to the chipper little eight-millimeter film and filmstrip projectors the children were accustomed to: and to this machine, to this massive terrible black gear-mass, elfin Miss Petrash ministered with a screwdriver and a flashlight, tightening here and there and sticking her nose and fingers into various dangerous-looking orifices. "Sit down," she said, directing the children to their seats on the floor with an impatient hand. "Since we have failed in our attempt to create beautiful music, I have acquired from the university a film about a symphony orchestra." A titter of excitement—no work for an hour! "Quiet, please," Miss Petrash went on, grunting now with the effort of adjusting some stray flap of metal. "I certainly hope we all can learn something from this."

They waited in silence for five additional minutes, and then Miss Petrash turned at last to the windowed side of the room and gestured to the students seated there to draw down the shades. In the darkness of the classroom the monster awoke, and a blinding white light ignited the blackboard and a deafening fan rattled to life, enveloping them in a kind of electric sensory fog. And still Miss Petrash prodded, flipping switches and tapping anxiously on the side of the machine— Raymond Keech's offer to help ("my dad's an electrician") was met with a frantic shushing—until the thing clanked and shuddered and the giant reels heaved into motion. All eyes turned to the blackboard. No images appeared. Janet Peel stood up and tugged at the filmstrip screen rolled up behind the maps, and it slid down into the projector's beam, and the light intensified, but still no pictures. And then—it is a sound Mailman is loath to remember—a tremendous wheeze, a noise of awful strain and complaint, issued from the machine, and the children turned to find that Miss Petrash had somehow *become a part of it,* her head seemed to have *bonded with the projector,* and she began, incredibly, to scream. To scream! And once the initial shock wore off the girls began to scream along with her, and so it was almost impossible to hear her shouting "Unplug it! Unplug it!": and even after this cry had reached the boys sitting beside the outlet, it still took several horrible seconds before they realized it was directed at them, at which time they leapt from their seats and dived for the cord and together yanked it out of the wall. Meanwhile the shades had flapped open (thanks to Beverly Simms, who prided herself on her shade-opening skill), the lights had flickered on (the handiwork of Kenneth Weymouth, he of the speech impediment that forced him to pronounce his own name *Kemmeff Weymuff*), and attention had turned fully to Miss Petrash herself, whose unfashionably long hair, it was becoming apparent, had been swallowed by the film projector. Gasps escaped the students. The teacher, bent double, grunted and moaned and twisted her body, struggling to free the trapped hair; her breath was quick and shallow and her arms flailed helplessly at her sides. It was Mailman (how wonderful it felt to be the one to think to do it!) who grabbed a pair of snub-nosed scissors from the coffee can on the windowsill and came to the screaming teacher's side and detached her with a few quick snips: that's all it took, and Miss Petrash was freed.

Mailman stood behind her and stroked her back and told her it was all right, the thing didn't have her anymore (and it thrilled him to minister to her in the way Gillian ministered to him: to comfort, to touch, to whisper). The classroom fell silent while Miss Petrash stood, panting. The sight of her elicited new gasps: some of the hair had been *torn from her head*, and the scalp along with it, in a teardrop-shaped patch the approximate size of a quarter. Silent and still now, the film projector gripped the black strands of hair, which stuck out from its rollers and gears in gentle fanned clumps. Mailman took a step back. Blood was dripping down the side of Miss Petrash's face and into her ear. Slowly her hand rose to her cheek. Somewhere in the room somebody fainted and fell on the floor with a thud. And Miss Petrash's hand came away smeared red by her own blood, and her breath caught and she made a choking sound, and she turned to Mailman standing beside her with the scissors and trained upon him a look of fear and, yes, *accusation*. He felt himself starting to cry: what was happening? It was as if the machine had taken possession of her, the appalling giant wheels were moving in her head now and would not, could not, stop. He noticed her hands trembling, gripping her bleeding head, and they looked like the hands of a woman twice her age. It occurred to the shivering Mailman that his teacher wasn't a communist: she was a witch. A witch!

The ancient fingers shot out and batted the scissors from Mailman's hand. He stumbled backward into a desk, gouging his ribs, causing waves of numbness to race down through his thighs and calves. And meanwhile Miss Petrash had crumpled onto the floor, sobbing. She had lost it, that was certain. Within seconds other teachers had rushed in and helped Miss Petrash to her feet and led her away, and the teacher who had been left to supervise the class, a phlegmatic, snub-nosed woman named Mrs. Cantrell, listened to the children's really quite sympathetic version of events. Even Mailman, once he'd gotten over what had happened, was willing to forgive Miss Petrash her hideous glare, the one that had told him alone the truth about her: but he never got the chance. When she returned (with a bright white bandage and a new short haircut), her manner indicated that the incident was behind them and should not be mentioned again. So it wasn't. Days later he heard his mother telling his father (and his father reacting with the disproportionate enthusiasm— "Really? Wow!"—Mailman would one day learn represented a complete lack of interest in what he was being told) that the hair caught in the projector had *mousy roots*: and when Mailman asked her what that meant she slapped him for eavesdropping and then told him it meant Miss Petrash was a slut.

When he told Gary Garrity this story, Gary Garrity said, "And do you think about this experience during sex?"

"During— what! During *sex*? No!"

"Hmmm," Garrity said, unable to prevent a smile from ever-so-subtly transfiguring his froggy face. "So what *do* you think about during sex?"

"I don't think about anything! Or I think about the sex! That I'm having! What does that have to do with the Postal Service!"

"Well," the doctor said, "maybe more than you think."

Mailman is torn from his reverie by a gripping need to urinate. How long has he been here in the coffee shop, staring into the dregs in his cup, woolgathering? Too long. There's no restroom, so he's going to have to walk down to the public library. He gets up (easy there, bladder!) and says goodbye and thanks to Graham, and Graham says "I'm deeply sorry about your pastries, nothing like that will ever happen again," and Mailman says no problem, and Graham says, "Of course it was a problem. Don't insult me by lying. Just forgive and forget, okay?" Mailman says, "I forgive you." He walks down the street to the library, climbs the crumbling stone steps (the local shale falls to pieces if you so much as look at it askance) and sneaks inside. At the edge of the circulation desk there's a little wooden box that usually contains three keys, each attached to a rectangular piece of plexiglas, each piece of plexiglas magic-markered with the name of the appropriate restroom: men, women, wheelchair. But now all three are in use. Against his better judgment—he really really has to go and in fact doesn't think he'd make it the four blocks to the Square and the many restrooms available there—he sort of conceals himself behind a nearby post and waits for the restrooms to open. He watches people on the mezzanine pawing through the stacks, glances at the nearby computer cluster where teenage punks and homeless men are fiddling around on the Internet. They have these privacy shields on the screens so that unless you're peering right over the user's shoulder you can't see what he's looking at, fat lot of good it did him. Now there's a motion beside him, it's a young girl replacing the women's room key. Damn. Really has to go. Watches the girl walk away: ten years old maybe, skinny and tall. Something about her thinness, the depressurized-bladder nonchalance of her walk, makes him nearly wet his pants. He grabs the key she's left and heads for the back of the building.

"You! Stop, you!" shouts a voice, a familiar frightening caw. Without slowing his pace he turns and sees the person he wants least to see, the snorting bloodhound of a reference librarian who banned him from coming here ever again, and she's hurrying after him with a pencil raised in the air, her thick shoulders pumping and the large round head they support bobbing and nodding with the moral correctness of her mission. "Out, get out, no restrooms for the likes of you!" She's awfully loud for the library, people are watching them, but Mailman does not slow down, and he beats her to the door and locks himself in. He pushes down his shorts, sits on the clean seat (he doesn't stand up to pee in public restrooms, especially when he really has to go, as the splashing filthifies the place for other people), and begins to relieve himself. Thank God. Thank God. There is a pounding on the door and the librarian kind of shouts in a whisper "Your kind is not welcome. Get out," and Mailman says, "Sorry, I just had to go, I'll be out in just a minute."

"And the women's room, no less! I command you to come out."

He thinks, She *commands* me? Says, "Look, I'm almost done already, I'll come out in a second and you'll be rid of me for good."

"Out now or I'll call the police."

"Oh, come on, I'm already getting up, by the time they get here I'll be long gone and what'll you tell them, a man came in here and used the women's room? They'll say big deal, lady and will never again come when you call them." No reply to that. He flushes, makes sure everything's clean and neat, washes and dries his hands. Then he opens the door.

She's there, face pink with rage; she grabs him by the arm and jerks him the rest of the way out. "You have been banned, banned, banned. You will leave now." He resists, but she succeeds in dragging him out into the atrium where everyone's milling about, entering and exiting and waiting in line to check out their books, and all these people turn to watch him being yanked toward the door. "Out-out-out! Pervert!" She pushes him with surprising force and he trips-tumbles out through the automatic doors and is left standing at the top of the stairs still clutching the key and its giant plexiglas platter.

"Wait," he says, "the key," and she comes marching through the doors and snatches the key from his hand, and here, outside, her voice finds its full expression and volume.

"And a thief to boot! When I said out I meant out for good, you sick pervert, and when I say the next time I see you climb these steps I'll call the police, I mean that too. They'll come here and apprehend you and I'll have you taken in for sex crimes and you'll lose your precious little mailman job. And wouldn't that be nice, you'll have to leave this town in shame and I'll never have to see you again. So I dare you, sir, to come back and try your sicko games again"—shaking the key in his face—"and I will lay you low, and don't forget it."

"Look," he says, exhausted by humiliation, "what happened when you banned me was a misunderstanding, I was neither exposing nor abusing myself, it was that that day the heat wasn't working and it was cold and I had my hands in my pockets kind of moving them up and down so the friction would make them warm, and regardless of what was on the screen, wait let me finish, I know it wasn't a good thing to be looking at in a family kind of place like this but it was nobody's business but my own, regardless of that I would never do something so revolting as what you're describing."

She gets right up in his personal space now and growls "The heck you wouldn't! The heck! I saw it, your . . . thing! Lying exposed in your lap! And so did Lydia my trainee," and he says, "No, no, it wasn't what you thought, I told you this at the time, I'd gotten this deodorant at the health food place and it came in this kind of round pinkish container, and as it turned out the stuff wasn't even any good, it was all gritty, so the entire thing was completely for naught. But I had it in my lap because if I'd put it on the floor I would have forgotten it, and if I'd put it up on the table people would be disgusted by it, because who wants to look at some guy's deodorant? So that's what you saw, I told you, not any part of my body." And she says "Men like you make me sick," and marches right back into the library leaving the skateboard kids who'd been sitting on the steps to laugh at him and mumble things to each other behind their hands. Little shits. And her too, the bitch, doesn't even know a human penis when she sees one, or rather doesn't see one, and that's no surprise, who'd want to expose themselves to her anyway, nobody, that's who.

For the rest of the day he's got nothing to do, figures he'll go home, relax, maybe have something to eat, catch a matinee, then have dinner and see another movie that night. It's what he likes to do with his Saturdays, watch a couple of movies and then come home and go for a long walk and think about the movies he's seen. Loves movies (he thinks as he walks), the power of them, the tyranny, the way the real world all but disappears. Likes the classics: likes Wilder, likes Welles (doesn't care about the actors, only the people who put 'em on screen, the directors, the photographers): likes that one, which is it, *Touch of Evil*, with the bomb in the car, and you have to sit there and watch the people get in and drive down the road, and they're going to blow up and they don't know it, God, he could just shit. And your thrillers, your action pics, he'll watch one anytime, give him *Die Hard* 1, 2, and 3 and a bucket of popcorn and he won't move all day. He loves the way the movies compress time, months seem to pass when it's only been a couple of hours. He's talked to other people about this and they tell him they're never fooled, they're always aware that they're in a theater watching a movie and that time is passing: which is perhaps why he only goes to movies alone. Feels like he's lived three or four times longer than other people have because he's spent so much imaginary compressed time watching movies: more of his perceived life has been imaginary than has been real.

At home he sits on the couch fending off Semma's cats and thinks about Gary Garrity: the jerk: the way he presumed to know something about him, Mailman, just because he had a degree from a college certifying him to know things about people he didn't know. Always his *concern.* That solicitous *nod.* That knowing *frown.* "Yes, how interesting. Yes, I see." If anything, Mailman could have told *him* a thing or two, for instance if he, Gary Garrity, wanted his wife and kids to be a little better behaved during business hours, maybe he could possibly respect them just a tiny bit as human beings and not, as Mailman is fairly certain Gary Garrity did regard them, as case studies. Oh, he knows, there are probably shrinks who can *separate* their *professional assessments* of others from their *personal feelings,* that it is possible to stop thinking about shrinking once office hours are over, but he suspects strongly that Gary Garrity is not one of those shrinks. Alone in his leather swivel chair for an hour during a cancellation, surely GG thinks about Mrs. Gary Garrity and the Gary Garritys Junior, listens to their hysterical conflicts, the keening, the wailing, the shouts of the missus, "You little sonsabitches!" and thinks, If only I could get them on the couch. If only I could apply to them the theories and practices I apply to my patients. He likely regards them as *people with problems*, problems that could be treated: and his wife's unwillingness to seek such treatment as he deems appropriate is a further sign of her moral turpitude. This is doubtless what was going through the psychologist's mind during the silent moments of his sessions with Mailman, when the sounds of his family overwhelmed the prominence of Mailman's so-called rehabilitation. Not that Mailman minded the inattention.

So, sick of the cats (and sick, isn't he, with thoughts of Semma dead at the roadside?, of the way his hand stroking a cat reminds him of her hand stroking a cat, reminds him of her hand stroking him?, of the possibility that she might be alive if not for him, of the possibility that Jared Sprain might as well?, and my God, was that only last night?), he goes for a walk. Not a stroll, Mailman cannot stroll: he is aware that he looks almost ridiculously intense when he walks, but his attempts to walk slowly, with a certain looseness of limb, a certain pleased attention to his surroundings, have all failed, and he now accepts this extremely brisk near-jog as the only walking method he is capable of employing. He walks east to the hillside and north along its base, past the houses with cliffs in the backyard, intending to go all the way out to the high school, where the highway meets the hill, to walk west beneath the underpass to the lake and down its shore, then back east again to his house. The weather remains good: cooler than yesterday, clear, ideal walking weather: it gives him the feeling he always has when the weather is good, which is sadness, because he's all too aware that such weather cannot last.

Pretty soon Mailman reaches the lake. From this vantage point a few hundred yards from the park he can see the charred bones of the Chapin-Caldwell house smoldering, a thin line of smoke rising up off them, the whole surrounded by yellow caution tape, which is not stopping kids from circling it on their bicycles or ducking under the tape and slapping with open palms the hot black boards. He wanders along the shoreline, gazing into the abnormally clear water, the result of the invasive algae that coats the bottom and has eliminated all the rank stuff that fish eat; along the beach are fishing shacks and rotten docks and the occasional pile of quarry refuse. Pretty shabby, for a Finger of God. Miles from here, NestorFest carries on; he is pleased to be alone. He passes the zone of jagged brick fragments where the brick factory used to stand and comes to the chainlink fence behind which its foundation lies open, brimming with stagnant rainwater. He picks his way past the fence and reaches the park, and from there he heads home. The sun passes behind the sky's only cloud on its way toward setting, the cloud seems to throb like a heart. It's what, four-thirty? Where'd the time go? Already missed the matinee, got to check the paper for the evening listings. Dammit: he left his paper at More Coffee!. Since he's going to pass there he might as well stop in and get another. He's relieved to find the place empty of customers, and Graham gone for the day. He buys the paper from a Walkman-wearing clerk, rolls it up the way his was delivered this morning, tucks it under his arm—but what about his pit sweat? He pushes it down a little and presses it against his ribs with his elbow. But that hurts, faintly: he pushes it up again.

Maybe he ought to save up some money and get himself a secluded lake cabin, something up on the north end, away from Nestor, where the land is cheaper. Teach himself to fish, to hunt. Never have to see another person again. Walk around in tattered rags, like Robinson Crusoe. Sit on the beach and regard the water. He ought to think about retirement, actually: sooner or later they'll force him out: get an inspector to follow him around, count his footsteps, measure the distance between each one. They won't get him on efficiency, though; it'll have to be something else. His appearance. Unpressed shirts. Wrong shoes. Demeanor. "Attitude." He'll have to read the signs carefully, retire at the right moment, right when they're about to fire him: he'll get the biggest possible pension that way. No need to worry just yet, but good to think about it, to plan ahead. To contemplate the lake cabin.

Garrity said to him: "Tell me more about this plan of yours, this escapist fantasy," because Mailman had made the mistake of mentioning it to him. This was during their second session, a week after he spilled his guts about Rhonda Petrash and the film projector. *One more week,* he kept telling himself, *one more week.*

"It isn't escapist, it isn't a fantasy."

"This non-escapist non-fantasy, then. When did you first get the idea? Your father? Did you wish to escape your father?"

"I got the idea from Gorman."

Jim Gorman, high school English. Must be dead now. A giant, slickskinned man, a perspirer, six-five and Mailman would bet two-seventy-five: hair kept short in the military way even long after the war, this was, what?, 1961 he supposes. Well, they all looked like that then. The spaceman look, everybody impressed with Shepard and Grissom, pretending the Russians weren't winning the race. Gorman radiated heat, he was like a giant mulch pile, as if he'd accumulated matter and memory all his life with no way to release any of it, and in the center of him it had begun to burn and melt together, and take on a tremendous density and weight. He taught honors English, third year of high school. They read Homer and Virgil. Shakespeare. Milton. Back when that's what they taught in high school. In front of the class Gorman would talk-sing the lines with eyes closed, and occasionally a tear would form but never fall in the corner of one or both of those eyes: *Yet once more, O ye laurels, and once more / Ye myrtles brown, with ivy never sere* . . . Strange eyes, large and striking but somehow distant: in yearbook photos he gave the impression of a man who could see into your very soul but in person you could see the eyes were always in motion, taking in everything but the center of you, darting around your face, collecting the pieces of you but never seeming to put them together. More than once he told them of his secret ambition: he and Mrs. Gorman were going to throw it all over, they owned eighty acres in the North Country of Maine and would go there one spring, chop down trees, build a cabin, hunt and garden and fish, never come back out. They'd drop out of society, they'd make it on their own, like Natty Bumppo. The fat of the land. This was years before everybody else got the same idea. Gorman talked about it often, everything seemed to remind him of it, and now and then Mailman would think, Why don't you do it then? Why don't you just go: why are you telling a bunch of kids about it? In the other classes, in the cafeteria, after school, they would gather and gossip about the Gormans: Gorman was *all talk*, they said, he ought to *put his money where his mouth is*. Outside class they disdained him but in class they gave him their grudging respect: he had passion, he made them feel like they were part of history. For that short while, before the war with Gorman began, Mailman actually liked poetry.

Just after Christmas vacation the class took up *The Odyssey*. After having endured *The Iliad*'s exhaustive lists of ships and descriptions of battles, the psychological drama and adventure of the second poem was a relief, and the class grew excited and came to the lessons eager to talk and to listen to Gorman's booming recitation of some of the best bits. In retrospect Mailman's not sure what made him start the war: quite possibly the weather, which was unseasonably warm and sunny, or perhaps a change he'd begun to notice in his own appearance and demeanor: his shoulders had begun to fill, as opposed to jut, out; his voice had smoothed and deepened; his face had traded its weak-jawed triangularity for the rigid line of a strongbox. He'd lost his awkwardness before any of the handsomer and more popular boys, and though no girls seemed to have taken note of this (ah!, those dresses: the arms: the ankles), it seemed that they were right on the cusp of doing so. He felt actual confidence walking the school halls and strode from classroom to classroom feeling as buoyant and impenetrable as a battleship.

But at the time he'd seriously pondered none of this; he was aware only of a dim kind of convergence, a gathering of prowesses; and when he raised his hand in class on the day in question he didn't know what he was going to say, only that he was certain of his ability to say *something* worthwhile, words that would shape the sound of his voice into a glittering, diamond-hard thing through which the day's peculiar stunning light and heat would pass and fragment. Gorman (and is he remembering correctly that Gorman had about him, for the first time, the look of ebbing strength?, that Gorman's girth and volume had lost their impression of power and begun to resemble some freak gigantism, a failure of natural adaptivity?, that the teacher had become a kind of leftover?) held out his iron pipe of an arm (but—is it possible?—did the arm tremble ever-so-slightly, like Achilles' quivering spear wedged in a waning Trojan heart?) and pointed a pink finger at Mailman.

"Mister Lippincott."

"I don't get it. We've had three chapters of Odysseus's whiny little runt of a son and we haven't even seen Odysseus. Is there going to be some point to this or is Telemachus just going to wander around saying 'Daddy come home' for the whole book?"

There was a silence. Mailman had meant to be blunt, but not quite so cavalier; a couple of people behind him were snickering. "That's all I'm wondering I guess," he concluded, a weak finish to be sure: but a new dynamic had been unveiled in the room, and all eyes were on Gorman, whose face shone bright and wet in a slanting beam of winter sunlight.

"You don't like Telemachus, Mister Lippincott?"

"No, sir," Mailman said, realizing it was true: Telemachus was slack, womanly, neither warrior nor sage, a sniveling drone. The "sir" was a sop. "He's ineffective, a lousy son. He's a mental weakling." More snickering.

Gorman—and how could Mailman have known about Gorman's own son?, eight years old and mildly retarded, a bent and bony little old man of a boy with a leg brace and maxillary protrusion: how could he possibly have known, having not yet seen Gorman and his far-sighted ratlike squirt of a wife trying to get their son to eat french fries in a restaurant (as he would the following summer), blowing each one cool and dipping it in ketchup and angling the bloody end in the half-open side of the boy's randomly champing mouth?, how could he have anticipated the holy rattling racket the boy would make every two or three minutes when his wayward right fist, at the end of its bicycle-spoke of an arm, came thundering down onto the table in a gatling-gun rhythm, knocking water glasses and silverware onto the floor?, how could he ever have imagined that a waiter would approach them and ask if they could please get the boy to stop doing that because the other diners were complaining?: he couldn't possibly have known, anticipated, imagined; he could not, at the age of sixteen and in the first flush of intellectual and sexual maturity, have been expected to possess the empathy or experience to see any of it in his teacher's eyes—Gorman hung his head for a scant few seconds, and when it rose again it was a lion's head, afire with bloodlust, and Mailman was taken aback. His arm—Gorman's arm—was still extended, the finger at its end still pointing; now he upturned the hand and curled the finger, beckoning.

"Lippincott. C'mere."

A simple command, foolproof really, the greater man directing the lesser. Still, Mailman protested.

"Wha— you mean there? You want— I should come up there?"

The lion's head nodded, licking its chops. "C'mere."

There was no snickering now as Mailman stood up and walked to the front of the room to face his teacher. He stopped four feet from Gorman and hazarded a glance into those black eyes that for the first time seemed to see clearly, brutally, all the way through him. He could feel the heat coming off him, could see the dark circles widening under his arms. Mailman began to be afraid.

"Closer, Albert."

He obeyed. Gorman's outstretched hand fell and he gripped both Mailman's shoulders. The pain was deep and instant: his bones themselves protested, he felt the presence in his body of organs that had never before announced themselves. Then he felt himself being spun to face the class. He could see in his classmates' faces what his own expression must have betrayed: real terror at the magnitude of his lapse, as Achilles must have felt as he dragged Hector's corpse around the city of Troy for the third, fourth, fifth time: *now I've gone too far, and I will have to pay.*

Mailman paid quickly. He felt a sweaty hand—a filet mignon of a hand, so large it was barely a hand at all, instead some evolutionary throwback from the days before humans crawled out of the ocean, a massive fin or tail or pad of fat used for butting foes to death—fumbling at the back of his pants, and then the hand was there, in his underpants, parting the crack of his ass, tangling itself in the hairs there, bunching itself into a fist—*My God,* he thought, *what's he doing!*—and then the hand was out, and Mailman was nearly lifted off his feet, and the fabric of his underpants squeezed his testicles so hard that they, the testicles, seemed to consider popping out of their sacs and running for their very lives, and his penis, innocently dozing until this moment, was trapped in the leghole and clamped by the wedgie's sudden force. *My God! My God!* his mind was gasping, *a wedgie!* Mailman cried out, the entire class drew breath. One hideous moment later he was lying in a heap at Gorman's feet, utterly undone. His gorge rose and a thin stream of vomit splashed on the floor beside him. He felt the urge to shit but managed to keep his bowels in check. Silence roared through the room.

"Now, Mr. Lippincott," said Gorman. "Sit down."

But even in this beaten state, even gasping on the hardwood beside a puddle of his own sick, Mailman could hear the stunned surprise in Gorman's voice: now it was he who had gone too far (far farther than Mailman had gone); now Mailman, curled on the floor at his feet, had the upper hand. The war with Gorman had begun.

"Sit in your seat, Mister Lippincott."

Even if he was capable of moving (he was not), he would have remained in this position, visibly beaten, for a little while longer, because every second he failed to rise, every second of total silence that emanated from his classmates, was a second of triumph for him, Mailman, and a second of humiliating defeat for Gorman. This man—a teacher, a responsible adult!—had done *this* to a student! A mere boy! Did Gorman find a *child* so threatening that such intimate violence was necessary? Everyone in the room had their minds on a single thing: Mailman's equipment. For this, Gorman could blame no one but himself. No, Mailman would stay right here.

How long did he crouch there? How long was Gorman forced to stand at the front of the class with a crumpled student at his feet? It might have been an entire minute. "Get up!" Gorman demanded, "get the hell up!" And then—only after Gorman had closed the circle, from losing his cool to glacial triumph to doubt to the attempted restoration of decorum to once again losing his cool—only then did Mailman stand up, run his hands through his hair, and stagger—not back to his seat, but to the classroom door! The class reacted, letting out breath; Mailman felt their eyes turning back to Gorman.

"Get in your seat, Lippincott," Gorman said quietly, the voice of reason now: but Mailman was having none of it. The battle was on. He opened the door—

"*Get* in your *seat.*"

—and walked through it, into the empty hallway, where his feet fell heavily (Mailman was staggering, still nauseated and in pain, but he had the presence of mind to exaggerate the noise of his departure) on the linoleum. No sound from the classroom, where the door still stood open wide.

The hall monitor approached, a gangly senior named Steven Crouch. "Where's your pass?"

"Get it from Gorman," Mailman said and let himself into the boys' room, where he holed up in a stall to assess the damage. Later his classmates would tell him what had happened: Steven Crouch had asked the stunned Gorman, who still stood gaping at the open door, what Albert Lippincott was doing in the hallway, and Gorman, failing to meet the monitor's eyes, pointed at the pool of vomit and intoned, "He's sick. Send in the janitor."

That night Mailman called his sister: she was in drama school at Yale. He told her what happened and asked her what he ought to do about it. "Cup your little nuts in your hand and promise them it'll never happen again," she whispered, giggling: she was high, or perhaps acting the way she did when she was high (or, at any rate, acting the way she *thought* people acted when they were high). He said, "I mean to him. What should I do *to him*?" "Oh, *darling,*" she said (she'd taken to calling him *darling* during her senior year in high school, after she'd starred in *Anything Goes*), "you mean you want to get *revenge*?" "That's what I mean." "Well then you've come to the right place. Just a second." And then Mailman heard her telling someone what he'd just told her and repeating, "And he wants to get *revenge*." "Is someone there?" he asked her. "A friend. His name's Neil." "Isn't it late to have a . . . friend over?" Gillian laughed: "My roommate's at *her* lover's, we trade, the desk attendants don't mind, excuse me Neil but I'd like to retain *some measure* of bedclothes, dear." "You're in bed?" "Don't worry, Albert," she said, "we're all finished with the dirty stuff. And now your revenge."

But it was hard to listen, given what he now knew about his sister, that she was sleeping with men and didn't seem to care that he knew it: he tried to picture this one, Neil, in her bed, which he had seen on a visit neatly sheeted, with a quilt their grandmother had made draped squarely across it: this narrow twin bed of the same variety he used to sleep in with her when they were children, into which she was now folded with an entire living man, whose naked body she apparently had full access to. Were they naked now? Were they under the quilt?, with perhaps a foot or arm trailing out into the chilly winter air . . . ". . . and you would address it to his wife," Gillian was saying, "and pop it in the mail. But you have to make sure the handwriting is dumb and girly, or the trick won't work—she'd never believe he's fucking a smart woman on the side."

"What? You're saying send a letter?"

"From his lover, yes."

"How do I know if he has a—"

"Albert, darling, are you even *listening* to a single *word* I've been saying? It doesn't matter if he has a lover or not, the key is to make her *think* he does, to make him have to defend himself, and besides, they *all* have lovers, that's the only way men can marry."

"*All* married men have lovers?" he said, in disbelief.

"Well just about, I'd say. Believe me, I've talked—"

"Even *Dad*? Are you telling me that *Dad* has had lovers?"

"I've never asked him, Albert, but really, think about it: have you ever seen Mother and Father engaged in *any* affectionate act of *any* kind?"

"Sure, yes: I've seen them hug and kiss, yes," the words *hug* and *kiss* rushing to his head and making him feel woozy and sick.

"Yes, but it's always per*func*tory, it's a *sham*, a social grace, not real affection. I'm certain Father's had his share of affairs, God knows Mother has—"

"With who!"

"With all those men in all those pictures hanging in her room, the ones with their arm or *arms* draped or *wrapped* around her? Really, Albert, I can't imagine any of this is *news* to you, what did you *think* she was doing with them?"

"They're musicians, they're club owners in New York and Newark and Philadelphia. She told me, those people are professional contacts of hers, they help her with her nightclub act—"

"Albert, *please*, she gets the gigs because she *fucks* the owners, the bookers, the band. Did you ever notice she's at home on the weekends? What kind of *chanteuse* stays at home in *New Jersey* on Friday nights?"

"I—I don't know."

"The kind that *can't sing,* that's what kind. Not that I have a problem with Mother's *infidelity,* Albert—there's nothing wrong with a woman using what she's got to get what she wants. I don't have any illusions about my *acting* ability"—and a commotion ensued, the man in her bed seemed to be protesting and she told him to shut up—"but I have good tits and nice hair and I'm willing to screw the director, which I happen to be doing right now."

"You mean to—" Mailman began, but his sister was arguing with her lover and the telephone fell aside, leaving Mailman to listen: he was sitting at the kitchen table, his father below him in the lab and his mother singing (or not) in Philadelphia; he hadn't bothered to turn the light on and so he was in the dark, sweat trickling from his armpits down his sides and soaking the waist of his pants, and he leaned over, straining to hear: *If that's how you feel about— Don't be ridic— No, I'm not interested in some— You can go and—*: and he heard the slam of a door and the horrible sound of Gillian crying, muttering under her breath at *the bastard, I'll kill him* . . . Mailman said "Gillian! Gillian!" and there was no response, he shouted, "Gillian!" And then came the sound of the telephone being handled, that hollow percussive clatter, and the line cut off. Mailman was left holding the receiver in one suddenly cold numb hand and after a moment he set it on the cradle and began to flex his fingers. Footsteps sounded on the stairs and the basement door swung open, admitting the caustic odor of his father's ministrations.

"Hey! Was that your sister? What's up with— that is, how's she doing?"

"She's fine," Mailman told him and retreated to his room to write a letter.

"Really?" said Gary Garrity, sitting up a bit straighter in his seat. "You forged a letter?"

"Yes, *really*, what're you acting so shocked at?"

"Well, it's so . . . decisive. For you."

"What in the hell is that supposed to mean?"

Garrity grimaced, sighed, glanced at the clock. Mailman glanced with him. Thirty minutes gone, twenty-five to go. "It's just very devious, very confident. I'm impressed."

"Whoop-de-do," Mailman said. "I'm so gratified."

Garrity sighed. "Just finish the story, please, Albert."

He wrote the letter on composition-book paper, torn at the edge by the stitching that bound it, to give the impression that the writer was a student of Gorman's. A student none too smart, the kind to whom it wouldn't have occurred that composition-book paper might betray her position. He took his time, trying several drafts before he settled on the text, and then he practiced a girlish hand, neat and cute and proper. It wasn't hard at all, almost fun once he got the hang of it. He even began to develop an image of the girl, a dumb girl with dignity, with golden curls, tight sweaters, the works. He imagined her sitting on a hotel bed rolling her stockings down over her knees and her skirt ever-so-slowly up to the lower hem of her panties. Yes, this was going to work. When he was finished he went into his mother's dressing room (ignoring this time the bright photos that he once so enjoyed poring over, the carefree hedonist grins of the musicians and club owners and his mother's confidence and allure), found a suitable-looking perfume atomizer, sprayed a bit into the air and waved the letter through the scented cloud. Then he folded it, stuck it into an envelope and addressed it to "Mrs. Gorman" at Gorman's address. He got a stamp from the kitchen drawer and went out into the street and down to the corner where the mailbox stood. Would it be an exaggeration to say that the emotions he felt as he placed the letter on the weighted tray and let it clank shut, let the letter fall, were revelatory? Would it be too much to suggest that what he felt at that moment was the moral force of performing an irrevocable act, the utter *finality* of mailing a letter, and that these feelings filled him, quite instantly, with a yen for the irreversible power of the mail system? It would not: this is what he felt.

The letter read:

Dear Mrs. Gorman,

You dont no me but I am having an affair with your husband Mr. Gorman. I am telling you this because I am gilty and you should no. You do not no me and would not no my name if I told you it so that is not important. What is important is that I am ending it because its wrong and because I feel bad. I am sorry.

Sinceerly,

Unonamous

In addition Mailman wrote another draft with crossouts and revisions, crumpled it up, uncrumpled it, rubbed it in the dirt and on the pavement and surreptitiously dropped it in the school hallway between classes. He regarded this as a beautiful touch, and it was. In this version of the letter the girl had referred to "your husband James" and had crossed out the "James" and filled in "Mr. Gorman." What he had realized was that there could be no real damage if the "affair" played out in isolation; Gorman could convince his wife that the letter was a hoax. But there was no such possibility if everybody else was talking about it too. It would come to Mrs. Gorman from two directions: through the mail and through the grapevine.

Within two days rumors were all over the school. Everybody thought they knew who the girl was. Several names circulated but only one stood out: Candice Strout. Other suspects denied the accusation; Candy Strout was rumored to have replied, "I dunno, *am* I having an affair with Mr. Gorman?" In fact Candy was a student of Gorman's in his low-level English course, which, though given the presumptive title of Introduction to Literature, was actually more of a remedial reading class. Mailman heard through a boy he knew whose older sister, held back for a year, was retaking Intro-Lit, that Gorman had completely lost control of the students. Candy Strout sat in the front row in complete disregard of the seating chart, stuck out her ensweatered chest, and swung her unstockinged leg provocatively for the entire fifty minutes while lasciviously winking and raising her eyebrows at Gorman. Notes were being passed, and on some days entire conversations were held in the back of the room by little groups of girls who, when Gorman demanded that they face front and stop talking, turned in his general direction, tsked loudly while rolling their eyes, and went back to what they were doing.

If any of this bothered Mailman's conscience—and from time to time it did—he simply revisited his memory of the wedgie, the pain and nausea and humiliation of it, and his regret would disappear. On occasion he could relive the experience so clearly and powerfully that, in sympathy for his former self, a queasiness would develop which would require several breaths of fresh air to dispel.

Meanwhile his English class continued with Homer. Gorman was subdued, to say the least; the passion seemed to have gone out of him, as if he were trapped in Circe's cave along with Odysseus. He spent all his lecture time either facing the chalkboard or mumbling into his open book. Never once did his eyes meet Mailman's. For the duration of one class, this didn't seem so strange, but over the course of a week it became ominous: was Gorman failing to make contact with everyone, or just Mailman? And if it was just Mailman, was it out of guilt over the wedgie, or because—and this is what he feared, and what would soon obsess him—*he knew Mailman had sent the letter*? Careful study over several class periods convinced Mailman that Gorman was snubbing only him; he raised his hand just like everyone else when a question arose, but always it was another student who was called upon to answer. Gorman was on to him, and suddenly the letter seemed idiotic: how could he have thought Gorman wouldn't figure it out? There was no one else on earth (at least, as far as Mailman knew) who would have done it. And if Gorman had not yet confronted him, then there must have been something else up his sleeve: the next volley in the war. And so Mailman braced himself.

But the volley, when it came, was silent. Two and a half weeks after the letters, people had begun to grow weary of Candy Strout's antics (the kissy face, the eyelash-bat, the pout); there were students who no longer believed she was the one, and some who had fully internalized the fact of the affair, so that it no longer seemed surprising. The fake early draft of the letter had been lost; Mailman never knew who'd found it and by now it was likely to have been confiscated by the principal: and if the principal was going to fire Gorman (which was Mailman's goal, he had to admit), he would have done so by now. Most likely there had been a meeting, a denial, an agreement to discover the culprit. *Whoever did it will brag eventually,* the principal probably said, *they always do.* And Gorman would be tempted, wouldn't he?, to reveal Mailman's name. *I know who did it,* he'd be dying to say; but he wouldn't. He couldn't, because of the wedgie, the wedgie everyone had seen and which might, with effort, also be used to remove Gorman from his job. And so Gorman was sitting tight, biding his time.

One day there was a pop quiz on *The Odyssey*. Mailman thought nothing of it: after all, he knew the book inside out, even liked it. The questions were easy—essay questions, matters of opinion—and so he waxed intellectual for half an hour and handed the thing in along with everybody else. Piece of cake.

The following day, when the quizzes came back, Mailman's was marked F. *Shallow,* Gorman had written next to Mailman's gloss on Penelope's moral dilemma. *Inconsistent with the facts,* was the response to his view of the slaughter of the suitors. And beside his paragraph about the cowardice of Telemachus, Gorman had simply printed WRONG. The unkindest cut came at the bottom of the sheet: a personal note that read:

Albert,

I am worried about your performance in this class. Every assignment so far this year has received a grade of F! You can still pass if you complete the appropriate work. See me.

Mr. Gorman.

But it wasn't true, he'd gotten an A on everything, the quizzes, the midterm exam, the essay! His classmates were filing out, clutching their papers nonchalantly as they chatted, and Gorman sat on his desk, staring—*staring!*—at Mailman frozen in his seat.

Son of a bitch, Mailman thought. So this is how it's going to be.

When the others were gone he said, "Liar."

Gorman smiled complexly: on its surface, a smile of complete and malicious confidence, a just smile, a vengeful yet righteous smile; yet the confidence was hypothetical: Gorman was not quite sure—could not be *one hundred percent certain*—that the letter, the rumor, the scandal, were Mailman's doing. The finger, the plump red finger that had beckoned him to his wedgie, beckoned to him again. And again, Mailman stepped forward. Except this time Gorman turned his back, walked around to the other side of the desk and placed the finger with a meaty thud on the blotter, where he had opened his gradebook. Warily Mailman leaned over and read. LIPPINCOTT, ALBERT. And after the name, inked neatly into the squares, no corrections, realistically rendered in a variety of different-colored inks: *F. F. F. F. F. F.*

"It isn't true."

Gorman shrugged. When he spoke it was with the grave calm of a boulder baking in the middle of a desert. "Why don't you bring in your papers, then, Albert? We can double-check."

But of course Mailman never kept his papers. He'd made a point, along with a few other boys who had wished to show not only their intelligence, but their *indifference* to about their intelligence, of insouciantly tossing his graded exams and essays into the metal waste-

basket on their way out of class: just their way of showing that *Yes,
this stuff is easy for us, so easy in fact that we take no pride in having accomplished it, because our eyes are fixed upon our shining futures, in the
colleges of our choice and beyond, into the professional world, so high
above this classroom that you won't even be able to see us from where
you're standing.* What fun it had been to pass through the door
without looking back: so certain were they of the effect their little
pageant had on Gorman that they didn't even need to see the expression of self-pity on his face in order to enjoy it. And Gorman had
noticed, all right. Oh, boy, had he. Mailman thought fast. Already
he'd gone down the wrong rhetorical road; "Liar" was a mistake, the
response of someone who knew why he was being punished. No, the
correct response would have been shocked surprise. But Gorman
wasn't all that swift: he could still be fooled. To buy a few seconds
Mailman whispered, "But . . ." Yes—it felt good on the tongue, like
a dose of castor oil, a punishment that was for his own good, and
the flavor of it spurred him to manufacture the correct emotions. Yes:
injustice. Persecution. "But," he said, a touch of vibrato beginning to
creep into his voice, "I don't understand—I remember those papers,
I got A's—there has to be some mistake!" And he looked up at his
teacher, into those dark unfocused eyes, and did he detect there . . .
doubt? Perhaps?

"There's no mistake," Gorman muttered as in the hallway a shout
echoed, and the laughter of boys.

"But why—why are you *doing* this to me?" *Too heavy! Rein yourself in!*

"I think you know what's going on here, don't you, Albert?"

He's jumping the gun. "It's a mistake—those grades are someone
else's."

"You can quit pretending. I know you did it."

"But I didn't, I aced those tests, I swear!" *Yes, feign misunderstanding.*

Gorman persisted. "You wrote those letters."

An honest man would not, Mailman knew, avert his eyes. An honest man would search the face of his accuser for a way into the truth:

he would not be afraid. And so Mailman steeled himself and said: "*You* wrote them! You wrote them in your gradebook!"

Gorman lost his cool. He slammed the gradebook shut (and what could produce a more pathetic sound than a softcovered thirty-page gradebook being slammed shut?: a gentle rustle and flap, like a dead twig falling out of a tree) and raised once again his finger and pointed it at Mailman. "I know you did it, Lippincott, and mark my words, I'll get you. I'll get you. I just want you to know one thing: your little ploy didn't work. June"—this must have been Mrs. Gorman—"knows better than to think I would have anything but a professional interest, *if that,* in one of my students. I don't know if you did it alone or if that Strout girl is in it with you, but I want you to know that she didn't believe it for a second. Not a single second. And she wants to see you exposed as much as I do. Just keep that in mind."

"Why are you doing this to me, Mr. Gorman?" Mailman said, marshaling a strength he didn't know he had. "First you . . . you hurt me in front of everybody, and you give me an F for no reason at all, and now this—you mean that, I mean, you think, you think that I started these . . . rumors about you?" Tears rushed to his eyes, beautiful actual tears, and he hadn't even tried. Miss Petrash would be proud. Gillian would be proud, better than that she would be *jealous.*

Gorman shook his head slowly, his eyes squeezed shut, and Mailman knew he had won. He knew that when the semester ended, the grade on his report card would be A. Gorman wouldn't get him, couldn't get him: he had nothing at all on Mailman, and Mailman had everything on him. To Gorman's crime, there were *witnesses.* Mailman gathered his books and pencil and went to the door, pausing only to half-turn and say to his teacher, "Just leave me alone, okay, Mr. Gorman? What did I ever do to you?" And with that he went out into the hall and into his life.

The following week, Candy Strout, newly licensed, was driving her father's Nash Rambler out of the parking lot of the diner on Route 1 where she was a waitress, when a wood-paneled station wagon veered out of the eastbound lane, crossed the yellow line and slammed into her at forty miles an hour. Candy Strout told police she saw a small woman with large eyebrows and straight hair behind the wheel, and a boy of indeterminate age, wearing extremely thick eyeglasses, in the passenger seat beside her. The woman dislocated her shoulder in the crash and broke several ribs; the boy pitched forward and split his lip open on the dash, a wound that required thirty-one stitches to close. The woman was, of course, June Gorman. Mrs. Gorman later claimed to have "lost control of the car." Since Candy Strout was uninjured, save for a bruised halo where the steering wheel had met her forehead, no formal charges were pressed, though the Gormans agreed to pay for the damage done to the Strouts' car. The incident would certainly have strengthened everyone's confidence that the letters had been written by Candy Strout (obviously June Gorman had been fooled), except that during the medical examination following the crash Candy Strout confessed that she was pregnant, not by Gorman but by a boy three years her junior who lived five trailers down. She admitted that she never did have an affair with Gorman, and was promptly fired from her job at the diner for being pregnant and for being involved in the entire Jim Gorman scandal in the first place. Everyone was soon convinced that the entire thing had been a hoax, and nobody could actually produce either letter anyway. And so the scandal was over.

It was more than a week later when Mailman sighted the Gormans while dining at the Old Road Tavern, a dark and "elegant" place in Pennington, where his parents had brought him to celebrate the double good fortune of his father's having won a research grant of some kind and his mother's having secured a regular weekly gig (Tuesday nights) at a club in Trenton, which would pay better than any job she'd gotten before (and which Mailman would later learn she had to perform *while stripping* down to a pair of sequined underpants and a set of tasseled pasties). The boy, Gorman's son, still wore a bandage on his lip from the accident and spoke, if you could call it that, in a grunting monotone only intermittently audible through the classical music and the clinky-clank and babble of people eating dinner. At some point during the meal the Gormans just gave up, their food half-uneaten, and Gorman paid the bill and they walked out (the boy lurching between them in a horrible robotic parody of human ambulation), passing right by the Lippincotts' table as they left without once glancing in their direction. It occurred to Mailman that the Gormans must be very good at that, at ignoring stares. His father watched them pass with an amiable detachment and—too soon, really, when they were probably still within earshot—said, "Ah, poor kid." His mother waited until they were gone to say, "Christ, thank God, it was like eating in the same room as a goddam pile driver"; and Mailman said "Excuse me" and got up from the table and went to the men's room and forced himself to vomit. It seemed only right that he should throw up, it felt wrong to have eaten and right to rectify the error. He'd never done it before, but it was easy: you just stick your finger down your throat like people say you're supposed to.

"So your rebellion resulted in profound guilt," Gary Garrity said, turning over and over in his hands a fat ceramic fertility figurine, complete with gigantic breasts and vertiginous vaginal cleft, that he happened to have snatched from the bookshelf behind him as he listened.

"No."

"No?"

"I didn't feel guilty, I was *right*," Mailman said. "He *deserved* what he got. I didn't know about his goddam retarded son, even if I had I might have done the same thing, the guy humiliated me and squeezed my nuts until I puked, and I gave him as good as I got."

"Interesting that your story both begins and ends with vomiting."

"No, it isn't."

"Sure it is. Vomiting is so like ejaculation. And I'm interested in the interlude about your sister. Was that really the first time you ever thought about your sister having sex?"

"Vomiting is nothing like ejaculation."

"Were you a virgin then, Albert?"

"None of your beeswax."

"We're not going to get anywhere if your responses continue to be so hostile."

"We're not getting anywhere anyway. One more session and then I'm never going to see you again."

"Oh, come on. It's a small town."

"*Voluntarily*. I won't see you again *voluntarily*. Not that I'm doing this"—he gestured around the cramped office—"by choice."

Garrity shrugged, planted his elbows on the desk, arched an eyebrow. "In life, Albert," he said, "the things that are good for us are rarely the things we desire. So"—settling back now, hands behind his head, his voice registering a highly unprofessional delight—"next time, you can tell me about Maurice Renault. Class dismissed."

By the time he gets back to his house it's almost evening, and he is forced to conclude that his walk has been a failure. His head isn't cleared, his senses are not restored. There is much of a Saturday left to waste. He goes inside and spreads out the paper on the kitchen table. Déjà vu: this is where he always reads his morning paper, except that this isn't his paper, it's another one, which he bought at the place where he left the first one. Things have taken on their intended shape: the day is healing itself before his eyes.

Okay, what's playing? At the Cinemas 6: *Triple Duty*, a sequel to a spy thriller; *Benny III: Rising Tide*, another sequel to the original politically correct picture about the brilliant dolphin; *It Hurts*, a love-but-probably-not-sex story; *The Court of Kings*, a lawyer movie starring that guy; *Five Lunches and Two Breakfasts*, a sex-but-probably-not-love story; and *Starbase Eleven*, a sci-fi pic. Too damn many options: he can't think, he's too hungry, so he'll pick up some dinner somewhere and decide on the movie at the theater.

But it's on the way there—just as he's merging onto Route 13— that a stray thought drifts in the car window, brushes his forehead and is torn away by a semi's slipstream. What is it? The movie? The dinner? Something he needed to do.

He has to pull over: it was right there, his thought, he can't let it get away. He signals, steers onto the shoulder, activates the hazards and rests his head on the wheel. Think. Think. Outside, cars rush by. Thinks about the things he thought about earlier: Gorman? Miss Petrash? The girl at More Coffee! (oh, God!, the girl at More Coffee!, but that's something to deal with another time), reading the newspaper: wait: something: oh no!

He got—this morning, the cats, oh!—*he got out of bed without going over the previous day's mistakes*—and worse than that, he woke without remembering to keep his eyes closed! If he were Chuck Balling, his vet ex-customer, if this had been 'Nam, he, Chuck Mailman, would instantly have been killed by the Vietcong! And he didn't chew his raw brown rice, a transgression he is about to magnify by visiting a *fast-food restaurant*, a veritable temple of bodily defilement—on the heels, no less, of croissants and bear claws.

He squeezes his eyes shut, gulps breaths of hot air, in an effort to dispel a sudden dizziness. How is it he can spend the day remembering things that happened to him when he was six, when he was sixteen, but fail to execute his only remotely healthy or productive daily regimen? Behind his eyes appears a pulsing, a shifting of light. Is he sick, now, to boot? The dizziness, the lights? He takes another breath and opens his eyes to find the light intensified, given definition: the red and then the blue sweeping across the interior of his car. It's a cop.

"Everything all right?"

A lady cop! Scrawny one, with smoker's skin, but she looks good in the blues, with the gun on her hip. He has to be careful here, doesn't want to give the impression that he thinks she'll be a pushover because she's a girl; he's seen it at the P.O., women overcompensate for what they believe (correctly he supposes) men perceive as the natural proclivities of their gender. So he acts real nervous. "Oh! Yes, I— I'm sorry, Officer, I was just pulling over. To try to remember. What I forgot."

Her face is freckled, bent nose, flat dull eyes covered by light-sensitive eyeglasses (now in medium-light mode, which is to say she can make eye contact, which she is doing). "License and registration," she mutters.

Mailman hands it all over, it's all in order, she looks at the picture and at him and examines the words printed on the papers. Pauses. Is she going to run him through the computer? She almost but not quite smiles.

"You're my mailman, sir."

"What!" he says, can't help himself. Clears his throat though there is nothing obstructing it. "Oh, say, sure, where do you live?"

"Downtown. I'm Peggy Mussman, Officer Mussman."

Sure, Mussman. He remembers the name. Peggy Mussman is not a letter-writer. On the highway an SUV full of college kids speeds past honking, their arms out the windows, "She got youuuuu!"; from their stereo blasts one of those snarly-voiced rock bands that sing songs about how they need a fix, or how they're a freak, or how their girl is a freak, or how somebody has sold out, and Mailman says, "Whoop! There's somebody for you to pull over," then realizes she's just trying to be friendly in her extremely curt way: "Sorry, I mean not that you're not doing your job, I mean thank you for noticing me doing my job, I take great pride, I hope you think I do it well, I mean, I hope you have no problems with your mail."

"No, sir."

"Anyway I pulled over because I thought I forgot my wallet but here it is, you can see I took my driver's license out of it."

She hands back the license and registration and says "Stay off the shoulder, Mr. Lippincott," and he almost says *How'd you know my name!* but catches himself in time.

"Yeah, sorry, it was the spur of the moment, I acted impulsively. Sorry about that." He's quite relieved; sweat breaks out on his forehead, his breath catches. She returns to her car, turns off the lights, waits for him to pull out. He does, but someone in the left lane is switching unsignaled into the right and honks; Mailman presses on the gas as the honker comes up illegally close behind him and the lady cop doesn't bother pulling out and chasing this insane maniac lawless asshole. Christ! What's the point of being a traffic cop if you're not going to pull over guys like that! Then he hits the hill and his car slows and the nut swerves around him still honking and gives him the finger. Second finger of the day! Mailman smiles and waves.

He exits at the top of the hill, pulls into the burger place. Orders chicken nuggets, BBQ dip, Coke, fries, and wolfs them in the car. In the windbreak between here and the old people's home, one squirrel with a bum leg chases another squirrel with no (or maybe a little stub of a) tail while a couple of crows watch the whole thing, screaming. Ah, the beauty of nature. When he's finished he has to push his trash deep down into the garbage can to keep the whole teetering pile from toppling onto the pavement. Driving off he can smell the garbage on his arm.

At the theater he buys popcorn, though he isn't hungry. Size: regular, which is to say very large: what he'd prefer is a cup the size of the smallest (aka "regular") soft drink cup, and he asks for same, but the counter girl tells him no, the soft drink cups are for soft drinks and the popcorn cups are for popcorn.

"But I don't want this much popcorn."

"So don't eat it."

"But I don't want to pay for popcorn I'm not going to eat."

"So don't buy it."

He buys it. In his pocket is a ticket to see the spy thriller, *Triple Duty*.

But first, the men's room. No door, just the labyrinthine hallway protecting urinating men from curious eyes, and then the rows of sinks, beside which he takes a moment to find a dry spot to put his cup of popcorn down. He pees: feels better: zips. When he gets back to the sinks there's a guy energetically scrubbing his face *right next to his popcorn* and so Mailman surreptitiously grabs the cup and brushes the top layer of men's-room-exposed and possibly soapy and wet popcorn into the trash, and hurries down the hall to his theater. *Triple Duty* is already in progress. On the screen, a menacing-looking man in black goes into a bank and withdraws a lot of cash (of course the bank manager must approve such a huge transaction), then leaves the bank and gets into a waiting car which drives away, and then a completely normal-looking man approaches and enters the bank and speaks to the teller, and she calls the manager over again and he comes over and says, "But . . . you can't be Andrew Fleming—Andrew Fleming just left here!"

Mailman settles back into his seat, distracted by his reeking, trash-contaminated arm—why didn't he wash it when he had the chance? Now he'll have to sniff the thing for an hour and a half. Cops, spies, and bankers are racing around on the screen, and Mailman leans his head back, trying to relax; he presses his knees against the empty seat in front. Comfortable at last, he lets out a sigh and that's when he sees six rows in front of him the graywhite sculpted coif of Maurice Renault.

The "great man"! He's here with his son, Kendall, a *poet* of all things in the meager NYTech English department. What a coincidence, he was just thinking about the old bastard, or thinking about telling Garrity about him, anyway. Things converge, they find one another in the void and engender a nexus, a clot. Mailman catches himself: that's a Renaultian concept if ever there was one: that things happen not because they just do but because they *want* to. This was the subject of his third book of popular science/philosophy, *Come Together*, the one that secured his fame, before the UFOs-are-real brouhaha and the PBS miniseries hullabaloo and the handsomest-man-in-the-universe embarrassment and the presidential visits, but after the *Natural History of the Solar System* and his first big splash, *It Could Happen*. That one was written when Mailman was still a student—Renault's student, in fact.

"That hat must have been a thrilling time, a golden age," Garrity offered from behind his desk. It was their third session. He was dressed in a Hawaiian shirt and a baseball cap, as if Mailman were the only thing keeping him from his yacht.

"Don't be an asshole."

"Moi?" Two fingers pressed to the sternum, the eyes wide and contrite.

"Do you want me to talk about it or not?"

"Of course I do. I'm your therapist."

"Oh, right. It's so easy to forget."

A disappointed scowl. "Who's being an asshole now, Albert?"

"Still you. And so was Renault. The guy was a nobody."

He was a nobody, Renault, a junior lecturer, a visitor to NYTech from his native France whose visit never got around to ending. He was Mailman's advisor: Mailman was assigned to him upon declaring his major in his freshman year. At the time he had never seen the man up close; he'd attended the big Physics 101 lecture like everybody else and when there were questions they were handled by graduate students. In the front of the classroom Renault seemed small, slight, dark, rough, like the cigarettes he smoked during class; his accent was penetrable, but barely. *Eeenairshal mass end graveetashonal mass air eequel.* The sight of two hundred fifty heads tilted slightly forward, swiveling like satellite dishes, attempting to decipher the garbled English vowels: that is the way Mailman remembers the early days of Renault. You'd see him wandering around campus like he was lost, stopping suddenly as he got an idea and pulling a little leather-bound notebook from his pants pocket (and what could have been more pretentious than a *leather-bound notebook?* Wasn't the incidental medium best for the recording of brilliant ideas?, e.g. the cocktail napkin, the back of the hand; Picasso drawing with a stick on a Spanish beach or Lincoln and the famous back-of-the-envelope Gettysburg scribble), then writing the idea down and looking around as if suddenly noticing for the first time the students and professors bustling past him. And then the notebook went back into the pocket and out came the cigarettes (in a silver case!: this was 1961, for the love of Pete, the silver cigarette case was deader than Vaudeville), and he would stand there placidly smoking, and you could see the thought bubbles forming over his head, filled with self-satisfied Gallic thoughts. During review sessions the teaching assistants would mock him, doing the accent, the stiff-legged walk, the little swirl the chalk-clutching hand performed as it approached the blackboard. The assistants loved to hate their professor; they were bitter to be stuck serving under such a minor figure when giants were lumbering about, unlocking the secrets of the universe. Their favorite Renault shtick was the succinct answer: undergrads would think up long-winded questions to ask while their TA stood patiently in the Renault pose: one leg straight, its foot flat to the floor; the other leg out at an angle propped on its heel; the right forearm held close to the body, resting on the belt, and in its hand the elbow of the left arm, at the end of which burned one of the trademark cigarettes (or in the case of the mocking TA, a pencil). The more long-winded the question, the more profound the expression of absence, the more hooded the eyes, the deeper the hollows of the cheeks, until, just before the TA came out with his comically brief reply, his face would appear nearly to implode.

"*Oui.*"

"*No.*"

Or—everyone's favorite, brought out only rarely, to preserve its freshness—the insouciant shrug, accompanied by the almost complete closing of the eyes, the absurd lengthening of the chin, and the faintest sniff.

Oh, how they howled at Renault, the gag Frenchman: the only people on campus who actually liked him were the kids in the English department, who had discovered that Renault was acquainted with— had lived in the same town as, went to the same school as, something like that—Albert Camus. And so he never went to the physics parties and receptions, hobnobbing instead with the literature students, in their coffeehouse, at their potlucks, at their poetry readings and critical lectures. Rumors flew that Renault was writing some kind of book, which struck the physics students as hilarious: either it would be in French, which meant nobody would read it, or it would be in bad English, which meant nobody could decipher it.

For a long time Mailman avoided him: halfway through his second semester he still hadn't spoken to the man in person, hadn't visited his office to be advised. Frankly, Renault didn't fit into Mailman's vision of himself as an undergraduate: in the waning days of high school, he had come to anticipate his college years as a kind of social and professional runway down which he would brilliantly roll, on his way to a spectacular launch into the stratosphere of Big Science; he would be the kind of student whose arrival into any conversation would effectively end it: "Here's Albert, he'll settle this." He imagined his hair as forever windblown, his corduroys worn at the knees, his voice a magnet to which all ears would be inexorably drawn. So he went to the dean, to ask to have his advisor changed. He wanted to work with the big guys, he said; he wanted to get out from under Renault.

"If you want to switch advisors," said the dean, "you have to get permission from your advisor."

And so at last he reported to Renault, during the lunch hour, when he figured the Frenchman would surely be out wandering and thinking and smoking; Mailman would simply tuck the permission slip under the door. And in fact Renault appeared to be out when Mailman arrived—the frosted window was dark and no sounds issued from the room—so he left the appropriate form with a short note paperclipped to it:

Professor Renault,
Could you please sign and return to dean via campus mail?
Thank you.
Albert Lippincott

And he turned and walked off down the hall, relieved of the burden of personal contact, his head filled with plans for the hour, a brisk walk, a sandwich, the fresh cold air of late winter. Then he heard the clatter of the doorknob.

"Come here, please, Meester Leepeencott."

Mailman slowed, slumping against the hall wall and the bulletin board affixed to it so that a few sheets of paper escaped their thumb-tacks and wafted down to the linoleum floor. He bent, picked them up, rethumbtacked them. Renault waited, standing half out of his office with the form and a cigarette sharing one hand. Then he raised his eyebrows and retreated, vanishing from sight. Mailman turned and went back.

"Seet," said the Frenchman, gesturing with the cigarette toward a wooden chair upholstered in worn green velvet and covered with books and papers, as his eyes roamed over the yellow form and attached note. Mailman paused, waiting for further instruction regarding the chair, but none came, so he lifted the mass of paper and dropped it from a height of several inches onto the already-book-and-paper-strewn floor, causing a loud smack to which Renault had no reaction whatsoever. Mailman slumped into the chair. The office was a mess. Books were piled indiscriminately on every surface: but no, the mess wasn't indiscriminate at all. It was a cultivated mess, an intentional one, designed to portray its architect as a man of great intellect, too busy thinking deep thoughts to concern himself with domesticity or in fact any aspect of physical reality—a chaos that mirrored the chaos of the universe (because that was the new thing: the universe wasn't orderly after all, it was a god-awful mess that nobody could sort out), which one was led to believe was being contemplated daily in this very room. The only clean surface was Renault's desk, a blocky scratched oak hand-me-down that bore a lamp, a telephone, a legal pad, a pencil, and a gigantic ashtray filled to the brim with cigarette butts. *He could empty the thing, for Chrissake,* Mailman found himself thinking. *How much trouble could it be?*

"What ees thees . . . document?" The form flapped in the air before Mailman's eyes. Renault had one leg crossed over the other as far as it could go, in a casual pompous knot; his face registered only boredom.

"I want to switch advisors. I want to work with the theory guys."

Again Renault gazed at the form. He lifted up the attached note and peered underneath it; he turned the paper over and over. Then he lay it facedown on his desk, on top of the legal pad (covered, Mailman could see, with English words, written in a surprisingly careful hand, now largely obscured by the form), and leaned back in his chair, and looked at the ceiling, and drew from the cigarette and expelled smoke, and stood up and went to the window (tinted brown from smoke), and inhaled and then expelled more smoke so that it struck the window and spread across it and dissipated into the corners of the room (surely there was an equation for that? That is, for the behavior of the smoke cloud as a whole and not the individual atoms, to which, it was now known, Newtonian physics did not apply), and shook his head, and returned to his chair which creaked loudly beneath him, and set down the cigarette and leaned forward and expelled smoke from the corner of his mouth, and put his hands on his knees and said:

"No."

"*No?*"

"No. Sorry. Goodbye."

"But why not?"

And now Renault did something he had never actually seen Renault do, only the teaching assistants, which was to elongate his face and raise his eyebrows and half-close his eyes and *shrug*, a gesture so comical that Mailman knew Renault had *actually seen* his own TA's mocking him, had seen their famous "Renault shrug" and had taken to doing it himself, in mockery of his mockers. He followed up with a dismissive little wave, a gesture not at all self-mocking but in deadly earnest, and he turned in his chair, picked up the form with his right hand, and held it out to Mailman as he returned to work with his left. For a moment the only sound in the room was the scratch of pencil against paper. The form hung in the air between them, trembling slightly from the motion of Renault's writing. In the end, Mailman did not—could not—take it. Instead he stood up and left, kicking over the pile of books and papers he'd cleared the chair of when he entered. Only when he was in the stairwell, on his way out of the building, did Mailman hear the sound of the closing door echo through the empty hallway.

Gary Garrity seemed to find this story highly entertaining. He leaned back in his own chair, Renault-style, and grinned a closemouthed, shrinky grin, and nodded, and chuckled, and said, "Oh, that certainly does sound like Doctor Renault."

"What the hell's that supposed to mean?"

"He has little patience for little minds."

"I thought you were supposed to be making me feel better about myself."

"Only you can make yourself feel better about yourself, Albert."

"Oh, don't give me that shit, please. How much time do we have left?"

"Fifteen minutes." Garrity, actually, seemed to be feeling pretty good about himself, his hands hooked together behind his head, which nodded agreeably, in appreciation of its own prowess. What is it, Mailman wondered, about these guys and their desks? You put a guy behind one and he turns into a prick, or rather his *inner prick* is given free rein. Garrity waggled his eyebrows. He said, "It was *It Could Happen*, wasn't it?"

"What was?"

"What he was writing, at his desk."

"I have no idea."

"Aren't you glad to have been there for that? You can tell people you saw Renault writing his first book, the book that would win all those awards . . ."

"Jesus Christ," Mailman said and stood up. Behind him the clock ticked in its square of bookshelf. He turned and grabbed it down—

"Hey!" said Gary Garrity.

—and thinking of the atomic clocks flown around the world, the clocks intended to confirm Einstein's theory of general relativity, which in fact they did, seeming to "lose" several fractions of a second relative to the (relatively) motionless clocks on the ground, Mailman spun the setting dial until the fifteen minutes had elapsed. "There," he said, "time's up."

"Albert, surely you are aware that three full sessions are required. When Len Ronk asks me—"

"Oh, for crying out loud, are you going to rat on me? Well, go ahead, then, rat on me. If it's that important to you. I'll lose my job, but if it's that important to you then go ahead. I'm leaving."

An exaggerated sigh. "Is that what you're worried about, Albert? Your job? I think there is quite a lot more at stake here than a mere job."

"Like what?" The clock still in his hand.

"Well, this cesspool, as it were, of unfulfilled ambition. Something inside you is decaying, Albert. Something died which you failed to dispose of properly, and now it is, if you will, stinking up your very self."

Mailman raised the clock above his head intending truly to smash it. But Garrity cringed, threw his hands up over his head, whimpered. "Here," Mailman said instead, "catch": and he lobbed the clock. It described a gentle arc in the air.

Mailman didn't stick around for the catch: he was out the door and out of Garrity's life for good. He stomped off the porch, passing Mrs. Gary and the Minigarys bickering over a board game and stepped out into the street muttering curses. He was through with shrinks. They never told you anything you didn't already know.

If, on the other hand, the young Mailman believed (he certainly hoped) that he would never see or speak to Renault again, he was in for a disappointment. Renault was going to haunt him for life, up to and including this very moment, here in the movie theater. Mailman considers (as, on the screen, Andrew Fleming, the hero, chases bad guys in long leather coats through the streets of Seattle) how *French* Maurice Renault was then, and how *American* he is now: does anyone else notice this? Probably, though they certainly wouldn't regard such a transformation as unsavory, the way Mailman does. Americans love when foreigners turn into Americans. They love it when an immigrant says "I love America!" in a comical foreign accent. "Go Yan-kees!" That's what we like to hear. But Mailman always hated Renault, hated him more the more American he got. At least the French version was authentically *something*—authentically rude, authentically pretentious.

And then, of course, *It Could Happen* happened. Praised by Dyson, Mailer *and* the Book-of-the-Month Club. A true crowd-pleaser: engrossing, hopeful, amusing. Written in simple language, for the common man. The idea behind it was also simple. Using, as evidence, pioneering work on the frontiers of physics, biology, astronomy and philosophy (work that he, Maurice Renault, had no part in whatsoever), the book took the liberty of *predicting the future*. Guess what: there would be no nuclear war! The book was published soon after the Cuban blockade, and what the American public needed, and what it got, was a guy from somewhere else, a guy who presumably had some kind of outside perspective on our twisted culture, to tell them that, in his learned opinion, contrary to Khrushchev's vow, nobody was going to be burying anybody. In fact, everything was going to be terrific! The book predicted men on the moon, of course; that one was easy. It predicted men on Mars and Venus as well, space colonies, the spread of humanity and its wonders throughout the universe. It predicted the imminent harnessing of safe, nonpolluting nuclear power for peaceful use, contact with alien civilizations, an end to poverty and starvation in the third world. It did not predict Lee Harvey Oswald, or James Earl Ray, or Sirhan Sirhan.

Just about anyone could have written the thing, actually; but Renault, or perhaps Renault's publisher, played up the professor's mystique, made much of his loose associations with both science ("Maurice Renault is a distinguished professor of physics at the renowned New York Technical Institute") and literature (the Camus connection again), and photographed him in high-contrast light, sitting at his desk in his office, ribboned in cigarette smoke. At a meeting of some kind of campus club, he met and shook hands with fellow-immigrant-American and fellow-central-New-Yorker Vladimir Nabokov. Somebody snapped a photograph, the image was printed in the school paper with the headline EUROPE'S GREAT MINDS MEET IN NESTOR, and the Associated Press picked it up and used the photo anytime it ran a story on Renault. This despite the fact that Nabokov referred to the book as "a trifle, a schoolboy's fantasy" in an interview in *Time*. Nevertheless it was nominated for a National Book Award. It lost, but the book became a best-seller and the paperback would remain in print more or less forever.

Meanwhile, Mailman had gone ahead and pursued his desired course of study, lashing himself to the high-powered physics faculty, staying late in the lab scribbling on the blackboard with his pals (and getting to know the custodians: in the physics department, if you weren't on a first-name basis with the custodians, you were a nobody; and at Christmas it was traditional to throw money into a pot and buy them—Vic and Ed were their names—an extravagant gift, generally some expensive booze, which the janitors dutifully shared, on the spot, with the students) and attempting to avoid Renault. And yet he was always happening upon the man, even after he had completed the low-level courses, even after he no longer required Renault's signature on anything: always passing him in the science libraries (or the humanities library, the few times Mailman had gone in there to spy on girls), stumbling upon him in bars, standing behind him at the post office (Renault always seeming to be holding a package addressed to a literary agency or book publisher in New York City, marked URGENT! in his curlicued script), and once by mistakenly dialing his telephone number.

"Hello? Is this Grisman?"

"No, sor-ree."

"Is he— who is this?"

"Thees is Maurice, hello, who ees cal-leeng?"

He wondered how in the name of God he'd done such a stupid thing; Grisman's number was nothing like Renault's. He only knew Renault's because of the crank phone calls he and his pals had been making:

"Hi, this is Fred Golgi, from *Nature,* we're doing a poll. Is light a wave or a particle?"

"Hello, this is Erwin Schrödinger, I have your cat in a box. If you ever want to see him alive again, leave ten thousand dollars . . ."

In this manner, Renault seemed to *haunt* him: even after he was out of school, *especially* then, when the man would begin to publish books regularly; when he would appear on television to explain, "in layman's terms," whatever complex new theory was being offered by science; when he would announce, in the wake of Bobby Kennedy's assassination, that he would seek to become an American citizen; when he would come to host his own PBS series, *Out There*, and everyone in Nestor and everywhere else would begin to recognize him on the street: by that time Mailman, laid low by mental illness and intellectual unfulfillment, would feel *tortured* by the Frenchman, driven to distraction and rage. By 1970, when Mailman had already been delivering mail for several years, Renault had formed his American identity. The jeans (always old, faded, except on the TV series, where they were new, pressed, and dark blue); the brown leather belt with the gigantic buckle (what was depicted thereupon? It varied: sometimes an olive tree, sometimes a tractor, sometimes a breed of dog. Girls, students, would boldly gaze at the buckle, sometimes leaning over and bringing their faces close: "Oh, Professor, that's a *nice* one"); the soft chamois shirts with the enormous pockets that he kept filled with pencils and pens and erasers, and later a pocket calculator, then a graphing calculator, and now a handheld computer; the scuffed brown shoes and sweat socks. His accent became less pronounced, but sometimes, when he employed a particularly overt Americanism, it made him seem somehow *more* American, as at the end of every episode of *Out There*: "Join me next week, for another exploration of what is out there . . . *far* out." He was the kind of brainiac populist hero this country loves to hold oh-so-tightly to its hollow breast, a smart guy who *cares* about us, an academic who won't *talk down* to us, a brilliant man but *modest*. Imagine! Renault as modest! Perhaps the nadir of Mailman's Renault-loathing came a few years back when he heard a couple of kids on the Square talking about someone they knew who was smart: "Yeah, he's sharp, but he's no, like, Maurice Renault." Not Einstein, the old standard—Renault! As if, because being smart is what he's famous for, and because he is the most famous living smart person, *he must be the smartest person in the world.*

It was this resentment, this bottomless disgust, that led Mailman,

one cool September day in 1977, to rupture the delicate membrane dividing his personal and professional lives. Renault was in his feathered-
hair phase, his UFOs-are-real phase; it was the age of the Lubbock
Lights, Project Bluebook, *Close Encounters of the Third Kind.* It was the
year he published *Come Together,* a very short work of popular philosophy and astrophysics, which suggested that the universe was about
to start contracting, and as it did, its constituent parts would tend not
toward entropy but toward greater order, and human beings, both
conscious and *subconscious* of this change in the rules of existence,
were themselves beginning to join hands, to come together, which
explained the civil rights movement and predicted the end of the Cold
War. The science behind it was as idiotic as its philosophical under-
pinnings, and this time the critics didn't hold back: his own col-
leagues, people who encountered him daily at the physics department
coffee urn and had done so for fifteen years, wrote that the contrac-
tion of the universe was not, in fact, happening, and human beings
did not believe, either consciously or "subconsciously," that it was.
But once again Renault had correctly read the public mind, and the
book, for better or worse, became a feel-good best-seller.

By this time Mailman's Person-They-Fuck years were long over
and his mail route, though undesirable to most (it was the West
Heights route, which roved over hill and dale from one forested mansion to another, necessitating more walking, with a heavier load, than
most carriers were willing to undertake), suited him just fine. One leg
of the route carried him over the Zabriskie Bridge—Nestor's "secret"
bridge, which was no secret but was remote and difficult to find—and
thus past Renault's house, a neo-Victorian barnacle that hung ass over
the Reston Gorge, the least accessible and second deepest of Nestor's
five gorges. The old bastard was always home, it seemed: lately he had
convinced NYTech to let him hold his classes at night, so that he could
hack away at his books for the first five or six hours of each day. And
so, as often as not, Renault met Mailman at the front door, always

friendly, perhaps hoping to be recognized, hoping for Mailman to say something like, "Mister Renault, I'm really glad to have the opportunity to deliver your mail." But of course Mailman never said anything: Renault didn't seem to recognize him, despite the unfortunate circumstances of Mailman's breakdown more than a decade before. And now, in 1977, Mailman was, and had been for three years, faced with having daily to face his unwitting nemesis. Nothing could have been more humiliating.

Then, one afternoon, Mailman found himself standing at Renault's door (later it would not be possible to stand at Renault's door: his fame would precipitate a flood of pilgrims to Nestor who would bother the "great man" at all hours, and so a tall fence would be erected, and an iron gate with an electronic entry system, and an intercom would be installed, and if you wanted to get directly to the "great man" you'd have to scale a good hundred feet of sheer cliffside to do it), holding what was obviously a piece of fan mail, something from a child, it seemed, and his, Mailman's, revulsion finally reached its apex of intensity (or so he thought at the time), and he took the letter out of the bundle—

What am I doing? What am I doing?!?

—and slipped it, quite easily, into the pocket of his jacket.

For a few seconds he paused, catching his breath. The only sounds were the distant roaring of the creek far below, and the occasional passing car, out of sight behind the hedge, and the honking of geese heading south, and the rustle of leaves in the trees. No one appeared at Renault's door. He turned and peered up the hillside: he was hidden from the neighbors by a screen of woods. No one had seen him. The felony he had just committed went unpunished. The balance of the world had not been upset. He extended his hand to the mail slot and dropped the lightened bundle of Renault mail into it. He heard the mail thump on the floor, and then the clickety-click of a dog's paws on hardwood, and then the dog's placid panting. Mailman leaned over and lifted the metal flap: there stood the dog, watching. It sat down, then lay down. Mailman let the flap fall and turned around and finished his route.

At home he sat at the kitchen table with the letter lying flat before him. His divorce was not precisely recent—it had been almost a year and a half—yet the house still bore the marks of Lenore's departure: the unbleached squares and rectangles of wallpaper where her family pictures had hung, the filthy dishrags he could never remember to wash, the wooden table smudged and smeared and unpolished. He stared at the letter. The return address read:

> *David Fleener*
> *12 Myrtle Crescent*
> *Otis, Ohio*

—this in an immature hand, with a single scribbled correction (Miyrtle). The mailing address was that of Renault's publisher, thoroughly X'ed out and replaced with the words PLEASE FORWARD and Renault's home address.

On the table beside the letter lay a steak knife. Mailman picked it up—the knife—in his right hand, the letter in his left. He nudged the tip of the knife under the flap (thoroughly licked and sealed, with a child's exhaustiveness), and then pushed it farther, and a bit farther. A good sound, a knife slicing through the fold of an envelope, and he didn't have any second thoughts until it was most of the way open, and by then it was too late. Later he would remember this moment (he is remembering it now, in the movie theater, although this time the memory is bending, bleeding, for Mailman is falling asleep) and muse that it was amazing what a person could get used to: things that one day seemed terribly taboo might the next seem routine. But now, his body warming with his heart's sudden pounding, he simply set down the knife and removed the letter from the envelope.

Dear Professor Renault,

My name is David Fleener. I am nine years old. I have a tele-
scope and every night I look out the window. I am looking for
space ships and I will tell you when I see them! I love your
books! You are my favorite author. My mom thought I was too
young to read them because they are about science, but I am
good at science, and I want to become a famous scientist like
you. I will study alien civilization when we find them, which I
hope will be soon. Thank you for writing your books. I would
like some advice on becoming a scientist if you will give me
some.

> Your friend,
> David

Mailman was not thinking about Jim Gorman, about the fake letter he sent Jim Gorman, as he got up from the table and rummaged in
the junk drawer for an envelope and a piece of notepaper. At this point
he wasn't thinking of anything at all, save for the text of the letter he
was about to compose. He sat down and knocked out Renault's reply
in one draft, and it felt perfectly natural.

Dear David:

I am glad you like my books, but I would not necessarily recommend a career in science. In fact, I must implore you to abandon
your ambitions. You think I'm smart, and I'm flattered that you
think so, but only the truly brilliant can succeed in any significant way, and you and I are just not among the blessed. Furthermore, the aliens probably won't be coming—that is something
whimsical I came up with for the sake of the book—and if they
do there's every chance they'll kill or enslave us. I hate to disap-

point you, but the world is a terrible place, and quite unfair. There's a saying we have back in France: *c'est la vie!* That's life!

Thanks for writing!
Maurice Renault

And he sealed it up and addressed it and stamped it and strode out the front door to the nearest mailbox (only a couple of blocks; this was in the days before the Postal Service started tearing out the friendly blue mailboxes) and dropped it in. *Ahhh!*

It wasn't until later that night—specifically, the dead of it—that he truly understood the implications of what he had done. Surely any middle-class mother worth her salt would respond to such a letter, would she not? Certainly she would take the famous scientist to task for upsetting her poor son? And so in a couple of weeks Renault would receive a letter from somebody named Alice Fleener, or whatever; he'd open it up and a line would catch his attention—*dare you suggest that my son isn't smart enough to*—and startle him, and he would look again—*will not be killed or enslaved by aliens, how could you*—and he would get on the horn to Otis, Ohio, and thus to the bottom of this terrible misunderstanding, because of course Maurice Renault would never discourage any child from embarking upon a career in science, no matter how stupid he was! *Au contraire!* Because the next Einstein (or, hey!, even the next Maurice Renault!) could be playing Little League or flattening pennies on the train tracks right there in the Great American Middle West! And it wouldn't take long, once the formidable Mrs. Fleener sent the letter back to the good professor, for the two to figure out that an impostor was involved: and perhaps then, at last, Renault would recognize the handwriting and realize (in one of his trademark intuitive leaps) that his mailman used to be one of his students. And the next morning when Mailman arrived at work the inspectors would be waiting.

Mailman leapt out of bed, pulled on his jeans and ran barefoot out into the cold empty streets, all the way to the mailbox on Sage. He stood before it, panting; he peeked inside.

But there was nothing to see, even if the box's contents could be made out in the darkness; there was nothing he could do. The letter to David Fleener was long gone, collected by the venerable Lincoln Purdy, Mailman's mailman. For a thrilling moment he imagined driving to work and finding it, sifting through the bins until it appeared, like a winning lottery ticket, in his hand. But it was too late. It was on a truck, heading for Elmira, and by daybreak it would be sorted and on its way to Ohio.

The slot clanked shut. A punk bicycled by, spitting in the grass. There was nothing to do but go home. He slept that night, though his terror would only increase in the coming weeks, gripping him at the throat while he ate, oozing out through his pores as he walked from house to house, setting his hands atremble as he sorted the mail—until, about a month after he sent the letter, he would begin to think that he just might possibly get away with it. And after two months, he would become a bit surer, and after six he would feel almost positive. He got away with it! Somewhere, a tiny tumor was growing in the hulking body of Renault's popularity—nothing malignant, mind you!, just a little cyst was all, a benign little polyp—and there, among the friends and family of young David Fleener, the man was known as a creep and a spoiler. It was such a small thing, so insignificant in the long run; yet Mailman felt its enormous power, the way they must have felt tapping the atom. Pretty soon he found himself standing at the stove, suspending a love letter over the teakettle, and a few weeks later he had the bedroom cleaned out and set up as a kind of lab. He practiced: he set himself envelope-cracking tasks, the tougher the better, until he could open almost anything, and close it again without a trace. And now, of course, he is very, very good at it, except sometimes (as was the case last night) he makes small mistakes.

"Pardon me? Pardon me?"

A hand on his shoulder. He wakes, snaps to attention, his face is numb with sleep, and drool has dampened the right side of his face. "Wha—"

"It was not a good movie, yes?"

From the hand (large, firm, knuckles dusted with white hair) he follows the arm to a shoulder, over which looms the famous face, handsomely cragged, beneath the white hair.

"Time to go! We should be sleeping through it too, ha ha!" Behind him, his son nods, chuckling. The poet.

"Ah," says Mailman. "Ah, thanks, I guess I did nod off there—"

"Fleming got the serum, and the bad guy," the son says. "In case you were wondering."

The theater is empty now, save for these three.

"Do you remember me?" Mailman asks.

Renault removes his hand from Mailman's shoulder. He stands back, fingers on chin, elbow in hand, and hums quietly, appearing to think. He frowns, nods. At last he stands straight, and smiles. "No, what is your name?"

"You never knew my name," Mailman says, hauling himself to his feet. "I used to be your mailman."

FOUR

The Marriage of Mailman

—

Sunday morning: he opens his eyes. No, wait! Shuts them, quick.

Stiff and sore, wedged mummily onto his cot, he covers his face with his hands and sighs. Two days in a row he's blown it and forgotten to keep his eyes shut. If this were 'Nam he'd have a smoking hole in his noggin by now—but it isn't 'Nam, it's Nestor, and he has a routine to work through: chewing the raw brown rice, analyzing yesterday's mistakes. So he rolls over, disgusted with himself, and feels around on the nightstand's lower shelf for the rice container. He steadies it with his thumb while his fingers work at the lid. And then the lid comes free and the rice container falls over and he hears rice spilling onto the floor.

Dammit, dammit, dammit! He slumps back on the cot. Nothing's going right. Even keeping his eyes closed is an actual *effort*, they seem to *want* to open all by themselves, and he must remain absolutely alert to prevent them from doing it. Last night his encounter with Renault had left him as exhausted as he'd ever been in his life, his eyes had slammed shut like storm doors the second he slumped into bed, and all he wants now is to sink back into that sleep and forget about his routine, forget about his mistakes, about the rice. Suddenly it all seems like a horrible burden.

But that's all the more reason to stick to it, right? If it were easy, it wouldn't be building much character, would it? Now his facial muscles tremble with the effort of keeping the eyes shut, they are fatigued after only thirty seconds or so of effort. Thank God there's no intruder in the house, no trigger-happy assassin, no psycho.

There isn't, is there?

He scans the eidetic frame of his memory, trying to recall what he saw during the split second his eyes were open. The room full of shadowy morning light filtered by a thick curtain. Two of the cats sleeping on an army blanket in the middle of the floor and the other walking tail-up toward the door. What else? Wallpaper design: intertwined tea roses climbing, from floor to ceiling, a patterned stake. What else? Something: a shadow where he might expect light: something near the door? Behind it? Yes, a shadow, the outline of something, of a man.

Nah. Not possible. No sounds of entry woke him, the cats placid, no foreign smell. Or is there? Besides the remnants of cat urine, besides his own unshoweredness, the smoke smell from the clothes (still on the floor at the bed's foot) he wore to the burning of the Chapin-Caldwell house. Something else. Musty man-scent. Not supposed to be here. A shadow, tall as a man, or perhaps a man hunched as if to spring. Its edges undefined: is he in a dark coat? Yes. My God: an intruder. The girl from 200 Keuka, she reported him, and they've come—the inspectors—to tear up his house in search of the missing mail. But that's absurd!, it's the weekend, Len Ronk wouldn't send his dog out for the paper on a Sunday let alone arrange a raid: and yet, maybe it's out of Ronk's hands. Maybe the higherups have other ways of working. It's been a minute or more since he opened and closed his eyes and in that time the intruder could have crept closer, could be at his bedside now or snooping in the mail room. He lies motionless, feigning sleep: but that's stupid, of course, the intruder knows he's awake, has seen him wake and spill the rice. His, Mailman's, only present advantage is that though he knows the intruder is here, the intruder does not know that he, Mailman, knows that he, the intruder, is here. And so it is possible to attack, to throw back the covers and fly at the intruder with everything he's got, with every ounce of strength and guile and dexterity. Well, then: time's a-wastin'!

He tosses back the covers and leaps out of bed and opens his eyes and flings himself at the door. Even before he trips over the sleeping cats he realizes he's deceived himself, that there was and is no intruder and no shadow stands behind the open door and no strange odors fill the room, and then he trips over the sleeping cats (they let out a sound like a bedsheet being torn in two) and falls, twisting his body so as not to land facefirst against the door; instead he is caught under the left arm by the doorknob where (he remembers as pain explodes there) he hurt himself somehow a couple nights ago.

On the floor he presses his face into the carpet and screams. Jesus fucking Christ! It hurts! Grips with his right hand his left arm, holding it tight against the wound, what a fucking pain! Feels like his entire cardiopulmonary system is going to be sucked out of this awful flaming void, and he tastes the gritty cat-trodden weave of the carpet (musty, gamy: going to have to clean or replace it) and rolls over onto his back, and the throbbing howling pain continues. Lies there panting, waiting for it to subside. He's willing to bet he broke a rib. A few days before he and Lenore moved into this house, he fell coming out of her bathroom and broke a rib. Not the same one as now, a different one, lower and on the other side. Didn't realize at the time that it was broken; it didn't feel all that bad. But when they started packing and hauling, the muscles worried at the fracture, creating soreness and a swelling and a rhythmic stinging ache, and there was no relief except to sleep in a certain position or walk perfectly upright like a soldier. Of course she was a nurse (well, a psychiatric nurse) but there was nothing she could do except tell him to take it easy, and so he watched her lug and unpack all their boxes. Humiliating for him but she was very sexy to look at in her sweaty shorts and tee shirt, he kept saying things like "Hey, if you're hot, just take off your shirt, nothing I haven't seen before," to which she replied that no, she was perfectly comfortable, and his injury would not be well served by the rigors of sex. Fair enough. Yet he asked her—this was when the unpacking had neared completion—begged her actually to do a little dance for him, a sort of striptease, there was nothing untoward about it, he said, being as they were married, and it was something she'd never done for him before, and was certainly something he'd like to see. And she said that there would be many years of very exciting activity in this house in the future, even the near future, but sorry, she didn't take requests, it wasn't her kind of thing. Which of course he already knew. Which of course was part of what he liked about her in the first place, no embarrassing pandering to the needs of men: a necessary skill, he supposed, if you're a nurse (and quite, it strikes him, now the opposite of Semma, which contrast was part of what he liked about *her*). All those lonely men with only Lenore to provide relief from pain, no doubt they demanded other things of her as well, or thought she ought to provide them. Sponge baths, for instance, surely they asked her if maybe she would— just a little to the— maybe a little extra of— but when Mailman asked her if this was so she said, sorry, I don't want to talk about that. Which Mailman also admired her for: this integrity, this unwillingness to betray her patients (most of them as vulnerable, emotionally speaking, as he'd been), which he would later come to see as niggardly and cold.

Well. There on the floor he experiences regret. How is it that he came to despise the things he most loved? Maybe he didn't love them to begin with. Maybe admiration is not so much like love after all. Maybe admiration is a kind of hatred, actually. Is it possible not to begrudge people the things they're best at? Not for him, he supposes.

In a while he tries getting up. It isn't so bad, maybe because the wound is high on the ribcage, not down by the abs. Limps to the bathroom still clutching his left arm with his right. Crunches three aspirin and after a moment crunches two more. Looks at himself in the mirror. Looks bad: well of course he does! He's always sworn he would never be one of those men who looks at himself in the mirror and longs for his lost youth, for his dark full head of hair and flat stomach and toned arms and legs. And really those aren't his problems. His hair's been thin since he was a kid, and he is very healthy for a man his age. The skin's not as taut as it used to be but so what? And his color's bad this morning because of the fall and the broken rib. And it's early. And he still hasn't caught up on the sleep he missed Friday night.

He goes into the kitchen and makes coffee. There's no Sunday paper in Nestor so he turns on the radio and waits for the news break. Sits, drinks the coffee, eats a bowl of cold cereal. Ads are on. Dentures. Eye surgery. End-of-life care: *Doesn't your loved one deserve the best? You can't go it alone. That's why Forest Glen Home is here.* Only the old and sick are awake at this hour. Finally the news. A Japanese earthquake. Fighting in Kashmir. *And in national news, Ford announced today the introduction of the most spacious SUV yet* . . . Is this news? This is a press release! . . . *Scientists announced that your dog may be smarter than you think!* . . . What about poverty? What about the growing prison population? . . . *Sources say the pop star's baby is doing just fine* . . . Screw it. He turns it off, slouches in his chair, lays his head on his arms. Feels like a fool for caring. Here he is, a middle-class American mailman, working for the government, pretending to give a shit about poverty. He never volunteers for anything. He's never even been inside the Nestor soup kitchen, and it's three blocks away. He stares into space, listening to the cats moving around the house. He imagines he can hear in their furtive motions a hint of resentment. He wishes he had Semma to touch him, to calm him down. He wishes he had Lenore to feel under his arm and tell him to relax, and then go around the house doing for him those things he would otherwise have to do himself, while he sat watching and admiring her. He wishes he could go back and start over with her, meet her again, not in the hospital but somewhere else, in a park, at a bar, at a party. On an even footing. Instead, he was pathetically weak, helpless and immobile as an infant, Lenore pitying and mother-strong.

They sedated him after he attacked Renault. This part he does not remember, it was all told to him later. The police said he was very lucky that Professor Renault had not pressed charges, that all he wanted was a letter of apology. The day Mailman came out of it he had no idea what they were talking about, he didn't recall having encountered Renault at all recently and was deeply disturbed to be told that he had. And yet he did not, that first day, find it at all odd that he was in a hospital bed, and that people—policemen and doctors—were gathering around him asking him questions, and that his wrists were bound to his bed by knotted cloths, and that he was holding forth at length in this white room with padded walls. This did not strike him as odd. It was—it must have been—the medication they were giving him that made him so agreeable. Everybody knew his name and approached his bed with such kindness, such tenderness, even the cops, and to Mailman that seemed exactly right. He thinks he remembers his first glimpse of Lenore: the room empty of people; the dim, caged electric light; the sound of a distant muffled shout from somewhere in the building; and then the door opening (padded, it looked like a mattress on hinges) and admitting a darkhaired nurse carrying a small paper cup and a pitcher. She filled the cup with water and brought it to his lips. Her face was light-skinned, slightly lopsided, faintly pocked from some past case of the measles or chicken pox or acne. Eyes black (though not really black, he would discover: brown, but very dark), large, expressive, but expressing nothing just now. He smiled. She didn't. She put the pills in his mouth and let him drink again. She said, "How are you feeling, Mr. Lippincott?"

This was after someone "representing" the college had come and gone, after the police. Nobody had yet asked him how he felt. He said, "Strange."

"You're on a tranquilizer. This is the hospital."

"The mental hospital?"

"Yes."

She began to leave.

"Nurse."

"Yes?"

"I kind of want my hands."

"The doctor will decide that, Mister Lippincott." Again turned to leave.

"Nurse!"

She turned.

"What's your name?"

She hesitated before saying, "Nurse Inness." And: "Dinner will be in an hour." And left. He thought about her for a while when she was gone, and again after she came and fed him.

Next thing he can remember is his doctor talking to him. "Professor Renault has spoken to me. He expressed his hope that you could be placed in a conventional room. If you make sufficient progress, we shall honor his request." Lenore came and went countless times, saying little. Then one morning he woke up in a room without padding. A pitcher of water and a glass (both plastic) sat on a metal table beside his bed. The table was bolted to the floor. Instinctively, he tried to get up, and was surprised to find that he was able. He was wearing a hospital robe. He felt clean. He went to the window (barred, the glass—or was it plastic as well?—thick, distorting the scene) and looked out. He recognized West Campus and Reston Gorge in the distance, a shady cleft in a wood. Soon the doctor came in and sat down on the bed. What was his name? Guest. He was, basically, short. This was his defining characteristic, though he lacked the short man's compensatory belligerence. His head like a smooth river stone, the nose wide and flat. Hair gray and plastered to his head, faintly shiny from some kind of goop. He sat down on Mailman's bed and introduced himself and said, "Look at me, Mister Lippincott."

Mailman looked.

"How many fingers am I holding up?"

"Your hands are in your pockets, Doctor."

The doctor nodded. "Ehhhxcellent," he said. "Tell me, Mister Lippincott, what is it that you were looking at, through the window?"

"Reston Gorge," Mailman said, and though he didn't know it at the time, this is what kept him in the psych ward for another two months. If he'd given it any real thought he would have known that this was the wrong answer, but he was tired. So he told the doctor he was looking out at Reston Gorge and the doctor pulled out a notepad and wrote something ("Reston Gorge (!!)," no doubt). And then Guest sighed and said, "Tell me about your thoughts, Mister Lippincott—your thoughts about Reston Gorge."

"Just, I don't know, it's right there near campus, this amazing natural feature, and I've never been down in it. Have you, ever?"

The doctor spoke quietly, so quietly that Mailman had to lean toward him to hear. "At one time there was a trail. It's closed now."

"Too bad."

"Mister Lippincott, are you aware of what happened? Do you know where you are?"

"I'm in the hospital. They told me I attacked Renault, but I don't remember that."

"Tell me what you do remember."

And then he did remember. It wasn't as if it *came back* to him; it hadn't really gone anywhere, it wasn't even hidden in memory: all he had to do was look at it and notice it was there. "I got some crazy idea," he said, "I burst in on Renault in the lecture hall. I guess I was pretty excited."

"Doctor Renault claims that you, Mister Lippincott, attempted to . . . bite him."

"It doesn't sound like something I'd do."

"I'm afraid, however, that it is what you did, Mister Lippincott," the doctor said, with what seemed to be real regret. "A class was in session.

The students witnessed it." He cleared his throat. "You realize, Mister Lippincott, that this is the mental health wing of the hospital?"

"The psycho ward."

"So to speak."

"Well," said Mailman, "I guess you think I need some treatment."

"Yes, I most certainly do."

Suddenly his exhaustion overwhelmed him. He was not simply sleepy but enervated, wrecked. He reached for the windowsill and his hand flopped around uselessly. He whispered, "Doctor, may I sit down there?"

"I beg your pardon?" Guest said, standing.

"On my bed."

Guest came to his side and took his hand and led him step by step to the bed. For Pete's sake! It was as if he hadn't slept in weeks! And then he remembered that he hadn't, not for any significant duration, he'd been up most of the night every night for a month, scuttling around in the library like a crab. The doctor sat him down and lifted his legs and swiveled him into a prone position. Mailman tried to pull the sheets up over his body but his arms just lay limp at his sides. "Wow," he croaked. Guest tucked him in and leaned close, smelling of shaving cream and toothpaste and coffee and rubbing alcohol. He placed his hand on Mailman's forehead. That hand was hot as a coal! He said, "Sleep, Mister Lippincott. Nurse Inness will come to check on you and bring your medicine."

He groaned some kind of thanks. Or tried to. Sleep came quickly. When he woke, every bone in his body was sore, right down to the marrow. He thought: My God, have they shocked me? Have they juiced me? He'd heard about that, Jesus Christ, can they just go and do that?

"No, no electroshock for you, Mister Lippincott," said Nurse Inness, who stood beside him with a gleaming aluminum bowl. He could hear the water sloshing in it, slapping and scraping its sides. He wondered how long he'd been asleep.

"About sixteen hours. It's almost dinnertime. I was reluctant to disturb you but I thought I could wake you with a bath."

Ah—the bowl. She was going to give him a sponge bath.

"I've already finished, Mister Lippincott."

And now he could feel it: his body having been touched, the skin breathing a bit more deeply, the water still evaporating, taking the heat along with it. He shivered. She pulled the sheets back up over him and a blanket too. She could read his mind!

Lenore said, "No, your lips. You're talking."

Then he fell asleep, and this time he dreamed, spectacularly, vividly, he was enthroned, he was some kind of king, and they were bringing it all to him: everything!, they were bringing him everything! Men, slaves, bearing all the wonders of nature, clouds and mountains and trees and rivers. They brought him the waves, carrying them in on their shoulders, the waves crashed and rose and curled and crashed again as the slaves' thin bodies trembled underneath. They brought him the planets and the stars and sun, these amazing men, bearing objects of such hugeness and power that wracked and burned and bent them, and yet they endured, they bore the awesome weight of creation, all for him. Incredible! And at last it was time for him to eat, he could smell the feast approaching, could see the legions of men, dark, loinclothed, their eyes bright with terror, shouldering these huge brass plates, so massive it was impossible from one side to see what lay across on the other. And he felt a hand on his shoulder and it was Nurse Inness.

He cried out. She shied. "Mister Lippincott?"

"Oh!" he said. He shook his head. "I'm sorry, I was dreaming! How long was I asleep?"

"About ten minutes," she said.

"That's all?"

Before him a tray was presented upon a wheeled cart. Chicken cutlet in a ponderous white sauce, chopped into sub-bite-sized pieces; niblet corn; Jell-O; a cup of water. He said, "Is there any bread?"

"No bread, sorry." She had recovered her composure. "I'll be in again shortly." And she began to walk away.

"Wait!" he said, and the way she stopped, turned, her hand on the doorframe, was very attractive. "Can I have a radio? I always listen to the radio when I eat."

"No. Not yet."

"'Not yet'?"

She hesitated, as if considering how frank she could be. "The doctor doesn't want you to become agitated. You're very weak right now."

She was right. He tried to pick up a spoon. There was no fork, no knife. The spoon was heavy. She came to him and scooped a piece of chicken onto the spoon and brought it to his mouth. He chewed. It was hard: his jaw ached. "Stay," he said.

"I'm sorry, no. I have other patients to attend to."

But she continued to help him eat his dinner.

Right now, in his kitchen, finished with his breakfast, Mailman considers how long it takes to feed somebody an entire meal. Eating your own meal is easy, it's all automatic, you can read the whole newspaper while you do it. The arm and hand are coordinated with the jaw. But to feed someone else it is necessary to concentrate, to take care while inserting the morsel, to take note of when the chewing has stopped, to inquire if a sip of water is needed. Feeding another person involves looking closely into that person's face for at least ten minutes. This is a long time to look into someone's face. For the first five, he tried to catch away Lenore's gaze, to bring her eyes to his using nothing more than the intensity of his looking. It was all he was capable of doing; his eyes were the only part of him that didn't feel tired. It was a game, the only one he could play. She resisted for the longest time.

A lot of psych patients must do it, strive to make that simple and subtle connection; her defenses would have been strong. He had seen these people, on the way to the crapper: desolate, lonely, exhausted people. Worth defending yourself against. Yet she met his eyes, she allowed him to look into hers. This despite what she thought she knew about him, what she believed he had done! With every bite she turned away to pick up more food, and then turned back and again met his eyes and allowed him to look at her. This he remembers perfectly well.

Of course everybody falls in love with his nurse. When he had finished eating he said, "When will you be back?"

"I'll look in on you throughout the evening. I'll take you to the bathroom."

"Thank you. Nurse?"

"Yes?"

"Tell me your first name." He knew it already—had heard a doctor use it—but he wanted her to tell him.

She didn't say anything. But cocked her head, just a little bit. Then she turned and left. What had she been thinking of saying? A warning? "Don't become attached to me, Mr. Lippincott." Because not only was he a patient of hers, not only did that disqualify him from the running, she also had a boyfriend, or rather a fiancé. She wore a ring, anyway. Mailman noticed when she came back that night.

"When are you getting married?"

She frowned. "June," she said. It was autumn now.

"Another June bride." He said this, just to have something to say.

"That's right."

"What's his name?" he asked her.

But she only said "Open," and placed his pills upon his tongue.

The following day his parents arrived from Princeton. NYTech must have called them. Both looked grave and frightened. In addition, his mother appeared annoyed, his father confused, as if he'd expected to be led to a little office or lounge, rather than this room. "Well, Albert," his mother said, kissing him on the cheek (but not otherwise touching him; she held her handbag with one hand and with the other restrained it from swinging into his face), "how did this happen?" She was wearing a sort of cocktail dress, pink with short sleeves that flared up at the shoulders, giving her an unintentionally military air. Her hair was bundled high on her head.

"I don't know exactly," said Mailman.

"We had to go through three goddam locked steel doors!"

His father approached the bed but there was nowhere to sit, so he took a step back and looked around the room. Then he smiled a small smile at Mailman. "Son," he said.

"Dad." Edgar Lippincott still taught at Princeton, but had scaled back his course load, leaving him more free time. Or so Mailman's mother had told him, suggesting with her tone of voice that this scaling-back had been suggested—recommended—to him by some higher power. Perhaps as a consequence, the old man (actually only in his forties, but already he seemed old, had seemed old even before Mailman moved out of the house) carried an increased air of distraction about him, as if he now spent much of his time figuring out what to do with his time. His gray shirt was stained around the collar and smudges encircled the sleeves at the elbows, as though he'd had them rolled up while doing something dirty. He smiled again. "I, uh . . . no chairs," he said.

"Jesus Christ," said Mailman's mother, and she turned to the door. "Nurse!" she shouted. "Chairs!" She turned to Mailman shaking her head. "They think you're going to smash a window and slit your throat on the pieces."

"I wouldn't do that."

"No," she said, disdainfully. "Not you."

A nurse—not his own nurse, not Lenore—brought two aluminum army chairs and set them on the floor at Mailman's bedside with a startling clank. When she was gone (but not, he suspected, very far gone) Mailman's mother pulled them back a few feet and sat. In a moment his father sat beside her. He reached out toward the bed and Mailman had a moment of alarm—Is he going to take my hand? Will we hold hands? What do I say if he does this?—but he only fiddled with the crank that controlled the position of the mattress. Mailman felt his head being lowered and then hoisted up again.

"So," said his mother wearily.

"Yes," said Mailman.

"Mm-hmm," said his father.

His mother leaned forward, her hands outstretched, the way she might accept a basketball. Not that she'd do that. She said, "You bit a man's *eye*? That's what this is all about? Are you out of your *mind*?"

"No, I—I didn't know what I was doing, I guess."

"When I bite somebody in the eye I know exactly what I'm doing."

"Sorry."

"*Sorry*, he says. You *are* nuts, aren't you. I hope you said *sorry* to the man you bit."

"I didn't actually bite him," Mailman said. "I guess I . . . tried to."

Mailman's father lifted his head suddenly, as if hearing a distant alarm. "Who'dja bite?"

"*Tried* to bite. Professor Renault."

There was a silence. His father said, "Really?"

"A professor?" said his mother.

"Yes."

There was another silence. Mailman adjusted the sheets. He liked these sheets: they were substantial, with a real heft, and kept him plenty warm, even without the blankets. A breeze was blowing in so he covered himself to his neck. He could see goosebumps breaking out on his mother's bare arms. She was underdressed for the October weather, but then, she generally was. She said, "Edgar, shut the goddam window already." Mailman's father obeyed.

"Look," she said, leaning toward him, revealing a black lace bra that gripped her freckled chest. "They told me you were suicidal, all right? We're supposed to be cheering you up and telling you life's terrific and that we'll take you home with us when you get out."

"I'm not suicidal!" It was true, he felt good. Goodish. He thought about Nurse Lenore a lot, that alone was worth living for. Suicide! Not him!

"Yes, you are. You told them you wanted to jump off a cliff."

"Into a gorge," said his father, reclaiming his seat.

"What! I didn't say that!"

"You stood at that window," his mother said, "contemplating suicide."

"No, I didn't!"

Now his mother was getting angry. She leaned farther forward and leveled a bony finger at him. "Look, you. Just do what they tell you, all right? I don't know what kind of loony game you're up to here, but knock it off. We drove up here six goddam hours."

"That includes rest breaks," his father said.

"I'm not suicidal! I don't have to go home!" Talk about depression: moving back in with his parents! What would make him really happy just now would be learning that they were letting him out, say, three days from now, and telling him he could resume his classes. This last—his classes—didn't actually seem very appealing to him right this minute, but he was confident they would, soon enough.

"Well," said his mother, "God knows we don't want you home either—"

"Oh, that wouldn't be so bad," his father said.

"—but that's what they're telling us is best for you. So you can be 'supervised.'" She shook her head. "It's just like your goddam potty training."

"I wouldn't mind you at home one bit," his father said.

"You just caught on all at once, in one afternoon. I just sat you down on the toilet and you pointed your pecker down there and pissed and dropped a turd. You thought you had it all under control. But the moment something didn't go your way, it was piss and shit in the pants. God! I tried putting you back in diapers but you screamed and kicked and promised it wouldn't happen again, and then it would be all right for a while, until 'Waaaaaahhhhh!,' something would get you going and the pants and underwear were soiled. We didn't have an electric washer yet because your *father* was afraid of the appliance man—"

"Oh, that wasn't it," his father said, "I just—"

"—and I had to *scrub* your shit and piss out of your clothes, not that it ever really came out. And then I had to go and *sing* every night, exhausted because *you* thought you could take care of yourself. Well, I should have just let you, if you were so goddam independent, I should have let you wash your own shitty pants."

This he had heard before. "Well, I can take care of myself. I had, I guess it's a, a nervous, ah, breakdown. I'm fine now though. Actually, I sort of like it here, a little. I like my nurse."

"The tart who banged the chairs?"

"No, someone else."

"Well good," his mother said. "You don't have to deal with *her* all day."

The nurse, clearly having heard this exchange, strode in and told Mailman's parents it was time for them to leave. When they were gone it occurred to Mailman that no one else had visited. Perhaps they didn't know he was here. Or maybe it was more than that, maybe they were glad to be rid of him. Or they were scared of him: surely it had gotten around, what had happened in Professor Renault's lecture. And now the doctor thought he was suicidal and they were planning on keeping him here! For how long? He got out of bed and paced, in his baggy cotton pants and tee shirt. After a while he went out the door and into the ward. The nurses' station was unmanned. He could see through a couple of doorways: people with tired faces studied the ceiling. Others stumped up and down the halls. He bounced on his toes a couple times and then hit the call button. In a moment Nurse Lenore appeared, all but running when she saw him. "What is it?" she said. "Where are your parents?"

"They left. Listen, there's been a misunderstanding."

"What?" She had taken him by the arm and was leading him back toward his room.

"Somebody told my parents that I'm suicidal. I'm not suicidal."

"I know you feel better right now, but those feelings don't disappear so easily."

"No, no," he said, aware that his voice was rising in pitch and volume, aware of what effect this must be having on her. He calmed himself, said, "No, I never was suicidal. I mean, the doctor asked me what I was looking at out the window and I said 'Reston Gorge' and I talked about walking down in it, not jumping into it, I would never do that."

They were in his room now. She led him to the bed. "No," he said, "can we sit in the chairs? I'm sick of the bed."

"Nurse Seeley was supposed to remove those when your parents left."

"Just—please. Look, please, I need to talk about this. This isn't fair."

She sighed, crossed to the door and shut it. They sat. He told her how the talk had gone with the doctor and she listened, nodding slowly. How good it felt, to be listened to: most of the world's problems, she would tell him as they lay in each other's arms in her bed six months from now, could be avoided if people actually listened to what other people were saying, instead of pretending to listen while formulating what they themselves were going to say next, which is what people usually did. *Not me,* Mailman would tell her; *I don't think at all before I say something,* and they would have a good laugh about that, but this exchange would define their relationship for years to come: her obsessive attention-paying would become annoying, maddening even; his tendency to speak without thinking would grow chronic, reckless, disastrous. Now (that is, right now, alone in his house, washing his cereal bowl and coffee mug as he remembers how he met Lenore) he thinks: Should have seen it coming. Might have been able to change things. Damn shame, that; he misses her. Or rather misses the things about her he still likes (okay, loves) even as he is glad to be rid of the things he stopped being able to stand years ago. If he'd loved her right he would never have had to get involved with Semma, and lost her too: instead of one wife he's got one ex-wife and a dead girlfriend. Back then, in the hospital room, as she listened, nodding: then, he was absolutely certain he was falling in love with her, and the idea that she should marry her fiancé, whoever the hell he was, was inconceivable. How could it happen? he thought. Look at us! Look here, we're looking at each other, she's listening! That she was a nurse, that it was her job to comfort and care for him in his fragile (though not as fragile as they thought) state was of no importance: something *different* was happening here. They sat there, and she sighed, and looked at the window, and said, "I'll see what I can do, Albert."

Albert! She called him by name! His first name! "Thank you, Lenore," he said, and she didn't correct him, didn't say, "Nurse Inness, please." She tried to leave but he stopped her: he said, "What's his name?"

"Whose?"

"Your fiancé."

She looked at the ring on her finger, as if just now remembering it was there. "That's not an appropriate question, Mister Lippincott."

"Albert! You just said Albert just now!"

She shook her head. She said, "His name is David."

You mustn't marry him, he nearly said. She looked down at him with curiosity and mild alarm.

"Lenore?" he asked her.

"Your chair," she said quietly. "You'll have to get up, so that I can take the chairs."

Two months! Nothing could have been duller. He begged them for his radio and he finally got it, and damned if Kennedy wasn't shot that very day. Jesus fucking Christ! The nurses ran through the ward weeping, confiscating every radio in the place, and he was not unhappy to see his go. (And over the years, when people asked him, as everybody would ask everybody, "Where were you when Kennedy was shot?," he would always say sick in bed with the flu: and so nobody would ever ask him what it was like to emerge from the psych ward into a changed world, a world more paranoid, a sadder world: and the answer would have been that it never seemed quite real, that he could never square the panicked voices on the radio—voices that might as well have come from his own head—with the genuine artifacts of the outside: with Jack Ruby, and the Zapruder film, and Johnson in the White House.) Meanwhile, he slept a lot, he took his pills, and as his discharge grew closer he saw less and less of Nurse Lenore, whose professional attention had come to be diverted elsewhere, toward needier patients.

When the end was near he began to make overtures. "I'll miss you when I'm gone." "I'll miss you too, Mr. Lippincott." A sweet sting: she'd miss him, but she didn't call him Albert anymore. But she had!, she had! "Can I come by here and visit?" "I don't think Doctor Guest would approve of that." "But you would." "Don't, please." "Don't talk to you? Or don't visit?" "Don't visit me here." "So we can talk, then. Can I visit you elsewhere? Where do you live?" "Not far. But don't visit me there either." "What about the phone? May I call you when I'm discharged? Can we keep in touch?" "I don't know." "That's not a 'no.'" "No, I guess it isn't a 'no.'" "Okay, then, I'll stop now—I'll quit while I'm ahead, and I'll call you, all right? No, don't answer that, it's too direct a question." "I think you should take your medicine now." "All right, all right."

Honestly he thought he would just collect his belongings and walk out the door. He had fired off his apology to Renault and put it in the mail ("Dear Professor Renault, I'm sorry I tried to bite your eyes, I promise it will never happen again, Yours sincerely, Albert Lippincott"); they were going to give him a prescription, they were going to set him up with a therapist. To these sessions he would never go—nobody could force him—and he would quit taking the pills. And up to the very last minute he believed, truly, that the entire suicide matter had been cleared up, that he would be going home, to his apartment halfway down the hill from campus, where his books and clothes were. But it didn't happen that way.

"Your parents are here." This wasn't Lenore, Lenore was off that day. It was the other nurse, the one who'd banged the chairs.

"My *parents*?"

"Your mother and father. They're here to take you home."

"I live ten blocks away."

The nurse shook her head, inexplicably annoyed, and admitted his parents into the room. They were trim, darkly dressed, like undertakers. His mother wore white gloves. White gloves, in the loony bin! "All right, Albert," she said, "the car's packed, let's get out of here."

He looked from one to the other, not yet quite panicked. "What are you doing here?"

"We're here to take you home. No theatrics, please, can we just hurry along?"

"I was looking forward to walking."

"Two hundred and fifty miles?"

At this his father laughed sharply. The laugh trailed off into giggles as he searched a high corner of the room.

"I'm not going *home* home," Mailman said. "I'm going *home*. To my apartment."

She rolled her eyes. "Well, *they* want you with *us*."

"But all my things, my books—"

"Everything's in the car, Albert." Now the more familiar Mom was beginning to emerge: wrinkles fanned around the eyes; the muscles in the face tense, rendering her more beautiful. "It was all together, in a closet. They told me they moved you out weeks ago. Somebody needed the room."

He gaped. It's a trick! It's a trick! He turned to his father. "She's making this up."

"What? Me?" his father said, flinching.

"You went to my apartment? They moved me out? My room-mates? My *friends*?"

"Well," said Edgar Lippincott. "I . . . I guess so. It would seem that way, yes."

"Satisfied?" his mother said, openly annoyed now. "God forbid we should be allowed to enjoy collecting you, Albert. To think I canceled a gig for this!"

But Mailman would have none of it. He insisted on dropping by his old place. How many times, during his convalescence, had he fantasized he was there, reading his books, listening to the radio, under the warm light of his desk lamp, the only lamp he'd ever owned, that he'd brought from his childhood bedroom, the one with the dirty yellow shade, its lining cracked and shrunken from heat? Many, many times. That vision had sustained him through the hard dull hours. Nobody said goodbye as they passed through the heavy steel doors of the mental ward. The physical world was as he'd remembered: not quite adequate: the sky and trees inscrutable, filled with secrets. Wordlessly they drove through the streets in the outsized powder-blue Oldsmobile they had bought when Mailman was eleven, which had looked and smelled within a month of purchase like it was inhabited by a family of miniature goats, until they reached the shared house where Mailman had lived. He dashed in while they kept the car running outside. The door was unlocked. "Hello? Hello?" It was eleven in the morning, always it was empty at this time of day, when everyone was at class or in the lab. He climbed the stairs—what a feeling! to be free to climb stairs again!—and ran down the hall to his door, which he threw open upon someone else's life: clothes he would never wear, strewn on the bed and floor, books he would never read (Literature! French literature! Could it be they had admitted one of Renault's cohorts into the house? Turncoats!), and the lamp, *his lamp*, burning wastefully on the desk. "Bastards!" he shouted, and he swiped the lamp and stomped down the stairs and out onto the porch. There were his parents, eyes forward, waiting without particular urgency, his mother's hands ready on the wheel and his father's head pressed against the side window. There were few places he wanted to be less than in the back of that car, but where else was there to go? Who would take him in? He could play upon the guilt of his former friends and insist they accommodate him on the living room floor, but my God!, the humiliation! And so he made his feet follow one another to the car, and he made his hand open the back door, and he made his legs fold themselves onto the seat. No words were exchanged as the car pulled off the curb, none were exchanged as they left town along one of the many sad country roads that snaked out of Nestor, roads infested with the cheapness, the dowdiness that so characterized life in central New York, from which Nestor was a refuge. And yet these tarpapered houses, these broken cars and rusted appliances leaning in yards, tugged at his heart like a dog at a pantcuff, begging him to stay. *I'm sorry,* he told the houses and cars and appliances. *I promise to come back.* And in his mind he said the same to Lenore, beautiful pale Lenore, *I will be back.* The month of June lay heavy on his mind, like a wet towel: he couldn't let it happen, he had to steal her away from that man, her fiancé. David. That gave him, what, how many months?

"What's today's date?" he asked his parents, the only words spoken in an hour.

"December first."

Okay, so let's put the wedding on June first, to be safe, which gives us . . . "Wait a minute," he said. "When's Thanksgiving?"

"Last Thursday," his father said.

"I missed Thanksgiving? I was in there for Thanksgiving?"

His mother turned in her seat. The car kissed the shoulder before righting itself. "The doctor *said* they gave you *turkey,* Albert, don't you remember?"

"Well—yes, I guess. I mean, I thought— It's just, I didn't know—"

"We went to Hal's, you know that old place?" said his father. "We ate turkey clubs with gravy. They were half-off."

"*You* went, Eddie," his mother said. "You went *alone*. I had the stomach flu."

"Oh, that's right."

"'*Oh, that's right*,'" she said.

"It was no fun. Everybody was upset. About the President." He craned his neck to face Mailman. "Say, do you know— did they tell you Kennedy's dead?"

"Yeah."

"Poor Jackie." He shook his head.

"That's right," said Mailman's mother, with a theatrical sarcasm that reminded him of Gillian, "now the poor woman has *nothing*."

Then there was silence again. They didn't call me!, he thought. Nobody called me! Lenore didn't say Happy Thanksgiving—but then again, she had the day off, he remembered it now, the bad nurse served him his supper, he asked where Lenore was today and she said four-day weekend. Of course: she was with *him*. With the fiancé and his family, at *his* table, in *his* arms. His *bed*. Oh, it had to be stopped, really it did. He had to get to a phone! But not now: he had hours to go, here in the car with his silent parents. This was what it was like to be a child: hurtling forward with someone else behind the wheel. Like Jackie on the plane to Washington with LBJ.

Well, that was the future for you: always of someone else's making. The whole country had a new future now, a grimmer one, filled with ritual violence and shared misery. It sounded interesting, all right. He would have liked to be a part of it, but they started it without him.

Now, in the kitchen, he stands listening to the last drops of water draining from the sink and stares out the small soiled window at a squirrel rooting at bulbs in the neighbor's garden. He sighs. What is this, *nostalgia*? For *that*? For going home with his *parents* from the *psych ward*? No, for the feeling of desperation, for that terrible sense of need. For passion. Only passion he's felt lately is rage, or anxiety, the way he gets himself worked up over a whole lot of nothing, like Friday and the radio contest, his pursuit of the Gray Fox.

Ah, hell, got to do something, can't stand here all day feeling sorry for himself. Of course: the parade, the festival parade. He'll go down to that, and then a nice dinner on the Square with revelers and rock bands and religious freaks and hippies exerting themselves out-of-doors. So he wipes down the counter and heads to the bathroom for a hot shower. It's plenty warm this morning but for some reason he's cold, even his fingers that have just been submerged in hot water, as if the blood's not getting all the way to the tips. He undresses, everything but his shirt: and he realizes that he's saved it for last in order to postpone the pain he'll experience lifting his arms up over his head, for his left side is throbbing from his injury and the recent insult to it perpetrated by the bedroom doorknob. So he snakes the right arm out of its sleeve and uses it to shrug the shirt up to his shoulder and over his head while the left arm hangs limp. Then he uses the right hand to tug the shirt off. There! He turns toward the shower and gets a start when he sees himself in the mirror: his left side is purpled all up and down the ribcage and pain flares with his sudden intake of breath. Christ! What a shiner! He hit it hard as hell but this seems all out of proportion, obviously there's a crack in at least one rib, maybe more, and the whole side seems to be swollen somewhat. He opens up the medicine cabinet (his reflection swinging away) and takes out the aspirin before he remembers he already took five, which ought to be plenty, especially now that he's had some coffee, which has the effect of speeding up the flow of blood. Reluctantly he returns the aspirin to the cabinet.

Shower feels good. Again he appreciates his wonderful shower head with its copious drenching spray. Lenore had liked the old one, the stinging, punishing one; she had actually enjoyed the sensation. She'd emerge from the shower as smooth and red as a cranberry, and if he could catch her, this was a good time to lure her into bed, when she was completely clean and unembarrassed about her body (about which there was no reason for embarrassment, in his opinion): and then, if the seduction worked and they went at it, she would shower again, restoring herself to that previous state but sapped now of energy from the sex and the effort of washing, and she would curl naked under the sheets (if there was time) and take a short nap, never longer than fifteen minutes. Which is why he didn't press the issue of replacing the shower head, when she was around. The sexual opportunity it provided was one of the very few that existed, as both of them were forced to adhere to absolutely inflexible schedules, that of the mailman and nurse, leaving only scant gaps for sex, most of which were fraught with anxiety anyway, over the job they'd just come home from or were about to leave for.

Sex with his wife. Misses it. Don't want to think too hard about that now. Unlike Semma she was difficult to get into the mood, but once she was in the mood (and really he liked getting her into the mood) it was— it really— they—

No. Don't want to think about it.

Hot shower, that's what's now at hand, he scrubs his every part thoroughly in the time-honored order and whistles a tune, the Nestor College fight song. The cats have heard him whistling and they scratch and meow at the door; he ignores them and concentrates on getting himself clean.

His room in Princeton was as he had left it, which is to say basically gutted. A single bookshelf with science fiction paperbacks lined up on it, Asimov and Clarke and Heinlein (and how he hated them now!, ever since Renault had taken up the yoke of hokey futurism); a mattress fitted with a fitted sheet, topped with an uncased pillow and a loose throw blanket; a poster of a mushroom cloud at Los Alamos; a closet with nothing in it; a scratched metal desk with three pointless pencils in the top drawer and in the file drawer a broken telephone he had tried and failed to repair. And now his lamp, and his possessions from the house in Nestor, still in the cardboard boxes his former roommates had found to contain them. The foul smell was gone, the air redolent only of old wood and dead bugs. That first day back he lay on the bed and stared at the ceiling trying to think of what to say to Lenore when he called her. His parents left him alone, except for his father's awkward delivery of pills. He knocked three times and mumbled unnecessarily "It's your father" and pushed the door open and set the pills and a glass of water on the corner of the desk closest to the bed, and sat for a moment on the aluminum desk chair and said "Good to have you in the house," and "Home again, eh?" and "There's always a place here for you." These overtures seemed as chilly, as charmless, as a picture of a snowstorm, but later Mailman would realize how hard it must have been for his father to make them, to speak so plainly and honestly with real (if uncomfortable) sentiment, and he would regret not responding with anything more than a grunt. Once his father was gone, Mailman swept the pills off the desk and into his hand, then crouched on the wood floor and fed them one by one into a knothole, which he had used all throughout childhood as a place to dispose of things secret or undesirable (other pills from other illnesses, swear words scrawled onto crumpled little balls of notepad paper, tiny hard turds from his underwear, a playing card with a naked lady on it that he found in a bus shelter and could no longer bear to look at) that were doubtless still down there. All day he lay still, no longer under the effects of his medicine, waiting to turn back into a crazy person. But all he turned back into was himself. It gave him to wonder if he himself was not just a little bit crazy—if in fact madness was not a simple you-is-or-you-ain't but a gradient, a continuum upon which he was generally somewhat south of normal, but had briefly bottomed out on, plunging past the South America of sanity. Maybe. Maybe. When night came he slept and when day broke he was starving and felt more or less okay. He went down and ate some cornflakes and drank some coffee while his parents sat on either side not looking at him. And when his father had gone off to the lab (the one that paid him, not the one downstairs) and his mother had retired to her boudoir, he picked up the telephone and called NYTech hospital.

"Nurses' station."

"Is Lenore in?"

"Who's calling?"

"Albert."

It was a risk. He could have said David, but that would have made her angry; he might have said "a friend" or "an old friend" or "Just tell her it's an old friend," but the desk would not have bought it. So he told the truth. He didn't think she would come, but she did. She didn't say hello, just picked up the phone.

"Lenore? It's Albert." *Love me,* he silently demanded. *Love me.*

"I know."

"How are you?"

"I'm fine."

"I miss you."

She let out breath. "I hope you're taking your medication, Mister Lippincott."

"I'm not. I miss you."

"You should continue on your medication."

She stopped talking, but she didn't hang up.

"I've been thinking about you all the time. I spent all yesterday lying on my bed in my old bedroom looking at a poster of a nuclear explosion and thinking about what I'd say when I finally got you on the phone. I was lying there wondering if I would go crazy when I stopped the pills and I didn't. I'm all right. I couldn't stop thinking of you."

Again she sighed. "I can't talk to you now."

"You can talk to me later?"

"No."

"Let me call you at home. What's your home number?"

"I'm sorry. I have to go now."

When he hung up he immediately called the operator and got her address and phone. He started calling an hour later and continued throughout the evening. Nobody answered. At around eleven o'clock he pulled a chair over to the kitchen counter, climbed up, and stole thirty dollars from the Yuban coffee can where the grocery money was kept. In its place he left the discarded envelope, with the words I.O.U. $30, ALBERT written on it. His mother was off somewhere, his father downstairs. He chose a few articles of clothing from the boxes in his room, took his toothbrush and comb, packed them in a duffel bag. He left a note ("Thanks, gotta go, Albert") and walked out the door. There was a late bus to New York. He took it. He slept in Port Authority and in the morning boarded the bus to Elmira, and from there the bus to Nestor. When he stepped off in Nestor it was midafternoon, the sun was bright and glaring and the air cold. He had enough money for a cab but he wanted to hang on to it—he had no apartment here, after all, and no job, and he would likely meet some resistance trying to get back into school. So he slung his bag over his shoulder, wrapped both arms around his body and walked the twenty or so blocks across downtown and up the hill to the NYTech hospital. He went inside and set his bag down in front of the reception desk and asked the receptionist to get nurse Lenore Inness on the phone and tell her that Albert was here to see her. Then he took a seat in one of the upholstered chairs scattered around the lobby and waited.

When she came down she did not make for where he was sitting but instead went straight out the doors, beckoning to him as she passed, her face bearing a trembling blankness, like the face of a statue shaken by bombs. He followed her out the doors and around the corner where he had seen her white skirt vanishing, and found her there, in the dark ambulance bay, standing straight, crying silently. "What—" he managed to say, and she glared at the pavement and said, "You have to leave."

"I can't."

She sighed. "I know."

But he was going to. There was only so far he could push it, and he'd pushed it that far, and he was going to apologize and leave.

And then she threw her arms around him, she pulled him to her. Her hands were hot on his back and her face hot against his face and he pulled back to try and kiss her—but she turned, shaking her head, and took a step back, leaving her hands on his shoulders. "This is terrible," she said. "I am a terrible person, Albert, I'm sorry."

"There's nothing to be sorry for."

"I have accepted *gifts* from his *parents*. They sent me on vacation. Oh, God," she said, "everything is going to pieces."

"Do you love him?" he asked, in the selfish expectation of a no. But she said, "Of *course* I *love* him, Albert."

And now he backed up a step and her hands fell from his shoulders, brushing his chest. "But then—" he said angrily, "but why are you—?"

"Because!" she shouted. "Because! Because!" A distant siren erupted into nearness and an ambulance swung around the corner and pulled into place beside them. She shook her head and ran off, not to weep in some corner alone as he thought, but to the opening doors of the ambulance, her face aflame with tears, so that she could attend to the needs of the sick.

He went in and grabbed his bag from the reception desk. He walked away, back toward campus proper, toward the house he used to live in, hoping vaguely that they would admit him, or at least that they hadn't changed the lock on the front door. But he knew they wouldn't, they had. He had lost his marbles, after all, and might be dangerous. "God damn!," he said, and continued to say it as he walked, until he came to an empty phone booth. On impulse he stopped, picked up the receiver, called Gillian, collect.

"What, already!" she shouted, for he had told the operator to let it ring until someone picked up. He stood there as it rang, emitting despondent little clouds of visible breath and feeling sorry for himself. By this time Gillian had moved to New York, where she held down three waitress jobs and acted when and where she could. Already she was too old to be a starlet, but, at twenty-four, not too old to be discovered, to become, as they say, semifamous. And so she kept herself very, very busy. Now she sounded annoyed and out of breath and he wondered what he had interrupted her in the middle of. She accepted the charges.

"It's me," he said, redundantly.

"Oh, *Me*. Hi there, *Me*. What's new with you, *Me*? Hey, everyone, guess who's on the phone, it's *Me!*"

"Am I interrupting anything?"

"Only my wonderful little charmed *life*. And may I ask where you are? I have a message here from our beloved *father*, he thinks you've come to stay with me. Have you? Are you downstairs? I don't have anything here to eat, I've been fasting for a casting call—ha! fasting for casting!—and have figured out a way to digest cigarette smoke through my *lungs*."

"No, I'm back in Nestor."

"Oh, Albert, darling, don't try to bite that poor man again! Mother told me, only last *week* mind you, that you'd flipped your lid. I'd have come to see you if I'd known, but all I can do now is tell you that in this neck of the woods, a bit of madness is actually rather *chic*."

"That's good to know."

"So why *aren't* you here, I could introduce you to the most dastardly people, you'd *love* it."

Something about the thought of living with his sister—where would he sleep? the bathtub? the floor? under her bed?—stirred and terrified him. He said, "There's a woman—"

"*Yeeeeessss . . . ?*" said Gillian.

"—who, I guess you could say I'm in love with her. She's engaged."

"Oh, dear. Not to you."

"No."

"I have to tell you that this is very sweet. You're in love with her. All right, then—my God, what's that horrible noise?"

"It's a bus. I've been kicked out of my house here and I don't like my roommates anyhow. I guess that's why I'm calling, I don't know what to do. I'm on a street corner." Saying this, his jaw began to tremble and his eyes fill up with cold tears. "I don't have anywhere to stay and I don't have any friends. And I think this woman, she's a nurse, she was *my* nurse, in the psych ward, might love me, but she's engaged. I don't know what to do." He sniffed, wiping his nose with the back of his hand. Dammit—no tissues. Fluttering on the ground outside the phone booth was a paper napkin from a deli, but when he bent down to reach for it, the wind picked it up and blew it away.

"Oh—oh, my," Gillian was saying. "This is a problem. Where is this fiancé of hers? Does he live with her?"

"No."

"So where is he?"

"San Francisco."

There was a beat before she burst out laughing, a bluejay's laugh, impatient and mocking and delighted. "Well then there's no problem at all, is there, Albert? You go to her, you go to her house! To hell with Mister Sanfrancisco, go over there and knock on the door and say 'Here I am,' and just walk right in! That's what I'd do—in fact, dear, it's what I *do* do. And don't apologize, don't say"—and here she put on a deep dumb voice that sounded nothing like his—"'Uh, gee, I'm sorry to just sort of show up, I know this is inconvenient for you but I was wondering if maybe I could spend the night on your sofa.'" It *was* something he would say, though. "Just walk in, tell her you've come for her, or better yet don't say anything at all, just put yourself near the door and walk toward her, and she'll back away and you just go right in. Guaranteed you'll wake up in the sack with her."

"That's not necessarily what I'm—"

"Oh, for Christ's sake, Albert, for once in your life be honest with yourself! You want to *screw*! It's nothing to be embarrassed about!"

"It's not that I'm embarrassed, it's just that m-m—making love is not what—"

"*Fucking!* That's what it's called—let me hear you say it."

202 • J. ROBERT LENNON

"No."

"Say it! Say it or I'll come up there and fuck you myself!"

That very nearly stopped his heart; his mind produced the improbable image with such stunning clarity that it almost seemed like a memory, of himself and his sister—*fucking*—on a bed, oddly enough the daybed with red sheets in his mother's boudoir where he had never even sat, let alone committed incest, Gillian on top of him grinning, heaving, his hands on— and her hands— and their— and— and so aroused and disgusted was he by this fantasy that he gripped the receiver and shuddered and smacked the glass wall with his palm and screamed "*Fucking!*" so loudly that the students waiting in the bus shelter fifteen feet away jumped in their seats and turned startled to face him, their eyes stripped bare, their hands flying to their possessions on the seat beside them.

Quickly he hung up. My God, he thought—now she's done it, now she's really gone too far, she's planted this awful thing in my head and now it will never, ever go away. His hand was still on the receiver; bright pink, white around the knuckles, it looked like a trick hand from an advertisement in the back of a comic book. It took him a good minute to gain control of it. Then he picked up his duffel and walked back to the hospital and waited four hours until she got off work. When she did, she saw him, shook her head, walked past, and so he got up and followed. They walked twenty blocks, Mailman mere steps behind Lenore, glaring at the narrow hips beneath the gray wool coat, and when they reached a squat old apartment building she held the front door for him. They went up a flight of stairs and into her apartment. She put down her bag and, with a resigned sigh, kissed him. By nine o'clock they were rolling around on the sofa in their underwear, groping one another, though that's as far as it went, then. He woke up several times in the night to the sound of little gasps: she was sitting wide awake in her bra at a small oaken desk, working at her typewriter and crying. "Lenore?" he said, and she commanded him to go back to sleep, and he did.

———

He dries himself off (gingerly) and steps out of the shower, opens the door for the cats. They bustle in and hop into the stall. He dresses (gingerly). Looks at the clock—almost ten. Hours have passed and he can't think of how he spent them, maybe standing in the shower thinking, maybe looking out the kitchen window into the neighbor's yard. What day is it again? Sunday. (Hears the recurring radio ad for NASCAR: *Tioga County Civic Center, Sunday* SUNDAY *SUNDAY!*) He is really getting off the track: botching his morning routine, losing time: what does it all mean? At any rate he'll have to get it back together tomorrow, because it'll be Monday and back to the grind. He contemplates his mail route with relief. It hasn't exactly been a restorative weekend. It will do him good to be stepping where he's stepped before. Work: something to look forward to. For now it's out the door (grabbing first his camera from the kitchen counter) and down to the park where the parade is getting ready to roll.

June 4. The day is too nice. Sunshine is only really enjoyable after a day of rain, the trees and grass seem to like it, first the coolness of water evaporating from their leaves and then the deep penetrating heat. But this sun, coming after days of sun, disturbs him: too much of a good thing. It's too cold for the shorts he put on but in half an hour he'll be glad he did. In the park, bums are still asleep in ratty sacks under the trees, the cops haven't yet arrived to rouse them. Probably they're all lined up along the parade route. He walks down the path, shadows of the sycamores chilling him, to the City Hall parking lot, where participants are milling in a manic way, holding cups of hot coffee (the air cool enough, just barely, to render the steam visible) and eating donut holes; their mouths are white with confectioner's sugar. In a corner of the lot is the high school drill team in their white uniforms (red piping and gold buttons up the front, between the breasts, short white skirts over bare legs and heavy high white boots); he finds a bench and watches a baton twirler, a thin girl with a ruddy pimpled face, throw her baton higher and higher into the air. She is blued by a giant maple's shade, but the baton launches itself up into the sun, where it catches white fire and splatters light against the bricked rear wall of City Hall. The girl has noticed this phenomenon: she catches the baton and flings it again, harder this time, so that it spins faster, hangs longer in the blue sky; she turns her head to watch the baton's reflection flashing on the building; then she looks up in time to figure its trajectory and snake her long arm out to catch it. Her friends are clustered ten feet away, huddled in little groups gossiping; their shrieks of laughter are audible from here, compressed and flattened by the hazy air: but the thin girl is oblivious to them; for the moment she is free from anxiety; she spins the baton in one hand, walks in a tight circle, lowers her arm down almost to the asphalt and *flings*, and the baton rockets high above the shadow-line, so that this time the flashing first appears on a green metal air duct that juts from the roof, the flashes unsullied by brick, clear and watery and bright. Quickly Mailman snaps a picture, fitting the flashes in at the top of the frame, the girl's arm at the bottom: and then the flashes cascade down the wall again—Mailman is following them closely, the girl gone for a moment from his thoughts—until the baton strikes pavement with a rubbery bonk. The girl lets out a sharp scream: like Mailman, she got lost in the game. She forgot that the baton would fall. Her arms cover her head, and when the baton has stopped moving she laughs, picks it up, rejoins her friends. She is swallowed by the throng of girls.

On his bench Mailman experiences a tightness in the chest; when he exhales, his breath catches and he gasps as if stifling a sob. As quickly as the emotion came over him, now it disappears, so quickly that he couldn't describe it if asked to, so quickly he can't be certain it was there at all. But it was, he can feel the slack aftermath of it, like a filament that has broken, releasing its weight.

A marching band has entered the lot now; one of the drill team girls runs up to a band member and embraces him. Good to know they're not all dating football players. There's a cluster of old Volvos to which sandy-haired, large-hipped women are affixing enormous crinoline tutus. He has a rush of irritation: there's a certain kind of townie he can't stand, the kind who are responsible for the Volvo Ballet: the tradition-generator, the encourager of official town recreational activity, the gratuitous protestor: the kind of person who can't let a single pleasant community event occur without commemorating it with a tee shirt. Their shenanigans tend to become the subject of public debate instead of the issue that they have initiated the shenanigans to protest, and the very reasonable views they hold are discredited due to their behavior, and public opinion swings in favor of the opposition, who are not the protesting kind and have hardly said or done anything to support what they think.

But could anything be awfuller than the Volvo Ballet? Is there anyone who is not embarrassed at the sight of these clunky gas-guzzlers executing clumsy K-turns in the middle of Sage Street, while the "Blue Danube" crackles out of a loudspeaker? Is there anyone who does not wince when the mayor smashes a bottle of champagne on the fender of the leading Volvo and makes his little speech? Mailman's hands have curled into fists, he is pounding his knees as he thinks about it, goddam these people and their soy flour and sandals and weedy gardens full of crows!

"It's *you*."

She's beside him on the bench: his conscience, Kelly Vireo. She's gently panting, wearing the same shorts and tank top she was wearing at the coffee shop yesterday, only now there's a brown stain around the hem, tomato sauce or gravy, blurred by ineffectual napkin-daubing. "Oh! I—"

"*Hitting* yourself. You're going to do . . . permanent damage that way."

"No, I was just—"

"Remember me?" she says. "From yesterday?" Smiles.

"Sure, we were talking— you were telling me about—"

"Your aggressive . . . *behavior.*" She gestures with her head at his knees where he's been pounding. "I guess on your off days . . . you take it out on *yourself.*"

He feels he ought to speak but doesn't know what to say. He looks down at his knees—indeed, they look bruised—and at the grass between them.

"I have to . . . ask you something," she says, suddenly and suspiciously sweet. "Will you get mad?"

He shakes his head no.

"It's about my mail. I write a lot of letters. Like, to friends? Who live far away? Like I have this girl. That's my . . . childhood friend? And sometimes when I get letters from her? The flap's all wrinkled . . . and easy to open. Like I can just pull it right open. And other times? The envelope is totally normal. Except . . . that *thing* . . . it's like the mark they put on the stamp? . . . it doesn't say New York. That's where Lisa . . . my *friend* lives? But it like says *Nestor* . . . like it was mailed here? Instead of there?" Her eyes, clear and sane enough by themselves, don't seem to be working together; each appears to be focused over one of his shoulders. "I just want to know . . . like, what all that's about? . . . because my mail always used to be totally . . . *normal*? Before I moved into that building? What's that thing called . . . that thing I was saying doesn't say New York?"

"The postmark."

"Right, that. So . . . what's up with this? Should I, like . . . get in touch with the post office about this? Maybe I should ask that guy? Your friend? Ronk. Ask him . . . what to do." When she is finished her mouth remains open; her chest rises and falls.

He clears his throat. It seems to please her, this mighty scraping, this hacking. She bats her eyelids. He says, "I don't think . . . I don't think you have anything to worry about. About your mail."

"That's . . . *funny,*" she says. "Because I have this idea that somebody has been . . . reading it? Like . . . steaming open my letters? And sealing them up again? Or maybe using a . . . totally new envelope? Because this one time, my friend I was telling you about? Lisa? Who has known me since like *first grade*? Spelled my name wrong on the . . . you know, address. Isn't that . . . *funny*?"

"That is funny," he says.

"It seems awful . . . funny to me, yeah."

He is waiting for her to come out with it, to accuse him, but she simply sits there beside him, swinging her legs, like a child. Her lips are moving, he can hear the sound they make, a gentle flapping. And her eyes now appear to have fallen totally out of synch; one of the two is roving like a marble in a box. He sits up straight—he is pulled up, in fact, by a sudden memory of Maurice Renault's eyes, a memory he has not had in many years, if (could it be?) ever, the sight of those wide shocked eyes as he climbed onto the lecture stage, those eyes so round and bright and wet, that would be such a pleasure to sink his teeth into—and he says, with a shudder, with a sort of choking sound, "Well, probably it's somebody in your building, it's easy enough to break into the mailboxes, as you noticed. If you don't want to confront the person directly then you could call or write a letter to the postmaster."

She seems saddened by his response. He is mildly nauseated by a wave of anxiety. Really, who has he hurt by reading her mail?: so he knows now about her ritualized weeping sessions (candles, black hankies, dirge rock), about her aversion to dampness and thus showers and baths, about her effort to depilate her upper lip with solvent, which resulted in the faint puddle of pink skin around her mouth that he is right this moment looking at. Big deal! If anything he is helping her, he is helping by understanding. Isn't he?

She stands up. She leans over him, again exposing herself, and he realizes that it wasn't intentional last time or this time either, she wasn't and isn't trying to throw him off his guard, she just really honest-to-God has no idea how she comes off, she doesn't know how slovenly and grubby and miserable (and sexy—now, *stop* that) she looks, with her rimmed unmakeuped eyes and straight dirty hair and stained tanktop and (how could he have missed this?) *clogs*. The eye, the terrible eye, wheels in its socket.

"You're . . . *ffffucking* with me," she's saying now, baring very slightly her uneven teeth, panting like a bloodhound. "You are trying to ffffuck with me . . . and I am not . . . gonna *take it*."

"But I'm," he says. "it's just—"

"I'm gonna get you . . . one way or another."

She has run out of things to say and just stands there, biting her lower lip, her hair half over her face. Somewhere, blocks away, the marching band begins to play a Herbie Hancock song. A weak cheer reaches the park over the buildings and trees. Her head turns slightly at the sound; for a moment she looks like a squirrel. He can imagine her—it's so easy to picture it—with her hair matted and gray and her body shrouded by a torn green sleeping bag, he can see her snoozing on a greasy length of box cardboard under the maples, or in line at the back door of the Episcopal church, waiting for her soup. He thinks of her father, the squatter. By now the dot-commers will have kicked him out and knocked his building down: where has he gone from there? To a shelter, to a job office? Or down to the wharf to drown himself?

He says to her, "Kelly."

At this her head snaps back to him; her eyes come into focus. "Who told you my name?"

"Listen . . ." he says.

"Who *told* you . . . my *name*?"

"I'm your mailman, I know everybody's name."

This is too much for her. She shakes her head, purses her chapped lips. "You're . . . history," she mutters between them, and she begins to back away.

"No, hey—" he says, and he gets up and reaches out, and she slaps the arm away, hurting him, and she turns and runs. Mailman watches her sprint onto Sage (parade-prepped and eerily empty of cars) and toward the library, her clogs alternately slapping against the sidewalk and her heels. He lifts his camera and snaps her picture before she disappears around the corner. And now a new sound fills his ears: the "Blue Danube," trickling out of tinny speakers, and he can see the first Volvos pulling around the corner of Sage and Franklin a block and a half from here, and alongside the road the first spectators are cheering them on. He sighs, rises: surely it is his civic duty? He walks to the curb rubbing his slapped arm, and peers up the street with everybody else. The lead Volvo is the oldest and rustiest, a discontinued beige, the tutu awkwardly stretched around it at fender level. It weaves in the street as if piloted by a cartoon drunk; an arm juts out the window acknowledging bystanders, the hand cupped, like the Queen's. This is not the dance: the dance begins at the Square. This is the warmup. Behind the lead car snakes a line of Volvos, all colors and years, mostly sedans; behind them the majorettes are visible, and the marching band, the floats. The bystanders clump and cluster as the lead car passes; it lures them south along the street and they bunch into a crowd. Soon the crowd reaches Mailman and he is pulled along with it, walking briskly, then jogging. The jogging doesn't feel half bad, his aspirin has kicked in, his side throbs only slightly with each step, but he is left in a funk (don't think of the eye, Renault's eye, how good it would have felt had he been able to bite it) by the thought of Kelly Vireo. He's ruined her morning and afternoon. The crowd draws through the light at Center Street—yellow sawhorses block traffic and cops turn cars away on both sides—and ahead is the grandstand, spanning Sage, rickety as a pup tent and lousy with bunting. On bleachers some of the county's leaders—city councilors, judges—appear to be sitting, uncomfortable in the direct sun; a few have "dressed down" and wear shorts and golf shirts; others are in suit and tie or a business skirt and jacket. The mayor stands before them at a makeshift lectern, his red hair lurid in the slanting morning light, waving with both hands: Mailman wonders what he's standing on, a milk crate maybe, because he looks almost as tall as a regular guy. Beside him, wan and frazzled, his combover blowing into his face, stands festival organizer Saul Bean. Now the late crowd is slowing, meeting up with the early crowd already waiting; there is a bit of jockeying as the newcomers, having witnessed the parade's birth and feeling proprietary about it, nudge and jostle the already-theres, many of whom have been standing for hours to guarantee themselves a good spot and a chance to appear on television. The Volvos assume a straight line in the middle of the road and behind them the parade extends, in patches of color and noise, all the way north through the presidents' streets. There is hooting, there is arm-pumping. Mailman finds himself squashed between an unusually tall, thick-necked woman with a toddler on her shoulders, and a trio of high school girls jumping up and down and shouting *Woooooooo!* at random intervals. They fall against him in a steady rhythm, jabbing his ribs with their elbows. Watch the wound! Watch the wound!

Saul Bean mumbles into the microphone; he is clearly out of steam. He refers to the mayor as "a man who needs no introduction" before collapsing onto the bleachers. The mayor again raises his hands in the air. "Hellllloooooo Nestor!" he screams.

Some people cheer. The teenagers persist in their *wooooo*ing. Most people say hello back in vaguely enthusiastic voices.

"I'm very pleased to welcome you to . . . NestorFest 2000!"

More cheers. Mailman doesn't like the mayor's voice, the way he drops and hushes his vowels, trying to sound official; the way sibilances seem to distort on his tongue, the way he enunciates his plosives, overloading the microphone and causing the PA to feed back.

"At only the halfway point, this has already been a banner year for Nestor," the mayor says and pauses to make room for a cheer that doesn't come. "The new library is about to open, with three times the computers it had in its old location"—that's right, Mailman thinks, our success as a town can be measured by the *number of computers*—"and with a brand-new state-of-the-art solar-powered heating and cooling system." Small cheer from an isolated part of the crowd: librarians no doubt. "And our new Southwest Business Park has already caught the attention of dozens of out-of-state companies who are considering *bringing* . . . their *business* . . . *here*." Silence. "And so I think it's appropriate that this year's NestorFest theme is 'Looking Toward the Future,' because truly that is what we are doing, and what . . . *you*, citizens of Nestor, have helped . . . *me* . . . to accomplish! Because, Nestorians, the future truly is ahead of us . . . it is only waiting for us to come up right behind it and *grab* it"—and here he startles everyone by reaching out suddenly with both hands and making a grabbing motion; there is a small gasp; his hands knock against the mic and a terrible *pock* goes up from the speakers, rendering his next words almost inaudible—"and *grab* it we will." A bit of clapping. "Many," he says, seeming to be launching a new topic, "believe that the small town, as an American institution, is something that should be *put under glass* . . . something that should be *frozen in time*, like some kind of historical book or something in a museum. But friends, I want to tell you that *Nestor* . . . is *not* . . . an an*tique*. Those who fear change will say that because something is *old* . . . then that something is *good*. But we know better, citizens of Nestor. We know that to stay alive, a town must make *progress*. We must show our neighbors in the surrounding counties, our neighbors of the great Adirondacks and the western forests and the great city downstate, that we are not *stuck* in some *dusty old museum*."

And now the first boos—historic preservation boos, anti-development boos, open-space boos—begin to rise from the crowd, and the mayor sternly peers from side to side, as if trying to identify the troublemakers. "No, we are making progress, and that means . . . invest-ment in *technology* . . . an increase in *commercial development* . . . and a new focus on clearing the books of *antiquated laws* that may stand in our way." The boos redouble. At Mailman's side the tall woman is boo-ing with a disturbing intensity, leaning forward, distending her lips. On her shoulders her child joins in. More boos erupt in bunches all through the mob. The mayor is frowning. Well, what did he expect, Mailman thinks, he won the office with only twenty-five hundred votes, to his opponent's twenty-three, out of the, what? thirty percent of registered voters who bothered showing up at the polls: and this crowd, the festival crowd—they are not his supporters. They are *letting* him talk. They're here for the *Volvos*. Suddenly the Volvo ballet seems kind of all right, not a bad idea at all, really. Kind of sweet, when you think about it. The mayor again raises his arms, appearing to be gently *patting* the crowd. "With our new *attitude*," he says, "with our new *pride* in our community, we truly are 'Looking Toward the Future,' *ahead*, into the twentieth century!"

A few people manage to laugh at the mistake before one of the Volvo drivers gets the idea to honk, and before long others begin honking, and the honking takes on a rhythm—*honk honk honk!, honk honk honk!*—that serves as a cadence for the crowd, who begin to chant "*Throw! Out! the Bums! Throw! Out! the Bums!*" until the mayor can no longer be heard and the city officials behind him begin to gather their purses and hats and glance around for an escape route from the grandstand. A few stand up; Mailman can see them mouthing *excuse me* to the people beside and in front of them: they seem to think the speech is over. But the mayor doesn't. He raises his arms in the air yet again—it's worked before!—and speaks into the microphone, but his words are drowned out by the crowd. Mailman photographs this memorable moment. The Volvos' honking is no longer in unison, the chants have unraveled into random shouts and whistles, and over the noise it is possible to hear cars starting their engines. Now the smell of exhaust reaches Mailman—Christ, people, we're all going to be gassed to death, move the hell out of the way!—and he backs up, it's too crowded to turn around and walk normally, he just sort of nudges his shoulders into the people behind him. "Easy!" "You're falling backwards, mister." "Hey!" "Look out, look out!" He comes to rest against a brick wall behind which, he happens to know, is a store called Not Just Candles.

The grandstand is half-empty now (the mayor would likely say that it was half-full, ha!). Champagne, forgotten, the Volvos have begun to move, people are clearing out of the way and the parade turns the corner onto Main, heading west toward the park. Here, on the first block of West Main, the ballet begins. Mailman can't see it clearly—he's looking at the backs of the cars, whereas up ahead along the true parade route Nestor's citizens have packed the sidewalks for a good view—but he gets the idea: in unison, to the "Blue Danube," each Volvo bears right to the curb, backs up to the opposite curb, pulls forward in a half-circle to face that same curb, backs up to the original curb, then pulls back onto the center line and honks: *beep-beep!* They will perform this maneuver for the next half-hour. People will continue to love it for that entire time. Meanwhile, directly before him, the parade continues beginning; each parade element waiting to make the turn onto Main can be seen assuming its official parade position and expression. He watches the drill team getting into place, then responding to their leader's whistle; they twirl batons and manipulate fake white rifles. Where's his friend, the skinny one?: there she is, her stick-on smile like a DO NOT DISTURB sign, her baton a blur before her. You'd never know she was the one; you'd never think she'd spent those minutes before the parade standing apart, launching her baton into the sun. You never would know it.

It's a good place to watch from, though most have already left. He leans more heavily against the wall, letting the rough bricks gouge his back, and witnesses the conversion of each parade participant from private citizen to public spectacle. Marching band members approach the corner as hankie-toting dorks and emerge onto West Main in postures of dignity, as self-effacing participants in a mass endeavor. The Dairy Princess, slouched on her float, approaches peering into a compact, snapping gum, fluffing her hair like the fifteen-year-old C-minus student she is (of this incarnation Mailman takes a picture); she adjusts her breasts, as if it were she, not the cows, whose bounty were being celebrated: but she turns the corner as a comely and stately representative of the county's farmer-owned dairies. It occurs to Mailman that though he hates parades, he likes this: the moment of transformation, the abandonment of unselfconsciousness. He stands there for an hour until all the parade has passed (at the very end, a NesTrans bus, packed to the gills with drivers, he bets every one of them drunk, crawls through the intersection and nearly fails to navigate the turn, one tire squeaking up onto the curb, and Mailman takes a picture). The street empties of onlookers. City workers pull up in a flatbed truck and begin to dismantle the grandstand. A group of twenty or so developmentally disabled adults are led onto West Main wearing orange caps and vests printed with the words SuperCrew 2000!; they carry plastic trash bags and metal claws on poles. They fan out across the width of West Main and begin their slow progress toward the lake, the claws scrabbling along the pavement. Mailman photographs them. When they are out of sight, cops arrive to direct impatient traffic along the route, and when Sage is cleared of the grandstand, down Sage as well. By now the parade has probably reached the lake; a final picnic, with barbecue and volleyball and frisbee and illegal swimming, will be getting under way any moment. But here, downtown, NestorFest is over.

Mailman is depressed. Not that he likes NestorFest. He raises his camera to his face, looks through the viewfinder, but it's only the street corner. Its crosshatched image gives him an empty feeling, a near-portent, and he shivers and realizes belatedly just how tired he is, and how sore. The aspirin have worn off. His feet are swelling in his running shoes and his legs feel heavy and stiff. What's happening? Has he been standing on this corner for *years*? It isn't often—he is an active and healthy man, remember?—that he feels old, that he is able to detect the signs of aging, but suddenly it's all upon him now: the parched skin, the thin hair, the shallow sour breath. It's his schedule, that's what it is, he has strayed too far from routine, what with the extra day off and the botched letter and the abandonment of the wake-up regimen; and while he was getting his bearings, his fifties have come roaring up and tackled him. Goddammit!

He pushes himself off the wall and begins the walk home. The sidewalks are emptier than usual, owing to the gathering at the lake; he passes More Coffee! on the opposite side of the street and waves to Graham who waves back and then beckons for him to come in: there aren't any customers in the store. No, thanks, Mailman conveys with a shake of the head, and he makes a gesture with his finger, like a little toad or something hopping over a rock, *tomorrow,* I'll be there *tomorrow.* But Graham either doesn't understand or perhaps understands but doesn't accept, and he holds his arms out at his sides and looks around in dismay as if to say, But there's nobody *here,* can't you *see* that?, I'm losing money *at this very moment!* And all Mailman can do is shrug, he doesn't have the energy to cross the street, let alone talk to Graham, and besides he hasn't brought money with him, and Graham lets his hands fall with exaggerated resignation and hangs his head and shakes it to and fro and walks mummily down the corridor and out of sight. Within seconds the neon *open* sign is switched off.

Back at his house Mailman collapses onto the cot and takes five aspirin and is asleep within minutes. When he wakes he feels refreshed, if a bit stiff and achy. The clock reads 3:17, but it's dark. Dark, he thinks, in the middle of a June afternoon? And then he realizes it is *morning,* that it's *Monday* already, and he doesn't have to report to work for *hours.*

He sits up. The neighborhood is so quiet he can hear the creek flowing three blocks away and the highway ten blocks away. The cats are all asleep. He, Mailman, is brilliantly, horribly awake. A hard object is digging into his hip; he feels around for it. It is his camera. He puts it on the floor. Now: it's not *morning*-morning, but he is awake: so he ought to eat his rice. So he picks up the container and counts out the grains and pops them into his mouth. He lets them rest on his tongue for a few seconds and then chews. Maybe it's just a bad handful, or (more likely) he's simply never noticed it before, but he doesn't much like the way the raw rice tastes. It's rather bitter, it lacks the mellow nutty flavor of cooked rice. It is gravelly and sticky in his mouth, a sort of coarse paste, and suddenly he is thinking of silt, Mississippi River silt, fanning out through the delta, filled with champing wriggling water bugs and the bones and scales of fish and the debris of a hundred towns all the way to Canada, cigarette filters and syringes and car parts and sweaty old tee shirts and the dust from the bottom of the dog food bag: and he can taste it all in this rice paste, this revolting mass in his mouth, and he wants to—he absolutely *must*—spit it out, *immediately*. So he leaps out of bed (narrowly missing—this time—the sleeping cats) and across the hall and into the bathroom, where he flicks on the light and spits the gray gunk into the sink. He turns on the water and tries to wash it away, but it *sticks*, little clumps of it *cling* to the basin, and he must *touch it* with his bare fingers to help it along. And then, for a moment, he thinks he is going to vomit. He is not a vomiter, Mailman; he prides himself on a strong constitution, on a stomach of iron. But he nearly loses it right there in the sink. Easy does it, now. He cups his hand under the faucet, sloshes water around in his mouth, spits it out. Better.

But not great. All is not right. He realizes that he hasn't eaten anything since yesterday morning—well, there's your problem! But when he tries eating breakfast, the coffee smells like an ashtray and he has to force down his apple-cinnamon O's. He waits awhile, a good twenty minutes, to make sure it's going to stay there, and it is, so he takes some aspirin, showers, pats dry, dresses, and goes back to the kitchen. Now it's four-thirty. Could the paper be here yet? He checks: it isn't. Shit. Well. He supposes there's work to do back in the mail room, letters to be opened, copied, read, resealed. But instead he steps out onto the stoop in his uniform and bare feet and sits. He rests his arms on his knees and his head on his arms.

Next he knows, he's hit in the shins with something—hey! a kid is bicycling away, what'd he throw?—that turns out to be the newspaper. Looks up at the sky: overcast with streaks of blue here and there. It's light out: true morning. He has time to notice a headline—MEMORIAL SERVICE FOR LOCAL "ARTIST"—before it occurs to him to check the time. Looks at his wrist but hasn't put on his watch. Goes inside, finds it among the discarded clothes (since when does he just toss his clothes on the floor?), puts it on. Ten to seven. Yikes! In moments he's in the Escort, puttering down the street.

On the way up the hill his eyes begin to itch, and he rubs them. Drivers honk, swing around him comically revving their engines. Where are you going so fast? he wants to ask them. Is there really something so important somewhere outside Nestor? Do you have some kind of emergency appointment in Daleville Corners? In Smiddy? In Nine Points? And yet he, Mailman, is late, and would be going that fast if he could, would be sweeping around the losers going at the speed he's presently going. But that's different: he's a mailman.

All's normal at the office but activity seems colored by the weekend preceding: people possessed by the brisk defeat of a workday following a good time: hands upon the work but thoughts still on the Italian sausage covered with fried onions and peppers, or the quiet lapping of water against moored boats at the marina, or the bare shoulders of your wife or husband. Whereas Mailman's mind is on (once he is through contemplating what's on other people's minds) his pastry embarrassment at the coffee shop and throwing change at the Gray Fox and Kelly Vireo's slapping clogged feet and the headline still facing up on the passenger seat of his car. Memorial service, eh? Ought maybe to go but on the other hand maybe not, wouldn't want to encounter that poor crazy girl there. Say, was Kelly Vireo Sprain's lover? Could have been, why didn't he think of that sooner? But already he doubts it, Sprain appeared so sexless, cerebral to the point of not seeming to have a body at all, unlikely to entertain outside passions. But maybe she loved him. It could have been.

He punches in (7:08, lost a few cents there but at least he didn't have to dodge the 6:45 coffeeklatsch), heads for his station, eavesdrops on the way:

"—lost his lunch on the tour boat—"

"—in this sort of you could say pantsuit—"

"—what you gotta do, or rather be, is reasonabler—"

"—so I said, 'Sweetie, you'll just have to sissy in the weeds'—"

"—pouring goddam syrup in it—"

"—cracked my patella—"

"—burn victim—"

"—fattest dab-nagged poodle I ever saw—"

The raw mail's waiting. He sorts it, now and then glancing around the place, taking in the whole, the vastness never ceases to amaze him: ceiling all the way the hell thirty feet up there and us down here only six feet tall, tops: all empty space to heat, except of course for the catwalk. Remembers the inspectors. Are they there now? Are they watching him watch them? Shakes his head, turns back to the work. Not much point in worrying about that.

Through the backless backs of his cubbies he sees Ronk walking up and down the adjacent row like a warden, his giant belt-loop-mounted ring of keys jingling at his side like a rottweiler. He's unusually sculpted today, his hair shiny with hair grease, his shirt tucked in on all sides, as if in compensation for the weekend of disheveled merriment. On one pass he glances in Mailman's direction and their eyes meet: Mailman raises his eyebrows, gives Ronk a here-we-are-at-work look, but Ronk has something else in his glance, and Mailman gets a sudden unpleasant feeling about what the rest of his day is going to be like. In a moment Ronk is behind him, leaning into the cubicle, trying to be surreptitious, but his jingling keys give him away. Mailman says without turning, "Morning, Len."

"Albert. What are these accountables doing lying out here?"

He turns. "Mary must have dropped them off." Turns back.

"Well here they are, you better pick 'em up." Jingle jingle.

Mailman reaches behind him and picks up the letters.

"These nixies here?" Ronk says now.

"Uh-huh."

"What's wrong with 'em?"

"Bad addresses."

"Gonna give 'em to Peter?"

"No, I'm going to eat them."

Pause. Jingle. "You know, I expect my carriers to take their duties seriously."

Something's going on. He turns around fully to face Ronk. Why do so many people who can't hide their thoughts have such large heads? Mailman says, "It was nice bumping into you and Darla. Did you have a good time?"

"I'm surprised you didn't remember her, when you met her," Ronk says.

"I did remember her. She didn't remember me. Did you have a good time?"

"Yeah, we had a ball." He clears his throat; licks his lips while glancing from side to side, as if in search of somebody to back him up. "I think what we have here is your typical dodging of the issue."

"Okay," says Mailman. "My duties. I do take them seriously."

Ronk steps back, as if Mailman has taken a swing at him. "Okay, okay, you're right, don't get all bent out of shape. All I'm saying is watch yourself, all right, Al?"

"Got it."

"You want I should bring these to Peter?"

"No, I'll get them."

Ronk picks up the misaddressed letters and slaps them against his open palm. "Ah, I'll save you the trouble." Mailman watches him weave among the sorting carriers to the nixie clerk. Ronk hands over the letters, points in Mailman's direction. Peter shrugs, raises a hand to Mailman. Mailman raises his hand back.

When he's finished sorting he gets himself a rolling cage and loads up his trays. He passes Peter on the way to the parking lot. "What'd he say to you?"

"'These were lying around at Al's station.'"

While he's loading his truck he sees Ronk's car in its special space at the far corner of the lot, and notices that the door is open and a shod foot is hanging out of it. Mailman returns the cage to the dock and when he comes back the foot is gone. He gets in his truck, pulls out of the lot and onto the Wayne Road extension. A look at the rearview confirms what he suspected, which is that Ronk is following him.

They do this: follow you around, making sure you abide by all the rules. Happened to him a few years back when they sent a guy to time him, to take notes on his appearance, his demeanor. Guy asked him quiz questions, what-would-you-do-ifs, asked *what he ate for breakfast that morning*. Those were the days of "going postal," when everybody thought the mailman was a hair's breadth from freaking out. Of course he, Mailman, did freak out once, didn't he. He wonders if he used his turn signal coming out of the lot.

Light turns green, he pulls onto 13 and stays at fifty-five on the dot. Sons of bitches want you to be lightning-quick but if you go over the speed limit you get a black mark. Cars line up behind him, one guy passes and pulls in front way too close and then has to slow down for an exiting truck, so that Mailman must quickly apply the brakes; he honks shouting obscenities that go unheard. Will the honk be held against him? The sudden slowing?

He pulls off the highway downtown and parks legally on an unmetered block, gets out, opens the back door, empties a tray into his cart. Peers up and down the street, looking for Ronk's Buick. There: wedged between a Volvo and a Beetle in front of Hal and Etta Meese's house. Mailman bets Etta Meese is watching Ronk just now, from behind the curtains. He hoists the cart up onto the sidewalk and starts off toward the corner and remembers suddenly (too late) that he's left the truck unlocked. Goes back, locks it, then realizes he's left the cart unattended thirty feet away. Another black mark. Rushes back to the cart. Soreness under the arm. Aspirin's wearing off: goddammit! Left the bottle at home! Easy enough to get, if not for Ronk: Mailman gets a break according to the rules but doesn't want to lead the little toad anywhere near his house.

So: all morning Ronk's on his tail, following him from street to street in the Buick, evidently thinking that he can't be seen: the car's smooth brown snout comes sniffing around corners, nudging into parking spaces, nuzzling curbs on both sides of the creek. Its air-conditioning fan is audible a mile away. The wuss! Can't even enjoy a warm spring day without climate control! And of course Mailman makes mistakes, tiny ones: leaves packages exposed on porches for people he knows will be back in minutes or are inside pretending not to be home; he has to go back and reposition them or (once, when the package appears to be filled with QVC jewelry) even leave a yellow slip from his pad. Jesus H. Christ! Management! These guys haven't done real work for so long they've forgotten what it's like: the dual imperatives of customer satisfaction and regulatory perfection are often mutually exclusive. Some people want to be your pal, some people never want to lay eyes on you. Some people want a yellow slip and some want their goddam jewelry left on the front porch. Old Tom Effening's on his porch, waiting for him, accepts his mail, rifles through it. Effening says, squinting down the street to where Ronk's car is stealthily approaching, "Who's the geek in the Buick?" "Carrier supervisor. He's following me, checking me out." "What, making sure all your buttons are polished?" "Exactly." "Want me to fuck with him?" "Thanks, no, I'll just get in deeper trouble than I'm probably in already, no." "Suit yourself." And in he goes to open his mail and jerk off to thoughts of his teenage neighbor. Helluva guy, heart's in the right place.

In a few minutes Mailman's done with Creekedge; it's almost eleven (late! He's running late!), time for his break, which he definitely needs today, given the ache in his side. He throws the cart into his truck and parks (legally!) in the lot next to More Coffee! and walks in the door. Out of the corner of his eye he can see the Buick pulling in beside the mail truck. He is crossing the line, at this moment, from irritation to actual anxiety.

Graham is behind the counter staring at himself in the side of the toaster oven, running his fingers through his hair. "I got gray," he says.

Mailman says, "Listen, have you got any aspirin?"

"I can't give you any. It's against the law."

"But have you got it?"

"I *got* it," he says standing, "but I can't *give* it to you, because you are a *customer* in this *establishment*."

"Look," Mailman says, "I am in very serious pain and I need aspirin, maybe we could step outside, onto the sidewalk, since there is nobody else here, and you could give me some aspirin as a regular human being, and then we can walk back inside and you could sell me some coffee as a businessman, okay?"

Graham sighs. "So you're extorting aspirin out of me? Fine. If I lose my license to operate, that'll just have to be the way it is." He reaches under the counter, grabs a bottle and heads for the back door. Mailman goes to the front and they meet next to the building. Graham hands him the bottle; Mailman opens it and with shaking hands removes four or five aspirin and crunches them in his mouth. Bitter: gorge rising! But no, it's under control, he can feel his blood rushing to pick up the drug and begins to feel better. "Hey!" says Graham. "Somebody's messing with your mail truck!" It's Ronk of course, walking around the truck with his notebook, scribbling infractions with a stubby pencil. "Supervisor," Mailman says. "Yeah?" "Yeah. Look, sell me some coffee, would you?" So back they go into the shop, Mailman through the front and Graham through the back, and Mailman is given his coffee which replaces the bitterness of the aspirin with a rounder, more congenial bitterness. The two men stand at the counter watching Ronk through the window.

"Watch this," Graham says. He turns, plucks the receiver off the wall phone and dials 911. "Yeah," he says, "I'm calling from the corner of Hoover and Sage. There's a guy in the lot by the park who's trying to break into a mail truck."

What! Mailman spins toward him spilling hot coffee on his hand which makes him jerk his hand, which spills more coffee. Masters himself, sets down the cup (its corrugated cardboard "Java Jacket" loses its grip on the cup and slips down to the counter, which it strikes with a dainty *pock*), shakes his hand in the air to cool it. Droplets of coffee spatter on the tables and chairs. "No! No!" he says to Graham, who's still on the phone. Graham turns his back, waves Mailman off, plugs his ear. "You don't understand, I'll get in trouble, they'll nail me for it, really, I mean it—" Now Graham waves him off more vigorously, flapping his arm with real vehemence as he gives his name and address and thanks the receptionist on the other end. He hangs up.

"What in the hell'd you do that for?" With a wad of unbleached paper napkins Mailman daubs his hand and arm.

"Fucking middle management," Graham says, his face in an attitude of pure delight. "Guys like that make me sick. Little motherfucking nitpickers and their red binders full of updated regulations, fuck 'em." Mailman is astonished; he has never seen this Vengeful Graham. He's *licking his lips*, for crying out loud.

"You have some experience—"

"Don't even talk to me about it. Don't even *talk* to me about it. I would happily take the entire managerial class and roast them alive."

They lean against the counter looking out the window. Ronk's on his back now, examining the underside of the mail truck: as if Mailman is responsible in any way for the maintenance of the engine or whatever the hell's under there! It is when Ronk has again stood and is trying all the doors to see if they've been left unlocked that the police pull up behind the truck, lights flashing, and hop out of their cruiser.

"Ah, here we go," says Vengeful Graham.

Wordless shouts can be heard as Ronk is slammed facefirst against the rear door and then, when he struggles, thrown onto the pavement. One of the two cops—a woman!, that ought to do a number on poor Ronk's masculine self-confidence—straddles his butt and cuffs him with one fluid motion while the second cop radios for backup using the radio attached to his shirt. Graham nudges Mailman; some of the old self-defeating tone creeps back into his voice as he says, "You better put a stop to it. Pretend you don't know what's going on."

"Right," Mailman says. He gathers himself and bursts out the door and trots across the street. "Hey, hey, now! What's going on here?"

"Sir, stand back," says the male cop: Hispanic kid, clean-cut, his toughness like a fresh new shirt with the creases still visible.

"This is my truck," Mailman says weakly.

"We got a call, sir. This man was trying to break in."

"That's my supervisor you've got there." He is surprised to hear a note of real concern in his own voice; he hopes Ronk hears it too. Poor Ronk looks so uncomfortable there, with the lady cop standing triumphant over his body. Graham has made fools of these three. Shameful.

"Sorry?"

"My boss, my carrier supervisor. His name's Leonard Ronk. I know him."

"Why would he be trying—"

"I was *attempting*," gasps Ronk, glancing backward over his hogties, "to *conduct* . . . an *inspection*."

The cops appear baffled: everything seemed so clear. "So he's . . ." the kid says to Mailman, "this guy's some kind of . . . supervisor, you're saying."

"Yes."

"Let . . . me *up!*" Ronk says.

The cops exchange glances. They don't want it to be true, this mistake they've made. Mailman hazards a look over his shoulder, at the coffee shop; Graham cannot be seen. "Look, maybe you should just let him up, it was an honest mistake, but . . ."

"Okay," the kid says, decisively now. "Okay, right. Officer Linden, why don't you help Mister—this gentleman here—and I'll just call in that the matter is resolved." He turns away, speaks into his radio. A crackling voice responds. Mailman goes over to where Ronk is being helped off the ground. The lady cop is brushing gravel off his belly; he slaps her hand away and faces Mailman, rubbing his wrists.

"Wow," Mailman says, "are you all right? What are you doing here? Did you follow me here?"

"Shut up," says Ronk, his forehead an Adirondacks of wrinkles. "If I find out you have anything to do with this, you'll be running a sorter for the rest of your life." Mailman feigns astonishment. "If *I* have anything to do with it? Why would—" "Don't, Lippincott: Don't." "Don't— I mean, what do you mean? You think—" "I'm serious." Mailman feels himself warming to this position, the victim's victim: "I just want to make certain that you know that I would never . . ." "Never what? What were you going to say?" "Never do anything like this, like—" "Like what? What happened here?" And now the tables have turned: Shit!, now he has to say something. "All I'm trying to do is respond to what you said, which is that if I have anything to do with this, etc., etc., and I want to say that I don't have anything to do with it, and I can't imagine what could be done, by me, to make this happen, since it seems to me these officers happened to be driving by and noticed what they thought was an illegal action taking place in the vicinity of a government vehicle, which as you know I very passionately protect the sanctity of, so I don't know why you would blame me, let alone think I have any idea what you yourself were doing here." There.

"Inspection."

"Well, all right then, that explains a few things."

"Actually," the male cop is telling them, "we got a 911 call. From a citizen."

Ronk turns back to Mailman with a tiny bit of his smugness restored. "Huh, I wonder who that was."

"Well, there— see what you're doing, you're trying to intimate something about my potential involvement in this thing, which as I mentioned I am not— or, rather, I don't, I mean, have anything. To do. With it."

"You said."

"Right."

There are apologies from the cops, handshakes all around, just-doing-our-jobs, Ronk assuring them that there will be no complaint to *their* supervisor because if there's anything he understands in this world it's the necessity of doing your job. The cops agree, thank him with obvious relief and get back in the cruiser, leaving Ronk and Mailman alone in the parking lot, standing between the Buick and the truck. "Now, as for you," Ronk says, removing from his pocket the notebook he'd been writing in, "I'm noting a number of infractions here, first of all that you're not taking maximum advantage of parking points as described in 323.21 of your *Duties and Responsibilities Manual,* by which I mean you need to maximize the number of relays that you can carry out without a vehicle move. And you left a couple of parcels on porches when 322.311(a) clearly states that—" "Wait a minute," Mailman says, "those packages were safe, people don't steal from porches around here, and the one that was valuable I left a slip for, so I don't see—" "Just a sec there," says Ronk and goes to the car and brings out his blue binder. In a moment he's at the right page. "Okay, 322.311(a): 'Parcels must not be left in an unprotected location such as a porch unless the mailer participates in the carrier release program by endorsing the package "Carrier—Leave If No Response" or the addressee has—'" "Sure," says Mailman, "but there's an unwritten agreement, I mean you know everybody does this, these people don't want to have to go all the way out to Wayne Road just to—" "All I'm saying here," says Ronk, "is basically that there is no such thing as an unwritten rule, either it's written or it isn't a rule, and also you didn't let me finish reading you 322.311(a) which goes on to say that 'Parcels must not be left where adverse weather can affect them.'" "But the porch roof." "Snow could blow in, or rain." "It's a sunny June day!" "So you can predict the weather? Are you a, what are they called, meteorist?" "Meteorologist." "Whatever."

Ronk continues to enumerate Mailman's violations, inconsistencies, etc., for several minutes, and as he does so Mailman closes his eyes and follows the aspirin's path into his stomach where the acid dissolves it, and from there to the little finger things on the stomach wall that deliver the crushed drug to the bloodstream; and around the body it flows, into the heart and out, and at last to his wound, surrounding and pacifying it (there, there), until the pain goes out of the throb and the throb itself recedes, slows along with his calming heart, and all that's left is a pressure, a presence that is almost comforting, like a handgun holstered just above the elbow, like a newspaper rolled up and clutched on the way to a café, like a woman's arm linked with his, like a rubber-banded stack of catalogs stowed while the opposite hand lifts the mailbox door: the swollen place like a little painless friend there, a thing nestled, which can do him no harm. When he opens his eyes Ronk is still talking, and still talking, and Mailman thinks of him lying facedown with the lady cop sitting on his butt (her own butt bunched beneath the polyester uniform pants, the two butts touching: and in no other situation could this conceivably have happened to Len Ronk) and smiles slightly, very slightly, not enough to arouse suspicion that he, Mailman, might not be taking him, Ronk, seriously.

Half a mail route, one lunch, three hours of catching up on stolen mail, thirty pushups, four or five situps (it hurts too much to do more), one dinner, four more hours of stolen mail, five more aspirin, one hundred seventy-nine (give or take a couple) sheep over the fence, seven hours fourteen minutes' sleep, twenty minutes of reflection (with eyes still closed!), twenty grains of rice, five more aspirin, one bowl of cereal, one cup of coffee, one newspaper, five miles in the

Escort, one punched timecard and half an hour of mail sorting later—at 7:32 on Tuesday morning—Mailman turns to a tap on his shoulder to find a stern, slick-haired, bespectacled face behind him, before which is suspended, in a smooth pink hairless hand at the end of a dark blue sport-coated arm, a shining brass badge that reads UNITED STATES POSTAL INSPECTORS.

"Mr. Lippincott? Mr. Albert Lippincott?" says the face behind the badge.

"Yes?"

"You'll have to come with us."

FIVE

The Postman of Uchqubat

He can't help but notice (there is nowhere else for his eyes to go) that the guy missed a spot shaving this morning—a little obtuse triangle south-southwest of the right-hand corner of the mouth, an unlikely region of stubble, like the last patch of forest the developers neglected to bulldoze. Perhaps they stand at attention under Mailman's scrutiny, these hairs, for the firmament beneath them twitches and crimps, and their bearer raises his free hand to scratch at them. If he is surprised to find them there, he gives no outward sign.

And is Mailman, in fact, surprised to find the inspectors—because there is another one, tense and sunglassed, crowded in behind the first—standing here, awaiting his cooperation? No, he is not. Was it all, in fact, leading up to this? Yes, actually, it was. It's so clear now: the moment he secreted Renault's fan letter in the pocket of his jacket, an invisible, inaudible clock began counting backward, gathering speed as it went, and here it is at zero, where he always knew it would end up.

The irony is that he quit once. A month and a half he was gone, a month and a half during which he read nobody's mail but his own, and sometimes not even that. He should have stayed quit, of course, he knew it even then. But you always think it will be different this time: this time I'll just have one beer, one cigarette; this time I'll treat her right; this time I'll keep my cool. This time I won't read other people's mail. Instead he went back, and here he is, and here are the postal inspectors.

How it happened was: in 1994 he had heard a radio story on the involvement of the Peace Corps in the creation of new national infrastructures in the former Soviet republics, and on a whim (or not so much a whim as a fit of pique—at himself, at his romantic failures, at Len Ronk, at Newt Gingrich and the so-called Contract With America) he called them for an application, and on the application he said that he could help set up a national postal service for whichever country needed it. He didn't speak Belorussian or Kazakh or Georgian or whatever, but if they would give him a translator, he was certain that he could get a lot done. He was fast, experienced, intelligent, accustomed to considering the problems of large, theoretical, multilayered systems; he had a degree (he lied) in physics from the New York Technical Institute, he'd worked for the Postal Service for nearly thirty years. Also he was not a spring chicken fresh out of college, he was (at the time) a fifty-one-year-old man; he'd had some life experience (oh, had he ever!); he did not make such decisions lightly; he could report for duty immediately, just send him the plane ticket. Signed it, stuffed it, licked it, popped it in the box.

After a couple of weeks (he remembers, as the badge wavers in the air before his face) he started to expect a reply. He doublechecked his mailbox daily, and after a few weeks of that, started checking the slot in his own carrier's cubby that corresponded to his address. Nothing. In a month he had lost hope, and within two months he barely even remembered he was waiting for a reply, and within six months he had forgotten, and within a year he had remembered again and gotten angry at the callous disregard for his time and emotions that the Peace Corps was displaying, and he fired off a nasty letter to the president of the Peace Corps organization about playing with his feelings. It was never answered, not even with a form letter; and within a year and a half he had forgotten again, this time so completely that, if he heard somebody mention the Peace Corps, or another story on the Peace Corps appeared on the radio, or if he saw a poster soliciting applications to the Peace Corps, not only did he not get upset, he in fact did not even notice, having buried for the time being any ambition to donate his time or energy to any causes, anywhere on earth. And then, almost two years after applying, he received a bulging envelope from the Corps and, remembering everything, opened it suddenly, recklessly, the paper tearing so unevenly that the material inside was itself bent and torn, and with a kind of horror read that he had been accepted to serve a two-year stint in the Peace Corps in Kazakhstan and would be expected to report for duty in less than two months, at which time he would fly to Istanbul and from there to Almaty for training, and then take a thirty-six-hour train ride to some small city where a car would pick him up and drive him to the town where he would be working.

Two years! he thought. Absolutely not! Two years! Who did they think he was, some kind of callow twenty-year-old with time to fritter away on self-aggrandizing international shenanigans? Forget about it! he thought, and flung the torn papers and their envelope onto the foyer floor, where they lay for the rest of that day and most of the next, at which time he picked up the letter and read it again.

Because the more he thought about it—really, he had to think it over seriously, didn't he?, because this was exactly what he'd wanted back then, two years ago, and he couldn't simply dismiss what he once thought was important—the more it seemed like a good idea, the more he became convinced that he should do it, would succeed at it, and return to the United States having accomplished something truly worthwhile: because what democratic nation could exist without a postal service (though the letter had said nothing about that, in fact told him outright he would be, among other things, teaching Kazakhs the English language, but no matter, he would get on the horn and get that taken care of)? What, otherwise, would bring the people together: the tyrannical, empathy-crushing medium of television? Not if they knew what was good for them. Shortwave radio? Nah, too esoteric, too unreliable. The telephone? Well, maybe the telephone, if they even had them out there, the hicks. However you sliced it, though, this was a Good Thing to do, with the Good Government, as opposed to the government of covert wars, of diverted funds, of propped dictators and coddled tyrants: a genuine, American, bootstrap-tugging Good Deed! He could see himself erecting the first post office in some chilly agrarian outpost, raising the walls with other bearded men (because he'd grow a beard, in that harsh clime) and women (that is, with regular women, not with bearded women, though God knew there were probably a few of those), stuffing those walls with fiberglass insulation donated by Home Depot and airlifted in by crop duster (Thank you, Dmitri! he heard himself shouting as the plane wobbled out of sight over the horizon), painting those walls alongside villagers who had become his friends, and one of whom had perhaps (you never know) become his lover: a slim, high-cheekboned young beauty whose dream was to study architecture in St. Petersburg and then return to transform her home village into a kind of testing ground for her brilliant designs, à la Frank Lloyd Wright and the American Midwest, and who would marry Mailman (for life was hard on the working man here, and few retain their health and good looks for long, and so Mailman would look pretty good even to a nineteen-year-old). They'll build their own house, a "dacha" he supposes they're called, on a couple hundred wooded acres (or whatever they measure land with over there), where they'll hunt elk or something, or better yet bear!, and grow beets and brew strong coffee in one of those tall ornate brass things with the steam coming out of it, he can't remember what they're called, and they'll recline nude before the fire upon their bearskin rug and screw with the kind of abandon only possible when you're an earthy rural Kazakh nymph who has discovered the passions of the mind coupled with an equally passionate American mail-carrier-cum-national-postal-infrastructure-expert.

In other words, bring condoms. Also (according to the packet of crap they sent him that he couldn't possibly imagine reading in its entirety): insect repellent, sunglasses, sunblock, American dollars, music, something to read, a Russian/English dictionary. Clothes that anticipate extremes of heat and cold. Sleeping bag, backpack, boots, electricity converters, rechargeable batteries, maps, a deck of cards. Jesus Christ! It was going to take him the entire two goddam months just to pack! And then there was the medical questionnaire, eighty-seven questions, to all of which he answered no, no, no, sitting on the foyer floor with the contents of his envelope spread around him: he just wanted to scrawl NEVER BEEN SICK over the whole thing in black magic marker and send it back to them but he knew they'd just send it back to do again, the bureaucratic weasels. No, instead he painstakingly filled in each little oval with his number two pencil, indicating that he had never once suffered from fibromyalgia, goiter, removal of spleen, esophageal varices, or hydrocephalus (either with or without shunt). Does he have difficulty walking two blocks on flat terrain without experiencing shortness of breath, leg, joint, muscle or chest pain? Hell, no! Did they even read his freaking application? He's a *mailman*. Does he ever have difficulty climbing two flights of stairs while carrying groceries or other items? *Try a couple hundred Land's End Christmas catalogs!* Have you ever attempted suicide? Hell, *hell*, no!, though try asking goddam what's-his-face, the head quack from NYTech, and see what answer you get! The only iffy one was the one about psychiatric care slash counseling, as in had he ever received any, to which he answered no, figuring that, in the case of Gary Garrity, (1) it was against his will, (2) it was necessary for his *job* (and good riddance to it!), and (3) he was in no way helped by the experience, i.e., he was not actually cared for or counseled; and in the case of the unfortunate and unnecessarily extended hospitalization of his youth, he was basically just pumped full of drugs and sent home with Mom and Dad. So much for the questionnaire. Also, because he was old(er!) he was going to have to go get a physical, which he was encouraged to schedule immediately with the physician of his choice, which in Mailman's choice was actually no physician at all, but since it was required, if entirely pointless, he would reluctantly comply.

That night he called up everyone except Len Ronk to tell them that he was leaving the country in two months and wouldn't be back until 1998. "Well," said Lenore, "we'll sure miss you," to which he replied, "Ha! I'm sure you and Mister Doctor Payne will be up late nights counting the days until I come back." (By now their friendship had settled into a pleasant jokiness that made it possible to pretend not to take seriously those things that were the most sensitive and painful, which jokiness Mailman would not, he thought, during his two years abroad, miss one iota.) "That's right," she said, and he said, "Actually, I'm supposed to get a physical, could Frank maybe check me out and give me the thumbs-up?, they think since I'm over the hill I'm not going to be able to hack the rough-and-tumble post-Soviet life, and I have to get a so-called expert to tell them I won't cry wee-wee-wee all the way home." "You're awfully frisky this evening, Albert." "Never felt better in my life," he said, and it was true, he'd taken to hoisting barbells before bed and when he woke up in the morning, a practice which was to be short-lived but during its brief duration gave him a heightened sense of personal vitality he would much miss in the months to come. "I'm sure he could fit you in later this week." "Why, his customers dying off?" "Ha-ha, Albert. What I'm saying is that he's very fond of you and I'm certain he'll be willing to do you the favor." "Favor! You mean he isn't going to charge me?" "No, I didn't say that." "You think he's fond of me, do you?" "Sure. He certainly doesn't begrudge me the years you and I spent together, and since he loves me and knows that I chose you, he knows that you must be a person of some—" "Please, don't make us both sick, you're sounding like a VD pamphlet in your old age." Heavily she sighed. "This is exactly what I ought to expect when I'm doing you a favor." "Your *husband* is doing me the favor." "Whatever."

He called his mother in Florida, where she and his father had moved precisely to avoid having to care about such things, and told her he was leaving the country. "Jesus Christ," she said and handed the phone to his father. "Hello? Who is this?" "Albert." "Oh, hi. Say, have you read this—that is, seen—this article in the *Times* about new kinds of glass? Seems they're making this new glass— up your way— for computers— the screens— very thin and lightweight. No glare." The rustle of paper. "Funny thing is, a friend of mine came up with something like this— this was back in the days of vacuum tubes— in those days we never thought— or rather, it didn't occur— that everything we came up with might be worth something someday, it was just this thing he came up with." "Dad." "If we'd had a little foresight— that is, if only— we'd all be filthy rich right now. What's that?"

"I was calling," Mailman said, "to tell you I'm joining the Peace Corps. I leave in a couple of months." A confused silence. "No, you're too old," his father said finally, "aren't you? They wouldn't— I mean— you couldn't get in." "Well, I did. As it happens I'm not too old at all." Another silence, this one punctuated, punctured even, by *hmms.* "Well, where are they— where are you going?" "Kazakhstan." "You mean Russia?" "It's nearby. South. South of Siberia, actually." His father laughed. "I should sure hope so! I should hope you're— that is, that it's south of Siberia! Well, bring your winter coat!" More laughs. Mailman said, "Ah, listen, I don't think I'm going to be able to get down to Florida before I leave." "Well, we just saw you—what was it— last year?" "That's right." "Well, how long are you going to be gone?" "Two years." More rustling. "Well. Do you want me to put your mother back on?"

He left a message for his sister and then headed for the bathroom to relieve himself but before he reached the door the phone rang. "You're going to *where*, darling, are you *insane*? This isn't 1975, there's a *bull market* on!" "Kazakhstan, and no, of course I'm not—" "I can't imagine anything *duller*, Albert, there won't even be a *movie* theater there." "But," he said, "well, see, that isn't the point, the point is to serve the— and to, to, improve the infrastructure of the— and the public health system and so on . . ." But in fact he hadn't considered that at all, not getting to see any movies for two years, and to be honest (not that he was being honest out loud) the thought was more than a little bit disappointing, devastating even. No television, he wouldn't miss that of course, but movies were another story. "Anyway, there'll probably be some kind of movies there," he said, weakly, "maybe a Gary Cooper flick or some dancey Leslie Caron thing, or something of that nature." Sure, he thought, why not, the theater would be dirty, the film would unspool every once in a while and people would groan while the octogenarian projectionist fastened the ends back together with duct tape . . . but his sister was laughing at him. "And coffee! Oh, my, let me ship you some coffee while you're there, dear, or you'll go utterly mad." "I'm sure they have decent coffee," he said, "it's a cold place, the people have hard lives, I'm sure they can appreciate a good cup of—" "Albert, darling, you can't even get a decent cup of coffee in *Westchester*, I'm quite confident you'll find nothing but the most unpalatable *swill* in Kracklestan or wherever it is you said you were shipping off to."

"Kazakhstan," he said. Then she went on to tell him about a man she was seeing who showed up drunk at her apartment at four in the morning with a woman he claimed was his second cousin but who was obviously a hooker he had picked up on the way over, and this man wanted the three of them to engage in some kind of ménage à trois but Gillian was having none of that, thank you, so instead the man had sex with the hooker on the sofa while Gillian sat up in bed reading a three-month-old copy of *Premiere*. "Goodness knows how difficult it was to concentrate but I gave it the old college try."

"That's disgusting," Mailman said, "do you mean the three of you, that's what he wanted?" And she said, "Well, dear, that wasn't precisely the *revolting* part, was it?, it was that he wanted us to do it with that *woman*, you ought to have seen her face, she looked like she'd been attacked by a kindergarten art class." "You mean you would have— if, I mean, it hadn't been the . . . the hooker but somebody—" "Well it isn't as if it's something I *love* doing, Albert, it's nothing I would think to do and then go out and draft a *team* for it, but on occasion, all right twice to be exact, the activity was suggested to me and I decided there was no reason not to shall we say *give it a whirl*." Now his need to go to the bathroom was becoming urgent, but he wasn't about to interrupt the conversation for that. "And was it— did you do it with— was it two men, or—" "Once with two men, or boys rather, this was back in college, obviously they were on board only so that each could watch the other do it to me, frankly it was a little creepy, the watcher sort of gently *stroking* himself while the other porked me and occasionally *glanced* over at his *pal*. And the other time was ten years or so ago when I was in this production of *Play* in some hideous sort of rat-infested garage or warehouse, and a man and woman from the audience came up to me afterward, very glamorous, I'm sure they were *somebody*, and offered to buy me dinner, and I was very appreciative of this at the time. Anyway, they brought me to the Café des Artistes, you know, the place with the nude *nymphs* on the walls, which should have told me something, and then after dessert they just came right out with it, it was the woman who said it, she'd barely opened her mouth the whole time except to shovel in the arugula, she said 'We'd like to fuck you,' and to be honest I really was rather taken with the man, and the woman had a certain I guess you could say *mystique*, what with her black lipstick and plucked eyebrows, so that while I don't ordinarily swing in that direction I was more than happy to give it a stab. Which I did. A worthwhile experience, though I wouldn't recommend it to *everybody*." "Oh." "Hoping for some action in Wackystan, Albert? A child bride, perhaps, you could bring home to fill that lonely house of yours?" "Me? For Chrissake, no, I only—" "The smell of borscht every night and hot sex every morning at five? Sounds like the life to me, dear."

A few days later he reported to his ex-wife's husband's practice on Sage Street, a small former drive-up bank building with a pharmacist working the teller window, next to the Hair Port and across the street from the Women's Community Center. In the Women's Center window was a sign that read CENTERING WORKSHOP. Frank's office was filled with people but he waved Mailman right in; his lower-middle-class New Jersey accent elbowed through the room, pushing all other ways of talking aside. "Had it with this goddam country, Albert? Can hardly blame you. The things they do that pass for foreign policy. You got to get on a plane and go do everything yourself. Don't you. Damn right you do." Elaborately cracked his knuckles. "Whaddya need here?" "A physical," said Mailman. "Ah, hell. They're just looking for an excuse to keep you in your place. Especially you. Government worker. They don't like you proving you can do things on your own. Take your shirt off." Payne was a stocky man with stiff black hair that flowed along perfectly normally for entire inches and then veered off in unexpected directions; Mailman had never once seen him touch his hand to it, which is something you saw men doing all the time these days. He looked a little like Lenore, the same wide-eyed ready expression, except that in the case of Frank he didn't actually seem to be seeing anything. His best feature was a strong chin. It wasn't going to win any awards but it was a good one, and anyway to the best of Mailman's knowledge there were no chin awards to win, even if it sometimes felt like there were. Payne listened to his heart and asked him to cough and breathe and felt up under his jaw and armpits. "Ah, hell, you're fine. Ever been sick? I mean seriously? Nah, you've never been sick." "No." "Then you're not going to be sick in the next couple of years." For a good ten seconds Payne stared at him without seeming to notice he was there, nodding, nodding. Mailman took the opportunity to wonder, as he did every time he saw Frank, exactly what variety of sex he had with Lenore, and how often, and with what results. He'd long considered Frank an anywhere-but-the-bed kind of guy, but couldn't see Lenore accommodating him. She had to be in charge. For her it was bed, period. But maybe it wasn't, anymore. Maybe she'd changed. Goddammit, he ought to be kept apprised of new developments, it ought to have been in the contract. He said, "So is that it?" "Yeah, that's it," Payne said.

On the way out Payne gripped his upper arm. "Hey. Let me ask you something. Come back in here."

"What?" Mailman said as the door swung shut behind them.

"Do you think? I mean, did Lenore? Ah, I don't know . . ."

"What?" Mailman said. Payne was rolling his eyes, his hands palms-up before him tipping up, down, up, down, as if determining the relative weight of two oranges.

"Did Lenore say anything to you? Lately? Anything funny, is I guess what I'm saying."

"Funny, what kind of funny?"

Payne made fists. He punched the air, half-turned apparently in order to look at a poster with a diagram of the respiratory system on it. "Nah, never mind. Maybe it's me. Nah, it's me. It's me. I'm sorry. I'm a prick. You're fine, Albert, lemme sign some papers."

"No, really, is everything all right? Are you all right? Is Lenore—"

"Look, Albert"—and now Payne had turned around fully so that his back was to Mailman, and he was removing his coat to reveal a white oxford shirt and black pants—"I'm going to be doing you a favor here. So I'm going to ask you to do one for me. And that's to never again mention what I just asked you. Least of all to Lenore. You got that? I've got a big fat mouth. Sometimes all kinds of stupid shit comes out of it. Lenore's tops in my book and I'm sure she's tops in yours too. So we're just going to let this one slide. Just let it slide, all right?"

"All right."

"Okay, I got huddled masses out there. Let's get cooking."

That night he sat at the kitchen table drinking coffee and intently thinking, what?, what the hell was it?, this thing that was happening to Lenore or that Frank thought was happening to Lenore, and what did it mean? She'd sounded normal on the phone: or was that an act, some kind of herculean effort to disguise her crumbling marriage? Or maybe Frank was losing it, and Lenore was going to leave him and maybe (maybe!) come to his, Mailman's, place "for a couple of days," just until she "got her bearings" . . . He stood up, pushing back the chair so that it barked against the linoleum, pounded the table saying "Could it be? Could it?," glanced around at the sorry state of the house, how ugly it was, said "No, it can't be," sat down again.

But what if it was? God, what would he do about Kazakhstan if she came back to him now? Would he give it up, keep his route, live the comfortable life? No—she could come with him, together they'd bring infrastructural integrity and public health to the struggling post-Soviet republic . . . They'd return thinner, tanner, looking years younger, Frank would have lost his practice, he and Lenore would be his only friends. In fact they'd invite him to come live with them, he could have the mail room, for there would be no need of stolen mail with Lenore back in Mailman's life. But Frank would turn them down—no amount of prodding would convince him—and in time the poor man would go to pieces and hang himself. God—always knew he was a loose wheel—something about the chumminess, the line of patter, that was just too glib, too facile—and after the funeral Lenore would cry "Forgive me, Albert, I should have stood by you, I didn't know . . ." and Mailman would take her to bed whispering, "Don't cry, no, no, it's all right, I was wrong to let you go."

"Goddam!" He stood up, bolted for the phone, dialed her number. Frank answered. "Whaddya want, Albert, she's in the shower." "I just want to talk to her, can you get her?" "What's so important? She can call you when she's out." "I just want—can you just get her please, Frank?" "No, I told ya, she's in the shower. This isn't about what I said today, is it?" "Jesus Christ, no." "It is, isn't it. Albert: what'd I *just say* to you? What did I *just ask you* not to do!" "Look, it's not like that, it's just you got me worried about—" "Okay, look, Albert, you wanna know the truth? Here's the fucking truth. We were in the thick of it the other night. In bed, you know. And I said something. To be completely candid it was somebody else's name. This girl I used to go out with in college. 'Cause I happened at a certain particular moment to think of her. This picture of her just flashed through my head. And Lenore was like, 'What the fuck?' And I had to explain all of this to her. It was really embarrassing, all right? And when she talked to you last night I was thinking, hell, maybe she's really pissed. She's telling Albert about it. She gave me the silent treatment last night, and then today I said what I said to you. Except when I got home all was forgiven. So everything's hunky-dory now, all right? Are you getting all this? You're getting all this." "Yes." "Good. I feel like a fucking idiot telling you all this. But I guess that's what it takes to keep your goddam mouth shut." "I wasn't going to say anything to her." "The hell you weren't. Now go to sleep." "Wait, I—uh—I'm sorry about—" "Yeah, yeah." "You'll still— you know, my physical—?" "Yeah, I'll hand in your goddam papers, Albert. Go to sleep." Hung up. So did Mailman. At least now he knew: they did it in bed.

Weeks passed. He got a letter saying everything checked out and we look forward to seeing you on September 12. Perfect: right before the election, Clinton-Dole: he'd register his distaste for the candidates by leaving the country. He should have felt elated, instead he felt lightheaded, as if a rope had been cut and he'd been carried off by wind. Now there was only Ronk to inform. A couple mornings in a row he walked right up to Ronk's desk to tell him but couldn't bring himself to cough it up. "Whaddya want?" Ronk said, and Mailman would say "Huh? No, nothing, just looking at this vacation schedule, sorry," or "What? No, just— there's something in my shoe," and walk off. Meanwhile he got himself a big backpack (a hundred bucks!), and started checking things off his list. Over days the bag filled up. He bought sunglasses, boots, boxers, gloves. From a used bookstore on the Square, a beat-up paperback of *Anna Karenina*—when in Rome, as they say! And the rubbers of course, just in case. You never knew.

As the day grew closer he began not exactly to panic but to implode. He felt like all of this was going to squeeze him to a point and he'd vanish from the earth, vanish from his house or apartment or yurt in Kazakhstan (whatever they were going to put him in) and never be seen or thought of again. Nights he put on his backpack full of stuff and humped it around the room, around the house, and in the last week or so around the neighborhood, reading in the light from the street his *Central Asia Phrasebook,* trying to learn Kazakh. "*Men . . . araq . . . ala . . . laymen.* I would like alcoholic drinks. *Maghan . . . tez . . . qutqarew . . . mashëynasë . . . kerek.* I need an ambulance. *Jana . . . shprits . . . istetsengizshi.* Please use a new syringe." Lenore was going to find somebody to take the cat (just one, back then) and would keep an eye on the house. His mail would be forwarded. He was really doing it! Holy Moses, what had he been thinking? But it was right, it was the right thing to do, he would grow and change and help a fledgling nation get on its feet. Yes! It was good, it was right. Please use a new syringe.

Every night it became harder to sleep as he tried to anticipate every problem, plot out his every move in response to whatever dilemmas might arise; every night he slipped more deeply into fear and despair as entirely new branches of possible disaster sprung into being: physical injury, incompetence (his own and others'), loneliness, frustration. Madness. Imprisonment. Death (his own and others'). Each day it became harder to make it through his route; he began to feel weary about halfway through and dragged himself down the last few blocks, lifting the bundle of letters and magazines and parcels and catalogs with quivering slowness, like an old man. And then it was the final week, then the final days, and at last the final hours of his last day of work, for tomorrow was Sunday and he would be flying to Maryland to meet his fellow-Corpsers and organize for the flight to Almaty. It was only as he pulled his punch card out of its slot and thunked it into the machine that he remembered he'd forgotten—or rather had forced from his mind—that he hadn't bothered to quit his job. From the punch box he could see Ronk sitting behind his desk in his chain-link-fence-enclosed office, sorting through a pile of mail, his bald spot casting a honeyed glow under the fluorescent light, and he, Mailman, shuddered. Shit, shit, shit. Ronk. Ronk. He replaced his time card, stepped aside, took deep breaths, girded himself for the explosion to come: but his feet never moved, at least not forward. He stepped back—back into the loading bay, back into the parking lot, back to his car. It appeared that he wasn't going to talk to Ronk in person. It appeared that he was going to . . . what? Leave him a note? No, then Ronk could call him tonight, he could come to the house to accuse and berate . . . how about a phone call? How about a phone call to Ronk's voicemail, after business hours? A voicemail he'd hear first thing Monday morning, before the carriers arrived, so that he'd have plenty of time to get somebody to fill in? Yes! The least inconvenience for everyone (except perhaps Ronk: but he would be spared the effort of chewing Mailman out), the least shame for Mailman. And so he went home, finished his packing, ate dinner, took a long walk, took a shower, listened to the radio, reread the newspaper, and made the call: Hi, sorry, I won't be coming in tomorrow or ever again. Sorry for the inconvenience, I just . . . I just found out at the last minute I'm headed for the Peace Corps. Goodbye and thanks for everything.

Perfect! It was over! He'd quit! When he came back he'd have to find another job, but that was two years from now and not worth worrying about. He went to the bedroom and got his jammers on and was just settling in for a final sleepless night when the phone rang. He got up and went to the kitchen.

"Hello!"

The stream of invective that emerged from the earpiece was loud enough to inflict an instant ringing in the ten-to-fifteen-kilohertz range, which would haunt Mailman all night long, long after it receded to a barely perceptible buzz. He'd never heard Ronk quite so worked up before. "Sorry!" he found himself shouting, "Sorry, sorry, sorry! I couldn't help it! Christ, will you quit it!"

"Never!" Ronk was saying. "Your ugly face!" "Make you pay!" "Have you prosecuted!" *Prosecuted?* For what? And what was Ronk doing at the office at this time of night?

"Working!" he shouted. "Working! And I'll have to do it again and again now that you've decided to go gallivanting off—"

"Working on what? It's nine-thirty at night!"

"None of your beeswax!" Calmer now.

"Do you always work this late?"

"No. Sometimes. None of your beeswax."

"What about your wife? Doesn't she—?"

"Shut up, Lippincott! Shut up! It's none of your goddam beeswax!"

"Okay, okay." But was it true—did Ronk always work late into the night, was Darla even awake when he came home? Was this why Ronk never showed up until seven-thirty or eight in the morning: because he'd just put in a twelve-hour day? Mailman had a momentary impulse to call it all off, to apologize to Ronk for trying to quit, for treating him disrespectfully, for causing him suffering. But Ronk continued, in that voice of his, that managerial squeak, and the sound weakened Mailman's regret and steeled his distaste.

"FYI, it's harder than you think being a supervisor, and you can bet I spend a lot of extra time keeping the bigwigs happy so the likes of you'll maintain efficiency and not go off killing people. So lay off it."

"I'm off it."

"And you can't quit because you're fired!"

And then, miraculously, he slept, dreamlessly, and woke refreshed just before dawn, and showered, and dressed, and fed the cat for the last time, and called his cab and gathered his things and waited by the door. Well, this was it. Goodbye to his house, to his life; goodbye to Nestor for a while. Would he miss it? Would he miss America? These months he had been so intent upon preparing to leave that he didn't have time to hate his country with his usual passion, and now he felt the way he might at the latter edge of a long

irreconcilable argument: it all felt silly now, all the things he despised
about America: hit radio, two-hundred-foot parking setbacks, vegetar-
ians, bottled products packed in decorative boxes, the brash ugliness
of the flag, obesity, baseball caps. So silly to care about these things,
little things really, nothing that ought to get in the way of a long and
productive relationship, a relationship from which he was about to
take an extended leave. *I'm sorry,* he wanted to say, *I'm sorry to be leaving you,* but who was there to say it to? Who would give a shit? And
with that he snapped out of his melancholy—it's true, this country
doesn't give a shit about me!—and the cab arrived and he got into it.
Screw this hellhole, he told himself, and to the driver he said,
"Airport!"

"You told me on the phone."

"Right, sorry."

He didn't watch as he left his town. He pretended to sleep in the cab,
and in the concourse, and as the plane left for Washington. He did not
look out the window at the lake receding, at each portly maple dissolving into a sea of green. He did not gaze upon the handprint of God.
But he felt it vanishing behind him, undoing itself like a stray thought.
He felt the Nestor of the mind give way, leaving only himself, a self in
transition, a ship between ports. In Washington a bus awaited; he collected his bags and was led to it. The bus was filled with chattering
twenty-two-year-olds; he spoke to none of them. Are these the people
I'll be with? he thought. The girls with the long straight hair and cargo
shorts (though it is a cold day today, for September); the boys with
their tiny little beards encircling their loud mouths; the voices excited
and confident. Beside him sat a small woman of about thirty. He said,
"These are all Peace Corps people, right?" "Yes," said the woman, "I
think so." "Are you going to Kazakhstan?" "Thank God, no. Vanuatu."
"What do you mean, 'Thank God?'" "I mean Kazakhstan is supposed
to be the worst. Except maybe some places in Africa. You know, the

pollution." "Pollution?" "The oil wells, the factories. Why?" she said. "Are you going there?" "Looks like I am." "Oh!" She scratched her cheek. "Well, good luck. I'm sure it's not as bad as people say."

They were dropped off at what looked like an abandoned airport hangar at the edge of a suburb; a giant sliding door stood open and they walked inside. Greeters flanked the entrance. "Where are you serving? Right over there." He went where he was told, to a buffet table with a sign taped to it—KAZAKHSTAN in bubbly capitals—and a girl there, her skin as smooth and unblemished as a puddle of spilled milk, said, "Name?" "Albert Lippincott." She rifled through a stack of papers and he thought, *She won't find me, it will have been a mistake, I can go home.* "Here you are, Lippincott—welcome, Albert, here are your fellow-trainees, please have a seat." She handed him a HELLO MY NAME IS tag with his first name written on it in the same bubbly caps and he stuck it to his chest and shoved the paper backing into his pocket. There were about twenty people here, almost all of them half his age, sitting cross-legged in little groups across a thirty-foot-square space; all around them throughout the hangar similar groups had gathered around similar tables marked by similar signs. He chose the oldest-looking person, a roughly complected man who might have been forty, and sat down at the perimeter of his cluster. The man was talking breathlessly, his hands forming shapes in the air, his giant forehead bunching itself above shifty eyes.

". . . so I had to ditch on this little gravelly beach covered with dead fish, and I stood there watching the pieces of the canoe floating away down the river. I turned around to see what the situation was behind me and the canyon wall, it was like, oh, shit!, no way was I going to scale that thing especially without my gear. So anyway I had to sleep there that night, it got to be like ten degrees and it started raining and I realized, either I'm climbing that cliff or"—and here he gazed around the circle at each and every listener, the girls all riveted, the boys leaning back on their hands wearing skeptical scowls—"I'm dead . . . fucking . . . meat." Nervous laughter. The man turned to Mailman and stuck out his hand. "Chris Boynton, sir, and you are?"

All heads turned to Mailman. He took the hand. It encircled and squeezed. "Albert Lippincott," he said.

"Meetcha," said Boynton and the kids all mumbled hello.

"So what happened then?" came a girl's voice.

"Well," Boynton went on, describing his death-defying scaling of the canyon wall in the pouring rain. The story went on for a long time. Somewhere near its end, one of the boys took out his Kazakhstan handbook and began to page idly through it.

Others joined their group, the young men with their rock-band tee shirts and close-cropped hair; the women muscled and bright-eyed and tan, wearing those same cargo shorts that carried no cargo except their excellent legs. Was this a prerequisite, the nice legs? Did they include this on their applications?

"Hi, are you our training leader, or what are you?" It was one of the women, this one a bit smaller than the others, with thick though not unattractive glasses which magnified her eyes and the eyebrows above them. Her name tag read MARSHA.

"Albert. No, I'm just . . . a guy."

"I'm Marsha. Wow, so, like, why'd you . . . ?" She raised the eyebrows until they escaped the magnification of the glasses, roosting on top of the frames like tiny toupees.

"Join at my age? I don't know. I'm a mailman." *Used to be* a mailman. Christ!

"That's so cool. I used to go to UMass but I graduated with a business degree? And I moved to New York and got a job at Smith Barney, but I had to buy new clothes something like every week and woke up at something like five to get a train at six to be at work at seven and I got home at something like eight at night and I thought, what am I doing in the rat race, you know?, when I could go help people. So I put all my money into a mutual fund and quit and joined the Corps. I kind of can't wait to get there, you know? There're like entrepreneurs, who want to start businesses, except they don't know anything about economics or anything, because they used to be in the Soviet Union?, you know, where they didn't have a free market or anything. So I'm going to teach them how to start businesses. I mean, here I was with this business degree, you know, just doing like nothing with it except making myself money, and my friend told me about the Corps and that you could do business stuff, and I thought, who would have thought I could do good with my business degree? I mean who would have thought?"

"Not me."

"No, me neither! I mean, wow!" She sighed, her face fell, her body slumped against her backpack which lay on the ground behind her. She closed her eyes and sighed again. In a while she opened her eyes and they came to rest on Mailman, who had been gazing at the ceiling of the hangar trying to figure what kind of wattage you'd need to light a place like this, and he sensed that she was awake and turned to her. "Nervous?" he said. "Yeah." "Ever been out of the country?" "I had a semester in Paris when I was a junior. You?" "No, never." It was true, Mailman had never even been to Canada; in his family, only his mother had the wanderlust, she talked for years about a world tour she wanted to mount—in Europe, she said, people actually appreciated the kind of singing she did, they wouldn't talk loudly and drink to excess and hit on each other during her performance there—but of course nothing ever came of it, she never went anywhere.

In a short while a severe, hairless man wearing a hooded sweatshirt approached their group and brusquely announced that Kaz 2 (that, presumably, was what they were called, their group) was ready to bus to the airport for their flight, and would everyone please gather their belongings and follow him, no dawdling, because if one of them was late then everyone would be late and it would be two days before they could get on another plane, and that's two days of work they would miss. This sounded far too much like Len Ronk for Mailman's taste, but he followed. They loaded onto the bus, Marsha silent at his side on the stained synthetic leather seat, and they were issued plane tickets and herded off the bus and onto a concourse and then onto the plane, where it appeared that Marsha, again, was to sit beside him.

"Albert, what's your last name?"

"Lippincott."

"Oh my God, I get it, they like put us on here alphabetically, because my name is Loring?" They sat. Mailman gazed out the dusty scratched window of the plane. "Albert," Marsha said, "did you ever go to Vietnam?"

"Remember, I never left the country for any reason, let alone war, thank God."

"Oh, duh. I was just asking because my dad went and he's in your, like, generation." She took off her glasses and rubbed her eyes with the heels of her hands and then blinked blindly in the dim light. Mailman watched her: without her glasses her eyes looked unusually small, like peas set on a dinner plate. She smiled blearily at him and he smiled back.

They flew. It took a long time. They switched planes in Istanbul and as they walked across the tarmac Mailman considered that this place looked exactly like the place they just left, and he supposed that was the way it was designed; travel was its own country, the plane ticket that country's passport, its race the race of pale, haggard people dragging bags down gray-tiled hallways. The thought made him unaccountably sad. They boarded another plane, this time to Kazakhstan. Marsha fell asleep on his shoulder. He himself ought to have slept, it had been a good sixteen hours since he had, but he couldn't seem to do it; not that he was nervous (though he was), but his thoughts had changed gears, each unscrolling itself discretely and in its entirety, rather than in a fragmentary mess, and this phenomenon was strange and demanded his attention. He saw the thoughts arrayed on a gleaming wood floor, they were like rugs—Turkish rugs!—unreflective patches on the bright boards, clear and colorful, drinking up the light; in the corner he could see his unthought thoughts rolled and fastened with twine and tagged, and on the tags were written the contents of the thoughts—FOOD, SEX, CATS, MAIL—that were not on his mind just now but ought to be close at hand. And of course by now he really was asleep, he felt Marsha's small round hair-cushioned skull under his left ear and imagined that he could hear *her* thoughts unscrolling, could hear the rug merchant of her mind bartering, displaying one thought, putting another away, concealing the very finest and most secret beneath his table for some select customer, some ideal buyer who had not yet approached him but would, most certainly, someday.

When he woke they were landing. He was leaning now against the window and below him a dry brown ground rocketed past, a dirt-brown ground out of which jutted stiff grasses not waving in the roaring air stirred by the jet. Now of course came the first homesickness, not regret actually, too late for that, but simple longing. Beside him Marsha sat upright, her face expressionless, the glasses restored to it. She was not pretty, but attractive for her youth and candor, a narrow nose (which now she scratched with an index fingernail) overhanging thin pale lips (which now she licked). Ears in proportion to her tiny eyes. Hair dun, straight, short.

Her father's generation, that was him. Why hadn't they had children, he and Lenore? It had never been an issue; the subject had come up and both said maybe and it came up again and they said maybe again. But they meant no. It wasn't for them. But why not?

For Mailman, fear. Afraid of the possibility of harming them. There could be no going partway for him, only complete emotional investment, he could never be one of those fathers who work seven-to-seven, read the paper until eight, kiss them good night and send them to boarding school, then still play golf with perfect equanimity when they land in prison for dealing drugs. Nor could he be a touch-football-in-the-leaves kind of dad, a get-down-on-the-floor-with-'em dad, or a distracted but charming dad, or a stern but loving dad. He would be the kind of dad who thought: how long can I leave them locked in the bedroom before they piss or shit on the floor or find a way to escape? He'd be the kind of dad who thought: what if I just lied to them, if I told nothing but lies for years and years, what would it do to them? He'd be the kind of dad who thought: if they are girls, and if they grow into women, and if I then see them naked, will it turn me on? No way, for Mailman, to compartmentalize the old bean the way it was necessary for parents to do; no way could the world contain, say, his children and seppuku, his children and Nazi human-skin lamp-shades, his children and tactical nuclear weapons, his children and monks who set themselves on fire. These contradictions were fine for most people but not for him. And seeing his own personality traits warped by infant innocence, that would not have been bearable: to watch his own son's mind spin out of control while he tried to choose between a graham cracker and a zwieback?, to watch his daughter dri-ven to tears by her inability to put a cap back onto a washable marker? Forget it! And as much as it was possible to imagine Lenore's best qualities combined with his own, it was far more plausible to imagine the mingling of their worst: a child both self-negating and self-flagel-lating; a child both dirty-minded and embarrassed by sex; a child full of both love and hate. A human being whose introduction to human-ity was . . . *him, Mailman*! No. Absolutely not.

But then, perhaps their child would have been this: a nervous girl with tiny eyes, gripping (for indeed she was gripping) his wrist as the plane screamed, bumped, squealed, thundered, and at last rolled to a stop. A girl unashamedly wiping away a tear: a girl who could take it.

She turned to him. "Whew!" Released and then patted his wrist.

"We're there. Here."

"Yep!"

They were. Another airport, like the others, except now, in the dis-tance, mountains. Not American ones, weird ones, way too wide.

They rose up out of the horizon like exclamation points: You! Are! Here! Over the cabin a hush had fallen as the trainees felt themselves swallowed by the largeness of the earth, and then they were up and chattering and examining the contents of their pockets, the airplane suddenly claustrophobic, no longer large enough to contain them, their excitement, their ambition.

"Thank you for talking to me, Albert," Marsha said to him.

"I didn't. Not much, I mean. I just— well, yes. Thank you. You're welcome."

"Could we . . . I mean . . . over the next few days. Before we leave for our assignments. Could we stay sort of together? I don't . . . these people. They are a little, like, overwhelming."

"Yes, yes, sure, okay," Mailman said, reaching out to pat her shoulder, but he ended up squeezing it, sort of manhandling it, as if she were another man, a man at a funeral they were both attending. But she seemed to like it, it seemed to comfort her, and she reached out spontaneously—this was not something members of his generation did, unless they had been reprogrammed in their late teens and early twenties—and hugged him, quite hard actually, so that her sort of smallish breasts squashed themselves against his (he was embarrassed to notice) sweaty chest. She smelled sour but a good sour, like a sour cream, rather than an unwashed sour, though they were in fact unwashed. She said "Okay!" and turned and walked off down the aisle without him, apparently confident that they would meet at some future point in the morning (or was it afternoon? or evening?).

Which they did. They gathered in the ratty concourse (weirdly empty, this concourse, with floor tiles missing, fluorescent lights blinking, and nobody trying to sell anybody anything) and were met by a Kazakh boy—short, stocky, faintly Asian, he could not have been more than fifteen—who pointed to each and said "*Kuz*" to the women and "*Bala*" to the men, which Chris Boynton, handy know-it-all, told them meant "girl" and "boy." "Teach him how to say 'woman'!" shouted a voice, but nobody laughed. The boy herded them onto a bus (*this* bus? said the faces of the young people, we're riding on *this*?, as they settled into their torn and lumpy seats, redolent of the chickens whose feathers filled the cushions) and drove them to the "training location," a Soviet-style apartment complex on the edge of Almaty (then the capital) owned by the United States government, which Chris told them (but how could he possibly know?) was bugged. Evidently the American Embassy, in a gesture of local solidarity, had hired Russian workers to pour the concrete walls, and in a gesture of local custom the concrete was filled with thousands, millions, of listening devices. And so the building, rendered useless for official American purposes, was turned over to the Peace Corps. Still, they were probably being listened to. For some reason this did not seem disturbing to Mailman; it made him feel safe; if some emergency was detected by the Kazakh government's listening team (he pictured them hunkered in a trailer wearing gigantic WWII-era military headphones and small neat Vandykes), surely they would promptly report it to the proper authorities and everything would be taken care of. The building housed a low square auditorium with cinder-block walls and a gray linoleum tile floor (had he not recently seen this very floor somewhere else?), and a dozen "residence areas," which were low square rooms with cinder-block walls and gray linoleum tile floors. There were three cots in each room, thus everyone would sleep in groups of two or three (again alphabetically); Mailman and Marsha were paired with a doubtful-looking crew-cutted woman named Beth Obst, who crossed her arms, walked a small circle around their quarters and announced, "I want you to know I am uncomfortable sharing a room with you," meaning Mailman. "Me?" "No, *her*," Beth Obst sarcastically spat, rolling her eyes. Daily they gathered in the auditorium, where for eight hours professional trainers taught them how to survive two years in Kazakhstan. This included intensive Russian lessons, a little bit of Kazakh (the trainer, a stern, eagle-eyed woman, told Mailman that he would have trouble learning the languages, and she was right), and cultural indoctrination, e.g., they were to accept whatever was offered them, they were to be patient, they were not to interpret rudeness as rudeness but as reserve. They were not to expect to get up in the morning and "get things done." They were not to go out at night. If there were restaurants in the town they were assigned to, they were not to patronize them; instead they were to go to bars, or else people would despise them. They were not to express frustration. They were to lower their expectations. They were to prepare themselves not to breathe fresh air. If they drank at all, they should expect to get very drunk, or else they should not drink. They should not act as though they were doing anybody a favor. They should hoard plastic bags, because they would not get any at the grocery store. They should not expect to eat salad; they should be ready to eat nothing but potatoes and dill. They should defer to the elderly. They should not have sex with anybody, ever, but if they felt that they absolutely had to they should use a condom, and if they didn't they were taking their lives into their hands. My God! Mailman thought. Who are these people! Was he on his way to a prison? He began to acquire a mental image of the Kazakhs as truculent, violent, unforgiving; as he looked around the room at all the healthy, eager Americans he began to imagine that he would never see anyone like them again.

After the training sessions the trainees socialized; they remained in the auditorium or hung around outside to smoke, or else they played childish games in the hallways, rolling (for instance) a child's rubber ball that someone had found into a cache of empty shampoo and conditioner and saline solution bottles. An intrepid few ventured out into Almaty, against the trainer's advice; the streets were mud, it was rainy and cold and there were no taxis, but the trainees always seemed to come back happily drunk and full of new Russian phrases. Mailman didn't join them. Neither did Marsha, nor Beth. All three hung around the complex, often on their cots, reading paperbacks. Mailman had discovered with horror that the copy of *Anna Karenina* he had bought was in French, but Marsha lent him a mystery from her little pile of same. Beth read a thick book with a plain blue cover and occasionally snorted, whether in pleasure or disgust or both he couldn't tell. After a week Beth would occasionally look at Mailman or Marsha and shake her head and say "Man alive" or "Unbelievable" or simply throw her hands up in the air. One night Mailman came back from dinner (they all ate together in a grim cafeteria—cinder blocks, gray linoleum—where they were served culinary non sequiturs: roast pork on black bread one night, spaghetti with a thin bland tomato sauce the next, "hamburgers" made not of ground beef but coarse slabs of the stuff, white fat clinging to the edges) to find Beth packing. "Where are you going?" "Sorry, no offense, I can't take you two, I'm moving in with my friends." "But what did we do wrong?" She stood up straight, gripped her hips, sighed. "You're just a weird couple, I can't stand being around you all the time, okay?" "Couple? We're not a—" "Please, spare me." And after that he rarely saw her; she sat far away from them in the auditorium and cafeteria and held animated private discussions with two other women.

Now at night he and Marsha talked; their cots were separated only by a few feet and each could whisper and be heard by the other. She asked him about his life and he told her. Not much had happened in her life, so she talked about her father's life, his quiet job managing a grocery store that gave way to a tour of duty in Vietnam, and then his brief marriage to her mother that ended in her mother's death. It was a sad story, and Marsha a sad girl. She said to him, "I have this memory of her looking over a railing at a waterfall, a big one, like Niagara or something, except I must be wrong because she doesn't look like she does in pictures and Dad says we never went to a waterfall together." She said, "One time I was holding my breath underwater in the tub, and Dad walked in and thought I was dead and yanked me out dripping wet, and for some reason I decided to pretend I really was dead, so I did, until he slapped me and started blowing in my mouth, and then I cried. I was like seven." She said, "When I was eleven I found a family of cats and killed the mother with a rock because another kid told me to." She said, "I hate music. I can't think if there's music. I never went to school dances." She said, "I had a parakeet but I let it go." One night she reached across the space between them and felt for his hand, which he gave her, and she held it while they slept. A few nights later (they were nearing the end of the training period) she got out of her cot and knelt beside his cot and lay her head on his chest and he placed his hand on her head. That night she went back to her cot but the following night she didn't; she raised her head from his chest and then ran her hand, and then her hands, over it, and leaned down and kissed him and then pushed up his tee shirt and kissed his chest, and then took off her nightgown and her underwear. Mailman didn't know what to say or do, this was not something he had allowed himself to expect, and he had developed feelings for her very dissimilar to the ones that were being bandied about here. But he didn't resist, and it happened quietly. She actually fell asleep lying on top of him, for there was no room beside him, and eventually he had to wake her up and guide her back to her cot so that he could sleep. And then the next night it happened again, and the night after that, and by now Mailman had reconciled his fatherly feelings with his other ones and looked forward all day to the sex they would have at night. He thanked the him of a couple weeks ago for remembering the condoms.

The fifth night was their last. It was elegiac, even miserable. She cried. She told him that her father had been diagnosed with prostate cancer just days before she was to leave for Washington; she had wanted to cancel, to withdraw from the Corps, but he told her to go, ordered her actually, and she went. She had called him several times since, but he would tell her nothing; he said only that everything was fine and he was feeling fine and the treatment had begun and it was just fine. But it wasn't, she said, nothing was fine, he had forced her to abandon him, and what if he died while she was away? Well, Mailman said, prostate cancer has a high cure rate, they're supposed to be able to do wonders with— I know, I know, she said. Again, please, she said, I want to do it again, and they did, once more, and slept. In the morning they were bused to the train station. They had long ago received their assignments; they would be going their separate ways. Marsha and Beth, of all people, would both work in a large town not far from here; Mailman was going to a small town in the north, the town of Uchqubat. There he would serve alone, teaching English and yes, because he had asked, assisting in building and organizing the post office. Her train, the Tashkent train, left first. She embraced him on the platform and kissed him on the mouth, in full view of everyone. She said she would write. So did he. When she was gone, he didn't turn to face the remaining trainees; he waited with his back to them for two hours, until his train came and he boarded it.

He rode the train for a really long time. Hardly anyone was on it. Now and then a dark figure would stumble past his seat. He slept as much as he could, ate when food was available; stretched his limbs on each station platform in cities and towns whose names he couldn't pronounce: Saryshaghan, Qaraghandy, Arualyq. It was at this last that he disembarked. On the platform stood a single man with a gigantic beard and pale white skin; he held a sign reading ABLERT USA. Mailman shouldered his backpack and went to him, nodded. The man nodded back, then walked away. Mailman followed. He was led to a rusted-out car bearing several different brands and sizes of tire and a broken-out window filled by a neatly cut piece of chipboard. The car was running; it made a constant scraping sound, though not a disturbing one, the sound of a cat scratching to be let in. Mailman got into the back seat, since it was the front passenger door that had the board taped to it, and he didn't want to ruin the repair. The driver got in and said, "You go Uchqubat."

"You speak English!"

The driver scowled and shook his head. It was unclear what this indicated: that he didn't speak English, or just that he didn't want to. Mailman wondered if this was one of the many places where they despised Americans, and if so, which of the many reasons for despising Americans they subscribed to.

They drove. The road, as in Almaty, seemed to be made of mud, with intermittent slabs of broken pavement that hindered more than helped. Every bump brought a shattering crack from beneath; Mailman gasped at the sound, but the driver did not seem worried, even though something must surely be breaking, even though the roadside was littered with crippled, mired, or (in one case) burned-out cars. They had begun in the foothills of mountains but now the mountains were receding, and everything in front of them was flat and wet and gray, and got flatter and wetter and grayer the farther they drove. They passed dilapidated villages and farmsteads; cows or perhaps oxen stood dispiritedly around in fields. In time, some buildings rose in the distance and approached and surrounded them, and the car stopped. "Is Uchqubat," said the driver.

Mailman gaped. They were at the edge of town, where the mud road gave way to pavement (cracked, weed-choked); on one side was a row of apartment buildings with nobody around them; the low buildings on the other side, whatever they once had been, were abandoned. "Wait," he said. "You do speak English?"

"No English."

Try Russian, then. Mailman groped for the words. "I going where?" he tried to say.

The driver shrugged.

"*Myne . . . núzhen . . . nómir? Nómir.* Right?" My room, where's my room.

The driver pointed at the apartment building and then looked at Mailman; his expression was not without sympathy.

"Da. Uh . . . *Kluch?* Is that key? *Myne núzhen kluch.*"

Again the driver pointed. He spoke, too quickly. He pointed. He shook his head, honked on the horn a couple of times. It made a barely audible wheeze.

"*Ya ni-pónil*," Mailman said; that one he remembered. I didn't understand you.

The driver spat some curse, pointed, got out of his seat and walked around and opened Mailman's door and pulled out Mailman's backpack and dropped it onto the muddy pavement. He pointed. Mailman got out, picked up his bag, dug into his pants pocket. It was raining. He gave the driver a dollar; the driver showed no reaction to it, to whether he considered it generous or inadequate or what. He got back into his car and drove away. Mailman watched it recede down the ruined road into what he supposed must be the town proper, though the low clouds and falling mist obscured any buildings other than the ones closest to him. Understanding it was now time to move on, Mailman turned and trudged toward the apartment. In the vestibule a woman stepped into view, a skinny woman of about forty in a frayed brown sweater and cotton trousers, her gray hair pulled back asymmetrically by rubber bands. She had the kind of narrow, perfectly articulated face that straddled the line between starving pauper and fashion model.

"You are Albert," she said flatly. "Yes," he said. She led him up two flights of stairs to a dark hallway that smelled of urine (were there hallways that didn't?), and down it to a deadbolted wooden door covered by a fresh coat of green paint. She handed him two keys on a metal ring. She said, "Batya." He said, "Albert." They nodded and she walked away.

He opened the door. It was a single room, same cinder blocks, same gray linoleum tiles. One window. Mattress on the floor. Refrigerator. Stove, sink; a toilet in the corner that was half-concealed from the rest of the room by a makeshift wall. There was no toilet paper.

He walked to the toilet and peed into it and held his breath when he flushed. It worked. He went to the sink and turned on the tap, and water came out, rust-colored at first and then clear. He tasted it; it did not taste very good. He turned it off, but now it wouldn't turn off fully, nor did it drip; it ran silently in a narrow smooth stream as if frozen in place. There did not seem to be any hot water. The room's light came from above the bathroom mirror, where a fluorescent fixture intermittently flickered. Now he noticed that the building was not silent; he could hear people on the other side of each wall; someone talking on the phone in Russian to the left and someone washing dishes to the right. He wondered what time of day it was, what day of the week.

He sat down on his mattress, listing slightly to one side. He took some of his things out of the backpack and set them on the floor at his feet. From this vantage point he noticed that there was a dresser, positioned behind the door; he went to it and put his clothes in. There weren't many; most he had had shipped, as the guidebook recommended. He wondered when they would arrive.

Among his papers he found a crudely drawn map of Uchqubat with circles marking certain landmarks: his apartment building, the grocery store, a church, a bar, the post office. Also in the bundle was his schedule. He was to have arrived on the eighth of October. Presumably that was today. (A sudden pang: the election! the World Series! the turning of the leaves!) He was to begin teaching on the tenth, and meet with the postmaster of Uchqubat for a grudgingly scheduled consultation. He was both relieved and dismayed: there would be time to adjust, but what would he do for two days? Well, groceries. He found the pouch that contained his passport and money and fastened it around his waist, and then he stood up and put on his jacket and went out the door, locking it behind him.

He began to walk toward town. For a long time everything looked the same. People lurched by without speaking to him, mostly women with children or drunken men. Soon enough, though, he came to the place on the map marked CHURCH; here was the kind of building he had expected—the onion domes, the stained-glass windows, many shattered and cardboarded over. A man sat on the church steps eating a chicken drumstick. Mailman nodded hello and the man followed him with his eyes but didn't nod back. He passed rows of cottages with yards overgrown or paved with concrete. The windows were thick, opaque, warped; they reflected the street and Mailman walking upon it as a series of sinuous streaks. At a certain intersection he made a right turn and there was the grocery store, a rectangle of unpainted cement. He approached the door. It looked dark inside. But when he pushed, the door opened, and he stepped into a large low undivided space interrupted by splintering white wooden posts and counters before which people stood in long lines. At first he thought that he had made a mistake, this couldn't be the grocery store, there were no groceries. But then he saw them, stacked on makeshift shelves behind each counter, and in front of the shelves stood an attendant who listened to each customer's request and went to the shelves and took items down and handed them over. There was constant, if lethargic, motion; the customers—mostly stout, muscular women with their hair wrapped in rags—moved from line to line, sometimes collecting food or dry goods, other times seeming to collect nothing at all. Every once in a while someone actually left the store carrying something.

All right. All right, Mailman thought, let's just go for it, just jump right in and do it. What do I need? Everything. But first, toilet paper. He scanned the room for it and found it behind a counter manned by a heavily made-up young woman, otherwise pretty, who wore a stained and smeared butcher's smock. He got in line behind fifteen other people.

After ten minutes only two people had been served, and he began to wonder what the delay was. He peered past the other shoppers (not shoppers, shoppers were people who walked briskly around swinging bright crisp paper shopping bags. These people were . . . penitents, maybe. They looked like they were here to surrender something, not to bring something home) to the front of the line, where a middle-aged woman was speaking to the clerk. Mailman could make out only a few of the Russian words. "Thursday . . . came today . . . four." The clerk was shaking her head, gazing at the countertop. The older woman spoke again, more sharply. For a while the two of them simply stood there, both staring into space, avoiding the other's gaze. Then the older woman resumed the argument, holding out a slip of paper and pointing energetically to what was written there. Eventually the young woman shrugged, turned to the shelves, removed a box, and handed it to the older woman. The older woman shouted some oath and the younger woman again shrugged.

Similar altercations continued down the line. In half an hour Mailman was at the front. He tried to meet the clerk's eyes but she was looking everywhere except at him. He ducked down, tilting his head; he cleared his throat. Still she would not look up, busying herself with something under the counter. Behind him in the line something was muttered. He turned but nobody was looking at him. When he turned back he had the clerk's attention at last.

But what would he say? So preoccupied was he with the dramas of the penitents that he hadn't had the chance to rehearse; now he was expected to say what he wanted, in Russian. He did not know how to say "toilet paper." Instead he said loudly that his Russian not good was, and then he pointed to where the toilet paper stood on the shelves. It was sold in single rolls, without a paper wrapping. The clerk nodded. She asked how many and he told her six. She shook her head, then took a slip of paper from a basket and wrote something on it. She handed the paper to him. It showed the number 2 next to a word he didn't know. He looked up at her, pointed again to the toilet paper. She shook her head, pointed at the paper, pointed across the room, where a man stood behind a cash register, accepting the slips of paper. As he watched, a woman left the front of the cashier's line with a receipt and brought it to the end of a grocery line.

He brought his own slip of paper to the cashier's line, and in twenty minutes had reached the front. He was asked for money and turned it over. He received a receipt, went back to the paper line, waited half an hour and gave the receipt to the clerk. She scrutinized it for what seemed an unnecessarily long time. Then she stashed it under the counter, took two rolls of toilet paper from the shelf, and handed them to Mailman. The rolls had been damp once; they were warped by water. They appeared to have been gnawed, perhaps by mice. He held them awkwardly. He had no bag.

It had been almost two hours since he'd left his apartment, and he still hadn't gotten any food. He looked around. People seemed to be holding more than one receipt at a time—there!, that was it, you got your slips first, and then paid all at once, and then returned to the lines. That made more sense. What time was it? His watch was still on Nestor time, he had never reset it. He went to the back of another line where people seemed to be receiving spaghetti. He got to the front and asked for ten bags. He was allowed three. He visited the meat line, the dairy line, and the paper line again, because he realized he would need dish soap, and that's where it was. Outside it grew dark. He cashed out, collected his receipts, got his spaghetti. Then people began to leave. The clerks abandoned the counters. Penitents still in line gave up wordlessly and walked out the door. He went to the paper clerk and held out his receipts. "Tomorrow?" he asked her, in Russian. "Tomorrow?"

She shook her head. "Monday," she said.

Two days? With only spaghetti and toilet paper? He began to panic. "*Nyet, nyet,*" he said. He tried to tell her he had no food, he pointed again to the receipts. "I have nothing," he said. She shrugged. "Monday." She took off her smock and shoved it under the counter and walked out the door with everyone else. In a moment, Mailman did the same.

He carried home his toilet paper and spaghetti. When he tried to unlock the front door, he dropped one of the rolls of toilet paper and it bounced into a puddle. He retrieved it, squeezed out the water and pinned it under his arm. He got inside only to find that it was dark; the hallway bulbs were burned out. On the first-floor landing he stumbled over something large and yielding. As his eyes adjusted he realized it was a man, who rolled over onto his back and swiped pathetically at Mailman's legs. He climbed the rest of the way, ran down his dim hallway, fumbled at the locks, and at last fell into his room. The fluorescent light flickered and buzzed and in the adjoining apartments people argued and children cried. He set the rolls of toilet paper on the toilet tank, boiled tap water in a pot (he had found it under the sink) and made himself some spaghetti. He drained the water by fitting the lid unevenly over the rim of the pot (Thank God there's a lid, he thought), and ate the spaghetti quickly, before it could stick to the bottom.

When he had finished eating he rinsed his pot and set it on the stove, and he used the toilet (and the dry roll of paper) and brushed his teeth (he had brought only one tube of toothpaste and so used as little as possible, now that he saw how things were going to be) and lay down on the mattress. It was bare; no sheets had been provided. He covered himself with his jacket and read the last twenty pages of one of Marsha's mysteries. Then he got out his pen and pad and tried to write her a love letter. He crumpled up three drafts before he stopped trying. He got up, went to the sink and turned off the light. The blackness was total; the fields outside his window were devoid utterly of habitation. Perhaps he would be better off with no window at all; at least then he could imagine there was something going on outside. He felt his way back to the mattress and lowered himself onto it and closed his eyes. Some hours later, he fell asleep.

The next day he ate spaghetti for breakfast and walked, map in hand, into the town center. The buildings were Soviet-style cement rectangles with other rectangles nested in them. People on the streets ignored him; some looked Asian—the ethnic Kazakhs, he supposed—but most of them were Russians, and Russian was all he heard anyone speaking. He went to the school building at the far west end of the town. It looked like an American community college, with a wide expanse of the brown scrub that passed for lawn here, and a circle of shrubbery surrounding a bare flagpole. He peered through the

windows and saw chalkboards (that is, real chalkboards, of the sort
Gorman used to scrawl on in his frightening slanted hand, and that
Renault, the effete little frog, never once touched, despite the black
band of them that stretched across the room behind him, utterly
blank and unbesmirched, like a backdrop of vast vacant celestial
space) and plastic chairs with collapsible desktops, just like the ones
at home. Okay. Okay! This might not be so bad! He walked to the post
office, a small wooden building with a board nailed over the window
cage. He was to go there after his class, to meet the postmaster. Now
he was getting somewhere!

Back home, he ate more spaghetti, and while he was eating it he
noticed a telephone jack on the wall behind his bed. The phone! He
was supposed to have a phone! He stalked through his room holding
the pot, looking in and under everything for his supposed phone, but
there was none. They were supposed to give him one, goddammit,
and he wanted one! There were people he could call, people who
could send him things! He stormed out his door in search of that
woman—what was her name?—Batya.

Though it was Sunday and people were supposedly not working,
he had some trouble finding anyone in the halls or out in front of the
building. For a while he paced back and forth in the mud by the
entrance, waiting for anyone at all to happen by; then he noticed a
peculiar stain, a trail of stains actually, leading across the cement
stoop and in the front door. He opened the door and peered inside,
where the stains continued along the muddy carpet. In spite of himself he followed. They led past the stairwell door into the next block of
apartments, down that hall and into the next stairwell, which (mercifully) was lit by weak but intact light bulbs. Up the stairs the stains
brought him, and out at the second floor (a large puddle on the landing, and it was here that he finally grasped that these were blood-
stains) and halfway down this hall to a door. It was possible to hear
noises from inside: a woman shouting, a hissing sound, the thud of
something being rhythmically knocked against a wall or floor.

Of course he had only been here for a couple of days. Of course he didn't understand the cultural conventions, there was no telling what he might find—a trail of blood leading to a door behind which there was knocking and shouting, in Kazakhstan, might well mean something very different from what it would mean in his own country. But he had no choice, really, did he? A woman was in danger, was she not? The Mailman of several weeks ago might have called the police, but the Mailman of today—the Mailman who had abandoned the buffering presence of American affluence and provincialism—was operating closer to the bone, closer to the instincts of his distant ancestors. Hell yes I'm going to knock! this Mailman told himself and he pounded on the door. "Open up!" he shouted.

Footsteps. He jumped back, his hands before him in a defensive stance. The door opened and he felt himself flinch. It was Batya.

She raised one eyebrow, shrugged (the same shrug as the woman at the store: was this a national habit?), and turned around, leaving the door open and Mailman in the hall. He supposed he was being invited in. But where was her attacker? The banging continued unabated.

He stepped in slowly, expecting an ambush. Batya had settled onto a stool by a post where a telephone loosely hung, its wire trailing across the linoleum, under a rug and behind a sofa. She grabbed the receiver and said into it, in Russian, "The American is here." Then she resumed her shouting.

Mailman closed the door behind him. In the kitchen beyond Batya, water was running from the sink at full blast, and the blood trail ended on the floor, where it had massed in a large rust-brown puddle, at the center of which a large dog gnawed on what appeared to be a joint of rotted frozen meat. The dog was lifting the meat in its jaws and pounding it on the floor, then scraping it back and forth, smearing the blood in a wide arc around its head. As Mailman watched, Batya took a dirty rag from the sink where the water was running, squeezed it out and, still shouting, tried to mop up (but succeeded only in spreading around) the blood. Then she tossed the rag back into the sink and returned to leaning against the post, leaving bloody footprints behind her. The dog gnashed and growled and spewed fresh blood in all directions.

Mailman was still stunned at having found Batya, and stunned to be in another person's apartment, one that was not in any way "nice" or even "homey" but was actually furnished and decorated, with torn posters advertising American movies he had never heard of, starring people he had never before seen. It was a large apartment compared to his, with a living room and, down what seemed to be an actual hallway, one or more bedrooms. Children's toys lay about, scattered across the rug and piled in the corner around a cheap floor lamp, and there was a smell of baking food that served to (almost) obscure the sharp scent of blood. The food smell caused Mailman's stomach to lurch and twist, and his mouth filled up with saliva. He smacked his lips. He missed his house, his job, his truck. He missed his local misery, so warm and familiar compared to this foreign one.

Batya hung up the phone and began to shout at the dog. She picked up the joint of meat—Mailman could see sharp bones sticking out from all sides—and tossed it into a bloody bowl that lay nearby; then she opened the refrigerator (or perhaps the freezer; Mailman hoped the freezer) and shoved the mess inside. The dog whined. She reached into the sink and wrung out the rag and continued to wipe up the blood.

Mailman searched for words, Russian ones. "I help?" he managed.

"Speak English," Batya called out. "I practice."

"Where did you learn English?"

"English class. Also book."

He watched her clean for a few minutes. "I think the dog is bleeding," he said.

As if to illustrate the point, the dog stood up and trotted over to Mailman. It lifted its head and licked his hand, smearing it with blood. The dog's tongue was split, right down the middle; it dragged across Mailman's fingers in two damp strips. He said, "It's the dog's tongue."

"What is tongue?"

Mailman stuck his out and waved it around. "He cut it. His tongue. It's split down the middle."

Batya called the dog. It went to her. She crouched and looked into its mouth, then stood up and began shouting at it in Russian. The dog, shamed, stalked off and curled up in a corner of the kitchen. "It is bone," Batya said to Mailman. "Is bone from back of horse? Is, how you say, like knife?"

"Sharp."

"Yes."

"So you speak English," Mailman said. Batya continued cleaning. "Are you planning to go to America?"

"Toronto. We go to live."

"That's in Canada."

"Yes." She stood up suddenly, glancing around as if remembering something. She shook her head, then washed her hands off in the sink. She said, "Sorry. You come why?"

"Oh— I just, I was going to ask you about the telephone, I don't have one and I want to call somebody . . . there was supposed to be a phone in my room. But you have— that is, there are worse things to worry about with—"

She seemed to decide something and came across the room to him. "No no no, you are guest, sit down." She pointed to the sofa. "I get you drink. You want water?"

"Sure," he said, and she said "What you say 'sure'?" and he said "Yes, I mean yes" and she said "Okay, good" and got him water from the tap that was still running at full blast. "Do you know the water is running?" he asked. She shrugged. "Some of times turn it on, nothing comes out. So all of times it is on. So I know when water runs." He thought about this. "Do you mean that sometimes there's no water?" "For long time, yes. Today okay. Stay on long time." She sat down in a folding chair and put her own water glass on the floor. "You meet my husband and childrens. They come back." "I'd love to," he said. "Good. You stay eat." "Yes, all right." "You need phone. Okay, we find phone." The dog began to whine, loudly, over the sound of the tap. Batya shouted at it in Russian and it stopped. "I show mean to dog." She shrugged. "So. Welcome to Kazakhstan. Is no good. My husband work in the oil. The Americans, they make the drill, oil come up, everybody get works. But now already no oil left. People lose works. My husband lose soon. He is geologist."

"Did you grow up here?"

"No. Leningrad. He lose works, we go Toronto."

"And you run this building?"

"I am . . . manager?" She arched an eyebrow. Mailman nodded. "Yes," she said, "manager."

He sort of wanted to cry. After only thirty hours, sitting in a room with somebody, speaking the English language, was enough; the wistful pleasure of it was almost unbearable. And he missed Marsha, he missed her need to talk about herself, about her life, he watched and listened to Batya and he thought about Marsha, and worried about her, whether she was making a go of it or if she was as lonely and miserable as he was. And he was miserable, he was only realizing it now, he felt so old, so decrepit and meaningless and useless. Wait until tomorrow! he told himself. Tomorrow you'll teach, you'll do something worthwhile! But it was hard to believe that tomorrow would ever come or that he would welcome it if it did. On the contrary, he dreaded tomorrow, for he had nothing to eat for breakfast but spaghetti, and his class was at nine and the appointment at the post office was at noon with no break in between, and he could not imagine getting to the store with his receipts. And so today, because he had been invited to dinner by an English-speaking woman and her family, today was better, but the more time passed, the closer he came to having to leave here and return to his room to await tomorrow. And so he leaned forward and put his head between his knees and, indeed, began to cry.

For some time there was no reaction from Batya, which was preferable—he wished only to be alone for a few minutes in his private world of shame and misery—but after a while he felt a reluctant hand on his back and heard some kind Russian words, and really, this did feel better than no attention at all. Soon she got up and returned with a wadded-up handful of toilet paper, which he was pleased somehow to see was the same abrasive yet unsturdy stuff he had bought and then dropped in a puddle; he accepted it and daubed his eyes and nose and then sat up straight. He said, "I'm sorry, this is so embarrassing, it's just this whole trip, this thing, it's not what I was expecting, I suppose."

"No," she said. "I think Ivan earn many money and we live good, but now we must save for the emigrate."

"Your husband is named *Ivan*?"

She scowled. "Many man name Ivan in Russia."

"No, yes, I know, I know," Mailman said and blew his nose into the balled-up toilet paper. This seemed to startle Batya, perhaps noses were not blown in Kazakhstan, but there was nothing he could do about that. Her arm was around his slumped shoulders, and then he leaned back and her arm slipped off his shoulders and she stood up. "I make you coffee. You sit."

She busied herself in the kitchen. He heard the clank of pots and dishes and the sticking and unsticking of her feet on the blood-covered floor. Then there was a commotion in the hall and the door opened, admitting three people identical except for their size: a gaunt man with pale unblemished skin and thick dark hair that stood out in all directions, who wore a nylon windbreaker and torn blue jeans; a child of about twelve with a matching windbreaker; and another child, this one about nine and wearing a pink sweatshirt that read HARVARD COLLEGE MEN'S SWIMMING. The three glanced at Mailman and then greeted Batya with kisses and fast Russian that Mailman didn't understand a word of; then, without explanation, the man came over and sat down next to him and shook his hand with both of his own. "Ivan," he said. "Ivan. Ivan." And then, in Russian, "These are my sons, Sasha and Viktor. Sasha is the older." The boys came over and shook Mailman's hand. Then the younger sat down next to his father and the older sat cross-legged in the blood puddle and began to pat and scratch the dog. Batya yelled at him to get out of the blood and he moved over very slightly, to the edge of the puddle, and resumed his attentions. The dog seemed grateful, moaning and pushing its brown matted head into the boy's hand.

Batya said, "We speak English. That is Albert."

Ivan nodded. "Nice ta meetcha," he said.

"That's a good accent," Mailman said.

"My supervisor is from Jersey. Always he talks about Jersey. Batya tells you we go to Canada?"

"Why Canada?"

"Hockey. Batya's sister tells that people have a dish, a giant dish"—he spread his arms wide, so that Viktor had to duck—"and hockey on the TV all day long."

"Her sister lives in Toronto?" Mailman spied a clock on the wall and tried surreptitiously to reset his watch.

"Right. They have entire house. We stay there, have work, buy a house for our own. In Kazakhstan I make lot of money telling the Americans where to drill for oil, but not much oil no matter where I tell them drill, so we smart, we save up the money. So!" he said, patting Mailman's back. "You teach the business to people of Uchqubat!"

"Uh, no. I'm teaching English."

For a moment Ivan looked confused; then he shrugged as Batya had and said "Coffee!" and lunged for the kitchen.

Viktor spoke to Mailman in Russian. "Do you speak Russian?"

"Bad."

Viktor nodded. "Okay. I won't talk to you." He went into the kitchen and joined his brother.

After coffee they ate some kind of stew with actual meat in it, and Mailman listened to them talking, understanding little except that they were happy together despite being in an ugly place. For a while this cheered him but as the meal wore on he began to grow despondent, jealous of their ambition to move to Canada, jealous of the likelihood of improvement in their lives. Why couldn't he have made a decent life for himself in Nestor, a better place? A place with trees, with grass, with clean(ish) water? Why couldn't he have gone the distance with Lenore, in that good house, on that good street?

(And now, at this moment, in the post office, as he stares at the postal inspector's badge, he wonders why he couldn't have made something worthwhile with Semma either, a woman who loved life, who loved living, whose life he might have saved had he been able to love life, to love living, to love her—and it occurs to him, as it did then, in Batya and Ivan's apartment, that the problem wasn't Nestor, it wasn't Semma; it wasn't Len Ronk or cats or Maurice Renault; it was him. And it further occurs to him that this isn't the first time this has occurred to him, and he wonders why these revelations never seem to sink in.)

He considered (back in Uchqubat, his dinner steaming before him) that he would be here two years, living in the same gray room, looking out over the same dead fields. Winter hadn't even begun. Siberia was all too close at hand, a place people were exiled to, as punishment for crimes. His stew, which he had set upon with gusto, began to seem a little bit bitter, a little rancid; he thought about the multiply frozen and thawed dog bone in the freezer and began to feel a little sick. He excused himself, found the bathroom and threw up, hoping that their lively conversation would prevent them from hearing. If they did hear, they gave no indication of it when he returned. He didn't eat any more, so Ivan ate what was left on his plate. Afterward he and Ivan and Batya drank vodka (it disgusted him at first; there was nothing good about it at all!, but after a few glasses he couldn't get enough, kept grabbing for the bottle and pouring more in, and when he couldn't seem to do it by himself anymore they did it for him).

He wouldn't remember leaving. He must have gotten lost,

because he found himself lying in a hallway with a pool of spit staining the hall carpet next to his face, and the hallway weaved and darted like a dragonfly. He looked at his watch: two-thirty. He must have slept here. How far had he walked? He didn't know where he was. The nearest stairwell brought him to an exit, which seemed to be quite far from his own front door, and so he staggered to the end of the apartment block, let himself in, climbed the stairs, found his room. He fell onto the bed. Got to find my alarm, he said to himself; it's around here somewhere . . . His hand moved across the bedclothes, into his backpack, and stayed there, limp, until morning.

He woke in his clothes at a quarter to nine, groping in the sheets in a panic for—it wasn't certain for what, something from a dream, a thing of immeasurable importance yet horrible to behold, scuttling away from him while he slept. Got up, fell back clutching his head, got up again. No time to change his clothes. He did have the presence of mind to check his pouch for the receipts, the ones for the grocery; he would let his class out early and go to the store, but he'd need a bag—he upended his not-yet-entirely-unpacked backpack, and everything fell out onto the floor, including a handwritten note on a torn-out piece of spiral notebook paper that had previously escaped his attention. *Dear Albert*, it began; *love, Marsha*, it ended, but the rest would have to wait. He jammed the note into his pocket, slung the bag over his shoulder and ran out the door. The street was still muddy but the sky bore a mist-dulled sun. The potential for shine existed. He ran without concern (well, with concern, but with no respect) for the hammering in his head; he realized halfway into town that he was still drunk and paused to vomit in front of a row of cottages. When he stood up wiping his mouth a set of curtains threw themselves shut in a darkened window. "Sorry, sorry," he muttered and continued running, now faster, since there was nothing in his stomach to lose. He arrived at the school building at five past nine, found his classroom, walked in.

They were there. All men, almost all in jeans, almost all wearing frayed oxford shirts and neckties and old running shoes. They wore beards. Some Russians, some Kazakhs, all with their dark hair combed, their eyes tired and alert. When he entered, they laughed—it would have been impossible not to, Mailman supposed—at the English teacher with his muddy pants and stained shirt (stained with stew and vomit and coffee and dog blood), and the empty backpack hanging agape off one shoulder. "Hello," he said, "hello, sorry I'm late, hello," having decided on the train days before that he would speak only English. It would be a tough-love kind of class, they would have to learn by doing. There was a buffet table set up in the front of the room and he leaned against this to catch his breath. The men waited, very polite, glancing at one another but not talking; they all had notebooks before them and pens or pencils in their hands. Mailman sloughed off his backpack and jacket, turned to the chalkboard, picked up a piece of chalk. He wrote his name on the board. He said "My," pointing to himself, "name," pointing to the name on the board, "is *Albert*," pointing to the name a second time, this time running the finger underneath it (Jesus Christ, his *head*), following the sounds of each letter. "*Albert*," he said again. Then he went over to the first man in the left-hand row and pointed at him and said, "*Your* name is . . ." and waited.

The man said, "Josef."

"Good! Now say, '*My name is Josef.*'"

The man looked around, shrugged. (These shrugs! Mailman thought.) "My name is Josef," he said quickly.

"All right! Good!" And now the next man. "Your name is . . ."

"Excuse me, Albert," said a voice. It was Josef's. Mailman was startled, he didn't quite know why, not yet. He said, "Yes? Josef?"

"English class is yesteryear. You learn us the entrepreneur, okay?"

Mailman stood straight, his weight on his heels. "Pardon me? You speak English."

"Everybody speak English. English class is yesteryear."

"I think you mean *last* year."

"Yes. Last year. Now you learn to us the entrepreneur skills."

He looked around. The men were nodding. English class was yes-teryear. "Oh," he said, "oh, I'm sorry, I get it—I'm in the wrong room. I have an English class to teach, I'm supposed to be teaching English, I must be in the wrong room. I'm sorry." He turned, grabbed his bag and jacket, retreated into the hallway. Sheesh!, he thought, walking down the dark empty hall, opening the doors of dark empty class-rooms, what an embarrassment, but it's hard to imagine things going smoothly, hard to plan what with the language barrier, the distance, to schedule one class in one room in a small town in the middle of nowhere, surely this thing happens all the time—

"Albert!"

—somewhere here is the place, he thought, and the hallway stretched around a corner and into blackness, into what appeared to be a completely empty building. "Where the hell's my classroom?" he said. "Where the hell's my class?"

"Albert!" It was Josef, behind him, standing by the door of Entrepreneur 101. "Albert, is no English class, only entrepreneur!"

"But I can't teach that!"

"Come back! You learn to us!"

"I can't!" He leaned against a wall, cinder blocks painted glossy green. Josef leaned back into the room for a moment, then emerged and came down the hall to him. He took tiny, quick steps on short chubby legs, pumping his arms as he approached. He touched Mailman's shoulder. "Is okay," he said, "you learn the entrepreneur, we listen. Come."

"I don't know anything about business, Josef. I can't tell you any-thing."

"You are American. You know something."

"I'm a mailman. I don't know anything."

"Mailman is important. Here we go." He led Mailman back into the room. The men were smiling. Josef positioned him behind the table and returned to his seat. "Okay," he said. "You stay. We listen."

But already—though he stood before them, facing them, as if he were about to speak—his mind was far ahead, following his future path, out the door and down the hall and out into the street and into downtown, where he would get his groceries and bring them home, and eat, and get on the phone (Batya never gave him a phone! All right, then he would go back to her apartment and get one) to Washington and tell them forget about the class, you screwed up, I'm going to the post office and that'll be the thing I do here, take it or leave it. And then he'd walk to the post office where he would set things in order. Yes. This is what he would do. He smiled at the future businessmen of Uchqubat. "I'm sorry, no. Someone else will come and teach your class. I'm sorry." And he swept out the door with Josef's voice following him: "Al-bert! Al-bert!"

And now there was a sting in the air, and now the clouds had moved aside in the distance, allowing rays of sun to penetrate all the way to the dead flat ground; and the glowing brown land backlit the cement structures of Uchqubat, and he was filled with . . . not optimism, but its emaciated cousin, its manic-depressive cousin from out of town, a thrilling electric positivity as ephemeral as it was bracing. Cold! Sun! Physical activity! And with the aborted class behind him he began to feel *in his element*—here he was, walking down a sidewalk (though it was no more than the side of the road, really, strewn with frozen mudpuddles); here he was carrying a bag (empty, yes, but not for long); here he was on his way, if not directly, to the post office. This is what he came here to do. Yes.

The grocery was open, his receipts were honored. He was given food, and it took only two hours. Before he stashed them in his bag he held his three tomatoes in his open palms. They were not good tomatoes, but they were recognizably that sweet fruit; they were brownish overall but actually red in places, dotted with the bore-holes of insects but not too many, deformed by pressure against the vine or by their own efforts to cover their wounds. (And it was impossible not to think of Nestor, of the Nestor Farmer's Market, those teetering stacks of round ripe red tomatoes that he had always found so pretentious, so self-consciously *outdoor-markety,* so disgusting in their smug abundance . . .) But they were tomatoes! He could chop them, freeze them, use them as sauce! And with dill! And salt! Both items he personally owned and could use as he wished!

He strode home and boiled a potato and ate it while his spaghetti was cooking and drained the cooked spaghetti and threw in a chopped tomato and some dill and cooked it for a while longer, and then ate that. Yes! Mealy, glutinous, but yes! Spaghetti with tomato sauce! And it was only now, sated for the first time in many days, that he noticed a telephone—of all things, a pink Princess telephone, the receiver cracked and repaired with black electrical tape—sitting on the edge of his sink, its cord connected to the wall outlet: Batya had come through! Yes, things were beginning to go his way!

The line, miraculously, was clear (the streak continues!), he called the help number in Washington, he told a bright-voiced young woman what had happened. She clucked with sympathy. She told him about how the same kind of thing had happened to her friend. She said that he, Mailman, couldn't imagine how complicated it all was, arranging these things, and errors like this cropped up from time to time, and that he, Mailman, should just get over to the P.O., ASAP, and she would get all this straightened out, and he shouldn't worry himself over these bureaucratic details. And so he shrugged on his jacket once more (he hoped—no, he was certain!—that the clothes he had shipped, the warm winter clothes, would be here soon) and briskly headed for the center of town and the Uchqubat post office. He was beginning to get the hang of this place: bleak, yes; cold, yes; but homey, sort of, in its own way: "Where do you live again?" "Uchqubat! Uchqubat, Kazakhstan!" "Come again?" "Uchqubat! Let me tell you, it's like no place you've ever seen!" "And you're saying you *live* there?" "You've got it!"

The P.O. still looked closed, the window was still boarded; nothing stirred behind the door's frosted glass window. People walking by on the street (and yes, there were people walking up and down the street here, almost like in a normal town) came up to the window, rapped on it, shrugged, moved on. For crying out loud, a Monday at noon, if the place wasn't open then, when would it be open? The middle of the night? The postmaster (or whatever they called them here) was supposed to be a man named Vasily, that's all he knew. So he too rapped on the boarded window and called out, "Vasily! Vasily!" There was no answer. He tried the door. Locked. Okay, okay, someone will be along shortly, and if they're not, well, it's that very attitude that has made it necessary for me to come and lend them a hand. There was a cinder block standing upright against the wall of the building, so Mailman sat down on it and rested his hands on his knees, and as he shifted around, trying to find a way to make this arrangement comfortable, he heard (and felt) a crackle against his right buttock and reached into his pocket and pulled out the crumpled letter that Marsha had left him at the bottom of his bag.

For a moment he held it between his fingers, reluctant to open it. The sky before him was clearing, the sun's streaming rays raking closer to the center of town (there, now: it had just touched the apartment building at the town's edge, his building; fully lit, it gave the impression of efficiency, of warmth; and Soviet-style architecture, for just a second, seemed eminently sensible and satisfying), but he felt that, if he opened the letter and read it, the sun's rays would somehow be diverted, that somehow they would fail to fall on him and he would grow colder (for already he had grown cold). *Don't*, a voice told him. But of course he did.

Dear Albert,

I know we promised to stay in touch but now I am having second thoughts about that. What we had together was wonderful and I don't know if I could have gotten through training without you. But now it is time to move on. I will always remember the feeling of being with you. I never felt so safe or happy. But now is not the time for safety in my life.

Don't try to find me or write letters. I will not write back.
I'm sorry if this makes you sad, but it is how it must be.
love,
Marsha.

And of course the sun reached him and fell upon him, and of course it warmed him, it was foolish to have imagined otherwise. But his euphoria was gone. Well, he thought, that's the way with euphoria, easy come, easy go. He stood up. His joints cracked and groaned as if he'd been sitting there for hours, though it had only been minutes. He turned and looked at the sad shack behind him and thought: I hate mail. I hate it, I never want to look at another piece again. He hated mail, and he hated people—yes, because people were the ones who sent mail.

"Vasily!" he shouted and rapped again on the board, and at last, in exasperation, *kicked* the metal door just under the knob, and the door swung open and *something*—something so substantial that it took him a second to realize that it was a *smell*, and not a visible thing, like smoke, or an animal—came tumbling out: a smell foul enough to cause Mailman to step back, into the street, where a stray rattling Lada nearly clipped him. "Jesus Christ!" he said, and a woman passing by glared at him, but then she smelled it herself and reeled back, and returned the way she came, her destination rendered meaningless by the stench. Mailman approached with caution, peeking in the open door, and saw, or thought he could see, a figure slumped in a metal chair, its head tipped back, its arm hanging down over the side, bloated and blackened from shoulder to fingertips, and now (as he moved to the right, so that a rack of cubbies—much like the ones that surrounded his carrier station at home—no longer obscured his view of the body) he could see the feet, ah!, the feet were moving—but no, those weren't the feet moving, those were the rats that were gnawing upon them, their tiny claws scrabbling in the black pool of dried blood, and he saw now that Postmaster Vasily was dead, and had obviously been dead for some time.

What in the hell kind of place was this, that the postmaster could be dead, the office closed, presumably for days, and nobody would do anything about it? The kind of town where nobody expects to get any mail, he guessed. The P.O. had a sort of force field of reek around it now into which no one was willing to venture, though there were quite a few people on its perimeter, trying to catch a glimpse of the dead body. Mailman turned to the man beside him—a pale man in a shirt and tie and running shoes! One of his would-be students?—and said, in Russian, "Call the police!" This is one of the first phrases they were taught: "Call the police!" But the man only raised his eyebrows.

Soon enough the police did come, and an ambulance, and the body was hauled away on a stretcher and Mailman in the back of a police car. There were three cops, each of them wearing a slightly different uniform, as if the uniforms had been bought piecemeal, from different manufacturers, at different times. One of the three rode in back, with Mailman. Nobody said anything. At the police station they examined his passport, asked him why he had broken into the post office. They were slumped in their chairs or had their chins propped on their hands, as if nothing could possibly be more boring. And nothing could. By four he was discharged, by four-thirty he was back in his apartment, and the sunshine had vanished and it had begun to snow. When he picked up the phone, it was dead.

Please, he moaned into his pillow, *please!,* but he stopped when it became clear that there was no one to beg to, not even God, to whom, admittedly, he had never paid much attention. At least back in the psych ward there was Lenore. Here, there was only him, Mailman, a warm speck on the cold world that had been so indifferent to him in spite of the passion with which he had loved and hated it. Enraged, he rose from the bed, threw open the door, stalked outside and around back of the building and tramped into the empty field, now grayed over with the not-quite-white (for everything here was tainted by the oil fields) snow; he crashed and ripped through the dead summer grasses out to where the earth's skin was at its thinnest, where he thought he could feel its mantle mere inches from his own flesh, and he kicked at it and pounded it with his fists. *Damn you to hell! Damn you to hell, you fucking piece of shit!* He dug divots with the toes of his boots—these *stupid boots* he had paid so much for, because the stupid handbook *told him to*—and sunk his bloody fingernails into the worthless soil . . . Yes, it did feel good to let it all hang out like this, but nothing had changed; it was still him, Mailman, a speck of hot ash alighting on the tundra of existence. And he wasn't even Mailman anymore; he wasn't even *a* mailman. He was a man, nothing else, and where was the dignity in that?

Maybe he would have frozen to death out there if young Viktor hadn't seen him from the bedroom window and brought his mother out to check. The two of them came, narrow figures leaning into the wind, their eyes squinting against the giant poison snowflakes, and here they were: "Albert, it is cold."

"Yes."

"You come inside. Drink coffee."

"Yes, all right."

"Okay? You come now."

"Please," he said, and stuck his hand up at them; ungloved, filthy and blotched, it looked like a rock. "Please, help me up."

It was their phone he used to call Washington, and then the airline in Almaty. He told Batya he would pay them for the calls, he would send money, but he never did remember, and they moved away, he supposed, to Canada. He never saw them again, never even learned their last name.

Four days later he was home: home to Nestor, the palm of God; home to a cold and empty house that was more or less the way he left it, except maybe cleaner. Lenore had seen to that. The door to the mail room had remained locked. McChesney, the cat, still unadopted (Lenore had not quite yet seen to *that*), rubbed itself against him: this wasteful swath of life, writhing and darting. Barely three weeks had passed. October had arrived, the leaves were changing, and he'd be here for the goddam election after all (how could he take seriously a government with money enough to burn to send people like him to places like the one he'd gone to?), and the World Series too. Not that he cared. He dumped his things in his bedroom and lay down and slept for several hours. Then he got up, got into his car, and drove to the grocery store. It was night, but things in America were open at night. He parked (there were plenty of spaces), walked in the door (which opened for him, automatically). Warm air blew down upon him from overhead fans. Before him were bleachersful of fresh produce—apples, pears (for this was autumn), but also strawberries, raspberries, blackberries, kiwi fruit, watermelon, oranges and grapefruits and tangerines and tangelos and clementines and kumquats and citrons and lemons. Astonished, appalled, he retreated with his basket into the foyer, where snow shovels, ice melter, plastic toboggans were already for sale. He stood for a moment with his eyes closed—"Excuse me," said a man choosing a shopping cart—and breathed the mechanically recirculated air. He went back in. He walked to the cereal aisle: that's all he would need for now, cereal. Milk. Just those two things and he could leave. He walked up and down the cereal aisle, intending only to grab an appealing box and move on, but all of them looked so good: the loops, the flakes, the clusters, the nuggets, the tiny square lattices of oat or corn or rice, sugared or natural or with a touch of honey or with the goodness baked right in, or banana-flavored or banana-*bread*-flavored, crunchy and crispy in or out of milk, or fortified with eight essential vitamins and minerals, or with nine, or with twelve essential vitamins and minerals, or high in fiber or folate or niacin or bran, or with pieces of date, or with raisins or cranberries or blueberries or raspberries, in economy size or family size or regular or in single-serving boxes of eight, all shrink-wrapped together; name brands at normal prices or store brands at lower prices or generic plastic sacks at rock-bottom prices, or the ones that were two for the price of one, or the ones with toys inside or health booklets or contest entries or board games or puzzles or mazes or quizzes; the ones that promised an energy boost, or lower cholesterol, or lower blood pressure, or a healthy fetus, or a longer life; the ones up high for adults to buy, the ones down low for children to beg for, and behind him the hot ones, the instant ones, the one-minute ones, the five-minute ones, the cereal bars, the granola bars, the breakfast bars, the instant breakfasts, with pockets of fruit or creamy fruit or fruity centers or chewy-in-the-middle or crunchy-on-the-outside or good-anytime or the-kids-will-love-it or all-of-the-flavor-none-of-the-guilt or who-said-good-nutrition-took-time or good-on-the-go or great-on-the-run or perfect-in-the-car or at-home-at-work-or-on-the-road! And before him, directly before him, yellow-tagged for shopper's club members at a special one-time-only price, stood a white box that showed the cereal (in the form of flakes) cascading from an unseen source into a white bowl with a blue rim (and how light it looked! and how liberating! and how wholesome! and how delicious!) and below the bowl a computer-generated blue shadow, the barest smear of shadow that registered on the invisible surface (a counter, you would guess: a perfectly clean, bleached-white, unpitted, unscratched, ungouged countertop that only a professional, eight-dollars-an-hour, live-in cleaning person could maintain), and at the very top, the cereal's name in plain blue serif caps,

SERENITY

A CEREAL FOR WOMEN.

Serenity, he thought, a *cereal* for women. A cereal *for women*. Specially formulated for a woman's needs, promoting a healthy lifestyle, strong bones, the vitamins and minerals a woman needs. At work, at home, at play, Serenity is the cereal *for a woman's busy day*. He held the box in his hands, his man's hands, dark and blemished (the fingernails still dirty from the ground he clawed at days before) against the pristine white cardboard. The *cereal* for a woman's *busy day*. This is not cereal that a man could buy. This is cereal for *only half* the world's inhabitants. Yes! He understood! A cereal for women! The quietest laugh escaped him—really, you would have had to stand right next to him to hear it—and then a series of giggles, still quiet, still imperceptible, as were the tiny tears forming at the corners of his eyes which, as the eyes squeezed shut, began to fall, began to roll ever-so-slowly down his face, which, if you looked very closely, you might notice was sort of quivering. Yes: something was happening to Mailman, something had hold of him; it would not have been clear, just from watching him, what it was. And the longer you looked, really, the less clear it would have been. You might have seen the box begin to bend and wrinkle in his hands; you might have seen that box begin to sully and fur under his damp thumbs. You might have noticed his legs bending slightly at the knees. And if you walked into the cereal aisle just moments later—for that was all it took for this emotion, this nameless thing that had not been born in this country, to fully take hold—if you had approached then, you would have seen a grown man *trembling* in the cereal aisle, *crushing* a box of cereal and (could it be?) *crying!*, crying in the grocery store!, and you would have pulled your child or children close and kind of sidled around him, perhaps on your way to notify a store manager that some nut was crying in the cereal aisle and crushing a perfectly good, unpaid-for box of cereal, you just thought he ought to know.

As for Mailman, the figure on the tiled floor (not gray tiles, by the way, but gleaming white ones, mopped hourly), the other customers had stopped existing for him as this terrible fit exhausted itself, this fit of giggles and sobs and shudders, which led to a managerial escort through the automatic doors and into the parking lot, with a muttered request not to return, upon pain of repeated ejection and the involvement of the police, got it? Mailman nodded that he had got it, but the

fit wasn't over. It continued in his car, which he sat in for long minutes, engine running. He laughed, laughed, choked on his terrible
laughter, until at last it was done and he pulled out of the parking lot.
Where did Mailman buy his groceries that night? At the gas station.
There was plenty for him there, plenty for anyone who could afford it.

The next morning—a clear morning, the air fresh, the yellow and
orange and red maples dripping with pure, unadulterated upstate-
New-York rainwater—he called Len Ronk and begged for his job back.
He told Len Ronk that he was sorry; that he, Mailman, had been an
efficient, dedicated postal employee for half his, Mailman's, life, and
that he deserved another chance. (If it was possible to hear a grin
forming on Len Ronk's face, a grin of chagrin, of recrimination, of
deep, bitter satisfaction, then that is indeed what Mailman heard.) He
told Len Ronk that he, Mailman, knew that he, Len Ronk, didn't like
dealing with PTF's and that he, Mailman, was a known element, a
sure thing, and despite their, Len Ronk's and Mailman's, history of
conflict, he, Len Ronk, had to admit that he missed him, Mailman.

"The Sam Hill I do," said Len Ronk, and hung up.

But it was all right. The seeds were planted. He'd keep on it—
Ronk was a pushover, that's why he'd been chosen as a carrier supervisor. It might take time, but Mailman would be restored to his
rightful occupation. Until then, however, he would need something to
pay the bills, for he was not willing to touch his nest egg, and his
odds-and-ends account had been emptied for the purpose of buying
waterproof boots, a winter coat, Thinsulate™ gloves and woolen
socks, all of which he had had shipped to an address he was no longer
at, and which he was unlikely ever to see again. And so he picked up
that morning's *Nestor News* and perused, for perhaps the first time
ever, the want ads. What wouldn't he mind being? A librarian? A fry
cook? He'd never much thought about it; the switch from physics to
mail delivery was immediate and there had not been any reason to
generate a backup plan. Almost all the jobs were menial (hospital
orderly, assembly line worker, delivery van driver) or required elabo-

rate sets of skills and qualifications (professor of art history, mechanical engineer, surgeon); the ones that didn't fit into either category he circled with a pen. They numbered three. Of the three, only one gave a phone number (he suspected the others were out of town), and so he called it.

"Hello, Parking."

"Hi," he said. "I saw your ad for a parking patrolman. I want the job."

"Send us a cover letter and résumé."

"I'll do one better. I'll bring it up to you, today. How about that?"

"Suit yourself."

"Where are you?"

"Nestor College," she said, and gave him a building and room number. "Don't try to park in the visitor parking, that's for admissions. Don't park in the Blue Lot. The Red Lot is faculty, the Blue is student. You need a pass. You park in the Green Lot. You'll have to walk down to us from the Green Lot."

He spent the entire morning at the public library (this was before he was banned), first studying a book on writing a résumé, then waiting for a computer, then using it, then realizing he had screwed up, then waiting in line again, and then using the computer a second time. The result was what seemed like a solid effort, simple and direct and neat. He left the library, removed the parking ticket from his car and shoved it in the glovebox, then drove up the hill to Nestor College.

Nestor College seemed to consist primarily of parking lots. The center of campus was not a wooded grove, not a grassy quad, but a gigantic parking lot, the Yellow Lot (permit required); around it stood the campus buildings, postmodern pink-granite wedges recently built, in and out of which no one seemed to pass. After memorizing a roadside campus map he navigated the Escort down a series of narrow streets which wound through parking lot after parking lot, until he came to the final lot, a swath of asphalt planted in a scrubby wood: the Green Lot. Indeed, it was very far from Kings Hall, where the parking office was. He walked. It was all downhill and hard on his knees; the fall air was crisp, though, the trees half denuded, the smell of the leaves excellent. You could see the lake from here. On his way he found a stray sheet of paper lying on the ground. Presumably it had blown here from the stadium: it was a copy of the Nestor College fight song.

Nestor College Fight Song

P. Magus   1977

Nes - tor, Nes - tor a col - lege on a hill! Clear - ly best a - mong oth - ers of its ilk! Hail to our big bro - ther a - cross the way! We sat to you to - day, Hoo - ray! Watch us as we wipe out foes a - way! Nes - tor, Nes - tor, figh - ting to the last! Nun - ber one a - mong oth - ers in its class! Foun - ded be - side the old saw mill, Now we re - side on old South Hill. For cour - age and for skill! (Hoo - ray! Hoo - ray!) For our un - dy - ing will! (Hoo - ray! Hoo - ray!) For good or ill, we are a col - ege still.

It seemed a bit defeatist to Mailman, for a fight song. He knew the tune, he'd heard it now and then, on the Nestor College radio station (which broadcast mostly sneering rock songs and free-form jazz records that always skipped), and so he sang it, keeping time with his footsteps, the rubber making a satisfying rhythmic *whack* against the pavement (intact pavement! with no mud on it!). By the time he got to Kings Hall he knew the thing by heart.

The office in question was easy to find, it was just inside the front door. He handed over the résumé, expecting to leave immediately, but instead the receptionist told him to sit down and went somewhere out of sight to speak in low tones with another woman. While he tried unsuccessfully to make out what they were saying, he squirmed in an uncomfortable upholstered chair and glanced about, reading the posters hung on the walls. STD's ARE YOUR PROBLEM! said one. The accompanying photo was of a dark-skinned girl with her arms crossed and a scowl on her face, and beneath her it read, in English and Spanish, *He promised that he loved you. He said he didn't have one. It was somebody else's problem. Now it's your problem. See your school health official for information about preventing the spread of HIV and other diseases.* Beside it was a poster for a dance, hastily tacked up, he supposed, by a student and likely to be torn down by the receptionist once she noticed it: TOTAL MAYHEM RAVE BLOWOUT DANCE PARTY BOYS BRING YOUR BALLS BABES BRING YOUR BOOTY AND SHAKE IT TILL IT HURTS $5 COVER FIRST TWO DRINKS FREE HOT NIGHT WITH DJ CRASH MASTER GASH!

"Mister Lippincott?" It was a narrow head, peeking around the corner, a woman's, pretty face if a bit severe, no smile on her mouth but one in her eyes, or so it seemed. The head withdrew and he followed it; it turned out to be attached to a large bunchy body clad in extremely clean dark blue jeans, pumps, and a purple turtleneck sweater knitted in a "popcorn" pattern. "Hiiii," she said, letting out breath with the vowel, "Dana Pehhhters, glad to mehhht you, sit down, this is an ihhhnteresting résumé." Dana Peters's office was very tiny, more like a hallway, barely five feet wide, a desk and two chairs jammed into the far end. When they had sat down, she said, "So tehhhll me, Mister Lippincott, why did you leahhhve the post office?"

"I quit."

"I sehh."

Silence filled the room. Unbidden, the words were drawn out of him. "I tried to join the Peace Corps, but that didn't work out."

"The Peahhhce Corps, I sehhh, tell me more about that."

Haltingly he told her of the problems he encountered in Kazakhstan, the misscheduled class, the dead postmaster, the grim apartment. She nodded and nodded again: in fact nodded continuously as he spoke, no matter what he was saying.

"Would you sahhhy that you're an organized kind of pehhhrson?"

"Yes."

Nodding. Nodding. He couldn't stop himself; he went on: "Very much so. Obsessively, even. Don't like a thing out of place."

"I sehhhhhh," she said, touching her mouth with two fingers, seeming to stretch out the word as if it were a piece of taffy. "Yehhhs. And you did a lot of drihhhving at the post office?"

"Yes."

"Yehhhs." Nodding. This time he didn't fall for it. The fight song sprang into his head. *For good or for ill, we are a college still!* He tapped his foot.

"Wehhhlll, Mister Lippincott, I must hhhadmit that we are having trouble finding a suitable parking officer. Why don't I just check your rehhhferences and get back to you?"

"Ah. Okay. Sure."

"If we hihhhre you, can you start immediately?"

"Yes!"

"Yehhhs, all right then, thank you."

He thought that when he got home the phone would be ringing, but it wasn't, and he waited all afternoon, until five, and then went out for a cup of coffee (More Coffee! did not yet exist; the space was still a chiropractor's office) at the bagel shop, where the coffee was not good but there was always a place to sit, and he drank it, and then ordered a sandwich and another coffee (he handed the clerk his empty cup so that she would pour the new coffee into the old cup but she merely said "Thanks," tossed the cup into the trash and poured his coffee into a fresh cup: "I gave you that so you would reuse it," he said, and she said "Oh, no, that's okay, you can have a new one, they're just cups" and he said "But I didn't want a new cup, why waste a cup is my point" and she said "It's just a *cup*, Jesus Christ" and he said "Oh, just forget it," and she shrugged and dumped the fresh coffee into the sink), but he could only eat half the sandwich because he became convinced—the clerk had talked to the sandwich guy in low tones while he was making the sandwich, no doubt on the subject of their altercation—that she or the sandwich guy had spit in the sandwich, a suspicion that was only strengthened when he lifted up the bread to put this concern to rest and found that the smear of mayo, at its near-frothy perimeter, was almost indistinguishable from human saliva. But he was hungry, and so while he ate it he thought about himself out in a remote meadow picking a fresh untainted apple from a lone tree and eating *that*. But in the end matter triumphed over mind, as it always did, and he left the half-eaten sandwich on his table.

When he got home his phone really was ringing, even though it was nearly seven at this point. "Ahhhlbert, it's Danahhh, at N.C. Sorry to call so late, I'm at hohhhme now but I wanted you to know that the job is youhhhrs if you want it."

"Yes! Definitely!" he said.

"Well goohhhd. Report to me tomorrow morning at eighhhht. We have nobody at ahhhll on the job right now."

And so in the morning he drove to Nestor College loudly singing its fight song, and parked in the Green Lot and made the long trek down to Kings, where he spent half an hour filling out forms, which he exchanged for a slip of paper to give to the guy who was supposed to give him his uniform. He brought it to a dark supply shed on the northern edge of campus. The uniform was a faux-police kind of thing, with epaulets, and embroidery that read NESTOR COLLEGE PARKING AUTHORITY, and a sort of heraldic crest consisting of a little car with a flashing light and a halo of wheat around it. The pants were too big in the waist but had a Boy-Scout-uniform-style fabric belt with friction-activated buckle, which he cinched tight. Then he went to the garage to pick up the car he would be driving. It was an Escort, the same year as his own, white with a flashing light on top (not at this moment flashing) and the Nestor College Fightin' Stevedore on the hood and the Park-ing Authority crest on each door. All along the lower edge of the body and in the tire wells the paint had rusted away, and one of the tires was slightly flat. He was given the key and directed toward the gas pump, around back, and he pumped the car full of gas and the tires full of air (carefully using the pressure gauge hanging there from a piece of twine tied to a nail). He drove back to Kings Hall, parked in the COLLEGE OFFICIAL ONLY space (why not?) and went in to show Dana how he looked in his uniform. "My Gohhhd, what are you doing here, it's nine-thihhhrty! You're supposed to be writing tihhhckets!" He told her he hadn't gotten a ticket book, nor had she told him what precisely he was supposed to be doing, and she sighed, found him a half-empty ticket book, told him to go look for cars that didn't have the correct passes for the lots they were parked in, he would find the passes hang-ing from the rearview mirrors. Put the tickets under the windshield wiper and give the copies to her. Go home at six.

"Do I get a lunch break?"

"Yehhhs, but stay off campus and use your own cahhhr. It's a sehhhcret. We don't want the students to know that you leahhhve."

And so all morning, over and over, he drove down every row of all seventeen of the Nestor College lots, checking the parking passes; and when he saw one that was out of place he gave it a ticket. Nobody demanded anything of him and he ran the flashing lights all day long. There was nothing to think about; he strove to keep his mind off fantasies of sex (ticketing car, coed driver approaches, pleads poverty; M. tears up ticket in exchange for quick screw in back seat), humiliation, and shame (stains uniform with ketchup, seat of pants rips, Dana loudly fires him in front of campus tour group). At lunchtime he went to the gas station down the road and ate a slice of cheese pizza and read a copy of the campus paper. MECHANICS STUMP STEVEDORES. THE-ATER PRODUCTION IS BIG SUCCESS. NEW NURSE AT INFIRMARY. HALLOWEEN PUMPKINS SMASHED. He listened to talk radio, picked his nose, talked to himself, thought long thoughts. He wondered if Dana was married (nude? bed? sex? cats? dammit, get those cats out of there) and, if so, was her husband also bunchy of body, or do opposites really attract? A person with more presence of mind than he would have noticed whether or not she was wearing a ring. On the way back to campus he took note of the turning of the leaves, the browning of the grass, the amplification of election rhetoric (nah, scratch that), the suddenly urgent songs of the birds, and he wondered why he hadn't thought to do something like this years ago, why he'd stuck with the P.O. for so damned long; he decided he would have to call Ronk and tell him forget it, he didn't want his job back after all. This was just his speed.

Ten minutes later he found a beat-up jeep covered with bumper stickers advertising rock bands (if indeed that's what GOAT BOX, LEER-ING MIDGETS, THUNDERBRA, and CRUMB were, God only knew what else they could be) parked pretty much diagonally in the handicapped space in front of the student union, and he pulled in behind it and got out his ticket book and wrote down the license number. Then he went around the front to tuck the ticket underneath the windshield wiper.

"Dude! Dude!" Here came the owner, jogging toward him down the cracked cement path from the union, waving his hands in the air. It was the jog that got to Mailman: so *casual*, so *assured*, as if the *jog alone* were going to set everything right: as if this jog could convey a secret solidarity between its executor and Mailman, as if they were both members of a special rule-bending club and now that the official club jog had been performed everything would be okay. Goddam flare-pant-wearing so-called "scholars." Mailman ignored him and tucked the ticket under the wiper.

"Hey, *dude*, I'm back, it's okay, man." The kid was beside him now, panting gently (though unnecessarily: for surely the panting was a put-on, there was no way a twenty-year-old boy could become *winded* jogging the thirty feet from the student union; the only purpose for such a thing must have been to *inform* Mailman of the *gargantuan effort* that had been undertaken in the name of *minimizing* the amount of time the rules would be broken); Mailman could smell pizza on him (for that's all they ate in there—or was that his own pizza smell, from the pizza *he* just ate?) and the oily reek that was coming from his hair, which was long, and long-unwashed.

"Sorry," Mailman said, turning, and the kid's eyes were big and mock-earnest, because in his mind they were still pals. Now those eyes narrowed slightly: yes, the kid was offended!

"Dude, I'm *back*. It was only like a minute. Here I am, I'm taking off, here, you don't need this," and he plucked the ticket from the windshield and handed it to Mailman.

"Sorry, that's yours, it doesn't matter if you're here or not, I have to give you a ticket."

"Dude, it was like *one minute*. I was in there like *one minute*."

"It took me twice that long to write the ticket."

"What*ever*, what I'm saying is that it was like a *minute*, like it was *nothing*, it's stupid to give me a ticket for that." Now his hands were on his hips, chest out, he'd given up the panting and was beginning to get pissed.

"You can't park here if you don't have a handicapped pass."

"Aw, come *on*," the kid said, swinging his arms, looking behind him for some ally, some witness to this injustice: "And I guess you *actually saw* a like handicapped person driving by who couldn't get a space? I guess you've *ever seen* a handicapped person parking anywhere on this campus?"

"Sure." A lie.

"Aw, fuck it, take the ticket, I'm leaving." He tossed the ticket in Mailman's direction, walked around him, opened the door of his jeep, climbed in, revved the engine, and did a kind of jerky, eight-or-nine-point turn to avoid smashing into the parking authority car.

"If you don't pay," Mailman shouted over the squealing of the tires, "you won't graduate!"

The kid idled the engine and leaned out the window. "And so what if I don't? I don't need to graduate. I made more selling shit on the Internet this year than you made driving around in your stupid pig suit. Ya pansy." He pulled forward, barely missing the handicapped parking sign, drove up onto the sidewalk and grass (two girls, dolled up in designer sweatshirts and custom-distressed jeans, moved out of the way, and when he'd passed them one said "Jerk" and the other said "Yeah" but then the first one turned around and said "Cute" and the other giggled and said "Yeah" so they both turned around and gave him the finger and said "Jerk!" and he honked and waved, and they giggled some more) and out of the parking lot entirely. Mailman was left holding the ticket book; the ticket he'd written drifted across the pavement. Christalfuckinmighty, where was the gratitude, the appreciation for getting to live in the richest country on earth, the amazement at the enormous bounty of the American educational experience? The little bastard! And bastard was right!: to kids like that there were no parents, no authorities, no clue that anybody who came before them had to strive, work, suffer, fight, or die so that they could sit around in their dorm rooms drinking beer and playing Super Mario Brothers all day long! Little fuckers! Complaining to the dean because their Nazi slavedriver professor gave 'em a B-minus! Picketing the provost's office over the school alcohol policy! To the two girls passing he said, "There's nothing *cute* about breaking the rules!" And the two of them flinched, gave him a wide berth, and one looked back and said "You better watch it," and he said "Watch what?" and she said "Watch the way you talk, or we'll report you and you'll be out of a *job*," and he said, "Report me for what? For trying to do what I'm hired to do? For trying to bring some order to this stupid hole of a college?" "Look who's talking," said the other girl, "at least we're *going* to the stupid college, you just *work* for it." They walked away with their backpacks slung over one shoulder, as if the books the backpacks contained were *just books*, this entire educational experience *just college*, the whole big mess of action and reaction, pleasure and pain, love and hate and sex and death *just life*, it's *just life*, geez, don't be such a *jerk* about it. "I *am* a jerk!" he muttered. "So I'm a jerk, so what! At least I'm something! At least I have something to be! Little fucks! Spoiled little rich fucks! I'll fucking kill 'em all!" And he got back into his patrol car and slammed the door shut and tore off through the parking lot. "I quit," he said, racing through the rows of BMWs and Mercedeses and SUVs and Volvos, "I give up, the little shits," and he even went so far as to pull up in front of the registrar's office and sit stewing there for a couple of minutes. But he didn't quit. He didn't. Instead he got his old job back: kept calling Ronk, kept begging to be put back on his route, kept calling up the people he'd worked with for years and asking them to tell Ronk to please hire Albert back, until at last Ronk capitulated and put him on the job as a PTF until the guy who'd gotten his old route retired a few months later and Mailman—because none of the other carriers would dare swipe the route out from under him, even though it was technically their right—got it back.

But he shouldn't have. He knew it within weeks of starting up again, delivering mail. Opening it. Reading it. They weren't his friends, these correspondents. Thomas Effening, Jodie Steiner, Mark Poll. Saul Bean, Kelly Vireo. He didn't know them, only their penmanship, their habits of punctuation. He knew their saddest, most confessional selves: the lech, the slut, the delinquent. The stalker, the nut. Like characters in a book: but no, not even that. They were nothing but their own myths of themselves, shambling golems mounded together out of fear, out of self-loathing and arrogance and delusion and lust. And animated by a stamp.

They weren't his friends. But as long as he delivered the mail, they were enough.

He should have stayed quit. He quit for a reason, after all: he could sense it coming. And now, at the end of a heavy arm, gripped in hairy fingers, here it is. UNITED STATES POSTAL INSPECTORS.

The badge is lowered, stowed in a pocket. "Sir," the inspector says a second time, "You'll have to come with us."

"Hell no," he'd like to say, but of course he doesn't. He says "All right," and puts down what he's doing and follows.

SIX

Inquisition

—

They lead him not to Ronk's office but, like an oversized package, through the loading bay door and down the unlit concrete steps to a windowless USPS truck idling in a corner of the parking lot. "Where're we going?" he asks, and the one with the stubble says, "Shut up." "Syracuse," says the other one and then the first one says "Shut up!" to the one who said "Syracuse." "Sor-*ree*" is the reply. They're typical schlubs, sideburned, thick around the middle where the shirt buttons threaten to pop, cell phone holsters clipped to their belts and aviator sunglasses obscuring their eyes. The one who said "Syracuse" is short and has a bulbous nose with one nostril pinched and the other unusually wide; the one who said "Shut up" is taller (though you wouldn't call him tall), with jowls that curtain a narrow square head. Now Shut-up tells Syracuse to open the back, and this is what Syracuse does, unlocks the sliding door and hoists it up, for this is your standard mail truck except that instead of the usual shelves and bags of mail inside, there are upholstered benches bolted to the floor.

"What, I'm sitting in there?" Mailman says.

Syracuse says, "Uh, yeah?"

"But there aren't any windows," says Mailman, and Syracuse says "Yeah, sorry about that," giving him a little push on the small of the back. Mailman climbs in. It is just barely possible to stand up straight in here. "What is this all about?" he says. "What do you think I did?"

"Ask me later," says Syracuse, and from the front seats, muffled by the wall, comes Shut-up's voice:

"Quit talking to him!"

"Sorry!" shouts Syracuse, and then to Mailman says, "You heard him."

"*Quit talking!*"

"Sor-*ree!*" Syracuse screams and then mutters, "Jay-Cee in a sidecar."

"Nice guy," Mailman says.

"Shut up," says Syracuse.

"Shut *up!*" yells Shut-up.

Syracuse rolls the door down and Mailman hears it latch. He sits on one of the benches. The truck rumbles out of the parking lot (or so it seems) and onto Airport Road and east onto the highway. For a few minutes Mailman leans forward, listening for clues; he hears them discussing the possibility of a shortcut, Syracuse seeming to suggest they should turn off here, Shut-up telling him that isn't the way, Syracuse saying but it's a shortcut and Shut-up telling him to shut up. Syracuse says "Do you have to smoke those things?" and Shut-up says "You oughta try 'em, it'd shut you up for a goddam minute," and Syracuse says "And you could tone down the language too, if you don't mind," and Shut-up says, "Goddam, goddam, goddam." Mailman settles back in his seat and prepares himself for the hour-and-change of solitary confinement and likely series of humiliations that will begin the moment they let him out.

He spreads his arms over the back of the seat (ouch—the tenderness under his arm has not been lessened by this morning's five aspirin, and he realizes that he doesn't have the stuff with him, there is some in his car but none on his person, though a fat lot of good it seems to be doing him) and takes in his surroundings. There isn't much to take in. Bare walls (dented and scraped), bare floor (patterned no-slip rubber), bare ceiling. An overhead light that might illuminate an oven, but not a mail truck. His heart seems to hiccup in anticipation of panic. Stay calm. Stay calm. To his left a graffito reads THE GOVT KILLD MY WIFE.

What are they going to accuse him of? Surely they don't know about his little operation? Kelly Vireo has told them something—about Jared Sprain's letter, of course: that he shoved it into the box at something like midnight (it seems so long ago, that terrible night, though it's only been a few days: all that's left is this idiotic wound, this lump, which must be infected, or perhaps there's some kind of hematoma or something: better go see a doctor, though the only doctor he'd consider going to is Frank, because he never charges anything, except ever since the fake physical and the exchange about sex he's been too embarrassed to call). Maybe the letter's gone to Washington for lab work, maybe they tested the inks, the prints, the fibers, looking for his DNA in places it shouldn't be, for the pattern of his kitchen knife on the torn edges of the paper.

Nah—he's heard stories about mail that has been delayed months, years, decades by some quirk in the system: a forgotten sack of letters left in a supply closet; squirrels who lined their nests with wedding invitations; a draft notice stuck between floors in an apartment building mail chute; tax refunds that blew out of a carrier's sack and off a bridge and into a river, later discovered washed up on shore hundreds of miles away, dried by the sun, faded but negotiable, and delivered. And when people receive these long-lost letters, is it a tragedy? Are investigations opened? Are inquiries made? No! Celebratory newspaper articles are written, the Postal Service is lauded for its dedication, its respect for every single piece of mail! And so the Sprain letter will be passed on, and it will give the Sprain family solace, and all will be well.

Unless the feds analyzed it after all. Maybe they found a hair, a scrap of skin. Maybe they got a warrant to search his house: maybe this morning they staked it out, waiting for him to leave, and when he did they went in and broke through the mail room door (or just walked through, actually, for he didn't ordinarily lock it) and discovered everything, the equipment, the archive, all of it, and radioed to Syracuse and Shut-up: "We got him, boys—bring him in!" They are there now: rooting in his underthings, frightening the cats, loading his files into the evidence van. The case is open-and-shut. They'll lead him from the truck directly into jail, where he'll await his trial. "What do you have to say for yourself?" demands the judge. "I throw myself upon the mercy of the court," Mailman whispers. Down comes the gavel! Guilty! Guilty!

No, that's stupid, they're just going to grill him and let him go. But how is he going to get home? Will they drive him back? And what about his union steward? His union steward is supposed to be present at any kind of questioning, but Mailman cannot see how that's going to work, when his union steward is at this moment sitting at his desk blithely eating an Egg McMuffin and reading (his very own personally subscribed-to copy of) *Sports Illustrated*, unaware that one of his charges has been whisked away by cell-phone-toting thugs. There's a line you're supposed to use—I demand to see my union representative?—or is it I request the presence of— I demand that my— I refuse to . . . or something, anyway, that he'll enunciate loudly when the door is opened, and the two of them will have to throw in the towel and probably bring him all the way back to Nestor so that his union representative can be present. Oh, that'll be a fine moment: he tries to cross his arms in order to create a physical confidence, to accompany and enhance his mental confidence, but what with the lump around his rib area he's not completely able to do it.

And now he notices that it's rather hot in here, it being June outside and sunny, with said sun beating down on this metal truck running over a black length of highway—and he has begun to sweat, on the forehead and underarms and in the crotch. Thank God he put on shorts this morning. He spreads his legs a little to give the *cojones* breathing room: that's better. He returns his arms to the seatback, and he draws one, now two, now three deep breaths of the stale, metallic air, redolent not only of his own nervous sweat but of the nervous sweat of a whole generation of apprehended postal carriers. The breaths fail to clear his head. He takes involuntarily to panting.

And this lump. It ought to be checked out. Not by a doctor, necessarily, but by him, now. There will be plenty of time; Syracuse (the city, not the guy) remains far away, forty minutes at least. Funny, he always imagined it would be Elmira. He unbuttons his short-sleeved chambray USPS work shirt and shrugs it off and folds it onto the seat beside him. There—that feels nice. The sweat is evaporating. It's hard to get a really good look at the lump in this light, but he can make it out if he concentrates. It's really not as jarring to look at as it feels: like a little pitcher's mound, the gentlest arc. He cups it in his right hand—a bit of tenderness there, careful!—and it reminds him of the first bare breast he felt at seventeen, it belonged to a girl named Gina who went to his high school in Princeton, a professor's kid like him; he'd kissed her a couple of times or rather she him, for he had been too nervous to perform the initial pucker-and-lean. After a few nights of smooching in various wooded or otherwise shadowed areas, they found themselves in her parents' wine cellar while a grad student party droned on upstairs; they were all talking about Gary Powers, shot down that day over Russia. "What if they come down for more wine?" he whispered, but she laughed and said "They don't waste *this* wine on *students*"—and it was then that he said to her "Can I, uh, feel your breasts?" and she said sure and unbuttoned her blouse and unlatched her bra and exposed herself to him (they were wide, flat, and to him very surprising, for they did not look like the breasts of the women in pornographic magazines) with what appeared complete self-assurance, and he said "Oh, my God!" and felt her up for what seemed like six hours but couldn't really have been more than fifteen minutes. That's all the further it went though, when his hands wandered she pried them off her. Not unlike Semma, actually, giving and withholding at once, as if, were he to take it all, she would have nothing left.

Sitting here in the back of the truck with no shirt on, feeling his own swollen painful area, he has to admit he's a little bit turned on—he remembers the juvenile conviction that, if he were a girl, he'd just feel his own breasts all day long—until he begins to probe the lump with his pointer and index fingers and discovers that it seems to have a kind of deep *root* that snakes down between the ribs, and that the ribs—can this be?—seem to be *parting slightly* to accommodate the thing: they, the ribs, are *bowed away from* the lump, and he realizes that the lump is not simply a swelling muscle or the result of any contusion at all but a *separate object* that is quite simply not supposed to be there. Now he stops being turned on and begins to feel frightened: and the lump begins to sweat underneath his palm, or perhaps it's the palm that's sweating, at any rate there's a lot of sweat, and his hand slides around with the motion of the truck and the lump does not yield, it goes on being hard and red and painful there and seems to be sending its root deeper and deeper into his chest and the hollows of his gut. He feels nauseated, his bowels begin to loosen. He blinks stinging sweat out of his eyes. Oh, Christ, what a mess this is. He feels weak—as if he's going to pass out—so he gets up, steadies himself against the seatbacks, staggers to the door and crouches in front of the crack of sunlight and air running along the bottom. He breathes, momentarily grateful, until he realizes that the air is contaminated by truck exhaust—and he rears back and bangs his head on the hard metal leg of the rear seat.

When he comes to, he can smell spring air and the truck is flooded with light. Syracuse is holding his sunglasses in one hand and the door handle in the other; his eyes are tired red blobs set into fans of wrinkles. "Jay-Cee! What the heck happened to you?"

Mailman has his hand over his face, the light's too much for him and now his head is pounding along with his ribs. "Exhaust," he manages to say. "Banged head."

"Where's your shirt, fella?"

"Seat." He pulls himself to his knees and then stands, rubbing his face. He's dizzy. He remembers the lump, his terror is renewed. Cancer. Inoperable. Pain. Death.

Syracuse points to it and says, "That's a real shiner there, friend. We didn't do that to you, did we?"

"I did it to myself."

"Oh, okay. Well, we're here. Get dressed, we got some questions for you." Trying to restore a little truculence to his voice. Mailman gets his shirt, puts it on. He hears Shut-up behind him: "What the hell were you talking about back here?"

"Poor fella was lying here subconscious with no shirt on."

"Pervert."

"Nah, he hurt himself or something."

"I'll bet he hurt himself."

They are in a parking lot; in the distance, the buildings of Syracuse rise into the clear air, a lovely art deco skyline that would have been knocked down years ago, if anyone'd had the money. At the other end of the lot is a building, and it is toward it that they walk. The building is white stucco with small square windows behind which heads are tilted over desks. The three of them, walking, are utterly enervated. The journey seems to take all day. They enter through a back door; Syracuse takes Mailman by the arm and pushes him inside. "Whoops, did I hurt your arm? Sorry."

It's cold in here; Mailman begins to shiver. But Syracuse and Shut-up seem revitalized, their step a bit springier as they lead him down a long white hallway, past scores of closed doors, around a corner where the hallway continues and then around another corner and down a flight of stairs. They pass a few people dressed like Syracuse and Shut-up. A cleaning woman languidly mops the floor. At last they slow and then stop before a door like all the others, and Syracuse takes a moment to search his ring for the right key.

"Jesus effing Christ," says Shut-up, "lemme do it."

"No, I got it."

"C'mon, lemme."

"I *got* it." He gets it. The door falls open. Inside are two mismatched chipboard-and-patterned-Formica buffet tables surrounded by aluminum frame chairs. There are microphones hanging in two ceiling corners. "Siddown," says Shut-up, and Mailman sits down. "Not there." He points.

Mailman rises, shuffles, sits again. "Can you maybe turn the AC down a little?" he says. "It's freezing in here." Shut-up, leaving the room, says, "Feels pretty comfortable to me."

"No, you're right," Syracuse mutters once Shut-up is gone. "It's colder than a witch's boobie." Syracuse sits where Mailman tried to sit, and the two of them sit there, apparently waiting for Shut-up to come back.

"How long've you been a postal inspector?" Mailman says. The cold air has cleared his head somewhat, the throbbing in his side has slightly subsided. He seems to have control of his bowels.

"Nobody said I was a postal inspector."

"Look," says Mailman, "I really hurt myself, I didn't bring my aspirin with me, have you got any aspirin or other pain reliever, please?"

He pats his pockets. "Geez, sorry, fella."

"Well, if you're going to be asking me questions, I'll be a lot easier to get answers from if I get some pain reliever first, so maybe you can go find some for me."

"Nobody said anything about questions. Or hold on, did we?"

"Oh, for crying out loud," Mailman says, shaking his head, and suddenly Syracuse sighs and says "Okay, sorry, don't get your knickers in a twist," and goes out into the hall. Some kind of commotion ensues, words are exchanged, there are jogging footsteps. In a moment Shut-up walks in with another man, a taller, fitter man in a nicer suit, tanned, with a large jaw and a regal bearing, like a pelican. He sits down exactly opposite Mailman and stares at him. After a minute of this Mailman says "Hello, I'm Albert" and the fitter man looks over at Shut-up, who shakes his head. Soon Syracuse is back with a paper cone of water and a bottle of generic acetaminophen and hands both to Mailman. "Here ya go, chief." "Thank you," says Mailman, but he can't open the childproof cap without putting down the cone of water, which can't be put down, owing to the pointy bottom. He tries holding the cone and the bottle in the same hand, but the cone begins to collapse, and some water spills on the table. The three men watch his struggle with interest, as if this experiment were the true reason for bringing him here. Eventually Mailman is able to wedge the cone between his thighs while he opens the bottle, which contains exactly four tablets, regular strength. He puts all four into his mouth, spilling more water onto his shorts in exactly the area that would be damp were he to pee in his pants, and then he washes them down with the water remaining in the cone. He puts down bottle, cap and cone, rubs his face with his hands and says, "All right, what's all this about?"

The new guy, Mr. Fitness, snorts. "*He* wants to know 'what this is all about,'" and he and Shut-up laugh theatrically while Syracuse just sort of chuckles.

Fitness turns to Mailman. "Why don't *you*"—he jabs a steady finger—"tell *us*"—a thumb at his own chest this time—"what this is all about." And falls back into his chair, arms crossed.

Shut-up says, "Yeah."

Mailman looks at the three of them, arrayed around him like a thesis committee. He says "Well, I can't," and slumps back and waits.

After a few minutes of silence the three men begin to look at each other. The plan isn't going too well. At last Syracuse pleads, "Sure you can, fella, you're not stupid. I mean we're not stupid." Shut-up says "That was stupid," and Fitness says, "Shut up." Everyone shuts up. Then Fitness reaches into the pocket of his jacket and pulls out Jared Sprain's letter and holds it by a corner of its plastic bag, and says, "Does this look familiar to you?"

"Sure," Mailman says. Don't act suspicious! Stick to your story!

"Sure, that's a letter. It was sent to a customer of mine, this guy Jared Sprain. He's dead. I mean, he killed himself. Or so I heard. Read. In the paper." He looks around at each man, Fitness and Shut-up are subtly nodding. Syracuse is picking his nose. "After my shift I found this letter, that letter there, in the bottom of my cart. It was torn. I saw who it was for and—because he was dead, you know, or so I read, in the paper—I felt really bad about it. So I thought, I better deliver this letter, so I put it in the bag and brought it home, and that night I went over to his address and stuck it in the box. Except the boxes were—I had some trouble, they were hard to get open—and I made a lot of noise and the tenant must have woken up, or I must have woken her up, who lives behind them, behind the boxes, because she came out—she's this young woman—and gave me a kind of a look. But anyway I put the letter in and that was that." He pauses a moment, closes his eyes to dispel a wave of dizziness. "I hope you got it to the kid's family. I really do. It would probably mean a lot to them to know— that is, if he got a letter from a friend— or I mean whoever it's from, I assume a friend, but to know that he was getting letters from people who cared— assuming this is a friend who cared. So I hope they saw it before you took it like that."

"Why'd you have your keys at home?" says Fitness.

"I didn't. I sort of pried the box open."

"This girl," Shut-up says, "what's her name again?"

"I don't know her name."

"She says some of her mail got opened. She said somebody's reading her mail before she gets it. What do you know about that?"

"I know— this girl you're talking about, I don't know her name— she happened to see me in the park one day and I guess recognized that I was her mailman and told me that somebody was reading her mail. So I told her—she was wondering what to do, you see—she had to report it to the landlord at least, because probably it's somebody in her building who got her box open, and if that didn't work to call up the postmaster, who would look into it."

"What did you say her name was?" says Shut-up.

"I don't know her name."

"So," says Fitness. "*You*"—jab—"know the name of *this guy*"—jab jab—he holds up the doctored letter—"but you don't know the name of this girl, even though they're in the *same building*." Big jab. "How's that?"

"I don't know," Mailman says, "some people's names you remember and some you don't, there's no rhyme or reason to it, also this guy Jared I kind of got to know, he got a lot of packages and I brought them upstairs for him and always knocked, and he'd open the door to take the package and we'd talk. But the girl I never saw until that night I dropped the letter off—which by the way I know is unorthodox—I mean, now that I think about it I guess it probably is against the rules—but at the time all I was thinking about was getting that letter to his bereaved family, that's all."

Fitness says, "Jared Sprain killed himself June second." A dramatic pause. "And it was in the paper *June third*." He looks at Shut-up, nodding, and Syracuse suddenly looks up and nods too. "But you said you saw the article in the paper and *then*"—jab—"you dropped off the letter. But the girl—what was her name again?"

"I have no idea."

"The girl *claims* she saw you drop off the letter on the *second,* or in the early hours of the *third,* before the paper came out. So"—he pounds the table, causing everyone to jump—"do you want to revise your opinion?"

Does he? He has no idea. What's worse, revising his opinion or sticking to his incorrect story? He says, "Nnnno . . . I think that's the way it happened, that's how I remember it anyway. By the way, I demand— that is, I would like the presence— please, I demand that I see, that you see, my union steward. If I'm going to answer your questions. I request that my union steward be present, that's it."

The three exchange glances. Shut-up says "You had to say that at the post office in Nestor," and to Fitness says, "Didn't he?"

"Geez, I didn't think of that," says Syracuse. "Should we call up—"

"Right, you have to ask in Nestor," says Fitness. "When you left, you waived your right to your union steward."

"Respectfully," Mailman says, "I don't think that's right."

"Well!" says Fitness, throwing his arms in the air. "Let's look it up. Anybody got the rule book?"

"Sheesh, I dunno," says Syracuse. "I could check the truck?"

"No rule book, too bad," says Fitness. "Now, Mister Lippincott, about this girl, *what's-her-name.*" Significant pause. "You say you *never saw her* before that night, correct?"

"Yes. But I really think—"

"*She* says"—jab—"you'd had encounters before, when you'd made noise outside her room? And we have records that say there was a noise complaint?"

"Yes, well no, I don't remember ever seeing her there, and I never knew who made the complaint but I guess it was her, and about the noise, I tried talking to the landlord about those mailboxes but he wouldn't return my phone calls. And anyway, I really want to—"

"So!" says Fitness. "We got this encounter of midnight on the *second.*" Pound. "And the one you mentioned in the *park.*" Pound. "Is that it? No other encounters, you're saying?"

"That's right."

"And the coffee shop, right? You also saw her at a place called . . . *More Coffee,*" this with incredulous distaste, as if the name itself were borderline illegal. He pauses, pretending to brush something off his jacket, and then—suddenly!—turns, leveling an accusing finger: "Isn't that right?"

"I don't remember that, no," Mailman says, remembering it. "No, I don't think so."

"Hey," says Shut-up, "isn't that the same place he got the cops to tackle his boss? That coffee shop?"

"Wait a minute!" Mailman says. "That wasn't me! I didn't do anything like that! Those cops thought— I mean they saw him trying—

they thought he was breaking into the truck, I didn't have anything to do with that! In fact I saved Ronk, I went over and told them everything was all right! He ought to be thanking me for that, not filing a . . . a complaint, or whatever he did!"

"Who says he filed a complaint?" Shut-up says.

"'Scuse me, everybody," says Syracuse, standing, "I gotta powder my nose."

"Is that the same coffee shop where you talked to Kelly Vireo?" says Fitness.

"Yes, that's the one— or rather, I mean, More Coffee! is the coffee shop where they tackled Ronk but not where I talked to Kelly Vireo, or rather not the one where I didn't, because I didn't see her or talk to her, to my recollection. Which by the way, Kelly Vireo— I assume that's the name of the girl you're talking about, who I saw at the apartment in the park?" Huh? "That's her name is what you're telling me?"

Silence. Syracuse pauses with his hand on the doorknob. Mailman thinks: Now *you* shut up. But instead he says, "Because I didn't know that, but of course it's familiar now that you mention it, from the mail. Hers, that I deliver, I mean." It really is very cold in here. He shivers, coughs.

"Sounds to me," says Shut-up, "like the name is very familiar to you indeed."

Fitness is smiling, rubbing his giant jaw.

"Well," says Mailman, "only now that you mention it does it sound familiar, it's one of those things that, you know, you know it but you couldn't say it, but then someone says it and you say 'Yes, of course, I knew that,' even if moments before you couldn't have said it if your life depended on it. You know what I'm talking about."

"Yeah," says Syracuse with genuine sympathy and goes off to pee.

"Let's shift gears here for a minute," Fitness says suddenly, getting to his feet and beginning a very unnatural pace back and forth across the front (or side maybe, or rear—the room is so featureless that these distinctions are arbitrary, the only certain thing is which is the floor and which is the ceiling, and if they were weightless, floating in space, even this would come into question) of the room, his hands behind his back. Mailman takes note of the hands, the fingernails whittled down to the quick, the skin on either side white and peeled and picked, the tips and knuckles cracked from the dry, which is what happens when you wash too much. He senses it's not going well, wonders why he can't seem to stop talking. When people ask him questions, he talks: that's his Achilles' heel. One of them anyway—but that's no good, a person can't have more than one Achilles' heel, right? Even Achilles couldn't have had more than two, at the outside. "Tell me," Fitness says, "about your daily schedule. Let's start when you're leaving the Nestor Main Office in the morning. Your truck is full"—spins, points—"*of mail*. You start it up and pull out of the parking lot." Slaps the table. "Where do you go?"

"I go downtown and do my route."

"You go downtown. And you park? Do you park on the street?"

"Yes, sure, you know the routine—I park, I load up my three-wheeler, I start rolling around the neighborhood. I finish very fast. I have never had an efficiency complaint. Everyone on my route gets their mail by noon."

"Wow, that's fast." Fitness nods. Shut-up nods too, seemingly unsure if the nodding is supposed to be sarcastic. "Do you take a break?"

"Usually."

"Where do you go?"

"Uh, I stay in the truck, or have a coffee."

"You don't . . . stop at home?" Fitness says. "Maybe for a snack, to check your answering machine, anything like that?"

"Home? No, I— I have the mail, I have to deliver it, so I go— I park— what I just told you." Here they come—sweat, heart palpitations. A painful throbbing under his arm. He remembers suddenly his foolish flight from the cop at 200 Keuka and resists an urge to leap up and run out the door. Syracuse left it unlocked on the way to the men's room, right?

"So you don't go home and then go inside and do anything and then come out again? Nothing real important or anything, just maybe you take a crap or something?"

"Take— no, I just—"

"Because some people can't just take a dump any old where, you have to do it at home, on the old throne, right magazine, right atmosphere, am I right?"

"Tell me about it!" says Syracuse, returning to the room.

"I don't have that problem, no," says Mailman, though all this talk about it is making him want to go, and he shifts around on his seat, trying to avoid having to ask.

Then Shut-up says, "So Albert, are you still engaged in acquiring and perusing pornographic materials?"

There is a sudden, trenchant silence. Even Fitness seems surprised at the question. He straightens his posture and leans back against the wall, hands folded together, nodding slowly.

"P-p-porn— No! No, I—"

"When did you stop?" Fitness asks.

"Never! I— I never started, I mean—"

"So this nice lady from the library was *lying* to us?" He pounds the table again, but, since he is standing up, is forced to bend over to do it. "Is *that* what you're saying? About your *engaging*"—pound!—"in *self-abuse*"—pound!—"at a public Internet station?"

Mailman blurts, "I didn't! I didn't! That was my deodorant, I'd bought it but didn't ask for a bag, I never get bags because I just— but what I'm saying is I never did such a thing!"

A silence as everyone, Mailman included, digests this response. They obviously don't know what he's talking about. He considers how to rephrase it, how to explain the deal with the deodorant, but Fitness interrupts: "You *were* perusing a pornographic web site, correct? I hate to accuse you of something you didn't do, but I deduced that since you were using the computer at the post office to look at pornography, then the library lady was probably—"

"I did no such thing!" he shouts. "Never! I did not, never!"

But he did. He did, he did, he did! He regrets it now—it was not a pleasure, not even a guilty one; it was not satisfying even in the basest way; on the contrary it made his worst problems worse still, but it is all true, and more: he engaged in the perusal of pornographic materials, not only on the Internet but also in his home, and—and this is the worst, the thing that haunts him still—in the library. In *libraries*.

How did it begin? Innocently enough? No, not so innocently—it began in his mind, his sick, diseased mind, when he returned from Kazakhstan, in his (God help him!) fantasies, wherein he remembered the sex he had with Marsha in that terrible cinder-block room, on that terrible moldering cot, above those terrible gray tiles. All of those things—the memories of them—the deathly echo of their own footsteps in that room, the smell of Beth's Atomic Balm (what kind of woman would bring such a thing with her, keep it close to her at all times, on such a trip: that reeking salve, applied nightly to the poor girl's calves and shoulders, my God!): even *that* was a turn-on for him once he was back in the all-too-familiar inner sanctum of his house. And so he lay in bed nights remembering the sex—this grope, that moan, a smack, a stroke, a poke—embellishing their words and gestures and acts (not that so much embellishment was needed), rendering himself, his own personal apparatus, extremely uncomfortable, and so it remained until he was able to fall asleep, and in the morning he would wake to a sick sensation of unfulfillment, a slackness, a brackishness of the loins, and everything would move in slow motion all day long. And instead of growing weary of these thoughts, instead of working to push them from his mind when he lay down in bed each night, he craved them, embraced them: he prepared for his fantasies as he might prepare for a real lover, airing out the bedclothes and fluffing the pillow and tidying up his bedroom; some nights he even lit a candle (and when, years later, a naked Semma led him to a bed surrounded by fragrant flickering candles, it was to the hideous squalor of this fantasy that his mind involuntarily returned). The

entire thing had an air of *romance* about it, at least until morning
when he would wake feeling like the last muddied puddled remains
of a frogpond on the hottest day of summer. He let himself down easy
into the fantasies, as into a hot bath, remembering the entire story
from Peace Corps acceptance letter to shared room, taking each memory slowly, smoothing it out before him until the creases disappeared,
taking as much as half an hour before he got to the hands, the lips,
the hips, the tits. And only then would his mind get to fondle each
remembered encounter, touching up a bit when necessary, buffing it
all to a sweaty shine. The whole thing would take about an hour and a
half, his discomfort ecstatic, excruciating, perhaps even disfiguring.
And then the old bean would give out and sleep would come and he
would wake in what seemed seconds.

But it wasn't enough: he still craved. Not, for once in his life,
actual women on the actual street—he began to crave the fantasies:
not their flesh counterparts, the fantasies themselves. He wanted to
mine every remembered second for its every nuance, to sift through
the mountains of ones and zeroes for every sensation that he could
enlarge, dissect, deconstruct. But he discovered that there were limits
to his memories, limits to the degree to which they could be bent by
imagination before they lost their erotic potency: and so he began,
without really acknowledging it to himself, his search for some annex,
some appendix to his exploits, a way to start again without starting
again.

He knows—he knew at the time—that relief was possible, that
there was something he could do to truncate his agony if not obliter-
ate it; he knew that most men and women would have employed this
exact remedy long before, and forgotten the entire episode and gotten
on with their lives: but this particular remedy was not available to
him, or rather it was, but he was reluctant, loath even, to wield it, for
fear that the cure would be worse than the disease. He had done it
before—abused himself, that is, loved himself, brought himself off,
choked the chicken; jerked, stroked, beat, yanked, pulled himself—

only once, disastrously, and to attempt it now, even in his agony, would likely redouble his suffering.

Once he had masturbated, in fifty years.

He figured out how to do it in the bathtub at the house in Princeton: a chipped and permanently stained tub of uncertain provenance, bearing marks that could not help but bring former bathers to mind: the smooth uncrusted patches near the back where hairy abrasive buttocks doubtless once sat daily; the stratified calcifications along the sides where dead skin mingled with the microscopic carcasses of mites; the greased gummed black semicircle on the back rim from the rubbing of hair; the wooden ledge above, where soap slivers had been scattered, had hardened and flattened and been painted over: this bathtub was where he discovered that he didn't need to be watching his sister undress for his special feature to stiffen, in fact he could simply imagine her undressing, and if he touched it, his personal item, the result was a rising sense of excitement and panic and sensation not confined to the tumescent organ but extending throughout his midsection and spreading upward to his chest and shoulders and down into his lower legs and feet: at which time, invariably, he would stop, concerned that something was about to rupture. For six months this went on, his eagerness for baths and their increasing length much remarked upon by his mother. And then, at last, on an evening following a day (one of many) during which he had hid under Gillian's bed and watched her undress and fondle her own breasts in the mirror, he reported for duty around seven-fifteen and remained there for more than ninety minutes, left hand gripping the tub rim, his forehead dripping with sweat, stimulating his singularity, until he was nearly to the point where he would have to stop, and it was then that he heard his mother's feet on the stairs and voice in the stairwell muttering, "Jesus fucking Christ, the kid's been in there an hour and a half": and rather than stopping, he redoubled his efforts, losing control of the motion of his hand, the monotony of its effort snowballing into a blinding, involuntary jitter; and instead of knocking as she usually did, his mother threw open the door; and in his sudden panic something in Mailman indeed ruptured: so strong it was audible, the explosive expulsion of life: and his mother screamed and said, "What in the hell are you doing!"

Through a window and into the silence came a distant wisp of song: *Winston tastes good, like a cigarette should!* He looked down and found his chest splashed with evidence, and horrified he slapped it off into the bathwater, pulled the drain plug, and said, "I— I— nothing, I— there was, I'm sorry, I!" But by this time she was upon him and slapped his face so hard his buttocks lost their grip on the tub floor and he slipped; his head banged, he went under, swallowing the sweat-and-sin-stained water.

He felt himself yanked up by the arm, pulled to his feet. "Fags yank their crank!" his mother was screaming. "Are you a fag, Albert? Good motherloving God!"

"I'm— I'm—"

"What were you thinking of?" she shouted. She was still wearing her apron, having washed the dinner dishes; he felt the diamond pattern of the rubber gloves she wore as they seized his shoulders. Now she stopped, narrowed her eyes, leaned in close to his dripping hot face: "Were you thinking of Chip Jacks? When you were doing it, you were thinking of Chip!" On her breath was the ham they had eaten, the potatoes, the peas.

"Wha— no! Chip— I don't know what—" Chip Jacks? Chip Jacks the lawnmower man? The barechested dolt who cut the grass, whose sweaty shirt as often as not was mistakenly left behind, draped over the rosebushes? Chip Jacks who smelled like salami and whom Mailman had caught around back of their house, urinating out of a giant dick that looked like it had just come out of a casserole dish, and whose reaction to being caught was "Howdy, big Al, just pissin'"? *That* Chip Jacks? What the hell was she talking about?

She came in closer, her face inches from his. "Were you *thinking* . . . about Chip's *thing* . . . when you were *touching yours.*"

"No! No! Chip's ugly! He's a jerk!"

"Then *what* were you thinking of." There was a stain on her sleeve, a gravy spot in the red-and-white-checked gingham of her dress. The dirty water slurped itself out of the tub.

"Nothing! Just, I was just, nothing!"

"It *was* Chip!"

"No!"

"Then who?" She shook him, his feet slipped on the enamel, but her hands, her steely gloved hands, held him upright, and as her face worked he thought, probably for the first time: How did my mother get so old? "If not Chip, who?"

He might have said anything. He might have said his math teacher, he might have said Judy Garland, he might have said Paula Paolangeli, the girl next door. But he said the truth. Said it quietly, to be sure, the word displaced by his hung head and fractured by the room's echoes and by the water on his lips, but he said it, and she let go very very quickly, and took a single step back. The distant television said, *Don't tell anybody what the ending is. Keep the ending a surprise.*

"*What* did you say?"

Oh, Ralph, how wonderful! I can't wait to see it!

"Gillian," he said again, louder now so that Gillian herself might have heard it had she been listening downstairs, and this time his mother didn't bother demanding an explanation: she just punched him, he smelled rubber as the balled glove connected, and something in his nose gave way and he dropped into the wet empty tub with a sound like a gong. Christ!—several vertebrae rattled like Christmas ornaments, his tailbone exploded in pain, and he looked up, stunned, to see through the open door his mother's back retreating down the stairs. Blood had splashed from his nose and now it fell all around him, pinking in the damp and creeping toward the drain.

He sat, panting, in the sudden silence. Tears formed and fell. He sniffed, and blood backed up into his throat. Downstairs he heard his mother screaming, and then Gillian screaming, the words as terrible as any he'd heard, accusing, recriminating, blazing back and forth across the kitchen; pots hit the floor and walls, and dishes smashed. Doors slammed. Silence again, and then the sound of sobbing: Gillian? No. His mother. This he had never before heard: or rather he had heard it, but always disguised, always drowned out by music or dulled by a shut door. Could he have been blamed, an eleven-year-old boy, for sobbing along with her? Could either of them have been blamed for anything, if first their accuser witnessed this: mother and child sobbing, alone, in separate rooms, each unable to comfort the other? Nothing could have been sadder: but to Mailman, just then, all that gripped him was fear, fear that everything which previously had been held together (if only by the thinnest of threads) had at last broken apart. He was aware that he had been a disappointment but wasn't sure how, he was filled with hatred but not all of it for his mother (and for what, or whom, the remaining hatred was reserved was impossible to know).

And where was his father? In the lab, no doubt, downstairs, that creature without desire, without anger; a man beyond understanding and so beyond reproach. The distant television, as if in deference to this genuine drama, was silenced. He never abused himself again.

And maybe this was why, soon after Ronk reluctantly rehired him, he found himself sitting in the back of his truck, unable to resist some poor loner's subscription copy (freed, by mishandling, from its brown paper sleeve) of *Amateur Hotties*: page upon page of honest-to-God young-to-middle-aged women baring all for the ineptly wielded cameras of their husbands, boyfriends, girlfriends, whomever, and of course for the lonesome sex-starved jerkoffs of America. There at the corner of Hoover and Sage he sweated, panting, and flipped the pages; there before him lay all the T&A anybody could want, along with stretch marks, cellulite, cesarean scars, excessive hair, eyeglasses (!!), love handles, unusual piercings, psoriasis, eczema, all the undignified disfigurements that had never before been available to him except upon actual women, the few he'd known intimately (the complete list, if intercourse is what is meant: Lenore and Marsha, with Semma and Lily Gallagher still to come. That's it!), and it was these inconsistencies, coupled of course with the T&A, that really got his motor running. He'd had no idea that such things could be had, photos of normal people naked, regular folks helpfully illustrating the location and intended uses of their various body parts: if he'd known, for crying out loud, he might not be where he was, he might long ago have quit his job and devoted himself full-time to the perusal of such material, like a lab rat that has dedicated its short life to the incessant tapping of the lever wired to its hypothalamus. And that certainly wouldn't do. So he quit reading his customers' magazines (though not, of course, their mail) and tried to wean himself from pornography.

At this he failed. You could almost say it wasn't his fault. He was freeloading at the NYTech library on a Sunday afternoon, using their online database to look for an old issue of *Scientific American* he had read as a boy, which contained an article (he thought he remembered) on how to build one's own twenty-foot weather balloon out of plastic garbage bags, when he saw himself type the word EROTIC onto the line beneath the prompt ENTER KEYWORD(S). And then he saw himself hit the spacebar and type in another word, PHOTOGRAPHY. He looked over his shoulder—was anyone there? No, only the never-used though not-obsolete-because-the-database-was-full-of-errors card catalog—before he hit the ENTER key. It was a lark—a joke, almost—because what college library would carry collections of erotic photographs? What librarian would remove from its shipping box a book full of pictures of, say, nude male and female models rutting in broad daylight in the back of a 1979 Ford F250 pickup, and then affix it with a little barcode sticker, and glue a little envelope in the front, and type the title, *Fuck in a Truck,* onto a little card, and put the card into the little envelope, and stamp the card with the words NEW ARRIVAL, 14-DAY LOAN, and then log the book into the database and place it, in call-number order, on a shelving cart for the work-study kid to take care of? But what came up was not the message he expected—YOUR SEARCH TERMS HAVE

YIELDED NO MATCHES—but the following: 571 MATCHES FOUND. FIRST 20 SHOWN. HIT P TO VIEW NEXT PAGE. And following was a list as long as your arm, documenting the true depths of depravity to which academe had crawled.

Mostly they fell into two categories, the HQs, which was the human sexuality section, and the TRs, which was the art. The human sexuality books were special: one had to get into one's Escort and drive to the Library Annex at the edge of campus, and give a librarian one's driver's license, and say "I would like *The Mystery of Woman: A Photoessay*, please," and then said librarian would bring one one's choice, and level at one a look of loathing and reply "It's due back in a month" when what she would really want to say is "Do you just want to take it into the bathroom for five minutes, mister?," and so the HQs were out. This left the TRs, specifically TR 675, which (he quickly discovered) was the Library of Congress's code for books of "artistic" photographs of naked human beings, and which could be casually walked to, casually located among the collections of nature and fashion photographs, casually surveyed and selected among, and spirited away to some forgotten carrel or study room for intenser examination.

The "fine arts" library in Keene Hall, that's where they were keeping all the good stuff: the pictures of women sprawled in deserts, curled up in open steamer trunks, standing under waterfalls, twisted abstractly around poles and over benches and into fetal balls, the cameras sliding over belly and buttock and into each crevice and crack and shadowed sliver of flesh: all of them were naked and some of them were beautiful, though it was the unbeautiful ones that most interested him, these women unaccustomed to the camera's eye, to the presence of the photographer. Did they respond to an ad in the paper? a question in a bar? a handbill on the street? a tip from a friend? Did they undress in a restroom or behind a scrim, or did they do it before the photographer's eyes? Did they like it? Did they do it again? Did they sleep with the man or woman behind the camera? And here he thought of

Gillian: had she ever done this kind of thing? It seemed right up her alley. Was she here, now, in this library, in a book, nude? My God!

He asked himself these questions as he sat, his legs uncomfortably crossed, at a round wooden table beside a row of tall windows, the TR 675s in an uneven stack before him, facedown, to preserve some semblance of privacy. Sometimes his thoughts would drift: out the open window, across the campus and state and across the ocean to Marsha: what was she doing? Did she ever think of him? Why had she cut him off? And when his eyes had returned to the books he realized that something was missing: they weren't enough, somehow. They weren't direct enough; they were calculated, they had an agenda. The artist was a distraction. Yet he held out little hope for something better, because he was not going to walk into a store and buy *Amateur Hotties* or anything of the sort.

He spent three consecutive Sundays at the same table, the same spring breezes chilling his back and elbows and neck, tearing himself to pieces with the same books, and on the fourth he arrived to find a little man sitting where he usually sat, a bearded homunculus with aviator glasses and long gray hair, apparently waiting for him. "Hello," he was forced to say—he recognized the homunculus, an employee of the library, a suspicious little person who occasionally (and gratuitously) drifted down Mailman's aisle trying to peek at the spines of the books in his stack. "Hello," Mailman always said at those times, convinced that he was well within his rights to be sitting here looking at the naked women openly provided for him at tuition-payers' expense, and again, now, he said "Hello," and the homunculus frowned and shook his head, and from the other side of the stacks stepped two uniformed police officers—retirement-age college cops, not the real thing—who came right up to him, their faces stony, and one of them, prickly and upright as a ponderosa pine, said, "Your name please, sir."

"Huh? Me? Why?"

"This the guy?" said the other, fatter, seedier cop to the homunculus, and the homunculus said "That's him," and Mailman said "That's him, what? What do you want?" and the first cop said "This man believes you're responsible for vandalizing the restrooms in this library," and Mailman said "I don't even use them," and the homunculus said "Ha," and led the little group of them around several corners to a narrow door with MEN painted on it, and they all went in, and the homunculus showed them how somebody had torn the doors off the stalls and markered YOU ARE ALL HORES on the walls.

Mailman said, "How do you figure I did that? I hardly ever come here."

"You come here every Sunday," said the homunculus, "to read those nudie books, and then you come back during the week and trash my restroom."

"I've never once been in this restroom, and I know how to spell 'whores,' and what business is it of yours what books I look at, I even reshelve them myself."

"In the wrong order," said H., and Mailman said, "The hell they are." In the end he was taken to the campus cop station (underneath the student union and cafeteria, so that he could smell the boiled vegetables and floor cleaner and hear the stomp of hiking boots and whine of alternative rock as he was being written up), written up, and asked never to enter the campus libraries again. "But I'm a city resident and this is a publicly funded university," he said, and the fat cop said, "See if I care, perv." And Mailman said "Well, fuck you" and got up and walked out, the terrible words (barely ever spoken to anyone, let alone authority figures, they were filthy and potent on his tongue) left behind like a couple of turds for them to clean up.

The next day, at the P.O., he was looking up a nine-digit zip code on the postal service web site—a new thing at their office, it had replaced a stack of books of regulations, guidelines and useful facts, books that never broke down, crashed or overheated—when he remembered reading a newspaper article about the ease with which children could view Internet pornography. And so he clicked on to a search engine ("Webcrawler") and typed in the words AMATEUR NUDE and within seconds he was looking at photographs of a skinny, bespectacled, flat-chested teenage girl with her legs spread and a teenage boy's mohawk'd head buried in between her legs: and then another photograph, and another, and twenty more, and then a long list of names and descriptions of acts on which he could click to call up yet another naked person (young, old, gay, straight, fat, thin, whatever) or people performing various acts upon themselves or one another or upon inanimate objects or pets. The descriptions alone astonished him into wide-eyed paralysis: TWO UGLY BROADS + DILDO!; ME AND DAMIEN IN HOT TUB; TONGUE BATH BOYS W/GRAMMA; HOT RETIREE ORGEE; TALL + SHORT TOGETHER ORAL!!; NUDE FAMILY VACATION; BUTT ACTION VERY SEXXXY; CUM SHOT ON FACE; FUZZY KITTY FUX; I AM TEENAGE HORNIE. Quickly he switched the computer off and then waited a few minutes and turned it back on again, and when the screen reestablished itself the words PLEASE ENTER YOUR PASSWORD appeared and he slinked away, embarrassed, hoping no one had noticed him there. After that, however, he was hooked, and he started coming in early (long before it was time to punch in) or returning late to "do extra work," and over the CRT he could watch Ronk scribbling away at something at his desk, never once looking up to see what Mailman was doing, for he didn't care.

There was something about the crappiness of the pictures: the bad light, the smeared and distorted colors (not that the original colors were very attractive, the colors of skin never exposed to sun, of patched and tattered sofas, of shag rugs and unwashed sheets and walls in need of paint), the unwieldy jutting of elements from the frame, all made these images exciting to him, and more beautiful and honest than the pictures he'd been looking at in the art library; and he found that they conjured up, with surprising accuracy, the dank illicit couplings he'd had with Marsha. It was even possible to find girls who looked a lot like her, girls who wore glasses (yes, they left them on, it seemed to be a geek fetish) over small eyes and narrow noses—but they were never quite right, the shoulders wrong, the legs or breasts, the neck, the chin. He'd collected enough, however, to let them run together in his mind and with his memories of Marsha, so that they were all Marsha, and all of them fully animated, like memories.

Then the computer broke, and it was sent in to a shop, and it didn't come back for weeks: and in that time Mailman grew depressed and now missed not only the actual Marsha but the imaginary one, for the memories and fantasies quickly lost their potency without new daily infusions of pornographic images. That's when he went to the public library and began flipping angrily through the handful of art books he could find that featured nude pictures (most of them torn out and replaced by crude photocopies, a baffling sleight-of-hand, for how could a librarian xerox a picture that was missing?—presumably there was a network of librarians, calling one another on the phone, saying "I need a xerox of page 241 of *Photographing the Nude*," hard as that was to believe), all the while longing for the comforting thrill of Internet porn. And so, inevitably, he made the daring leap from the private stacks to the dozen public Internet computers, which occupied a single large table in the middle of the reference section, and which were always in use, and which a lot of bearded semi-homeless men were always hanging around waiting for their turn at: he made this leap knowing full well that he would be detected by somebody, a patron or librarian, despite the discretion-enhancing anti-glare no-peeking shields positioned over each screen. He did everything he could to prevent discovery: leaned in close as if his eyesight were poor, kept small the window that the web browser was open upon, lunged forward when anyone passed behind, as if to grab a pencil or scrap of paper from the little plastic box , when in fact he was simply blocking the view. He even laser-printed a few of the pictures, minimizing the browser the moment he hit PRINT and dashing to the printer at the table's end, to keep another patron from grabbing his pages by mistake. "I think those are mine," said one woman who had hit PRINT at approximately the same time, dashed to the printer at the same time;

"No, they're mine," he said, and as the first page began to curl into the drawer he grabbed the end, and so did she, and she said "Please let go," and he said "No, I hit PRINT first," and she said "How do you know that?" and he said, "I just do." But it turned out she was right, and thank God for it; she spirited away her completed résumé saying "Now it's got your thumbprint on it, jerk," and he was able to smuggle out his pages in peace, after paying ten cents per page at the reference desk (where, thank God, they didn't ask to see the pages).

Then one morning (a sunny Sunday in June, much like today— far too nice a day to be sneaking peeks at Internet porn, much as today is far too nice a day to be interrogated by dim-witted postal goons) he showed up at the library an hour before it opened, and so to kill time went down to the Square, had a cup of coffee, read the free weekly (JUG BAND REVIVAL!), walked around a little, went into the health food store, picked up a bag of brown rice, realized he really didn't need it and did he want to carry it around with him all day?, put it back and finally bought a little round all-natural deodorant stick that was supposed to smell like apricots. "You wanna bag?" asked the multiply pierced clerk, who made it clear by her tone that to answer in the affirmative would be tantamount to slitting the throat of an endangered owl right here on the counter, and so he said no. On the way back to the library he took the cap off the deodorant and gave it a whiff and it didn't smell like apricots at all—more like tropical-fruit bubble gum. He looked at the ingredients list. "Natural colors." "Natural scents." And still it smelled saccharine, sickly. He felt it with his finger: gritty. What a ripoff! What a mistake! His buyer's regret caused his feet to fall more heavily, his shoulders to pitch forward, and he reached the library in a kind of rage, waited by the door, walked in when it opened, and nabbed the first available computer.

Did he notice the reference librarian and her trainee? He must have, they were the only other people in that section, but there was no reason for them to come around to the far end of the table, unless they were systematically examining each computer to make sure it was working right, which in hindsight he supposed was exactly what they were doing. At any rate it took them a while, and in that time other patrons came in and sat down at computers, and Mailman, suddenly conscious of his deodorant stick, removed it from the table next to his mousepad and set it on the ground, then thought better (he would forget it was there) and put it, at last, on his lap and rested his left—that is, non-mouse-using—hand on top of it so that it wouldn't slip down between his legs and onto the floor by his feet, necessitating an embarrassing duck-and-crawl right here at the Internet station. He decided to search for new sites, typed in NUDE GLASSES TEEN and came up with a few, one of which he brought up onto the screen, and at that point (the girl displayed on the homepage—HOT NERD OF THE MONTH!—was wearing only cateye specs and running shoes and had the Atari symbol tattooed on her arm, and she was sprawled out on a bed in a tangle of Star Wars sheets, fellating an acne-scarred computer geek) the computer crashed.

That is, it froze up, with the nude nerd image on the screen, and at that moment he saw the reference librarian's trainee (kind of a cutie, actually, in a plump girlish sort of way, a shame things had to happen the way they did) staring at him from four or five feet away with a quizzical then stunned then dismayed look, and she whispered something to the librarian, who began walking warily toward Mailman. Mailman meanwhile wanted to turn the computer off, but the CPU was out of reach; they kept it stored under the table to save space; so he began to feel around with his feet for it, and this was when the librarian arrived, saw what he'd been looking at, and let out a small, controlled squeal of horror. "Get that thing out of your hands and leave this library immediately!" she spat in the loudest whisper he'd ever heard—for her librarian training ran deep, even at the height of her shock and anger. "What thing?" he demanded. "Your *thing*," she said, and her tone reminded him, jarringly, of his mother, "put it back in your *pants* and *get out*," and he noticed she was refusing to look either at him or at the screen. "I don't have anything but this deod—" he said, and she said "I *see* what you have, now put it away!" and he looked up and saw the trainee staring at him in disbelief, her lips shut tight and her chin quivering, her eyes flashing to his lap and back to his face. He stood, stashing the deodorant in his pocket—it wasn't entirely clear what was happening—and said "Sorry, this froze here, I didn't try to look at it, it just came up," and the librarian said "I don't think you need to explain, now get out before I call the police," and he said "Fine," and walked past the stricken trainee and out the door.

The librarian called to him from the top of the steps. "I don't ever want to see your face in this library again!"

"Fine!"

"I'll remember you! If you come in I'll have you sent to jail!"

But Mailman simply waved his hand, dismissing her, dismissing the library and the Internet and nerd porn and porn in general and sex in general, telling himself "I don't need this, I don't need any of it," as his erection diminished and his heart began to swell in shame and swing low in his chest like a strung-up corpse.

Now, in the interrogation room in Syracuse, he marvels that they know what he was doing: Ronk must have been paying attention after all, the librarian must have reported him after all, nothing was said at the time but it all went into his record, along with Kelly Vireo and the coffee shop incident and everything else he ever did. He says, "I want to see my file. I want to see what they said about me."

"Who?" Fitness says, as if he doesn't know what Mailman could possibly be talking about.

"All of 'em. Ronk, the librarian, Kelly Vireo, all of 'em. What did they say?" Something has happened to his voice; the three men are staring at him now. "What else is in there? How many people filed complaints? How about Effening, the old pervert, did he complain? Or Saul Bean! What else did they say about me?"

There is a silence. Mailman senses that he has lost whatever advantage he might have had. Fitness says, in an unwittingly flawless impersonation of Gary Garrity, "What do you think they said about you?"

Mailman sighs, takes a deep breath (goddammit, why hasn't the goddam pain reliever kicked in?), lays his head down on the table and says, "I think it's time for you to take me home." He is thinking not of his house in Nestor, but of his parents' old house in Princeton. He is thinking of his room, his posters, his paperbacks; his private thoughts, thought in his private bed, in his private hours. He is thinking of the arms of his mother.

As if reading his mind, Shut-up says, "Wittle baby wantsa go home."

"No, he's right," Fitness says suddenly, and Mailman lifts his head. Syracuse and Shut-up are watching Fitness with interest. "The poor guy looks tired, let's pack it in for the day."

"Really?" says Syracuse.

"Yeah. Hey, Mister Lippincott," Fitness says, coming around the table to where Mailman sits. "I'm sorry about all this, let's just break it up. I'm sure if you think of any of the answers to the questions I've asked you, you can give me a call, what do you say?"

"Okay," Mailman says.

"Okay, good." But he gives Mailman no name or number to call, and instructs Syracuse and Shut-up (calling them Flinders and Greg, respectively) to bring him back to Nestor. Syracuse seems pleased, getting up from his chair and looking at his watch as if calculating how much time he has left today to, say, grab a beer or play with his kids. Shut-up shakes his head. "Whatever you say," he mutters, and Fitness says "I say take him back," and Shut-up says "Yeah, I heard you," and Fitness says, "Good." Then Syracuse and Shut-up lead him out the door, down the many hallways and into the bright parking lot, where the truck waits. They walk to it and Shut-up begins to unlock the back door. "Forget it," Mailman says, "I'm not getting in there again." "Well you ain't sitting up front, that's for sure, so where are you gonna ride, the roof?" "I don't know, but not in there. It nearly made me sick to my stomach." "Aw," says Syracuse, "let him ride in front." "You want to let him ride in front, you can damn well do it by yourself while I go and get a goddam fruit smoothie." "Hey, that's all right with me, all I'm saying is what's the point of sticking the poor guy in the back?" "Well, like I said, see you later, have fun, I'm taking off." "Okay, fine," says Syracuse and he gets into the truck. Mailman gets in next to him.

"Geez, fella," says Syracuse, starting the engine, "I'm real sorry about all that. That was really rough."

"Thanks," Mailman says.

"I got my whaddyacall it out one time, what is that thing?" Pointing at his belly.

"Appendix?"

"Yeah. Ouch. So, you know."

Mailman doesn't, but he senses that sympathy is being expressed, so he says "Sure" and thanks him again. As they're pulling out of the lot Mailman says, "Did he say 'Flinders'?"

"Family name," says Syracuse. "Actually I'm not supposed to talk to you. Being as you're a suspect."

"Of what, exactly?"

"Don't push your luck," says Syracuse, affecting toughness. He reaches up and rubs his bald spot.

"I think I have a right to know what I'm accused of."

"I don't wanna talk about it anymore," says Syracuse, practically in a whisper. "I'm a nice guy, but I'm not that nice." He turns on the radio. After a few minutes he seems to be in a good mood again and starts talking to the announcer—it's a sports station—saying "Aw, c'mon, give us a break, ref" and "Where were you back in January, Spackman?" with a tone half-rueful and half-delighted, as if he's happy just to have the opportunity to be unhappy about the game. He throws the truck into gear and pulls out of the parking lot. The interrogation is over. Mailman quickly falls asleep.

When he wakes up it's evening, the sky is brilliantly pinking and they're pulling into the Nestor P.O. Mailman is wet, having perspired all through his shirt and shorts, and as he rouses himself Syracuse says "You were really tossing there, friend, are you okay?" and Mailman, his dream draining away, says, "I'm fine." "Where do you want I should drop you?" "Out back," Mailman says and directs Syracuse to the Escort. He's decided he isn't going back inside, ever. He's through, that much is clear. The truck stops, Mailman thanks Syracuse and gets out and starts his own car. He follows the USPS truck out of the lot, and when he and Syracuse go in opposite directions on Route 13, Syracuse waves and honks.

From the street his house looks diminished, forlorn, like an old shoe box with doors and windows markered on. He parks out back, goes inside, takes five aspirin and goes to bed. He wakes up in the dark, shivering; the window is open and cool air is pouring in and over his sweating body. He goes into the bathroom, strips off his clothes and looks at himself in the mirror. The lump does not look as bad as he feared, and he is somewhat relieved, and reverses his conclusion that the lump is of sinister origin and is dangerous. Still, a sound rises in his throat, a sort of whine, and he gags on a sob-in-progress as tears form and one of them falls. "Shitshitshitshiiiiiit," he whispers. He is falling apart: his body (though wasn't he, just a few days ago, thinking about what great health he was in?), his mind. His career, such as it is. He stands, waits for himself to get hold of himself and ten minutes later he is still waiting, really cold now, sweating and shivering, whimpering, the lump red and throbbing, eyes stinging, knees trembling, and at last he gives up (what in the hell is *wrong* with him!) and gets in the shower. He watches the water swirl around the drain, carrying off suds and hair and flecks of dead skin. He thinks about how far those pieces of him will travel, all the way around the world and back.

When he's out of the shower and dressed he pours himself a bowl of cornflakes and sits on his cot and thinks. Not much pain now, only a gentle throbbing, like an extra heart. Almost a comfort really. It's going on midnight. Almost Wednesday. He finishes the cereal, puts the bowl down on the carpet, gets up, kicks the cats out of the way, and goes into the mail room. He looks around at all his equipment, feels tears coming on, clamps down on them until they've passed. The hell with crying, he does it too much. He goes over to the file cabinets full of photocopied mail and opens one of the drawers and gets himself two big armsful of papers. He brings them into the kitchen and dumps them on the counter, next to the sink. He reaches up into the cabinet (oh-oh-oh-oh little twinge there, he doesn't like that, but in a moment it's gone) for a box of matches and opens the box and takes out a match and lights it. Then he picks up the first piece of paper and sets it on fire and drops it, burning, into the sink. He curls another piece into the flames of the first piece and it catches, and soon he has a considerable little blaze going in his sink, the flames leaping two-three feet in the air. Maybe the neighbor can see him, the window faces her house, but who cares, he figures, what's she going to do, call the fire department? He burns the whole stack and then goes back in the mail room for more, and burns that too. He burns it all, every piece of saved correspondence, and then he takes down his milk crates and one by one he burns their contents: all the mail of a personal or business nature he has ever received, he sets on fire.

By two in the morning he's down to the last crate. He hoists it onto the counter. The kitchen is blackened, ashscraps have flown everywhere, the floor is sootily footprinted. He reeks of char and burnt hair. In the crate are letters fifty years old and more, his own mail, addressed to him: postcards with scalloped edges and addresses without zip codes and the fine tidy handwriting of generations past. He considers. In a little while he brings the crate into the bedroom, sets it down. He returns to the mail room and starts loading up boxes of crap—his glues, his stamp pads, his hot plate and teakettle—then carries them out to the Escort. He opens the hatchback, he goes in for his photocopier, the one he has kept running perfectly for so many

years, he rolls it out to the Escort and heaves it in—really *dashes* it
against the other stuff, it's a good little machine that has served him
well, and the sound of its breaking, of its plastic shell splitting horribly open, is what tells him it's really over. It's all over, this entire portion of his life. He gives this some thought as he's driving down Route
13, as he exits at the moonlit park, as he drives past the municipal
mulching depot and the golf course and down to the lake, the road
going to gravel, and then to dirt. He backs up on the filthy little
teenage drinking-and-humping beach, opens the hatch and flings his
equipment into the fucking lake, his fucking copier and all of his
fucking shit; beside him a goddam Volkswagen Passat rocks back and
forth with the motion of the teens inside, and he says "Good fucking
riddance" and then leans over the water and shouts, "Good riddance!
Good riddance!" The ride back is interminable, brief as it is; he shares
the car with his excitement, his shame, his regret.

When he gets home he takes more aspirin (now not even looking
at how many he's got there in his palm, though he takes note of their
amazing whiteness against the soot-blackened skin) and goes to bed
dirty. For a long time he doesn't sleep. Instead he thinks about
Lenore. Doesn't understand why the things he didn't like about her at
the time don't seem like bad things at all anymore, in fact seem
almost like good things. They bought the house together, it was good
as new, been lived in only by a Nestor College professor who got fired
in a cash-for-grades scandal, but when Lenore first saw it she said "This
is a house bad things happened in, and it's a house bad things will
happen in again," which he thought was ridiculous. "But the price!"
he said to her. "And it's a decent place! And the garage! No digging the
car out of the snow!" "True," she said, "but I have a bad feeling."

Yes, he was able to wear her down, but this bad feeling: she always
was having this bad feeling: "Let's get out of here, Albert" (this was in
the car, in the state park, their pants off, her underneath him, coyotes
outside, mosquitoes inside), "I have a bad feeling about this place."
"Now? Now?" "Yes," pushing him off her, reaching for her jeans, eyes

darting side to side. He drove without his pants, in protest. As they were leaving, a pickup filled with angry-looking rednecks entered, and he thought one of them might have seen down into his naked lap (the penis curled there ashamed)—the rednecks turned the truck around, and for a moment he and Lenore both thought they would give chase, but it turned out they were just parking. At home that night she said she wanted him (did she really? Probably not, she was trying to be nice) but he said no and they slept without touching. Once she had a bad feeling about his wanting to swim in the lake, they were lying on the rocky beach, people all around, three lifeguards, and she said, "Albert, don't go in there. I have a bad feeling." "What! About what?" "I don't know. About the lake. I don't want you to go in there. Please." "I'm going in, it's hot, I've been looking forward to it all day." "Don't, please, I have a feeling." "Oh, for Chrissake," he said even though he wasn't really all that interested in swimming anymore, in fact he had been thinking of packing it in and taking her to Value Dairy for an ice cream, but now he *had* to go in, he wasn't going to listen to her garbage, and so he shucked off his shirt and dove into the water and swam for a half hour solid. When he got back to the beach she was gone; he found her in the car. They went home, she didn't speak to him all day, they slept without touching, she left for the hospital the next morning without saying anything, and only at dinner that night did she talk: "What is this? It tastes like spinach." Once they were walking along Sage toward downtown and passed a woman pushing a baby in a stroller; the woman smiled, Lenore and Mailman smiled, a few seconds later Lenore turned around and then a few seconds after that turned around again. "What?" Mailman asked her. "I don't know. That woman. A car just pulled over." Mailman turned, Lenore turned, they stopped and watched the woman hand the baby into the car and then fold up the stroller and put it in the trunk, and then the woman got into the passenger seat and the car pulled into traffic. "Oh, no," she said, and Mailman said "What?" and she said, "I have a bad feeling about this." They watched the car go by; a man was driving and another man sat in the back with the baby. "Those men," she said. "The father," Mailman said, "the uncle." "No, it's something bad, I know it." "They were just picking her up." "I know, but . . . something. I have a bad feeling."

For days afterward she scanned the paper for news of a kidnapping or murder but there was nothing. "It was nothing," he told her and she said "No, nobody knows she's missing, or found the bodies, I just know something bad happened," but nothing ever came up, and a few months later they saw the same woman and baby on the Square. "It isn't her," Lenore said. "Of course it is," Mailman insisted, "she had those bangs and that lipstick." "No, her hair was parted." "She had bangs! Jesus Christ!" "You hate me, don't you," Lenore said and he said "Oh, fuck it all," and stalked off to the little playground and watched two crew-cutted twin boys beat the crap out of one another. He met her later at home and she said "There is a problem in our relationship" and he said, "I know." But that time they worked it out.

Household habits: things left in certain places, ways of doing certain things, ways of responding to certain situations, things avoided or paid undue attention: these things bothered him. Always the silverware thrown into the tray indiscriminately, always the pot left on the stove where the residue dried and hardened. Always the teakettle burned black. How many'd they go through? First time was their first week in the house; he heard her put on the kettle and then he went out to buy lumber for bookshelves (which he never built). Came back, smelled something chemical, metallic, toxic. "What's that smell?" She leapt up from the sofa where she was reading a book on pediatric psychology. "My God! The tea!" They ran to the kitchen, the kettle was burned and slumped, the wall behind the stove stained by a vague gray cone, the stove itself (brand-new) blackened around the offending burner. She was ashamed; he comforted her, thinking, Jesus, how could somebody do that? Burned the next kettle while actually in the kitchen with it, talking on the phone to her mother. For some time they used that one to prop open the kitchen window, which had a broken sash cord. She used to put the kettle on and leave for work; he'd stop home on a hunch and find it, find the stove lit, the kettle scorched. He'd call the hospital: "You left the kettle on again! You could have burned the house down!" "Albert, at this moment I am late to give one of my patients his anti-psychotics so can we please talk about this later?" But later she'd say there was nothing to talk about, so she couldn't remember to turn off the kettle, big deal, she was sorry about the stove and wall. Always when angry he would say "One of these days you'll burn us alive with your goddam teakettle and there won't be any of these problems left to solve!" and she would say, "You'd like that, wouldn't you, we'd be enveloped in flames, howling in agony and you'd be pleased that you were right." Or bills: he'd ask if she paid them, she'd say, "What bill?" He'd tell her which bill and she'd say "Yes, I think so" but a month later they'd get a late notice. "So pay the late fee, big deal," she'd say, and he'd say, "It *is* a big deal, it'll ruin our credit, is that what you want?" "Oh, well, God forbid, our *credit*. Our very important *credit*, don't want to ruin *that*."

Or clothes. He did her laundry, always he neatly folded and stowed her underwear and socks, with the underwear on the left side of the drawer and the bras in the middle and the socks on the right, but she never would acknowlege the work he had done or the careful way he'd done it. Once he confronted her and she said, "Well sure I notice, and I appreciate it, but it's just one of the chores we agreed to split up and I don't see why you need a certificate of achievement for completing it, and as for the neatness, I appreciate that too, it looks very nice, Albert, but I end up just digging through there looking for the undies I want and it all gets messed up." But still he did it, still he arranged the underwear, now because it seemed to annoy her, to remind her (he imagined) of her own slovenliness and lack of gratitude, and finally she said "You can stop folding them like that, don't waste your time," and so from then on he threw them in roughly, letting straps hang out of the drawer and socks fall on the carpet.

Always it was work that was to blame, always it was "I'm sorry, Albert, but I have more important things to worry about than whether or not I'm praising you for washing dishes," or "I guess my patients are on my mind, Albert, and not your little problems, not to be nasty about it but there it is," or "There are people at the hospital with real pain, Albert, who I have to worry about, how would you have liked it if I'd been dismissive with *you* when *you* were in the hospital, what if I was distracted and disrespectful when *you* needed to talk?" Always throwing that at him, her compassion when he was in the hospital: "You're lucky I care about my job, you might not have fared so well." "You especially should be glad I'm so responsible with my patients." "God knows if we'd even be together, Albert, if it weren't for my attention to my work."

Which was the truth, he supposed, but the more times she repeated it the less true it sounded. It is hard to believe (he thinks, lying completely awake on his cot) that they were in love through all of that, or most of it anyway, but they were, they were in love. He loved her, he loves her still. Why did he get so worked up over everything? God knows he was annoying, always demanding attention for everything like a child with his drawing of a car or tree, "Look, Mommy, look what I did!" Always expecting to be rewarded for his affection and perceived generosity (but it wasn't real generosity, was it?, he was only getting his obsessive-compulsive rocks off, it was all for his own satisfaction), when someone who really was generous would have just done nice things for their own sake and expected nothing in return.

Like Semma, for instance. Like Semma, picking flowers by the side of the road to please him. Semma, whose generosity disgusted him just a little bit, didn't it?, made him feel like she wasn't quite smart enough to see through him. Lenore wasn't enough like Semma; Semma wasn't enough like Lenore.

Christ, he was a prick.

———

Two of the cats—Semma's cats—come nosing into the smoky dark of his room, looking for the third. Reunited, the three bat one another on the head with their paws for a couple of minutes, emitting low squawks and growls, before they all head out to sharpen their claws on the rug. Damn: the cats. Something will have to be done about them. He sits up, goes to the filthy kitchen, runs water in the sink until the larger ashes stop up the drain and the water begins to rise. He turns off the water, picks up the phone, calls Lenore.

"Yes, Frank Payne." Mailman can barely tell he woke him up, so practiced is the good doctor's salutation.

"It's Albert. Look, I'm sorry it's late, but it's important, can I talk to her?"

"Jesus, Albert, it's three in the goddam morning, but all right, whatever, I'll get her."

Lenore comes on, her voice pitched and lengthened by sleep. "Aaaalbert? What iiiis it?" Frank mutters and groans in the background.

"I'm sorry, I just need to ask you something, after this I promise I'll never bother you again for any reason."

She pauses, rendering herself alert. "Is something wrong?"

"No, not really, it's just that I'm leaving in the morning and I want you to do something with the cats. Could you? I don't have time, I'm hitting the road at first light."

"Where are you going?" Concerned now.

"I'm just— it doesn't matter. I'm going to just leave a big pile of food for them and a big bowl of water, okay? If you— they'll be fine for a few days, if you can't get over here before— if you can't— I mean, don't worry about it too much. Just do something with them, is all." He sniffs. Is he getting a cold? Or is he about to cry again? "And if there's anything in the house you want, it's yours, just take it. Not that there's much here."

There is a long silence. She says, "Albert, tell me what's going on," but without, to his ear, much conviction.

"Nothing, I'm just getting out of here, it's no big deal."

"But you're coming back."

"Well, sure, okay."

"Well, are you or aren't you?"

"Aren't I what?"

"Coming back!"

("Does he know," Mailman can hear Frank muttering, "it's three in the goddam morning?")

He clears his throat. "Yes!" he says brightly. "Sure!, I'll be back, I just have to get some sleep now. Sorry to wake you up, it's no big deal, just do something with the cats is all. Okay! I'll see you."

She doesn't believe him, of course. But she says "All right" and he hangs up. It's okay, he'd rather not get into it with her, it would just make things more complicated and painful and he'd just as soon spare her the agony. He heads back toward the bedroom and swoons a little—whoa, what's this?, probably too much aspirin—and steadies himself against the doorjamb before going back to bed. This time he sleeps. When he wakes it's still dark, but a different dark, quieter, more portentous; he can hear and feel his heartbeat in his head and in every limb. There's a noise in the kitchen, something tells him it isn't the cats, and when he sits up and looks around he sees there's a light coming from the hall. He remembers the man behind the door, his hallucination, and a little jolt of fear runs through him, but he catches his breath, calms himself. Calls out, "Lenore?"

She comes in, dimly backlit by the hall light. She's wearing jeans and a baggy sweatshirt with STANFORD printed on it. One of Frank's, no doubt. She says, "What happened to the kitchen? Was there a fire?"

He sighs, says, "I'm leaving for good, sorry to alarm you this way, but if I don't go I'm going to be fired and possibly arrested and I'd just as soon avoid all that and disappear. So I'm leaving in the morning, or rather shortly, because I guess it's basically morning already."

She turns on the bedroom light and they both squint. "Arrested?" Her face bears that expression of pity and doubt he knows so well—indeed, it restores to her face the flush of youth, the fresh and private pity of 1963, when she was his nurse—but now there is something new mixed in, actual fear, and he can't bear to see it. He swings his feet to the floor and stares at them.

"It's not important, please don't concern yourself with it. I'm sorry. Everything's all right, I'm just leaving, that's all. It's a good thing. I needed a change anyway." And as he says it he realizes that it's true, even though he only said it to have something to say, he does need a change, for his life has gone nowhere, his mind to waste, and for a brief second he has a flash of optimism, and he can't wait to get on the road. And then he remembers that they might actually look for him (though without any evidence of wrongdoing, why would they?—but they might), and his chest begins to hurt, and he feels very, very tired, and the enthusiasm goes out of him. Now Lenore comes to the cot and sits down next to him, and she leans against him. Her shoulder is softer than it used to be. Or is it that his shoulder is bonier? She says, "I'm sorry, Albert."

"For what?"

She sighs. "Everything. That I couldn't make your life better."

"Nothing's wrong with my life," he says.

But this makes her cry. As on that day in the ambulance bay, when he learned that perhaps she loved him. She has done it so infrequently since then. And so he puts his arm around her and pulls her sort of close (the lump is on his other side) and says, "It's all right, I'll be all right," and they sit there awhile. He remembers the months after she broke it off with her fiancé, those times when there was nothing he could say to make her feel better, and so sat beside her, their arms and hips touching, and said nothing at all. He remembers that this used to lead to kissing, to sex, and this is the way it feels now, as if this thing must lead to the other, and so he tries to kiss her. But she takes his arm off her, she moves over an inch. Of course. "I'm sorry," he says, and she says "I'm just sorry I can't give you what you want" and gets up and goes back to the doorway. "Oh, Albert," she says, "what is happening to you?" and he realizes what she means: not that events have transpired, forcing him to move, but that he himself is undergoing a change. That he is different. That she no longer recognizes him.

And it's true: he is different. Never before this week has he lingered over his image in the mirror, never until now has he examined with such intensity so many painful memories. Not since his adventures in Khazakhstan has his routine (a routine so intertwined with his idea of himself that he believed it *was* himself) collapsed so utterly. He looks up at her and she sees that he can't answer her, and she shakes her head. No words: so unlike their marriage. He understands that she has a way out now, she won't have to deal with him anymore, she won't see him on the Square or in the neighborhood or have to feed the cats for him. She will be able to enjoy her marriage and forget she was ever married before, and this visit, this final visit to him, will come to seem like a sort of closure (and how he hates that word, now more than ever: *closure*, as if things ever stop, as if anything can be forgotten), a poignant end to their long history together, an excuse to stop worrying about him. And despite this, Mailman is not angry, because the idea appeals to him as well. He will no longer have to feel guilty about forcing her to continue caring for him. He won't have to feel like a fool every time he asks Frank to bring her to the phone. He decides right then and there: he's never going to call her again. Enough's enough. Instead of answering her questions he says, "Well, goodbye." She lets out a muffled sob—it sounds like a cough, and she covers her mouth accordingly, as if trying to prevent any more misery from flying out into the room—and says to him, whispers practically, "Goodbye, Albert." She waits a moment, giving him one more chance to stop her, and then she walks away, her hand still over her lips. He listens to her leave the house.

He continues to listen for another fifteen minutes: not to Lenore, but to the hush of sleeping Nestor, its handful of sounds—insects, traffic, a train—only calling attention to the silence that surrounds them. Then he gets up, takes another shower, gingerly washing the lump, which is tender but not, for now, truly painful. He dresses, stuffs some clothes into a duffel bag (how liberating it is not to care what he brings and what he leaves behind!), brings it to the bathroom and sweeps in his bathroom stuff, zips the bag shut. He goes to the kitchen, dumps the big sack of cat food onto the floor, fills a metal salad bowl with water and puts it next to the food. He prepares a pot of coffee, searches for and finds a large travel mug in the cabinet, and waits for the coffee to brew. Come on, come on. It is Wednesday, June 7, 2000. Out his kitchen window dimmed by soot, the sun is rising. He wants it to rise on the new Mailman, the free Mailman, the Mailman of the highways, but the coffeemaker is indifferent to his urgency, squeezing the coffee out drop by drop, the same way it has every morning for twenty years. Hurry it up! He gets on his knees, peering through the glass, *willing* the coffee to brew, and at last he can't take it anymore; he yanks out the urn, letting coffee drip and sizzle on the blazing silver platter, and fills up his mug. He unplugs the still-dripping coffee maker, and for good measure goes around the house unplugging everything, the toaster, the lamps, the clock-radio (5:44 is its last message to mankind). Only then does he pick up his bag and mug and last remaining crate of personal mail and carry them out to the Escort.

What is left? Nothing. He returns to the back door, preparing to close and lock it: but then, on second thought, he doesn't. He leaves it open. The cats will leave too, and find their own place in the world. The last thing he hears, before he leaves his old life behind, is the coffee-maker, still hissing, as if it doesn't even realize it's been unplugged.

PART TWO

—

PART TWO

SEVEN

South

_____

When the sun rises, it is greeted by a beast as alien to downtown Nestor as the brontosaurus: a glistening, sinuous creature that creeps past churches and schools and silver maples, its spine aglow with motes of shimmering color; its cry a clamorous bleat; its motion so sluggish—so grandly, indifferently slow—that one could be forgiven for presuming it to be entirely motionless. Beneath a single scale of the beast's steely back, Mailman (the new Mailman, the Mailman of the highways) is presuming exactly that. He has been sitting here in the traffic jam for half an hour, barely fifty yards from the house he left behind, still in the shadow of his own silver maple, its branches spreading summerly over his block. His coffee mug is already empty. In front of him is a bumper-sticker-covered Volvo wagon (DON'T LIKE ABORTION? DON'T HAVE ONE!; KILL YOUR TELEVISION; I ♣ MY CAT), its cargo area packed nearly to the roof with cardboard boxes bulging with grubby children's clothes and toys; its driver, a gray-haired survivalist-type of indeterminate gender, bangs a plump arm against the Volvo's door in a hiccupping rhythm and peers through pinprick eyes at Mailman in the sideview mirror every ten seconds or so. Behind him, in a spotless black Toyota Camry, a necktied ex-frat-boy yammers into a cell phone, occasionally smacking his dashboard for emphasis and running his free hand through his hair with uncommon vehemence. The smell of smoke on his clothes is the only proof Mailman has that all that happened last night really happened; if he were to turn right at the next block and go home, he'd half expect to find the kitchen unbesmirched, his possessions all in place. He won't do that, though. He's gone for good, even if only by fifty yards.

The radio says sun. So does his view out the window, thank you very much. There's another antidevelopment demonstration around the Square, thus the traffic; the protesters are protesting the construction of a 'Mart, Wal- or K- he doesn't hear. Instead he is busy enduring a wave of remorse and loneliness—he won't be around for the next local controversy. Or the next Friday radio scramble, either. Ah, hell. But then again, you can't drive through life looking at the rearview mirror, can you, otherwise you'll smack into a phone pole, or worse yet a pedestrian, or a pedestrian with a stroller, and you'll be a child murderer, all for the fleeting comfort of dwelling upon the past. So forget it. It's forward only from here on in, no more maudlin memories, no more feeling sorry for himself and his pain, by which he means both emotional pain and the pain under his arm. And anyway pain is, by definition, always in the past, isn't it—the signal that a wound sends your brain is a fraction of a second old by the time it actually registers, like the light from a star that has already gone nova. So ignore the pain, it's old news, and let's get the show, or at least the car, on the road. He is, after all, a mailman. He knows the shortcuts.

When a break appears at last he turns off at Hamilton and drives west to the creek, follows Creekedge up to the high school access road, then cuts through the parking lot. The punks have arrived and are out leaning against their beaters, smoking and horsing around— isn't there some rule against this kind of behavior? Why isn't a teacher or at least a janitor out here telling them to quit the puffing and get their skinny rears into the building? They watch as he passes and one of them apes him, placing his hands on an invisible steering wheel, pretending to steer, eyebrows arched, lips pursed. He makes a left onto Onteo Vista, which takes him up the hill and through the college. Nobody's awake at NYTech, the semester's over, after all, and he coasts through the ghostly campus like a haunt, peering up at the clock tower presently under renovation, the tiny workmen clinging to scaffolds and ropes. I won't be here to see it finished, he thinks. I won't be here when the students return. Ah, stop that! He picks up speed, crosses two gorges, gets himself past campus and away, into the outlying provinces, not into the future but the absolute present.

Here it is: the oft-ballyhooed here and now. A country road, triple-stitched with power lines; barns and produce stands flashing past. A meadow-cum-junkyard bearing a painted sign, NOT FOR SALE GO AWAY; pastel trailers affixed with decks and garden pinwheels. Children waiting at windraked gravel turnoffs for an eventual school bus, for the start of summer. Mongrel dogs loping after nimble deer. Piles of burning weeds. Empty trash cans, rolling across the road. When the radio reports that a protester has been hit by a car, Mailman switches it off: that place, that life, is gone to him now. He is a slowly moving spot on a map, citizen of nowhere, denizen of roads. Townless, he is freed from the drear of routine, the prying eyes of neighbors, the bitter tongues of managers, the burden of familiarity. Now, if he offends or is offended, the party in question recedes at sixty-four miles per hour, never again to be seen. He is free.

Unless of course they're following him. Unless they were up in his tree all night with binoculars, watching him burn his papers. Unless they followed him to the lake, captured him on film ditching his copier: or worse, broke into his house while he was gone, before he'd destroyed everything. In which case there's evidence; in which case there's a case. Maybe he isn't so free after all. He pulls over at a farm stand and buys a little basket of strawberries, then sits in his car, eating, watching the road for suspicious vehicles. He thinks he's got them when a big black Chevy pulls in, but it's an old lady and her husband; he watches her hoist his walker out of the trunk and lead him to it.

Back on the road his tires sizzle against the pavement; he finds himself on Route 17, sclerotic artery of the Southern Tier. Mountains rise around him and shunt him east-southeast. All there is to do now is sit and stare straight ahead, and wait for tall buildings to heave into view. It will take hours. The wise choice would be to settle in, to become the car: a half-machine-half-mailman, devouring miles and quarts of oil in pursuit of a single goal: ahead. It is his wont to do this, no fussing, no radio, no snack stops; but today, for some reason, he cannot quell his agitation; and as the minute hand creeps around the dust-blurry dial of the onboard clock, his agitation only intensifies. By nine he feels ready to throw himself out onto the scrolling asphalt, and to prevent this he stops at a fast-food joint for some breakfast. In moments he is bearing a tray (coffee, juice, an egg and sausage sandwich on a toasted English muffin, French toast sticks with a little tub of maple-flavored corn syrup) through a haze of cigarette smoke to an empty table by the window. The stagnant Catskills gene pool is arrayed around him in all its brackish variety: a couple of hennaed old ladies playing cards, a bearded loony grunting at the want ads, a goth teen mom and her pale squirming squealer tucked into a stroller. All are smoking (except the baby), but he is surprised not to be bothered: his traveler's freedom has provided a sort of gas mask for his peevishness, a secondhand smock onto which he can wipe from his hands the foulness of humanity.

Without delay, he crunches into his egg and sausage sandwich. It is perfect: the crunchiness of the muffin's crust giving way, beneath his teeth, to the sweet cushiony mealiness inside, and then the lesser crunch of the muffin's crannied underbelly followed by the yellow, salted tang of the special sauce; and then, at last, the fenneled oil-rich juice of the patty that heralds the patty itself, hot and meaty and heavily grained. For a moment he is lost in the food. And then, washing that first bite down with juice, then coffee, he realizes why he was so anxious: he is not, at this moment, delivering mail.

Nine-fourteen on a Wednesday morning! And he's not delivering mail! He is struck by a momentary panic: people, postal customers, calling up the main office, "Where in the hell's my mail?" But of course *someone* is delivering the mail. *His* mail. Conceivably in *his truck*. Which is no longer his. Which never was.

He dredges a French toast stick through the syrup, but his heart isn't in it. The fact of his expendability—of the interchangeability of all mailmen—begins to sink in. To most customers, the mailman is only the hand that bears the mail, nothing more. In the old days, the days when people stayed home (women, he guesses he means), he stopped and talked: they knew him. Now nobody's around. Always working, always traveling. Mexicans cut the grass, machines wash the car, maids scrub the floors. That's why he is—was—so quick. No reason to stop. He remembers (French-toast-stick-bearing hand frozen betwixt mouth and syrup tub) the family mailman in Princeton—handsome fella, big eyebrows, big white choppers—hanging around the kitchen, drinking coffee, eating cookies. Hell, sitting down at the table, smiling at his, Mailman's, mother. Mom smiling back.

Was that it? Just smiling? "Afternoon, little Al," the mailman said, patting Mailman's head with a strong hand warm and damp from . . . from holding his mother's hand?

Can that be right?

He rummages in his memory for further evidence. He could swear he saw it: coming into the room to see them holding hands across the kitchen table, grinning like idiots. The quick withdrawal. The greeting. The head-pat. Was his mother really screwing the mailman?

When he glances at the clock he sees that something like twenty minutes have passed while he gathered wool. The smoking patrons have left. The clerks snap dishrags at one another, laughing. He takes a few more halfhearted bites of his sandwich and eats another French toast stick, and he finishes off the lukewarm coffee, having to sort of choke it down, before bringing his tray to the trash can. As he walks out to the parking lot, he remembers the mailman's Brylcreemed coif; his nervous, tapping foot in its scuffed black shoe. His mother's sleepy eyes as she said, "Albert, go outside and play." His schoolbooks thudding on the floor as they slid from their strap. His own route, the one on which he has been supplanted forever, is gone from his mind. *The mailman stole my mother's love.*

He returns to the highway. The Tappan Zee approaches, asserts itself as a stripe on still water, recedes behind him. *The mailman.* The Saw Mill River Parkway twists and dips like the dirt track it once was; faster movers honk and pass. *My mother.* He begins to experience fairly intense chest pains and a shortness of breath and profuse perspiration and wishes that he had remembered to take his aspirin out of the duffel when he was at the fast-food joint. His hands tighten on the wheel. Now Manhattan is revealed between copses of trees and over stone walls; gray tenements appear as if pasted onto gray sky. He merges onto the Henry Hudson. On the river, barges barge; New Jersey sleeps under a blanket of fog that Manhattan, its insomniac mother, has managed to slough off. Mailman is dizzy with pain and thirst. The road renames itself after Joe DiMaggio and he can stand it no longer, he has to get that bottle, he finds a construction pulloff where backhoes idle, and parks. Gets out. Leans over the open hatchback (there, poking out from under his duffel, is a fragment of the copier, a paper feed tray, that he forgot to fling into the creek) and crunches four of the bitter little pills without water, having first to suck off the bittersweet easy-swallow coating. His lump—growth, cyst, barnacle, swelling, protuberance, what have you—feels like a rolled umbrella he's been forced to pin under his arm owing to a misjudgment about the possibility of rain, and he thinks: Okay, that's not so bad, having to hold a rolled umbrella under my arm indefinitely, there are greater burdens a man might have to bear.

It is Eighteenth Street he thinks he wants, so this is where he turns. The shadows of warehouses envelop and cool him; his dizziness subsides. Somewhere he must park, so he circles, eyes alert for a brake light in the barricade of cars. He is reminded of that morning's traffic jam in Nestor; he is reminded of his pass at Lenore. He ought to be embarrassed by the pass—it *was* embarrassing—but he feels as distant from it as if it were a hundred years ago, in some gentler, subtler era, when such emotions mattered. Now there is only parking, there is only getting a drink of water.

At last he finds a space, close enough to a hydrant to have deterred more fearful drivers, but far enough away for comfort, for now. The space is on Nineteenth, in front of an art gallery that used to be a warehouse. On a loading dock painted glossy black sits a desk, where a burly, short-haired man in a black tee shirt is stationed. He placidly reads the *Post* (BAD COP GETS LIFE), while behind him large white canvases bear red words, their own lurid headline: SEX. DEATH. RAPE. GOD. Mailman pulls his duffel from the hatch and begins to walk; first detecting, then denying, then ignoring, a faint numbness extending from his right hip down to the ankle. Few people are on the street; they are working or, if unemployed, have not yet gotten out of bed. It's been years, but he finds the building quickly, a block from Broadway and Union Square: a fifteen-story smear of sootstained art deco, too interesting to demolish, to dumpy to restore. There in the directory box is her name, G. Lippincott (onstage she uses the name Gillian French), spelled out in little white plastic letters with an upside-down 7 standing in for the capital L.

He enters the lobby and is glancing around for the elevator when the doorman intercepts him: "Somebody expecting you?" he says, then adds "Sir?" in the same tone he might use to say "Buddy?," which is clearly what he'd prefer. Mailman doesn't like the look of the guy, a troll of a man in a red suit covered with gold piping and epaulets, exhaling his final breath of smoke from the break he's been on.

"My sister," Mailman says, "Gillian Lippincott, I'll just go ahead on up."

"Miz Lippincott ain't in," the doorman says.

"Ah, well, did she say when she'd be back?"

"No," he says, "and how do I know you're her brother anyway, not that I'd let you in even if you was her brother."

"What is this?" Mailman says, "there didn't used to be a doorman here, especially not one who stood around telling people to go away." The wide face crinkles like a pug's. "Well, I didn't say that," the doorman says, "but now that you mention it maybe you oughta get on your way." "That's all right," Mailman says, "I'll sit and wait, thanks, I've been here enough times." Although it has been a while, so long that he doesn't feel as proprietary about the place as he's pretending to; in fact he's more than a little uncomfortable. They *have* renovated, they've added an awning propped up on brass poles, they've added a nice red entryway carpet. He sits. The doorman leans over him, obviously pleased to seem tall just this once. "Sorry, you can't do that, Miz Lippincott didn't say nothing about a brother coming." "Well, she isn't expecting me, but I *am* her brother, just look at my face, for Chrissake." The doorman backs up a step. "You don't look much like her to me, so howsabout you just get outta here." But then he's distracted by another visitor and goes to the desk to direct her, and Mailman is almost 100% certain he hears her say "Gillian Lippincott?" and is almost equally certain the doorman replies "I'll call up to her," and the woman heads for the elevator and the doorman reaches for the phone.

"Wait!" Mailman says to the woman, who stops, startled—she's very attractive, he seems to recognize her—probably some actor friend of Gillian's. She says "Pardon me?" as the doorman mutters into the phone. "Gillian!" Mailman shouts in the doorman's direction, hoping to get his voice through to her, "it's Albert! Let me in!" and the woman says "Excuse me, but who are you?" "I'm her brother Albert, for Chrissake, tell her I'm here, this little gnome won't let me up."

"She never said anything about a brother." Now the doorman's hanging up, starts toward the elevator doors where the two of them are standing. "Just tell her I'm down—" Mailman says but then the doorman arrives and grabs him by the arm and gives it a sharp tug. "All right, that's enough of this crap," he says, and Mailman stumbles and the lump under his arm presses itself against the doorman's hand and the doorman lets go, fast, frightened but seemingly unsure of what. He recovers himself, begins to push Mailman toward the door: truculent little pushes with both hands that require only minimal contact with Mailman's body.

"And stay out!" the doorman shouts as Mailman stumbles out under the awning—a phrase intended to show anyone who happens to be walking by that *this* doorman means business, and if you're planning to execute one or another shenanigan in an apartment building, you'd better not pick this one, buster. There is a throbbing under the arm of course where the doorman bumped the lump, but the throbbing isn't one of pain, only pressure, for the aspirin have commenced with their excellent work. Mailman is, however, experiencing a shortness of breath, as if the doorman's contact has pressed the growth deeper into his body, obstructing the lung: his first few efforts to draw air are in vain, and he falls against the building's granite foundation clutching his throat and imagining a hideous and humiliating death on the sidewalk. But at last he can breathe, and he gasps, his hands flying out involuntarily as if to scoop the oxygen into his body. A pear-shaped woman walking a Yorkie traces a wide arc around him. He recovers himself, and is about to start formulating a plan B, when the glass door flies open and Gillian sweeps out onto the sidewalk shouting his name.

There is a moment, before she notices him, when he is able to observe her undetected: she has put on weight, but she also seems to have put on height, as if she has not aged but magnified. She looks left for him, then right, and he recalls her naked pirouettes before the mirror, and he says "Here," and she goes to him and embraces him, screaming, "What are you *doing* here, you poor *man*, that *awful* little desk jockey gave you a hard time, how *dare* he, oh it's so *good* to see you!" Mailman gets a good whiff of her neck, same sweaty old Gillian, smelling like a peach that a dog has been carrying in its mouth, the scent stirring him in ways both disturbing and reassuring. He extricates his arms and returns her embrace and she holds him out at arms' length and says, "Let me look at you—my God, you look like hell, what have you been *eating*?"

"It's not my diet," he says, "or not totally anyway, I haven't been feeling so hot and I lost my job."

"You poor man, lost your *job*, how'd it happen?"

"Long story."

"Well come *in*, come *in*, we'll take you upstairs and get you a *drink*, you can meet my friend, but first let's talk to that little *prick*."

In the lobby Mailman stands by idly, uncomfortably, while Gillian attacks the hapless doorman. "But Miz French," he says, "you said if any man came I'm supposed to kick him out, that's what you said, on account of—" "For God's sake, man, use your *discretion*, I didn't mean my *brother*." "But he don't look nothing like you!" "Enough backtalk!" It goes on like this for a couple of minutes, the doorman shrinking, his eyes darting back and forth among the objects on his desk—the stapler, the date stamper—and surely Mailman's noticed this before (though he can't remember ever doing so), but Gillian looks and sounds remarkably like their mother, a heavier version of their mother, her voice a full-throated rasp, her body shaking with the force of her manic, almost rapturous harangue. She is not, as she once was, graceful. She is something else: less lovely, more powerful. When she's through she says "Come on, Albert" and strides past him to the waiting open elevator (the sort of instant prop that tends to manifest itself for Gillian whenever needed, as if carefully maneuvered into place by unseen sycophants). Mailman tries to make sympathetic eye contact with the utterly deflated doorman (now plotting, perhaps, a way back into Gillian's good graces and the check she probably gives him at Christmas) but the man is bent over the desk, pretending there is work upon it that needs to be done.

In the elevator she takes his hands, again says "Let me look at you," again tells him he looks like hell. "I know," he says, "I know, but the thing is I lost my job, I've been depressed about that, I've decided to just pack it in and hit the road for a while." "For a while? Then you'll be staying here? In New York?" Her face registers an excitement, an eagerness, but his sister is an actor, and Mailman notices how quick she is to qualify that, by "here," she means "New York" and not "my apartment." And so he says, "Oh, I don't know, we'll have to see, I figured that wherever I ended up I ought to come see you first and talk it over." Her relief is genuine. She smiles, shakes her head, takes his face into her ring-covered hands (and when did she become a ring-wearer, an accessorizer?), pulls him a little too roughly toward her and plants a loud dry kiss on his lips. He is thrown off balance, and to compound his disorientation the elevator stops suddenly, and he is forced to send an arm out to support himself against the wall, where a metal bar has been installed, apparently for this very purpose.

She leads him into her apartment, where the attractive woman from downstairs is sitting at the kitchen table pouring whiskey from a hip flask into a steaming mug of coffee. He'd thought she was in her early thirties, but the natural light from the window reveals her to be closer to forty, perhaps even forty-five. "Annabelle Rauss, my brother Albert." "Hello," he says and holds out his hand, and she barely touches it as she says, "Pleased." "You've seen her on TV and on the stage, Albert, remember the miniseries about the alcoholic family, Annabelle played my sister who *beat* her teenage son with designer *belts*?" "Yes, of course," he says, though he doesn't, "what are you working on now?" "Trying to get a fucking job," says Annabelle Rauss. "Ah," says Mailman, and Gillian says, "Well, it looks like I'm the unem*ploy*ment shrink today, Albert just lost his job and he's come to New York to *moon* over it and rely on his sister's hospi*tal*ity." "And what aren't you doing anymore, *Albert*," says Annabelle in open mockery of Gillian's inflection, though Gillian doesn't seem to notice it.

"I'm a mailman," says Mailman. Was, he thinks but doesn't say.

At this the unemployed actress openly cackles, as if he's told a terrific joke. "You are fucking kidding me. A laid-off mailman. Now that's the bottom of the barrel." Gillian, to her credit, steps in and says "The same barrel you're *drinking* yourself to the bottom of, my dear?"—and before she can respond, "Now move your tushy and make room for my brother or I'll cut off the half-caf *and* the Jim Beam." Annabelle Rauss obliges with a shrug, as if the whole thing were not the very big deal that it almost certainly is.

But she has been silenced, and Mailman has nothing to say: so Gillian is forced to fill the gap with stories, addressed to her brooding friend, of her childhood exploits with Mailman, which cast Gillian in the role of the cocky-yet-tolerant big sister who simultaneously protects, loves, and is annoyed by her admiring younger brother. The incidents themselves are genuine (to the best of Mailman's memory) but exclude details which, were he telling the story (not that he would), he would feel duty-bound to append, e.g.: the time they went trudging through the woods looking for lost Indian treasure and got lost, so that Gillian had to employ her superior navigational skills to lead them home (omitted detail: afraid to pee outdoors, Gillian wet herself and had to leave her undies hanging from a branch, after which she whooped and danced through the trees holding her skirts above her head); the time Gillian sacrificed her dolly on the train tracks and the two of them staged a mock funeral on the railbed, complete with candles and fake mumbled Latin (omitted detail: Gillian held her palms over the candles until they blistered and blackened, and then she passed out); the time Gillian tied the two of them together to a tree trunk and couldn't get them loose and they cried and promised to marry each other and have babies (omitted detail: there was no tree, she had tied them together face to face, and they could easily have untied themselves if they wanted to). Mailman wonders if Gillian is intentionally choosing only those stories with latent sexual and masochistic content, or if she is so choosing unconsciously, or if *all* their shared childhood experiences had latent sexual and masochistic content. At any rate Mailman is growing uncomfortable and Annabelle Rauss bored, and soon she has gotten up and left with four or five enhanced coffees inside her, and Mailman is left alone with his sister.

For a while they just sort of sit there. Manhattan is outside the window, and it is mesmerizing, what with the birds wheeling around the buildings, so Mailman looks at it; Gillian clears her throat a few times, sighs, shifts in her chair. It seems to him that all the time they spent together as children, they spent playing elaborate roles, roles which are no longer appropriate. Which may never have been appropriate. What they have, in fact, is a very close telephone relationship. He glances up at the kitchen counter, where a smudged white telephone sits, ensnarled in hopeless twisted strands of cord, and he longs to talk to her on it.

"Well!" she says, patting her lap.

"Well."

"How long has it been, Albert?"

"Years, I guess."

She throws her arms in the air, as if suddenly remembering why he is here. "I suppose I'm going to have to ask you eventually, so I might as well ask you now: *wha-at haaaapened?*"

"I was fired."

"*Why*, dear."

He considers for a while before saying, "I just was."

"You know," she says, getting up and walking around behind him and putting her hands on his shoulders and idly rubbing them as she speaks, "I've been rather *worried* about you since we talked last week, thinking about the *hallucination* you claim to have had about your little ticker escaping and chasing you down the street, and I wondered if perhaps everything was not quite right in your head. You didn't go 'postal,' did you, dear?"

"No."

"It would be awfully *dramatic* if you had."

"I didn't."

"But you're unwell. Your body. You're *sick*."

"I suppose so."

"I know a fine doctor, Albert, a naturopath, quite *handsome* actually, I could have him over here in a jiffy and to be honest wouldn't mind seeing him slinking around the premises for a few hours . . ."

"No, I don't need a doctor." Still the rubbing, now onto the upper arms, the neck, the fingernails biting slightly into the skin. He shivers. At least they don't have to look into each other's eyes, which he supposes is why she's doing it. He feels the weight of her discomfort in her fingers.

"Are you *cold*? Do you want a hot drink? Do you want a bath?"

"I'm fine."

A heavy sigh from behind him. "God," she says, a new unguardedness creeping into her voice, though he can't tell if it's a put-on or not—he supposes that when you've spent your life pretending, everything becomes an act, with the character you're playing being more or less distant from your own—and she comes around him sliding her hand down his arm to rest in his hand and she sits down beside him, still not looking at him, and says, "God, Albert, listen to us, we've run out of things to say to each other already. What's happened to us?" And then he knows it's an act, which bothers him less than he might have expected.

"Nothing happened. We're just adults. We don't have anything in common."

"*Failure*, Albert," she says, now playing someone who really has failed, and this annoys him because his failure is absolutely real.

"You aren't a failure."

"I'm not the success I *expec*ted to be," she says, "after Yale and all that." She shakes her head, and he realizes that this is her way of sympathizing—pretending to be as low as he is—and so he lets her go on.

"By now I wanted an *Oscar*. A *Tony*. I wanted to write and direct. Did you know that I tried to write a play? Oh, all right, let me come clean—I tried to write *lots* of plays, Albert. One of them was even *produced*, my *God*, it was such a humiliating *bust*. I have not realized my dreams, not at all." And she lowers her head and shakes it slowly so that her gray hair (to his surprise balding slightly in the middle where the whorls meet, just like his) waves to and fro like the sudsy strands in an automatic car wash. He experiences a wave of frustration with her that threatens to undo the progress they have so far made.

But *what* progress does he want to make exactly? He believes there is some urgency, that whatever it is he hopes to recover (because that's what it is, a recovery, of some understanding they had when they were children that has been lost) ought to be recovered now or it might never be recovered at all. And so he squeezes her hand and leans over to plant a brotherly smooch on her bald spot, but at this moment she sits up (her inner director presumably having shouted "Cut!") and her large head crashes into his approaching face, and his lip mashes itself against his top row of teeth.

She lets out a sort of yelp and he jerks back, his hand flying to his face. "Christ!" he says and tastes blood. "Oh, Albert!" she coos, in a tone tinged both with sympathy and irritation, and she reaches out and touches his lips, his cheek; she leans close and (unable, it appears, to stop herself) kisses him gently, wetly, sweetly on the lips.

He is stirred. There is a stirring. Perhaps aware of this she sits up straight and he is forced to readjust his position on the chair, his equipment in his shorts, his brotherly perspective. He says "Ow." She says "Poor baby." The two laugh and her laugh is unscripted.

"I'm sorry," they say at once. They laugh again, their eyes scurrying to opposite corners of the room.

They continue to sit. Their chuckles evaporate.

Gillian bursts into tears.

She really does burst—there is a flying outward, an explosion, her arms jerking and her knees audibly bonking together, her mouth opening suddenly and cheeks distending with the movement of her lips, and her face is suddenly wet all over, as if the tears were coming out of pores in the skin—and she is moaning, mumbling, and he just sits there in astonishment and confusion. What in the hell is this? "I'm sorry!" she says to him through slobber, which she sucks back into her mouth, and since there are no tissues nearby she uses her wrist to wipe her runny nose and then deftly wipes the wrist on her dress. "I'm sorry!"

"What are you sorry for?" he says when she's quieted enough for him to speak.

"You came here for . . . my *support*," she groans, "and I give you *this*."

"I don't think I know what's wrong."

"You don't, you couldn't possibly," she says, and suddenly covers her face with both hands, and stands up, and goes to the kitchen and gets a paper towel and towels herself off. When she returns her face is dry but new-looking, pink, like a furled bud, and the wiped snot has hardened a little in a long smear across her front. She sits. "I'm sorry, Albert, I'm sure you think my life is exciting and successful"—and damned if she isn't acting again. But enough!, he's got to stop noticing.

"But the truth is that I'm depressed, I'm always depressed, and sometimes I can barely come to work, and sometimes I don't. I was just *fired* from a *play*, by a *director* I happened to have been *fucking*"—and here she gives her own breasts a sudden squeeze, for emphasis, a gesture he finds odd and, yes, stirring—"this little forty-year-old *twerp*—and now I'm out of work and out of sex and out of money, and I'm just an old lady with a bipolar disorder, just like all the other unfuckable gray-headed bitches in this stupid city."

"Oh," he says.

"I suppose with you here, it's like when we were kids and Mother would be angry and Daddy would be hiding in the basement, and you and I would sit in my room and say all those *terrible things* about them, about how we were going to kill them and get the money out of the bank and go on a long trip—I remember studying the way Mother drove the car, trying to memorize what all the parts did. I was tall enough by the time I was eleven, we could have done it." She laughs. Mailman is thinking: *Kill* them? Kill their *parents*? Did they really talk about that? He doesn't remember—probably they did, but it sounds like Gillian took it a lot more seriously. These days it really happens—kids kill their parents. But she goes on:

"Except the difference is that Mother and Daddy aren't the problem, *we're* the problem, we're just like them, aren't we?"

"I guess." Though he has rarely thought about it—he's thought about his parents, sure, but never his own similarity to them, which is of course beyond his control and thus beyond his ability to tolerate thinking about. Simply the thought of thinking about it now causes his neck to tense up, and he feels his head give a little involuntary tremble.

"We *hide* like Daddy, we *rage* and *fail* like Mother." She sighs deeply, flopping her body over the small table, which creaks on its tiny legs. And of course she's right: he sees himself at home in Nestor, in his felonious workshop, cut off from the sunny, law-abiding world; he sees himself lunging at poor Maurice Renault, his inspiration transmuted into anger. Of course, the mail room is gone now. Rage is all that's left. "*Doomed*, Albert," his sister is saying, "we were doomed from the start. We are *thwarted*. Always. Everything's *harder* for us than it is for other people."

"Yes," he says, and that much is true, it is harder for him. He doesn't think other people are all that much smarter than he is. He's as smart as Renault, for sure. But obstacles are always thrown into his path, and the obstacles are himself. He pictures himself encountering the obstacles that are himself: that is, himself walking down an open road, free and clear as far as he can see, and then suddenly there's something in his path: a head, a giant head, *his* head, it's scowling and old, and hot to the touch. He tries to dodge but the head is quick, it ratchets from side to side, it tilts and nudges and mutters, "Back, back." He throws himself into the head and feels its enormous nose punch his chest. Ow! And then he realizes that his growth is smarting and he pats his pockets for his pills. "Say," he says, "do you have some pain reliever? Aspirin?"

"What hurts?" she says after a significant pause, annoyed to have been interrupted.

"This— I have this thing— it's just a kind of bruise or contusion or something I have under my arm."

She leans forward; he draws back. "Let me see," she says. He says "No." She says, "Just give me a little look, what'd you do, get into a fight?" He says, "Car door, it happened that night I called you, I was getting in the car and caught myself on the corner, now do you have anything?"

She makes a face, gets up, leaves the room. He can hear her rummaging. "Oh, here," she says and returns with a large white bottle. "Tylenol with codeine. You can get it in Canada without a prescription."

He takes the bottle, shakes out a few pills, gets himself a glass of water and swallows, leaning over the kitchen sink. "How many did you take, Albert?" his sister asks him. He says, "I don't know, four or five." She says, "Good Christ, Albert, you're going to kill yourself, don't you know what codeine is?" He shrugs, sits down. "It hurts."

They stare at one another for several seconds. He is violating the rules of their relationship by expressing pain: this is supposed to be her shtick. She keeps glancing down at his chest, his arm: can she see the lump? His shirt is loose-fitting but he thinks she can make it out, make *something* out. In her gaze he reads irritation, curiosity, even concern. At last he says, "Let's go get something to eat, it's on me. Wherever you like."

"How *sweet* of you, little brother," she says, snapping out of it, "of *course* I accept, but first let me make a few phone calls." She makes them in the bedroom while he sits in the kitchen listening: she pleads with someone he supposes is an agent ("Surely there's some *haughty matron* I can play?"); she calls friends "just to catch up" but manages to mention offhandedly her desire, her need for work. "No," she says to one friend, "I left that production, Roald and I didn't see eye to eye, and besides, my work there was done, I reached the deepest levels after two nights." She howls with laughter, bursts into song, she schmoozes and seduces. There is no reason for her to do this now, except as a response to his gobbling of the Tylenol—but it's petty of him to think that, where is his brotherly respect? When she's finished—it takes an hour—they walk down the street to a Chinese place. It's no different from the ones in Nestor. Either the place is a comfort to her or she doesn't believe that he really has the money to take her out somewhere nice. While they're waiting for their food she says, "I hope you enjoyed my *performance*." "What performance?" he says, thinking she means for the waitress, which was very convincing, exactly like a woman ordering moo shu pork and corn chowder. "On the *phone*," she says. "I hope it was *fun* for you to hear what an old whore your sister's turned into."

"I wasn't really paying—"

"Because that was your *real* sister in there, the one who needs to *beg* to get what she wants. Just like Mother did, letting all those gold-chain Guidos fuck her so she could sing. The difference is that Mother *actually sang*, and I prostitute my *soul* for *nothing*." He says, "Well, it's part of your profession, isn't it, people expect you to—" and she says, "Oh, just fuck off, Albert, it's no wonder you couldn't keep a marriage together, you don't know the first thing about how to talk to a woman." This outburst seems to set things right, and she moves on to other topics, the crappiness of movies, the difficulty of finding a cab.

The food arrives. It looks and smells like every other Chinese restaurant meal he has ever eaten. Mailman supposes he ought to feel insulted, at least irritated, by his sister, but for some reason his emotions seem detached from his perceptions; his mind feels like it's suspended in a mason jar, somewhere far away. Little is said, except warnings from Gillian about the food: "Don't eat the red chilis." "Shell that first, Albert." At some point during the meal he notices that his hands seem very soft and large, and the flavor of the food is beginning to fade, and he can't quite tell where it ends and his tongue begins, and consequently he bites his tongue.

"Ousshhhttthh," he says through the mouthful of food or tongue or both.

"Are you all right?" Gillian says.

He manages to swallow. His words come out very slowly. "Must be the pills."

She is suddenly alert. "Well, tell me if you're going to pass out, so we can do it outside. I don't want to be kicked out of my favorite restaurant." So she really *does* like it.

"No, I won't pass out," he says and continues to eat. But after a few more bites he feels that he really *is* chewing on his own tongue, and he touches his lips expecting them to come away bloody, and when they don't he swallows and for a moment chokes and gags and has to hold the table with both hands to master himself. "Excuse me," he says before Gillian can comment, and he stumbles off toward where it looks like the bathroom might be, his tongue playing at the flap of skin on the inside of his lip where he bonked into Gillian in her kitchen, his feet seeming to stick and then unstick themselves from the carpet, the room swelling and blurring around him.

The bathroom—there is only one, and for a moment he's glad he's not a woman having to sit where so many men have inexpertly pissed—is dark and dirty and cramped. He bangs his elbow on the wall trying to get the door closed and almost falls backward over the toilet. There's a dead potted plant next to the sink. In the pot, surrounding the dead plant, are cigarette butts, a variety of brands, stuck into the dry dirt so that they all stand up: a new kind of plant, sprouting from the roots of the old. The mirror is smeared and splashed and his face looks puffy in it, probably from walking around in the heat. He blows his nose on a piece of toilet paper and it feels like a lot of other stuff is coming out with the snot, a generalized head-stuff that uniformly fills his skull. He feels like he's going to fall to his knees, but the room is too small for that. He touches his lump and it doesn't feel like anything at all; there is almost no sensation. He lowers himself, fully trousered, onto the toilet and sits there, and leans against the counter, and closes his eyes. Behind him the sounds of the kitchen are muffled by the wall: shouted Chinese (could be Cantonese, could be Mandarin, or Mandanese or Cantorin . . .), sizzling pepper steak, the banging of pots and splashing of dishwater.

A knocking brings him around, a voice. "Albert! Are you in there?" The voice is familiar: who? He says, "Lenore?" A louder voice, a man's, accented, shouts, "Mistah, what you doing in my bathroom?" He says, "Who is it?" and the first voice says "It's Gillian, my God, Albert, will you come out of there?" and he remembers where he is and says "Oh, sorry, God," and opens the door.

Gillian is standing there, her face red and sweaty, and behind her is a Chinese man in a stained smock holding a large knife. "What you doing in my bathroom!" he says, and Mailman says, "I'm sorry, I wasn't feeling well." "Come out of there, Albert," Gillian says between clenched teeth, and so that's what he does. The proprietor slips in after him. "You smoking cigarettes in my bathroom!" he says. "This no smoking restaurant!" Mailman rubs his face with his hands, says, "No, those were already there, I don't smoke." But the proprietor doesn't touch the butts; he stalks away without looking at Mailman or his sister.

Outside, the buildings seem to lean over the block, to sort of bend, and he puts his hands on his head. This feels good, so he keeps them there. He can hear Gillian, still inside, arguing with the proprietor, and when she comes out at last she says, "Thank you, brother darling, for *nothing*. Now I can never show my face in there again."

He removes his hands from his head, reluctantly. "Why not?"

"I could barely *trust* those people before today, and now I can't trust them at all. They'll put *something* in my *food*. And I had to *pay*, I think you should know, and you didn't even eat your *dinner*. My God, I thought you were *dead*, I thought you *offed* yourself."

"I'm sorry. I felt funny."

"Well you can imagine how *funny* I must have felt having to explain to that terrible little man that my *brother* had been in the men's room for twenty minutes and might be *dead*. For Chrissakes, Albert, I'm on their *blacklist* now." They are walking briskly, too briskly, back to Gillian's apartment; it is evening, with the sun show-ing itself only occasionally between buildings.

"I still feel strange."

"Well, and I believe I've already told you this, you look like *hell*."

No evening sun penetrates Gillian's apartment, and now that the light is gone the walls seem rough and dirty and the floor warped. His sister's few possessions—framed icons on the walls, a checkered tablecloth à la Little Italy, a brass lamp with a glass shade shaped like a lily—retreat into the half-dark. He is tired, and he says so, and Gillian says "Well I won't be using my bed for the next several hours, Albert, you can go ahead and take a little nap in it," and so that's what he does. He goes into her room and lies down on the narrow mattress (it's a twin, same size as the mattress he hid under to watch her undress) and lets his eyes, throbbing in their sockets like jellies, trace the room's shadowy corners. Dust up there, cobwebs drifting in an unfelt current of air. A dresser, and above it a mirror surrounded by clear bulbs, which seems familiar. And as he drifts away to sleep, he remembers: it's his mother's mirror, or one quite like it, the white chipped (or, as the catalogs he used to deliver would have said, *dis-tressed*) paint, the little flowery filigree at the top with a carved cherub in the center. He never could look at this mirror without seeing his mother's face in it: if he came to her door, even if it was open, she would catch his reflected eye and capture him with that gaze, and he would be drawn in to be punished or at least reprimanded for spying.

"*Never* stare at a *woman* who is in the *process* of restoring her *beauty*," she would say, or some version of same: but he never really believed she was talking about herself, that *she* was restoring *her* beauty; for he never thought of her as beautiful, instead simply angry, because she was always angry, and anger did not look beautiful to him. He supposes now that she was beautiful, he supposes there is a type of man for whom anger is lovely. He supposes his father must be that type of man. So why isn't Mailman? The women who attracted him never looked angry, though they often were, and happened to be good at concealing it. Lenore, so owlish, round of face and hips; stocky Semma (and how he misses her now: she would have taken care of him, he would never have had to leave Nestor, she would have admitted him into her house, her arms); bookish Marsha.

Gillian: he likes women who look like Gillian, whose face and body take after their father's: soft around the edges, no angles. He remembers once again her naked body dancing in her room, he remembers the glimpse of childlike women nude beneath the brown wrapper of a magazine he regretted delivering, he remembers his own narrow legs and chest and hairless crotch in the bath. Now he dreams and in the dream he is in the bath, and the water is filling the tub, and he tries to masturbate as the water draws nearer to his mouth, and the water covers his mouth and nears his nostrils, and he is stuck to the tub's bottom and the water covers him and he can't breathe.

He wakes to blackness (as in the mental ward on a moonless night) and experiences a moment of absolute, crushing loneliness before he senses his sister beside him in the bed, curled against his back; he can feel her legs pressing into his, and her breasts against his shoulderblades. Her nightgowned arm lies over his arm, beneath which his lump painlessly pulses (what could that be, deep inside his chest, but the barest hint of a twinge of the pain about to return, codeine notwithstanding?), and her hand covers his hands which in his sleep have knitted together into a tight knot. He feels the sadness leaching off her, the heat and sweat of it, and her breathing is regular but too fast for sleep. She shifts against him; he can feel her hipbones pressing into his back; her legs move slightly and he moves his own closer to them. He feels the need to not speak, as if someone might hear, someone might burst in and demand they separate, and for the barest moment he feels a wave of happiness, deep as the loneliness of a moment ago, that begins inside his fist beneath her hands and spreads through them both, and he gasps with the power of it. Then it's gone. He imagines the wave continuing to grow, to spread through the building, meeting other sleepers in their dreams. His sister kisses his neck. "Poor Albert," she whispers, and holds his hands tighter in hers, and she buries her face in his hair and kisses him again and says it again, "Poor Albert," and sighs. The warmth against his neck turns cool. She has been crying.

They are not children. There is an awareness that childhood is over and that they have to part now, and that Mailman must go to the living room and spend the rest of the night on the sofa. But there is the obliterating cover of darkness, and there is the warmth of the bed and their bodies, and there is the familiarity of their smells and the sensation of touching, and there is the sadness, which Mailman only now, in the wake of the wave of happiness and security, realizes that he shares. And so neither moves for some time, and perhaps one or both of them falls asleep, but there is a moment, some indeterminate point of night, when her hand slides away from his hands and moves to his neck and face, and her other hand (where has it been all this time?) grips his shoulder and her lips touch his neck again, this time wordlessly, this time with a unifying moistness and heat, this time for long seconds that seem to take hours to pass. And he shifts his left arm, which her arm lies over, so that he can—what? Push her gently away, he tells himself—but his hand lands on her hip, which shifts beneath her nightgown. And maybe he would turn over to face her, except that she disengages her hand from his cheek and chin and lets it fall across his chest, between the buttons of his shirt (for he went to sleep in his clothes), and up and over his ribcage and it comes to rest—to freeze, actually, to go suddenly cold—on the lump that throbs hotly underneath the fabric.

Suddenly there is space between them; she has jumped a full inch away, her hands hovering over his shoulder and chest; and now he curls in pain, groaning, and his bowels are beginning to loosen.

He crawls out of the bed, shuffles bent over down the hall, feeling along the wall with one hand while the other wraps itself around his heaving gut, and he stumbles into the bathroom, turns on the light, shuts the door, shucks off his shorts (the erection, yes, that he developed is already gone) and voids himself thunderously into the toilet. He moans, he whines: he can't help it. The codeine dullness is gone entirely, the line between him and outside-him is clearly delineated now, and he feels part of him becoming part of outside-him, and his body chills instantly, he has begun to shiver. This time Gillian does not knock, does not ask if he's all right. He finishes, he catches his breath, he cleans himself up and flushes the toilet without looking. The room is hazy with his foulness, his ill health. He does not look at himself in the mirror as he washes his hands.

Gillian is not in the hall or the kitchen, lit now by city light. Her bedroom door is closed. He goes to the living room, looks out the window at the cars and people moving below. Of course, he thinks, of course he will not return to the bedroom or even spend the night on the sofa; he is no longer welcome, and it isn't because of the improper intimacy, which anyway she started; it is because of his lump, it is his lump she finds disgusting and hateful, his lump that reminded her that what she was doing was wrong, was unnatural, because the lump itself is unnatural, and so he's going to have to leave.

Well, all right, he was going to leave anyway, this was more or less just a stop along the way to Florida, because really, how could he possibly make a go of it in New York? In Florida he can get a job, any old job, and he can stay with his parents for a while and just make a little money, he doesn't need much, and evenings he'll just walk or sit on the beach, and he'll get himself a library card (an unexpected perk!) and just sit or walk on the beach and read crime novels. That will be the life. He looks out the window to the traffic moving below, follows it to Rutherford Square and the spire of its small church and he thinks sure, that was always the only possibility, right?, it'll be like retirement (which he was going to do soon anyway) except that he'll have to have a job. So he goes to the kitchen, picks up his bag from the floor (awfully light: what'd he put in it?), gathers up his keys and camera and pile of change.

And now it is time to leave, except that he doesn't. He stands in the dark quiet apartment holding his change and keys and camera, listening, until he is able to make out Gillian's breaths, too fast for sleep. He pockets the change and keys, sounding that familiar jingle of departure, but instead of going he returns to the bathroom and pockets the Tylenol with codeine too, and then he pads quietly to Gillian's door and grips the knob. Her breathing is no longer audible. With his thumb he opens the shutter of the camera. Now he flings open her door, she gasps, and he can see her wet eyes gleaming in a stave of light. For a fraction of a second he knows what the killer must feel, the lunatic with his knife; it is the energizing gratification of absolute surprise. He raises the camera and takes her picture.

It won't come out, of course. Those wide, bright, frightened eyes will never register. But maybe they're in there, dimly etched on the film, extractable by a professional: those guilty, sad eyes.

He shuts her bedroom door, moves to the front door. He unbolts, unchains it in haste, fearful of Gillian's pursuit; he slips into the hall and pulls it closed behind him. He takes the elevator, gives the doorman a nasty look before realizing that it isn't the same doorman as earlier, says "Oops, sorry" as he exits. He struggles to recall where he parked, remembers, hurries there. Nineteenth Street is quiet; a newspaper truck rumbles past him. The car's still there, intact and ticketed. He throws the ticket on the ground but his brief *frisson* evaporates by the time he starts the engine. The clock on the dash reads 4:14. He drives downtown like a cabbie, changing lanes for the hell of it; even Canal Street sleeps, the storefronts blinded by corrugated, graffiti'd metal. In minutes he's into and through the Holland Tunnel; he races under several traffic lights, and here is 95 South, laid out before him like an airstrip. That was the hardest part of the journey: all this long day, all he'll have to do is stay on this road. He has only to trust 95 and it'll take him all the way.

The night air is dry and summer-dank, with the refineries' odors and the stench from the swamps eddying among the racing cars. He has come this way before—vacations with Lenore to North Carolina and the beaches of Delaware, and once, the last vacation they spent together, to Florida, to his parents' house—and the road seems to remember him, to unfold itself for him in its old familiar way, and this is a comfort. He needs a comfort, too, as the sun rises over New Jersey, unveiling mall and warehouse and auto salvage yard; for Route 95 is the site of his divorce. That final trip was supposed to allow them to relax, him and Lenore, to sort out their differences, but it was over before they even made it into Georgia. All along here, in Havre de Grace and Lorton; in Dale City, Ashland, Emporia; in Roanoke Rapids, in Dunn; in all these places and everywhere in between, words came out of their mouths, swirled through the open car—not the Escort, not then, but a green Volkswagen Squareback as drafty and insubstantial as if molded out of aluminum foil—in toxic wisps, and were borne away into the slipstream to lodge in the gutters:

"Maybe it's a matter of recapturing that original spark."

"Maybe we should sleep separately while we're in Florida."

"I still love you."

"When was the last time you enjoyed it?, I don't think you've enjoyed it in two years."

"I want you to be happy but I don't think it's possible for you to be happy."

"We could just work part time, we don't need the money."

"Oh, it's all the same stupid words over and over again, I can't stand it anymore."

"That's all we have is words, all we can do is say them."

Mailman had stolen glances at her while driving and she said "I wish you'd keep your eyes on the road" and he said "I want to see you, you look nice, let me look at you now and then okay?"

"I think you're looking at me," she said, "because you want to see whether I'm looking at you or what kind of look I have on my face, not because you think I look nice."

And he said, "Maybe you're calculating and competitive like that but I'm not, I only look to look, because I like looking, and not because I'm trying to read you or something like that."

And she said, "Come on, Albert, we both know what you're doing."

And he said (to the windshield, knowing he was full of crap), "I can't believe this, I can't even look at her without some kind of outburst."

"Let's just be quiet for a while, I need to sleep."

"I'd like to sleep too but I can't, can I."

"I told you I would drive if you wanted."

"I don't want to have to say I want it, I want you to just be nice to me and say 'Why don't I drive for a while,' but you're so thickheaded, you can't see when I'm in need."

"So now I'm supposed to read minds."

"You know damn well when I'm tired of driving, it's just that you hate my need, if I'm upset or tired or weak it completely disgusts you, you want me to be some kind of manly man that I'm never going to be."

"We've discussed this before, Albert, I see genuine suffering every day, I see men and women who fight against problems more terrible than any you or I are ever likely to face, and they do it without whining or sighing or expecting other people to pat them on the back and say 'It's okay, little person' all day long. So when you sit there grumbling about how tired you are and how you wish I would read your mind and start being sympathetic to your little problems, I have to admit that I basically cannot bear it. And now can we be quiet please."

"The medical professional has the last word."

"No, you have to, apparently."

"I don't think so," he said, and when she said nothing he said, "Ah, fuck you."

This is where things stood when they reached the I-26 interchange in South Carolina, where they stopped for a pee and to get a snack out of the machines, and Mailman went to the men's room and Lenore to the women's. Mailman peed—he watched his distorted reflection in the hex knob on top of the inflow pipe and did a few discreet face exercises, and zipped up and washed his hands and went out to the snack area—and he bought himself a package of orange cheesy crackers and a can of saccharine-flavored instant iced tea, and brought them back to the car, and he sat there in the car with the door open (it was autumn, overcast, cool, breezy) and ate his snack. Before long he was finished, and before long he had to pee a second time. So he went back to the men's room and peed again, and when he came out Lenore was still nowhere to be seen.

He approached a woman emerging from the ladies' and said, "Excuse me, could you lean back in there and see if there's a woman named Lenore, about yea high, black hair, pretty, sunglasses that sort of sweep up at the corners like this?" The woman shrugged, went back in; he heard her say "Lenore? Is there a Lenore in here?" and for a while there were no sounds at all, and no one appeared in the doorway. At last the woman came out and tried to dodge him. "What? What?" he said. "Is she in there?" "She's in there but I'm not supposed to talk to you about it. Just sit tight and she'll be done in the fullness of time."

The fullness of time! What in the hell was that supposed to mean? But he had no choice—he couldn't just go waltzing into the women's room—so he found himself a bench to sit on and sat on it.

He fell asleep. He'd been tired, after all, as he'd told Lenore. When he woke up he looked around for her and saw her head and sunglassed eyes in the passenger seat of the car. He said "Jesus Christ!," got up, went to the car, got in his side and slammed the door shut. She was reading a paperback book and didn't look up from it. "How long have I been sleeping there like some kind of idiot?" "Half an hour, I guess," she said, not bothering to shut the book or raise her eyes from it. "Well," he said, "why didn't you wake me up?"

And she said—very calmly now, and he didn't like this one bit, "You needed rest, as you said." "Well, now we're going to be late," he said, and she shrugged. He started the car. They got back on the road. She continued to read. He said, "What's that book?" "It's a self-help book," she said, which surprised him, because she usually disdained such things, saying they were exploitive, they gave a false sense of well-being to people who really needed a good shrink and some medication. So he said "Where'd you get it?" and she said, "Someone gave it to me." He let that one go for a while—she had friends, after all, friends he didn't know very well, any of whom could have given it to her—but the way she said "someone" bothered him and he asked, "Who? Someone just now, you mean?"

"Yes."

"In the women's room?"

"Yes."

What the hell? He turned to her with the intention of asking her this very question, but when he saw her hunched there, staring into the book on her lap, her knees pressed together, he knew that something had changed, perhaps permanently. It was as if she had erected between them a wall of bulletproof glass, like the kind at banks. Anything he wanted to get through would have to be slipped underneath. Quietly he said, "Lenore?" She said, "Yes?" He said, "What's going on?" She cleared her throat, opened her mouth, took a breath. Closed her mouth. Said, "Give me a few minutes."

She looked out the window, ten, fifteen, thirty minutes. Outside, kudzu blanketed the trees; it crawled onto phone lines, making them sag and tangle. He began to drift onto the shoulder; rumble strips warned him back.

"Well?" he said at last.

She sighed. She said, "I think I'm all finished."

"With what?"

"Marriage. Ours."

He held his breath, waiting for her to elaborate, but she didn't, so he let out the breath and said, "That's it? That's all you're going to say?"

"Yes." She dogeared the page she was on and shut the book. Mailman could see the cover. The title read *Just Say It*.

"You can't 'just say' our marriage is over. We have to at least discuss it."

"That's all we've done on this drive. We've said enough."

Now he was in a kind of panic. But why? There was a small part of him that really did want to break up—or rather, a constellation of small parts: patches of skin where she no longer touched him, the muscles that ached mornings after they stayed up late fighting, the part of his tongue where he could taste the hospital when he kissed her after work, an outpost in the subconscious where the hope of new love lurked. A Palestine of the heart, a divided territory of misery. But fear trumped it: he feared the unknown, feared loneliness, feared events spiraling out of control. "You can't," he said, "just . . . *decide*. I mean, there are two of us involved, you can't just . . ."

"I'm sorry but I can, Albert, and I think you already have, too."

He blurted: "I won't *give* you a divorce."

Though he was looking forward as he drove, though she wasn't facing him and was wearing sunglasses, he knew she was rolling her eyes. In response, he reached over and grabbed *Just Say It* (bulletproof glass, ha!) and flung it out the driver's side window: but that window had been closed in anticipation of leaving the car unattended at the rest stop, and the book bounced back and wedged itself between the door and seat, and so he rolled down the window (all the way, though he could have gotten the book out through a one-inch crack) and flung it out again. He acted with a sense of urgency, as if she were about to stop him, but she made no move at all, sitting quietly with her hands folded and her eyes facing firmly out the windshield. When the book was gone—he watched it flutter in the sideview and bounce and slide along the ground—he rolled up the window and, astonished and alarmed by the sudden silence, said, "There!"

"Well," she said, "I guess I'd read enough."

There was nothing left for him to do but grit his teeth and growl, which growl metamorphosed into a scream, and he shook the wheel as he screamed, and pounded the dash and honked the horn. Meekly, a lawn care van in front of them pulled off to the shoulder to let them by. They passed it. He said, "I'd like to go back there and kill whoever gave you that asshole book."

"That's stupid."

"It made you dump me!"

"It made me dump you three or four exits sooner than I otherwise would have."

"I hate you."

She sighed. "Oh, Albert," she said, and it was her work voice, the voice she had used when he was in the hospital, the voice he labored two months to turn so that he could hear her real voice: the voice she would use with a lover, with a friend; the voice of perceived emotional equality and shared understanding and mutual respect. He supposed those things were gone now: or, rather, it was handy for her to pretend they were gone, to relegate him to the ranks of the pitiable, to politely put him aside: "Time for your pills, Mr. Lippincott."

It gave him to wonder: was she ever fully committed to him as a nonpatient? Because she had not fallen in love with a healthy man, with a strong man: she fell for a troubled man, a man in need. And perhaps now, fourteen years later, he no longer met her definition of a man worth loving; he wasn't weak enough. Well, he would show her strong! He would cow her with his stony silence, his granite indifference! He would sit here and drive this car all the way to Sarasota without batting an eye, without muttering a single oath!

But as the miles unspooled beneath them, he lost his conviction: was there even such a thing as the work voice? Perhaps she *did not*, in fact, divide people into patients and nonpatients, perhaps her voice was *simply her voice*, and her very *nature* was to minister to other people, and she simply ministered more to those who needed it most, almost all of whom she happened to encounter at work, than to other people. And so this legendary nonpatient voice that he had sought in her was, in fact, nonexistent. Which suggested that she was more complicated than he ever imagined. Which would have been nice to know before all this happened.

He looked at her, searching for words, but there were none. He was too angry, not only at her for dumping him, but at himself for failing to see things clearly. All he could get out, once they were in Georgia, was, "What should we tell my parents?"

"Don't tell them anything," she said. "Let them enjoy your company."

And so they didn't tell his parents, and they had, of all things, kind of a good time. The four of them ate all their meals together, and Mailman's mother entertained them with stories (certainly edited, perhaps exaggerated, and maybe even made up entirely) about her exploits in the tri-state club scene, and Mailman's father amazed them with his mumbled tales of scientific discovery (his own and others'), and Lenore told a few incredible-patient stories, and Mailman remained quiet, because he didn't want to talk about the post office. And when Lenore and Mailman went out at night, they left together and then split up at the end of the block; Mailman sat sullenly on the beach having hostile thoughts about passersby, while Lenore (presumably) went off to the village to have fun. This was the tiny town of Slip Key, a palm-enclosed Gulf Coast settlement of a few thousand, wedged onto a narrow island connected to the mainland by a single drawbridge. There were plenty of restaurants and bars where an attractive middle-aged just-separated nurse with an independent income could have fun. When they reunited at the house at the end of the day (Mailman was always already there) Lenore looked like she'd been having fun. He'd say "Have fun?" and she'd say "Yes" and would go into their bedroom, the guest bedroom, and happily sleep on the floor. "You take the bed tonight," Mailman offered. "Oh, no," she said, "the floor's plenty comfortable for me"—as if unchaining herself from Mailman had freed up her generous, accommodating side, and now whatever came her way was perfectly fine, unless of course whatever came her way was Mailman. She slept soundly. He lay in the bed, silently enraged.

She drove the car back to Nestor. "I get the feeling you didn't sleep too much on the trip," she dissembled, and so he reclined the passenger seat and pretended to sleep for much of the drive, plotting behind clenched eyelids a fabulous future of parties, affairs, and awards dinners which she would be made aware of (sneakily, through mutual friends, as soon as he was able to make some) but would never be permitted to participate in. When they got home—it was a bright fall morning, the perfect kind of day for contemplating your exciting future, if you happened to think you were going to have one—she left Mailman and the car at their house and carried her still-packed bag to the curb, where twenty minutes later a taxi arrived to take her to a hotel. Within three days she had an apartment, and in a week Mailman saw her having coffee with a woman friend he'd never seen before. Both were laughing like maniacs.

Her lawyer sent him the papers, he signed them. She didn't want anything but out. Well, out, and half the house, which he occupied rent-free and agreed to pay full taxes on for as long as he lived there. Lenore wasn't "happy" they divorced, of course she didn't feel "free" or that "a great weight had been lifted from her shoulders" or that she could now "discover the real her" or "treat herself the way she deserved to be treated." Four years passed, after all, before she called him up to tell him she was marrying Frank.

Mailman was, he believes, really good about it. Just the way she said "Hi, it's me" when he picked up the phone—the faintest lilt of fake exhaustion, the tiniest hint of imaginary doubt—told him exactly what the call was about; he had seen them around, of course; he had been introduced to the good doctor during a chance meeting on the Square. Frank wore feathered hair and aviator sunglasses. They shook hands, and Mailman considered himself a good sport for doing so. He could tell by Frank's too-strong handshake that he had voted for Reagan. He even went to the wedding (city park, birdseed, Lenore's tiny mother squinting up at him as if she'd forgotten who he was). He even let Frank come over and help him fix up the house now and then, since Lenore's half was now Lenore and Frank's half, or at least Frank saw it that way. And Mailman even . . . *enjoyed* fixing up the house with Frank. Frank's stocky male confidence, his deftness with tools, was contagious; Mailman felt more masculine around him. (He wondered, perhaps too intensely, if Lenore felt more feminine around him.) Frank made a big deal out of their simultaneous New Jersey upbringings, pretending that being a professor's son in Princeton was in any way comparable to being a plumber's son in north Jersey. Frank actually seemed flattered by Mailman's attention and he never ever brought up the subject of Lenore.

Of course, Mailman did. "You went *where*? I thought she hated French food." "*What* time did you say you two went to sleep?" "Her birthday's coming up, and I was wondering—does she still like those little bath balls, with the goop inside 'em?" Frank always answered, however evasively, in a bright, measured tone, the kind you'd use with a precocious eleven-year-old. "Waffles? Nah, now that you mention it, she *doesn't* eat waffles." Until the day when they were replacing a section of roof—or, rather, Frank was, while Mailman lay on his back, gazing through a sycamore at passing clouds—and Mailman let out a little chuckle and said, "Boy, this brings back memories."

"Oh, yeah?" Pounding a nail through a shingle.

"Yeah. One time, it was the Fourth of July, we came up here."

"You don't say." Pound pound.

"Brought out some blankets. Laid 'em down." Always, talking to Frank, he started sounding like Frank. "Oh, boy."

" 'Oh, boy?' "

"Well, yeah. We, you know."

Frank quit hammering. "Know what?"

"You know, did it."

A thunderous silence.

"You know, on the roof."

Nothing.

He turned his head. "You two ever go out and do it on the roof?"

Frank stood up, tightened his grip around the hammer. For a second, Mailman really thought he was going to come over and pound his, Mailman's, head in. At last! The trumpets of his mind let out a brassy blast: here was the real Frank, the hothead from Hackensack! He knew it all along!

But all Frank did was drop the hammer, shake his head, and go home. It was at least a few minutes before Mailman remembered: they never did actually do it on the roof. She was cold, and the shingles were too rough.

Semma would have done it on the roof, he thinks. It is now midday, the highway is clear, the world is bright gray and smells a lot like a highway and a little like rain and just a bit like lilacs (though the lilacs are a month gone) and just the tiniest iota like the ocean. Semma wouldn't have gotten cold, Semma would have told him that skinned knees were a small price to pay for screwing on the roof. She would have bandaged them up afterward. She would have named the constellations. It is time for more medicine. He takes two codeine-laced Tylenol—he'll need more probably but he doesn't want to go through that whole hallucinatory mushiness deal again, especially not while screaming down the highway. He's—where is he? Pennsylvania.

That's Philadelphia he's passing, looking very much not the way he remembers it. It's got a skyline now. It used to be short. Now here are big postmodern office towers, doubtless largely unoccupied, which is the natural state of postmodern office towers.

In Wilmington, Delaware, he is forced to slow down below the speed limit (not because of the location but because of the hour, which is eight a.m.), keeping close to the car in front, constantly checking the car behind. His father taught him to drive—a terrible driving teacher, had no sense of the big picture, the way it is possible to *feel* the road, to digest all inputs through some kind of organic process. He could only describe the rudiments of driving in formulas and codes, something along the lines of:

III. A. 2. PARALLEL PARKING

1) Line up back end of auto with back end of auto parked in space in front of desired space. Engage clutch, shift into reverse;

2) Turn wheel a) clockwise if you are on the right side of the road, or b) counterclockwise if you are in the left lane of a two-lane one-way street, one-and-one-quarter turn;

3) Back up slowly until a) sideview mirror on passenger side if you are on the right side of the road, or b) sideview mirror on driver's side if you are in the left lane of a two-lane one-way street, is even with rear end of auto in front of the space desired;

4) Stop;

5) Turn wheel as far as it will go in direction you earlier turned it one-and-one-quarter turn;

6) Back up slowly until a) right rear tire if you are on the right side of the road, or b) left rear tire if you are in the left lane of a two-lane one-way street, is approximately six inches from the curb;

7) Stop;

8) Turn wheel as far as it will go in the *opposite* direction from direction you originally turned it in;

9) Back up slowly until auto is parallel with curb, making sure that a) front right end of auto if you are on the right side of the road, or b) front left end of auto if you are in the left lane of a two-lane one-way street, does not strike a) left rear end of auto in front of desired space if you are on the right side of the road, or b) right rear end of auto in front of desired space if you are in the left lane of a two-lane one-way street;

10) Stop;

11) Turn wheel in original direction until front wheels are parallel with orientation of your auto;

12) Back up until equal space has opened between your auto and auto in front, and your auto and auto in rear, making sure that parking meter is situated near a) front right end of auto if you are on the right side of the road, or b) front left end of auto if you are in the left lane of a two-lane one-way street;

13) Stop;

14) Get out; lock auto; insert coins into meter corresponding to the amount of time you wish to spend parked.

Mailman received this on a neatly typed sheet of paper, punched and bound with other similar sheets describing other automobile operations, in a three-ring binder bearing a note card with the words AUTO-MOBILE OPERATION printed clearly on it. His father presented it to him on his sixteenth birthday, saying, "All you need to do is memorize this. Let's just sit here in the driveway while you read it and then you can go for a spin." And so Mailman read the entire binder, trying half-heartedly to commit the whole thing to memory, but really there was no chance: besides, driving had seemed a simple thing to him, a matter of pointing the car where he wanted to go and stepping on the gas, and hitting the brake when he got there. He'd been watching his parents drive for years (his mother did not like to be driven anywhere, so when both parents were in the car it was she who took the wheel; on these occasions Mailman's father closed his eyes and hummed quietly for the trip's duration) and thought he knew exactly how to do it: but now, sitting behind the wheel at last with the giant binder open on his lap, it seemed far more complicated than he'd thought. He said to his father "I don't know if I've got it all down," and his father sighed and said, "Well, I've taken the day off. Why don't— that is, go ahead and read it. A second— again. Sometimes I have to read something ag— that is, twice, to remember it all." In this Mailman suspected he was lying. And so he read the entire thing again.

When he was finished his father took the binder from his lap, opened it on his own lap to the first page, and said, "All right! Let's go!" Mailman turned the key and pressed down on the clutch and threw the car into gear.

"Ah-ah-ah!"

"What!"

"Whad'ya forget?"

And so Mailman looked in the sideview mirrors and into the rearview mirror and checked both blind spots and signaled with his hand in which direction he planned to go when he left the driveway. And then, at last, he gave the car some gas and let up on the clutch and the car bucked and shuddered and died.

His father sighed. "It's all in the book," he said, smacking the binder ever-so-gently with the back of his hand. "You read the book. Therefore, you know better. Again, please."

As it happened Mailman didn't bother trying to get his license for some time: not until he'd met Lenore, in fact, who taught him how to drive in half an hour, by issuing instructions like "Okay, drive over there," and waiting until Mailman did it. Lenore seemed to believe that cars were inherently irrational; that they were liable, even eager, to resist your instruction; that they liked breaking down or embarrassing you or leaving you stranded; and therefore they should be humored. Mailman never once saw Lenore throw a tantrum in an automobile, though he had seen her suffer breakdowns, flat tires, and fender benders—the whole gamut. During one or another of their arguments about their marriage, Mailman once suggested that if she had the kind of patience with him that she did with their car, they might not be forced to argue about their marriage all the time, to which Lenore replied that, believe her, she would fuck the Volkswagen if she could find a way to get any pleasure out of it.

Funny how, despite half a lifetime of driving experience, Mailman still cannot relax for even a second out here on the highway. Always he worries about the other drivers (their nose-picking, their phone-answering, their radio-adjusting), the condition of the roads, the degree of wear certain parts of the engine might secretly have reached. This last is the clincher: under the hood is a mess of metal and rubber, none of which he understands in the least: hundreds of parts, all working in tandem, each depending entirely upon the con-tinued optimum operation of the others: a house of cards! Surely (especially in a car this old, especially in a car this cheap) something is about to break; certainly, at any given time, several parts are a hair's breadth from splitting, dissolving, bursting, cracking, melting, disin-tegrating or seizing up: and what, then, when that happens? He doesn't have a phone, he doesn't have AAA (it flew the coop with Lenore and the Volkswagen); he'd have to flag down a cop and get a tow truck and spend the night in some airport hotel while a bunch of cigar-chomping yokels chuckled over the open hood, charging him by the hour for the dirty jokes they were exchanging.

By late afternoon he's passed Baltimore, Washington and Rich-mond. Historic American cities, their harbors and battlefields and monuments tidily bypassed by the highway, so that it is possible to forget (if you ignore the traffic) that you are in a particular place at all. As he approaches Fayetteville, North Carolina, he imagines a series of ironic picture postcards, THE SELF-STORAGE WAREHOUSES OF AMERICA!, each bearing the name of a city and the identical photograph of long, low, corrugated-metal shacks ringed by chainlink fences. Soon he will

cross into South Carolina, the Divorce State, which he has not entered
since his split with Lenore. Fatigue gnaws at his shoulders and butt.
He digs under the passenger seat for his road atlas. Coins and candy
wrappers and gravel rain off it and onto his lap, as the car lurches
almost to the shoulder and then back into the lane with the bending
of his body. His lump protests and he promises to get himself something to eat and take a couple more of those terrific pills as soon as he
figures out how to avoid entering South Carolina.

But quickly he realizes that actually South Carolina is quite large,
and that to go around it would take him all the rest of daylight and
part of the night, and so he decides to plow on through, damn the bad
memories. And within ten miles he's decided that, in fact, he *wants* to
go through South Carolina, and furthermore he wants to *pass the very
rest stop where it happened,* and by the time he's reached Sumter he is
determined not only to pass the rest stop but to visit it, and park in the
same space where they parked that day, and buy the same iced tea
(though you don't see it in cans so much these days, and NutraSweet
has replaced saccharine, and probably it'll have fruit juice or at least
fruit-juice-flavored chemicals mixed in) and the same cheese crackers, and pee in the same urinal and sit on the same bench where he
slept while Lenore read the self-help book that made her dump him
sooner than she otherwise would have. He is gripped by a feverish
excitement at this project, this homeopathic experiment; it is the first
real goal he's had in days.

For another twenty minutes he doesn't remember the landscape
at all, it's just another scrubby length of America surrounding an
interstate highway, a lush, trailer-park-studded flatness, illuminated
unnecessarily by bright noonday sun. But soon he's reached the long
bridge over Lake Marion and he remembers the signs for Santee State
Park (they joked that day about Santee Claus, or he'd tried to anyway,
and she tried to laugh at him), and the sense of being suspended on a
ribbon that might twist and shuck them off in the slightest gust, and
the gulls swooping overhead, and the dump truck filled with pine

bark mulch they couldn't seem to get around, so that all the way across, the windshield was struck by shreds of the stuff and the acidic humusy tang of it filled the car.

And then he's there, the interchange is just ahead ("I need a break," he remembers Lenore telling him, meaning not from driving but from him), and here is the exit for the rest area. Except that it's blocked, by a row of those red-and-white-striped barriers that look like hurdles from a track meet, except really huge, and a sign reads CONSTRUCTION—USE EXIT 57 REST AREA. He ought to keep going, but he is determined now to retrace, regain his life. He signals and slows and pulls over in front of the barriers.

Beyond the barriers, the off-ramp is rough but clear of debris, and at its end, atop a gradual rise, the rest stop stands, apparently unchanged, its walls windowless, composed of coarse cement with giant pebbles embedded in it. There is the gas station they didn't visit (because they had bought gas in Florence, where an overzealous pump attendant with an underbite had scrubbed their windows until every last smear of bugstuff was gone); there are the restrooms. Well hell, he thinks. There it is, here I am.

Without giving the matter much more thought he backs up and pulls around the right side of the barriers, over the grassy verge that borders the ramp. He drives slowly, as if this will prevent him from being seen: but though he spies construction machinery on the hill, there doesn't seem to be anyone manning it, nor overseers overseeing, nor any police patrolling. Weeds are growing up through the asphalt in the parking lot and between the concrete sidewalk slabs, and little piles of rubble lay here and there, a bit of cement with rebar sticking up out of it, a clod of dug-up dirt with a half-dead sodclump on top. There is kudzu growing everywhere, half-covering the trash receptacles and the phoneless telephone kiosks and the restroom building, and the sidewalk is stained and split, and a big roof corner has dislodged itself from the building and slid into the mostly dead

row of untrimmed yews and broken onto the sidewalk and the handicapped parking spaces.

He parks. He figured it would be easy to find The Space but there
is no chance of that: it's all the same, just a long row of diagonal hash-
marks without distinction. He gets out of the car, stretches (codeine!
But I was going to take it with my iced tea!), sniffs the air, listens. The
air smells more of vegetation than exhaust, and there is too much of
it; it is too dense. It is the South. The sounds are more of the adjacent
woods (wind in trees, crows) than of highway. He walks toward the
restrooms.

The entrances are where he remembers them, but there are iron
doors he doesn't recall and these are locked, rusted, and covered with
spray-painted designs. Gang tags? Here? An empty charcoal bag rus-
tles in a breeze. There are soda cups with their bent straws and straw-
gripping lids shoved inside them, and there is a condom wrapper, and
there is a broken and torn plastic kite. Over there would have stood
the vending machines—there's a hole in the wall, unattached wires
snaking out of it, where their electrical outlet must have been, and
discolored rectangles on the ground in the shape of the machines,
one for drinks, one for snacks.

A dizzy sensation threatens to overwhelm him, and he plants his
feet more firmly on the pavement: he forgot to breathe. He draws
breath now, big lungsful of that soupy air, and lets it out slowly. His
fingers tingle, as if they have magic powers. Now, where was that
bench? There? Here? There is a yew next to the bench in his memory
which is now gone: but There is an empty square of dirt, and beside
the square of dirt are four metal plates embedded in the cement
where bolts might have gone. He had planned to sit on the bench and
close his eyes, the way he had that day; and since the ground is fairly
clean where the bench used to be, he sits down on that. Though the
day is hot, the cement is unexpectedly cool. He closes his eyes, unsure
of what he's supposed to be doing. He sings, in a faint whisper:

Nestor, Nestor, a college on a hill!
Clearly best among others of its ilk!

But the song's compromised enthusiasm seems to sap him, and he slumps, curling over into his own lap. He was never the best among others of his ilk. He was a lousy student, a duplicitous mailman. A rotten husband: demanding, ungrateful, uncooperative. And he realizes that the question he has been asking himself—would he have married Semma?—is the wrong question; the real question is whether or not she would have married him, and the answer has got to be no. Surely she saw through him. If Lenore'd been a little older, she would have seen through him too. The same way Kelly Vireo saw through him, and the postal inspectors. He is see-thru.

He wishes he had never left the highway and come up here. He opens his eyes. His mouth is dry, his head aches, his lump is throbbing so hard it feels like it might explode. Cars move on the highway, robotic in their dedication to their lanes. That's what he wants: to be back on the highway, himself a robot, all his movements automatic. He tries to get to his feet then, and, to his enormous surprise and alarm, fails to do it. His legs and arms are too weak, too stiff, and it hurts to bend at the waist. He tries again. Christ! What's going on here? He attempts another tack now, curling his legs up under him and getting to his knees: there, that's working. Except that now, with his head in motion, he is beginning to feel dizzy and a little bit nauseated, and breath is coming only with effort. Never mind that: just stand up. He does it. He stands up. But when he takes a few steps toward the car he is nearly overcome by vertigo. He gags (but does not vomit), he almost falls down.

Okay, okay. Deep breaths. How'd it get so damned hot? And his lump—not just his lump, his entire chest—is in pain now, and the world is wheeling around him. Get to the car, he thinks, there might still be some water in your water bottle, you can take the goddam codeine and have yourself a little nap. And then it's back on the road.

He makes it to the car, barely, slumping against it like a drunk and sucking in deep breaths over his heat-slick tongue. Jesus Christ, gotta get something to drink. He gets the door open and roots between the seats: there, in the plastic bottle, half an inch of water, no doubt baking hot now. He drinks it and swallows a couple of pain pills and sinks into the driver's seat. Ah! Better! He had no idea how tired he was.

When he wakes it's almost dark and his legs are still outside the car. The air is cooler, though the car's interior has retained its heat. His pain has receded, the dizziness has faded, and now the primary sensation is thirst: he has to get something more to drink. He looks out at the twilit highway, at the way half the cars have got their headlights on and half don't, and as he watches, a few more drivers switch theirs on, and a few minutes later just about everyone has got their headlights on. That's all it took, a few minutes, for everyone to decide to do it, to put their headlights on: and now everybody on the highway is doing this one same thing, and now everyone is visible. The same metallic beast he left behind in Nestor, but incandescent now, and swift. He picks up his camera from the passenger seat and takes a picture of the moving cars, the friendly, bright-eyed cars. There will be another rest stop soon, he'll get his water, his iced tea, whatever he wants. He closes his door and starts his own car and puts his own headlights on, and he drives down the on-ramp and around the barriers, and tucks himself into the flow of cars.

EIGHT

The Doctor

―

It's better in the dark, with traffic thinning and the car whistling along smooth road; each passing streetlamp discovers his hands, narrow and white against the black wheel. The dashboard floats before him, indistinct, like an object from a dream; its glowing components hover in the stale air, the speedometer needle gently wobbling around seventy-five, the engine thermometer steady in the middle as a senator. When occasionally the supermarket sprawl of north Florida falls away and the car is swallowed by moonless murk, he can pretend he has no body—no scratchy ass, no throbbing growth, no sticky throat or spitless tongue—only a brain in a beaker, forested over with electrodes, wired to brakes, to gas, to wipers and wheels. He can imagine he has no past and no future, no miles behind or before him, that he has nothing to look forward to and nothing to be ashamed of. And then the lambent molded plastic signs appear, and the convenience plazas; and the blue brights of Lexuses blind him, and he is again Mailman, and he is again on his way to see his parents in the middle of the night.

At Daytona Beach he takes the I-4 interchange (And how is this an interstate? he wonders, for the highway stretches ocean to gulf and never once leaves Florida soil) and some hours later he reaches 75 south and finds the road west that leads to the drawbridge separating him from Slip Key. The bridge is up, there is a line of cars. Most of them are SUVs, those burly relics-in-waiting; most of them are white. Under streetlight they glow like shuttles to the afterlife, and perhaps that's what they are, preparing to deliver their elderly pilots into their final rest. Mailman watches the lights of a boat disappear behind the upthrust slab of yellow-lined road and reappear on the other side, and then the road silently begins to fall, and the sound of revving engines reaches him through the open window. The air, redolent of hibiscus and exhaust, is thick and humid, though the radio has told him that the Gulf Coast is in a drought, that gardens can only be watered after dark, that swimming pools should not be replenished until further notice. There is a quality of coolness that implies the recent presence of heat, and he knows that tomorrow will be a scorcher, and that no rain will fall.

He has not called ahead, he has not gotten directions, and he hasn't been here since Lenore threw him over: and yet his hands (look at them there, so ghostly) turn the wheel at the appropriate times and his feet tap the pedals, and he begins to recognize the place from his memory.

But it isn't the same place, not by a long shot. This used to be a community of dilapidated cottages sheltered in copses of palm and creeping vine; now the vegetation has been cleared and the cottages cower under giant plantationesque hotels, concrete-block condominiums, terra-cotta mansions. Daylight-spectrum spotlights are trained upon these buildings, and phalanxes of sprinklers chatter in their graveled courtyards, drowning out (and probably drowning) the crickets; honey-coated cars are slotted into their parking places like candy bars in a rack. But a few things are familiar: the Old Navvy Bar & Grill (recently the defendant, according to Mailman's father, in a lawsuit with the clothing retailer Old Navy; and Mailman hopes its continued existence means that the Old Navvy, with its rope-wrapped-dock-post barstools and rudder-wheel-with-a-glass-top tables and fishing-nets-filled-with-starfish-and-sand-dollars décor, has won); the Emperor of Ice Cream sweet shop; the Lighthouse Dog, a hot-dog-and-hamburger joint in the shape of a squat (thus self-defeating) white lighthouse. Closed for the night, devoid of consumers, these places appear hollow and parodic, like the once-vital people who pack the local nursing homes, men who wore hats, who fished; women who sunbathed and baked.

Or maybe, Mailman thinks, that's a bit of a stretch for this hour, in this light, when you have to pee and you're about to see the elderly parents you haven't laid eyes on in years. Everything seems so portentous, yet so fragile, a wasp's nest before the match. Indeed, there is a buzzing in his head and under his arm, a swarm warning. He hiccups and tastes snack chips, and stifles a twinge of nausea.

Here's the drive-up bank he remembers turning at before, and here's the street sign—MISTY COVE, as likely a porn queen as an avenue—marking where his parents live. He turns. Misty Cove Road was graveled and meandering when last he visited; now it is straightened and paved, sidewalked and shrubbed, and gated estates dominate. Et tu, Misty Cove?

He misses his parents' house on the first pass, and then on the second as well. For a few minutes he wonders if perhaps they moved, if they forgot to tell him, or for that matter didn't bother, because what difference should it make to him, the child who never visited? His emotions swerve from forlorn embarrassment to ashamed relief: and then he sees it, or rather sees the bare dirt driveway squeezed between the high stone wall of one gigantic house and the tall iron gate of another, and sees the dented aluminum mailbox nailed to a wooden post, and he signals (to no one) and turns in, pausing first to open the mailbox and get the mail.

Somehow he knew there would be ungathered mail. His father's subscription copy of *Nature,* a bunch of envelopes from medical clinics and hospitals and insurance companies, lots of clothing and home-furnishings catalogs. There are advertising circulars for grocery stores and plastic surgeons and dentists and oncologists (only in Florida: the fly-by-night oncologist). So much mail—it is so depressing that he considers putting it back in the box. Perhaps that's what his mother did.

Their car, a leased (he assumes) brown sedan of large proportions, is parked before the house at a rakish (or maybe just careless) angle. The house itself is a one-floor bungalow on stilts, beneath which gravel has been spread; giant weeds have sprouted through the gravel and tickle the house's belly. Mailman parks, breathes deeply (guts, don't unravel; head, don't split), unfolds himself from the Escort. It has made it, all the way, with no trouble at all, unless you count a few quarts of oil as trouble. The same cannot be said for Mailman himself. He is trembling—out of weakness, hunger, pain, anemia. He takes one step and suppresses a column of rising bile, takes another and corrects an involuntary lurch. The third and fourth steps are easier, the fifth easier still. Yes—like the car, he has made it. He climbs the steps. He pauses on the landing. He really, really has to pee. Should he knock, or just walk in? Which will be the more upsetting to them? Probably the latter: and so, he raises his hand to knock.

But then a light comes on, and a figure becomes visible through the front window curtains, making its way toward the door. His mother. From her silhouette he can tell she has been awake all night, that she has been waiting for him. Gillian must have called. The front door rattles, then opens, and he is facing his mother through the screen door.

She is large. He forgot that. She's tall, taller than his father (and if his father's stoop has worsened, she is taller still) and upright as a monarch. Her hair is yellow, not the yellow of youth or of dye but the yellow of cigarettes and poor nutrition: but her bones must be straight and strong, for she is large. She is holding a cigarette in one hand and now she lifts it to her lips to smoke it. When she's done so, she pushes the door open.

"Hi, Mom."

"Be quiet, your father will wake up, and then we'll have him to deal with."

She moves away before he can embrace her, and he follows the grimy robe through the front room (the furniture is the same, old but comfortable, if you happen to be shaped like his parents) and into the kitchen. The kitchen is different: it has been redone. It's not bad, actually; the dark and hulking appliances are gone, there is some nice wainscoting painted sea green and trimmed in blue. Around the stove the bright new paint is grease-spattered and stained, but at least they cook. The table is ugly, chipboard with woodgrain contact paper laid over it, and the paper is peeling and cigarette-burned. A smoke-browned lamp glows upon it. It is a lamp from his childhood, a lamp he pressed his face to, in order to examine the shade's lambent weave. His mother is pointing to a chair, pointing with her cigarette, and how well he remembers this gesture!, the cigarette point!, which has always suggested a disapproval of the thing pointed at, with a bare-hand-point implying approval. It is unclear now what she disapproves of. Mailman, the table, the chair? Everything, he supposes. He sits, and she sits across from him, where her ashtray is waiting.

"You were sitting here in the dark," he says.

"Big whoop," she says, smoking. "Saves on the power bill."

"You have new neighbors."

"Never see 'em. Just their dumb-ass houses."

But she isn't frowning—she is almost smiling. He waits, and her near-smile becomes a real smile, a small one, but a smile. He smiles back. He says, "Gillian told you I was coming."

"She said you look like hell." She taps ash.

"Well," he says, "I don't know."

"You got fired."

"Sort of."

"What's that mean?"

"I don't want to get into it," he says. "I don't have a job with the

Postal Service anymore. I had to leave. I thought—I hadn't seen you in a long time."

"Well, here we are," she says, opening her arms. She closes them again, smokes, taps ash. "Stay all you want."

"Thank you."

Her smile, so like Gillian's, is gone now, but there is an easy quiet between them. Like everything else about her, the quiet is familiar; he remembers suddenly all the other conversations like this one they've had over the years. How had he forgotten that sometimes she was calm? That they liked one another? He remembers that the two of them used to drink coffee together, when he was a child, during the half-day he wasn't at kindergarten and, later, after school. Most kids had chocolate-chip cookies and milk waiting for them when they came home (though as far as he knows this may be a myth, one of those sentimental collective childhood memories that never really was); he had oyster crackers and coffee. Sometimes just coffee. Back then he liked his with sugar and cream—not milk but cream, which, if memory serves, people drank without much concern in those days. Why did he stop taking cream and sugar? It was his experiment in macrobiotics, when he started in with the raw brown rice. After that he took his coffee black. From then on, its flavor no longer reminded him of his mother. He remembers that he has to pee.

"Do you still drink coffee?"

He's startled; she has read his mind.

"I was just thinking about that. I take it black now."

She shakes her head. "What's the point of that? The stuff's a vehicle for cream and sugar." She smokes, she taps ash. "I remember Diane Puhl coming by one afternoon and finding you with a big mug of coffee in front of you. She said I was going to kill you with it." She smiles. "The stupid bitch. You know coffee calms down excitable children?"

"No."

"Well it does. You would've been bouncing off the walls. You got that from me. I wonder if you've gone a day without coffee in your entire life."

He thinks about it. "Today," he says. "I didn't drink any today."

It was true, he forgot to drink coffee. He doesn't recall this ever happening before, though he can remember days when he couldn't get his hands on any: the day the coffeemaker was broken at the P.O. and he missorted and misdelivered and stumbled over roots and crooked sidewalks and forgot people's names all morning; the day, in college, that he flunked a midterm exam when the household can went empty; the three days he spent camping with Lenore during which he snipped and sniped and muttered and caused Lenore to say, "That is the last vacation I ever take with you" (and it was, if you don't count the last time they came here). And yet he hadn't recalled those afternoons drinking coffee with his mother, until now. That's the problem with good, routine things: they blur together and lose the specificity of their goodness, and instead of the terrific coffee afternoons, all you remember is the day your mother knocked the percolator off the counter and scalding hot coffee splashed her legs, and she shouted the word *fuck* over and over and kicked the urn against the wall, where it shattered. And how she cut herself cleaning it up, and the blood and coffee and grounds that stained the floor.

"Albert."

"Eh?" Distracted, because now he has begun to remember the bathtub incident, the punch with the rubbergloved hand, his confession of impure thoughts of Gillian, and he thinks that he either needs that coffee or needs to go to sleep. But first he has to pee.

"Go and pee," she says.

He is startled. "How'd you know?"

She shakes her head, again sort of smiling. "I'm your mother." But before he can get up, she says, "Albert. Your father is going to say some things about me."

"Oh?"

"Yeah. Some of them are even true. Just don't worry about them.

I'm not crazy, not any more than I ever was. I'm just old. I do what I want."

He doesn't know what to say, and so nods.

She says, "No guest room, just sleep on the couch. Where's your stuff?"

"I have one bag. It's in the car." He pats his pockets for the reassuring shape and sound of the pain reliever. His side is aching now—not as sharply as before but more comprehensively, his whole left side and his upper arm, and his fingers are numb. Also it's gotten down to his abdomen, his bowels feel a little mushy, though that's probably from all the driving and bad food. His mother leans toward him, kisses his cheek, and he is a little bit surprised and repulsed to be touched; he remembers the way Gillian drew back, the way Semma held his wrists to keep his hands off her. She draws back with a new expression on her face, of slight alarm or perhaps distaste, though what she has sensed is unclear. She frowns, taking the full measure of him, and he stands embarrassed. "Mom," he says. "Okay, good night," is the reply, and she goes to bed.

He feels his way in the dark to the bathroom, which adjoins their bedroom. It is as he remembers it, except that it is dirtier, and is now covered with signs.

The signs are made of black plastic with white sans serif capitals embossed, like the nameplates tellers have at banks. They are attached to the walls with four screws, one in each corner, neatly countersunk in little white holes. One above the toilet reads:

THIS TOILET WILL NOT STOP RUNNING UNLESS THE HANDLE IS ADJUSTED AFTER USE. PIPES ARE NARROW: IF COPIOUS MATERIALS MUST BE FLUSHED, FLUSH IN STAGES. DO NOT FLUSH NONORGANIC MATERIALS BESIDES TOILET PAPER. DO NOT USE EXCESSIVE AMOUNT OF PAPER. CLOSE LID AFTER USE.

There is another in the tub, over the faucet:

WARNING: COLD WATER FAUCET IS LOOSE. COLD WATER WILL ONLY COME OUT IN A TRICKLE OR GUSH. EFFORTS TO ADJUST COLD WATER DURING BATH OR SHOWER MAY RESULT IN SUDDEN SWITCH FROM TRICKLE TO GUSH OR VICE VERSA, CAUSING DISCOMFORT OR INJURY. HOT WATER FAUCET WORKS NORMALLY BUT WATER HEATER IS SET TO A HIGH TEMPERATURE. TEST TO AVOID SCALDING. DRAIN TOGGLE IS NOT WORKING, USE RUBBER PLUG (HANGING FROM CHAIN). WIPE EXCESS WATER FROM TILES AFTER USE.

And finally one over the sink, beside the medicine cabinet:

FAUCET KNOBS SHOULD BE TURNED GRADUALLY. SUDDEN VIOLENT MANIPULATION MAY RESULT IN SPRAYING LEAK. WARNING: SINK IS CRACKED. REGULAR USE (BRUSHING TEETH, WASHING HANDS) WILL NOT RESULT IN FLOODING, BUT DO NOT PLUG DRAIN AND FILL SINK, BECAUSE FLOODING WILL RESULT.

For the second time today he thinks about the driver's manual his father made for him; he wonders where it is now. He didn't have it when he cleared out the house, that was certain. Maybe it's here somewhere. He shucks off his pants and sits on the toilet. He is horribly aware of his parents in the next room, his mother is likely awake, and he tries to keep his doings quiet, but it's no use: his urine explodes out with comical force, ringing against the side of the bowl like an alarm, and is followed by a loud and poisonous bowel movement, fueled by abdominal cramps. Jesus Christ! He washes his hands and rummages in the medicine cabinet for some matches. There are none, but he does find this screwed to the back of the cabinet door:

REMINDER: ALL MEDICINES MUST BE DISPOSED OF BY THE EXPIRATION DATE MARKED ON BOTTLE. CHECK DAILY MEDICATION LIST TO AVOID MISTAKES. RETURN ALL PILL BOTTLES TO THE CABINET. CLOSE DOOR WHEN THROUGH TO PROTECT MEDICATION FROM MOISTURE.

He considers getting back into the car and leaving before he has to encounter the old man. But this would anger his mother. He pops a few of Gillian's codeine-laced Tylenol into his mouth and washes them down with a few handfuls of water. They put his mind at ease, if not quite yet his body. Of course he'll stay. There is nowhere to go.

When he leaves the bathroom he shuts the door behind him, to seal in his stink; he hopes it will have dissipated by morning. In the meantime he'll sleep. He goes outside and gets his bag from the car and brings it back in, though there's nothing in it that he wants. He sets it next to the sofa, snugs it right up to the dust ruffle, and lowers himself (slowly) onto the cushions. His body hurts, yes, but it is in more or less working order, which given what he's been through in the past week is a real blessing. At least he isn't in the back of a mail truck with his shirt off, breathing exhaust fumes. All right, he thinks, that's a good parting thought before I shuffle off to dreamland, before I blow out the candle of consciousness, before Mister Sandman pays me a visit. Okay, then. Here we go: embrace me, Morpheus!

But he remains awake. He has no thoughts, but synapses are firing. Dendrites twitch, or is it axons? Lights flash green as far as the mind's eye can see. Electric pulses speed through their stations. Baffled passengers on the platforms, trenchcoats fluttering, grip their hats. It's racing, is what they say, his mind is racing. But what is the racing mind racing against? Against itself, he supposes, against time. He decides to try some deep breathing exercises. Here's one he read about once: you breathe *in*, and imagine things going *in*to other things, such as some spelunkers going into a cave, or a train going into a tunnel, or an ant going into an anthill, or data going into a computer, or a voice going into a room, or a dog going into a doghouse, or food going into a mouth—no, scratch that, it's disgusting—or water going into a drain. And then you breathe *out*, and imagine things coming *out* of other things, like a mouse coming out of a mousehole, or a tape coming out of an adding machine, or the President coming out of Air Force One (no!, not him!), or toothpaste coming out of a tube (damn—I didn't brush my teeth tonight), or pus coming out of a pimple (no!), or urine coming out of . . . urine coming . . .

Jesus Christ! Two breaths and he's more awake than he's been all day. Now he's got to brush his teeth, and he has to pee again, so he gets up (his body stops him halfway with a hideous twinge, a diagonal slash from his lump to his bowels, before releasing him to stand fully at last) and takes his toothbrush out of his bag and goes back to the reeking bathroom.

Where is the toothpaste? Nothing here resembles a tube. But there, standing on the counter, is a little upright plastic cylinder with a spout sticking out of it, easily mistaken for hand cream. This is the toothpaste? He examines the thing, trying to figure out how to work it. Thankfully there are Edgar-Lippincott-esque instructions printed on it in large type. HOLD TOOTHBRUSH UNDER SPOUT. PRESS DOWN GENTLY. So, all right, he does it, and a nice little candy-cane swirl of paste comes oozing out onto his brush. He wets it, he brushes: what the hell? The stuff is nearly flavorless, no mint at all, the consistency of fine sand. He picks up the container and reads: *Gerident. For denture-wearers and non-denture-wearers alike.*

Right—toothpaste for old people. He's heartened to learn that he finds it disgusting; clearly he is not the intended demographic. But his parents: not only does the retail establishment consider them old, they're going along with it. They saw this stuff at the supermarket and thought, *There's our toothpaste.* He again hopes they are sleeping, not listening to him scrubbing his choppers. When he's through, he pees and flushes again, in defiance of the drought, pushing his earlier output farther into the sewer system.

Back on the couch, he counts. One little sheep, two little sheep, three little sheep. Why not? The sheep trot up to the fence—he's got their fat-assed waddle down cold—but he can't make 'em jump. *Do* sheep jump? They're unaerodynamic, their legs are too short. And so after imagining a few sort of *levitating* over the fence—their little legs dangle, wobbling back and forth in a light prairie breeze—he gives up and lets them walk along it, the way real sheep might, and munch on the grass that rings the posts. It's a split-rail fence: he knows real sheep would be penned behind a wire fence, or perhaps an electrified fence, but how relaxing are realistically restrained livestock? The split-rail fence is idyllic, rough-hewn, it allows him to imagine the sheep scratching themselves against the coarse-grained wood. But wait: they're scratching a bit too hard, aren't they? In fact, some of them have got these bald patches, and their skin is pink and inflamed . . . oh, no! These sheep have scrapie, the ovine mad cow disease—they're doomed! And sure enough, as he comes to this grim realization, the scrapie-afflicted sheep begin to collapse, until they have formed a large fluffy pink-and-white pile at the edge of the meadow.

Ah, hell—he gets up and angrily puts on his socks and shoes. If he isn't going to sleep he'll take a walk; in the morning it'll be too hot to do much of anything except sit very still and concentrate on not sweating. He doesn't feel too bad now, thanks to the codeine (in the back of his mind he's aware that he has only enough to last him a couple of days), so he lets himself out silently and takes to the street.

It is the quietest hour of night. On the main road, no cars pass. He can hear the Gulf breathing. Everyone's asleep, he guesses, except for the very old, who pace with their walkers or lie alone in bed, mis-remembering the past or rewriting their wills according to who phoned them that day and who didn't. He wishes he weren't here, that the last week had never happened, that he was asleep in Nestor: but there is a pleasure, isn't there?, to being awake and aware when every-one around is deep in dreams or nighttime fantasy; he feels capable and energetic for the first time in days. Why, in the name of God? He hasn't slept! But at this hour you can convince yourself of almost any-thing.

The mansions he passes are identically different, girded with molded-plastic columns, carbuncled with mail-order gables. They are clean and crisply landscaped, their shrubs enforcing clear patterns across wide graveled gardens. The more of them he passes the more he thinks there is a single hand at work, a single landscaping company with a dictatorial supervisor (barrel-chested, sun-darkened, he wears the only beard in south Florida and a tee shirt bearing his own name): none of the yards shows any homeowner intent, other than the desire to blend in with the neighbors. There is the white gravel walk. There are the low spreading succulents and the tall teardrop-shaped junipers and the smooth black driveway with the clump of lush ground cover running along the side. The sprinklers are running—not *most* of them, *every single one*—and he figures that they must be on some kind of timer, a timer whose manufacturer has some kind of deal with the only landscaper in town. His footsteps begin to fall in time with their chattering (and he feels, oddly, sadly, like a mailman, a secret mailman of the night). And the cars—they are all new, all large. Is this what happens to the affluent and elderly? They shrink, losing body parts, losing height, while their cars swell? They counter their own increasing decrepitude with this depressing automotive virility?

There is a shift in light and for a moment Mailman thinks it must be dawn already, that he has missed the sunrise before he got a chance to go to the beach. He considers running there—it's only two blocks away, after all, and he can hear the advance and retreat of the miniature Gulf Coast waves—but he doesn't: the sky remains black and starspecked. The new light is coming not from the sun but from a police car that has crept up behind him. Perversely, pointlessly, he becomes convinced it contains Syracuse and Shut-up. He pretends not to notice. The car pulls alongside, meeting his stride; the window hums open. Mailman stops, tenses for battle.

There are two of them, the driver young, black; the passenger white and middle-aged. Mailman is nearest to the white guy, and is briefly alarmed by his face: he looks a hell of a lot like Mailman.

"Where are you headed, sir?" says this Mailman-cop. *You'll have to come with us.*

"Just out for a walk."

"Can I see some ID?" *Are you still engaged in acquiring and perusing pornographic materials?*

Mailman leans down, feels the muscles in his chest protesting, stands back up again. "Um, no—I don't have any. I mean, I'm not driving and I'm not going to buy anything, so I left my wallet—"

"Visiting?" the black cop says, leaning over his partner's lap. "Or do you live here?"

"I'm visiting my parents. They live on Misty Cove."

The black cop nods, scribbles something on a piece of paper. The Mailman-cop says, "Do you know what time it is?" and Mailman says "Sorry, I don't have a watch" before he realizes that the cop isn't asking him for the time. So he says, "Oh, I get it, yes, I know it's late, I couldn't sleep, I'm just out walking."

"Well," says the Mailman-cop, "are you aware we have a drought on?"

Mailman doesn't understand why he's being asked this. The black cop looks a little surprised too. So does the Mailman-cop. The black cop jumps in: "We've had some thefts around here . . ."

"Really?" Mailman says. "These places look like Fort Ticonderoga."

For a second he wonders if it was the wrong thing to say, maybe they would think he'd been casing the neighborhood, but after a brief pause they both chuckle. "Yeah," says the Mailman-cop. "We gotta check you out, though. You say your parents live on Misty Cove?" *Wittle baby wantsa go home.*

Mailman gives the address and their names.

"All right, you're okay for now. But don't let us catch you snooping." He watches the police car pull back onto the road and drive into the distance. The ground here is flat and the road straight, and he can still see their taillights many minutes later, when they've traveled nearly half a mile. Only now does Mailman notice that he is trembling faintly, as if from a mild electric shock.

He hurries past houses, seeking a street that will take him to the beach, but every roadcut is a driveway, barred by a gate. Finally he reaches a desolate intersection and turns west. He passes several apartment buildings that look like hotels and hotels that look like hospitals, and then the street dead-ends at a beachside cottage development, the sign posted at its trellised entryway reading NO PUBLIC BEACH ACCESS! Despite this, there is a sidewalk leading directly to the beach—he is standing in front of it—that seems to exist solely to taunt the swimsuited, towel-toting, sunglassed-and-sunblocked passerby. WE DARE YOU TO WALK TO THE BEACH FROM HERE! the sign might as well say. So that's what Mailman does, he walks to the beach, passing the silent beige bungalows and their empty screened porches, his quiet footsteps echoing mildly in the private alleyway alongside. At one point he hears the clink of ice and when he peers onto the nearest porch there is a man, dressed in white pants and sweatshirt, at work on what appears to be a bottle of vodka. "Morning," says the man quietly, confident that his voice will carry through the humid air, and Mailman says "Morning" and continues on his way.

There it is, the Gulf of Mexico, the entire point of this neatnik nontown, rippling in the near-dark. The sun, rising invisibly in the east, persuades the first hint of color into the sky, shames the stars into dimming. Mailman takes his shoes off and walks over the cool soft sand to the water. It is warm. It runs over his feet and between his toes. The waves are tiny, they are like the children of waves, and the sound they make as they roll in is like polite applause. An indefinite amount of time passes (there's the trick that the very old pay millions to be conned by) before Mailman feels a presence behind him. He turns.

It is a ghost. It is a haunt, pale white against the pale brown sand, and it carries a faintly glowing lantern. It seems to float a few inches above the ground. It says, "I'll bet you need a drink."

Mailman watches the ghost close in until it is almost upon him; he watches the lantern resolve itself into a liquor bottle and the white ghost-togs materialize into terry-cloth sweats and the blankness beneath them into thin brown feet. It is the man who said good morning, the man with the vodka. It *is* vodka: Mailman is being shown the label. He is being handed a tumbler filled with crushed ice. Mailman is not a drinker but these things look excellent to him, they look beyond excellent; they look perfect.

"If you're out walking around at this hour, buster, you got something on your mind. Lord knows I got something on mine."

This gives Mailman pause. There is a speech coming. But the drink looks so cool—the bottle is rimed with dew, his own hand swirls the ice in his tumbler—that he will acquiesce. What's a little speech between drinking buddies?

His ghostly new friend motions him back toward the dry sand, and they sit together with their feet on the far side of the high tide line, tempting the waves. The man pours them each a glass of vodka. As Mailman watches the liquor fall into his tumbler, the man watches Mailman; Mailman can see this out of the corner of his eye. When the glasses are full, Mailman turns to him, but now the man is gazing out at the sea. His face is brown like his feet and hands, with small, nutlike features; the hood of the sweatshirt covers most of his thin gray hair. He's probably about seventy. He licks his lips: Mailman can see that he wants to take the first sip, but for some reason won't do it. Hurriedly Mailman sips his drink (it tastes like Uchqubat), but this doesn't cause the man to sip his own. Instead, he says, "Look at that."

Mailman traces the line the water makes against the sky, as the cold vodka penetrates. Holy crap! It's strong stuff! Out on the water, though, there's nothing, no boat, no plane. "What?" he says.

"Whaddya mean, 'what'?"

"I don't see anything."

"I'm talkin' about the Gulf!"

"Oh."

Another sip. "Pretty soon I'm gonna go out there and never come back."

"On your boat?" he says.

"Nope."

There is a pregnant pause. Obviously Mailman's supposed to bite. "What do you mean, then?"

"Terminal leukemia, buster. I got just a couple months left. Can't hardly get off my chair, can't hardly sleep. Everything's all run together. When it gets too bad I'm gonna just walk on out there, and when I can't walk anymore I'm gonna swim, and when I can't swim anymore I'm gonna just sink. Use up all my strength so I can't come back. And that'll be the end of me."

Well, there's the speech. Mailman doesn't know what to say—what is there to say?—so he nods in what he hopes is a knowing way and takes another sip of his vodka. He takes in a little too much, though, and coughs, softly at first but then violently, and his drink sploshes over his hand. "Excuse me," he mutters, but the man goes on.

"Moved down here from Michigan. We used to summer up in the U.P. Big birdwatchers. Then Bibby—that's my wife—broke her hip and we figured let's go where we'll never be snowed in again. Well, we're not here a week when I start feeling all run down. Couple months later I'm tired all the time, and Bibby says, 'Ron, get yourself looked at.' So I go to the doctor. Enough of 'em down here. I go to this doctor and he does some tests and he says I got this blood cancer, and let's start treatment right away, except really there's no hope. Well, Bibby and me talked it over and figured if there's no hope there's no hope, and to hell with the treatment, gimme some morphine and let it come. And that was what we agreed on. Except now that it's decided and I'm a goner, she doesn't want to talk to me. I want to go through all the photo albums, fly the kids down here, talk over old times, that kinda shit. But she won't even look at me. Well I'll tell ya, when I'm gone, and it's going to be sooner than she thinks, she's going to wish she woulda looked at me a little more. She'll be miserable as long as she lives. And she's got some good years in her too."

At last he sips his drink. "The damn thing is, I don't have the energy to even pick up the binoculars. I guess I could get myself out to the sanctuary, Bibby could push me around in the wheelchair, but to tell you the truth I don't want it like I used to. The leukemia just took it out of me. Maybe that's why Bibby doesn't talk to me, she can see I already gave up. But it's not me deciding, it's the goddam leukemia." Again the drink. "At least walking into the ocean'll be interesting."

Perhaps he recognizes that he has some catching up to do, because he takes a few more sips of his vodka, and then he drains the entire glass. Mailman does the same. He imagines the sound of heavy footsteps in the sand behind them, the unsnapping of a holster, the crackle of a radio: "Mr. Albert Lippincott?" The jingle of handcuffs on their chain. Ron picks up the bottle and pours them both another round.

They sit still, drinking, until the sun has risen behind them. It is probably around five-thirty or six. The early walkers begin to appear on the beach, in their baggy shorts and puffy sweatshirts and white visors. Old, fat, they don't care what other people think of them because everyone else looks just as bad.

It strikes Mailman that he is—what?—fifteen years younger than this man? Tops. Ron minus one teenager equals Mailman. And already he feels old and washed up, already his life has lost its meaning, and if he were to live as long as Ron he would have to find something to do for *fifteen years,* and Ron isn't even all that old. What in the hell is he going to spend fifteen years doing? All his thoughts have focused on the immediate future, his prospects for some kind of job, for finding a place to live. But that's the easy part. There have been people on this earth—there are *currently* people on this earth—who are *twice as old* as Mailman. Granted, there's not much chance he'll live to be 114, but even if his life is only two-thirds over, he will have a very difficult time filling up the hours.

With this thought arrives a twinge from his chest; it races down his left leg all the way to the toes and up to his ear, which chills and tingles and registers a high hum. His bowels again loosen and he clenches them shut. Let's be completely honest, he thinks: something is *seriously* wrong with me. I do not have a broken rib. I have a problem that will require *surgery*. And I have no job, no insurance to pay for it.

He tenses his jaw against an upwelling of tears. *I am sick!*

It feels almost good to admit it to himself. He gives the words a trial run, telling people the bad news in his mind. To the kid at the gas station who says, "Hey, man, are you all right?" *No, I'm afraid I'm very sick.* To the woman on the street campaigning for the Red Cross: *I'd love to give blood, but I'm too sick.* To the doctor who tells him that yes, he is very, very sick: *That's what I thought.* For a moment he considers telling Ron, but he doesn't, because it would seem like he was trying to trump Ron's sob story, and because he does not want to equate, even coincidentally, Ron's terminal illness with his indeterminate one.

And if it does kill him, whatever he's got? How does he feel about that? Not good, certainly, but will he accept his impending doom, or fight against it? *Do I love life, or do I hate life?* Make up your mind!

"So," Ron says, "what's your story, partner?" In his voice is disappointment, whether over the approaching end of his life or over Mailman's lack of reaction to same is unclear. Mailman resolves to react, then, to give this man the respect he deserves.

"Oh, I'm just down here visiting my parents," he says. "They're still kicking." Although, he now realizes, he has not yet seen his father, who for all he knows may not be kicking at all.

"Down from where?"

"Upstate New York," Mailman says, and as the words leave his lips he comprehends, quite suddenly, how much he misses his house, and his mail room and its purloined letters, and his ex-wife and his town. He misses Nestor. That chilly paradise!, named for that heroic blowhard of myth! He misses the NestorFest. He remembers suddenly a manhole in the middle of Sage Street upon which the name of the town is misspelled "Nester," and he misses *that*. He may never see any of it again—that was his plan, after all. My God! he thinks, What am I doing? I love life, I love it! He twitches: his body wants to spring to its feet, run back to his parents', jump in the car and leave without saying goodbye—leave for Nestor, the place where everything happened to him, where his life was. But of course he can't do that. "Ah," he says, "I don't have a story. I mean, my life, it's no story. It's all fouled up. I tried to do a lot of things and they didn't work out. That's all."

"Can't be all."

"That's all. What'd you do? For a living, before you retired?"

"Garbage," says Ron. "Worked summers on the truck, then on dispatch, then I met some guys, some local guys who didn't like my boss on account of some bad bets he made, and I got to be boss." He waggles his eyebrows suggestively. "Then I moved to the home office in Lansing. Had guys running computers, trying to figure out the quickest routes. A big puzzle. I hate a mess. I loved thinking of all that garbage getting hauled away as fast as possible."

Mailman thinks about telling him that he was a mailman, but if he says that he'll have to say "was" and then he'll have to explain why he isn't a mailman anymore. He drains his second drink—my God!, vodka at six in the morning!—and makes to get up. "Ah, I gotta run," he says, "gotta go see my father."

"All right," Ron says. "Help me up then."

Mailman takes Ron's hand which grips back with surprising force. How could this man be dying? The bones underneath feel strong, the diseased blood coursing through them seems as hot and vital as anyone's. It makes him miserable: or, rather, miserabler. They walk together back to the bungalow complex and Mailman delivers Ron to his porch door. "Good luck," he says, though he's not sure what he means by it. Good luck dying?

"Thanks, buddy. Go visit the sanctuary. Come back and tell me what you see."

"All right," he says, but they both know he won't.

——

He walks back via the same route, the sheetrock mansions now fully illustrated by rays of sun: he sees new stucco already crumbling under eaves, and mortar chipped and eroded away; stone walls slipping and bronze plating wearing off the knobs and fixtures. Only the cars remain pristinely white, like the teeth of the very rich. As he passes a terra-cotta Alamo he watches a middle-aged woman, so blond she is white-haired, so tan she looks Mexican, climb into a creamy Lincoln Navigator, a bulbous vehicle, like a gigantic pill. The car makes no sound as it trundles off. Occasionally between mansions a cottage has remained intact, its sunshine cut off by the three-story buildings, a victim of abandoned zoning laws its owners must have thought would last forever. In the gravel (once white, now scuffed, lichen'd, oil-stained) driveways of such places sit reasonable automobiles, partially rusted Volvos and BMWs fifteen years old or more, their license plates scratched and bent under from multiple encounters with high curbs. They remind him of himself: outdated, decrepit, but still running.

When he is three-quarters of the way back, however, it occurs to him that he might not make it. He's a little nauseated, and his left side hurts so much, in so many places (thigh-knee-hip-gut-ribs-lungs-arm-neck), in so many different ways (ache-twinge-scrape-puke-burn-rasp-throb-crick), that he's half-convinced his parts are going to start abandoning ship, leaping to their deaths on the sandy sidewalk. He takes a break to lean against a mailbox (a mailbox!—you hardly see them anywhere anymore—but of course this one, he soon realizes, has been welded shut, rendering it quaintly useless: like him, like the Eastern Bandy-Legged Mailman, a charming relic) and catch his breath. The world slowly wheels. He is not shitfaced, not tanked, but slightly drunk—the kind of drunk that, if he weren't walking and if he weren't *sick* would be very pleasant indeed. He pants, he palpitates. He leans heavily over the mailbox's hot curved surface, waiting for his nausea, his soreness, to pass: and miraculously, both sort of do. He straightens, opens his eyes. The haze is burning off; already it is hot out. He takes a deep breath (chest pain), throws out a leg and then the other, nearly falls down, recovers, continues. Makes it to Misty Cove (come to me, baby!). Makes it to the house. Opens the front door.

Here is his father, scraggly-haired, dirtily pajamaed. Small. Solid. He is everything he used to be but more so. He looks up and his eyes are bright and mad, his face is red, not with sun but with effort. He's at the kitchen table with a lot of small pieces of metal and plastic in front of him, spread in an apparent chaos that Mailman knows from experience is not an actual chaos. There are wires, circuit boards, a square molded shell, screws, capacitors and resistors and what have you, there are several sizes and shapes of screwdriver, and a cake plate with smears of butter and toast crumbs on it, and an empty glass with orange pulp stuck to the sides, and the old man is holding a soldering iron and there is a white plastic cold-prevention strip bent over the bridge of his nose. He says to Mailman, "Thermostat. Couldn't— you know, the temperature. It was— never felt quite right. Had to— because— and now I've got the. Didn't know I could. Now, see, here's the secret:" And he pauses with his one hand in the air, gesturing, and the other hand with the soldering iron, gesturing, and a tiny ribbon of smoke rises from its tip, the ribbon kinked from his tremble.

"Hi, Dad."

"Mother said. But I was— and then I woke up. Your car. Noticed."

"I went for a walk."

"Did you— would you like some— I can make you?"

"I'll get myself something."

The first something he gets himself is from the pill bottle. He takes four. It's too many, but he's already popped them before he thinks of this, and besides, everything really hurts. He washes them down with bathroom tap water pooled in his hand and avoids looking at himself in the mirror. The water tastes moldy, or is that his tongue? He returns to the kitchen and makes himself a piece of toast he doesn't really want to eat. His father has pushed the electronic bric-abrac aside, jumbling it together: maybe it's an actual chaos after all. Mailman takes his seat, trying to look casual, wincing as he waits for the pills to kick in. He eats the toast. Despite the copious smears of butter it tastes horribly dry; the crumbs absorb his spit and leave the inside of his mouth sticky and rough.

He and his father smile at one another. Mailman's father's smile is direct, honest, open: he is always smiling, and he always means it, in a meaningless way. The constant presence of the smile has ruined it for others, except for, say, bank tellers, grocery clerks, bus drivers: people who don't know him and will only see him for a moment. Mailman coughs. The cough hurts, but it doesn't hurt as much as he expects it to hurt, so the codeine is working. Mailman's father gets up, makes tea. He says "Do you—" and Mailman quickly says yes, unwilling to listen to his father attempt another complete sentence. He has always talked like this, sort of, but it has never been this bad. Mailman watches as he makes tea. "Milk?" he asks. "Sugar?" Mailman quickly says no, though he wants these things. They drink. It's hot and good. He wonders why he isn't more tired.

In a moment Mailman's mother barrels through. Somehow she has gotten out of bed and dressed without making any sound—she's wearing a red cotton sundress and makeup. She passes through the kitchen without a word, her face filled with barely repressed irritation.

"Call your sister," she mutters, and vanishes. So Gillian does not hate him. After another moment they hear the large leased sedan start up and pull away.

"Your mother—" says Mailman's father. "She's— it's hard for her, living with me."

"I guess." Like a child.

"She's— I'm— used to be. But now."

"I know, Dad."

"So don't. Really, she's."

"I know." And he adds: "Last night she was sweet to me." *Sweet*, he thinks as he says it—when has he ever described her as *sweet*? But she was. "Where is she going?"

"Shopping."

With Mailman's mother out of the house, his father is making more sense, and with the sense has come a sobering; he is not frowning, but he isn't smiling either.

He has fallen far, Mailman's father. Edgar Lippincott came from money, a small precision glass fortune; his grandfather made microscopes and medical instruments and sold them to universities and labs. His father—Mailman's grandfather—took over the business around the turn of the century and ran it into the ground trying to mass-market hand mirrors and colored eyeglasses. Mailman can remember the faded opulence of his grandparents' gothic mansion in Main Line Philadelphia: the towering piles of the trade journals and foreign newspapers his grandfather liked to read; the mudded path that wound from room to room, warping floorboards and staining rugs, the legacy of an ever-present pack of shaggy dogs; the bitter stink of birdshit from the makeshift aviary his grandmother had created in the dining room. But his grandfather wore suits, his grandmother gowns. They clung to a pompous dignity.

Mailman's father studied chemical engineering at Penn; after the war he landed the Princeton job on the strength of a paper he published on metallic coatings for glass, the legacy of which (he was once fond of repeating) helped lead to the telescopes powerful enough to discover, in 1949, the second moon of Neptune. He was a whiz kid, good-looking (Mailman has determined from pictures), and spent his days within spitting distance of the world's greatest minds. He was eating lunch one afternoon at The Annex, a diner on Nassau Street, with a group that included von Neumann and Oppenheimer, when a waitress spilled a cup of coffee on his lap.

He married her. "I did it on purpose," Mailman's mother told him once. Looking at his father now, he wonders if it's true. Maybe not.

But it's a better story that way. His mother never fit in with those peo-ple, the Princeton people; the professors liked her too much and their wives despised her. There was exactly one dinner party at their old house, a chemistry department retirement send-off that Mailman's father had gotten railroaded into hosting. Mailman remembers a lot of furtive whispering among the women and winking among the men. "Where'd you get her?" he overheard a sneering, rat-faced egghead ask his father. "The Annex," his father answered honestly and smiled as if he got the joke when everyone around him roared with laughter.

There were no complaints when Edgar Lippicott cut his course load and withdrew into the cellar to tinker. His early retirement was accepted without a hitch, his pension remitted gracefully. They were glad to be rid of him. By that time, Mailman was already a mailman.

Mailman says (in response to the last thing his father said), "Grocery shopping?"

"Clothes." He squeezes his nose, tightening the anti-cold strip.

"Right. Does she still sing?"

"No." He grins. "Once— she doesn't— well. Ah. Doesn't, ah, like it anymore."

"Why not?"

Now the grin begins to crack. Mailman backpedals: "No, no, never mind, forget it."

"Ah," his father says, as if discovering something he wasn't look-ing for, and isn't happy to find.

"So what should we do now? What do you like to do?"

His father's tea is gone and so the old man gets up again and stomps—for the halting steps land heavily—over to the sink to deposit the empty mug and plate. He tells the kitchen window, "Something. To-day. Special." He turns, smiling again, and Mailman feels a complicated emotion, some ineffable combination of love and disgust that incorpo-rates the foreignest elements of the two, a love that is tainted with obligation and frustration, a disgust that is tinged with admiration and awe. His father is such a pitiable, tenacious creature, a brilliant fool, and here he wants to do "something special" for his son, an unworthier son there never was. Mailman says, "Of course, sure, let's get ready and go."

Mailman is still wearing the clothes he left his sister's in—the shirt she burrowed under to discover his lump, and a pair of long pants. He goes to the living room and rummages in his duffel until he finds a pair of shorts (thank God!) and an old but clean baggy tee shirt. He takes note as he stands that the sharpest of the pain is gone now, though even the near-overdose of codeine cannot completely dispel an overall feeling of weakness, of general malaise, like a fresh coat of paint on a rotting house. His body is struggling to support him. It wants rest. He goes into the bathroom, beating his father to it handily, and washes himself (not looking too hard at the lump, which has reddened and, yes, enlarged since he last examined it) with a washcloth. This he wrings out and hangs over the edge of the chipped and crusted tub. Back home it would quickly dry, but nothing seems to get dry here, he hasn't felt dry for a second since he entered the state, in spite of the drought. Back home he would be listening to the radio, driving his car up North Hill to the post office. He would have eaten, he would have slept. He dresses and shoves his dirties in the duffel and goes to the kitchen to wait for his dad.

It seems to take forever. He hears the old man moving from the bedroom to the bathroom and back to the bedroom, the journeys taking as long as the visits, the jerking footfalls thundering through the tiny house. A familiar wait: every now and then, when Mailman was a child, his father would remember he was a father and decide to take Mailman somewhere—"Let's go somewhere," he'd say suddenly, cheerfully, and then he'd vanish for as long as half an hour, puttering around, putting things in order, clearing his throat now and then as if about to shout some reassurance to his son. Only then would they get into the car. Typically they drove a long time, half an hour, before his father asked, "Where do you want to go?" And Mailman would say "I don't know" and his father would say "Well, think it over" and then Mailman would come up with something, anything, to break the silence: "Museum" or "Park" or "Ice cream" or "Miniature golf," and with that his father's mood would improve suddenly, he'd begin to chat, explaining some byzantine chemical or electrical process as if Mailman were not a child but some casual acquaintance from the humanities, and presently they would arrive at a destination, sometimes but not always the one Mailman asked for. They'd get out of the car and his father would look around and smile and say "Well" or "Here we are" and they'd stand there, and Mailman would have to say something like "Come on" or "Let's go" and for the rest of the afternoon the responsibility of deciding what to do was Mailman's. His father just followed him around, talking now and then, not seeming to understand that there was a traditional relationship between father and son that involved hair-tousling, a strong hand on a thin shoulder, words of advice. He didn't know there were roles to play, he didn't know the right lines and behaviors and emotions. Mailman can recall one summer night hearing explosions outside, rushing with Gillian to the window and seeing curtains of light unfolding themselves in the sky and draping themselves to earth, to the distant happy cries of delighted people. "Ah. Hmm," said his father, glancing at his watchless wrist, "must be the Fourth of July."

What kind of parent would forget to mention the Fourth of July? To what kind of parent would it never occur to throw a couple of lawn chairs in the trunk and motor over to the city park, where the rest of the town has gathered? The older Mailman got, the more this quality—this anti-quality—came to enrage him; it was easy to see it as a kind of silent hostility, a deep resentment masquerading as absent-mindedness.

But waiting now on the sofa in the living room, his feet propped up on his duffel, Mailman knows it isn't hostility and never was; it is, it was, innocence, a far scarier, far more dangerous thing. As he waits, he feels himself begin to sort of nod off, his eyelids twitch, his thoughts begin to blur and stretch: that is, he is imagining that the couch he is on has got the kind of retractable footrest found on certain chairs, and that he is pulling on the thick wooden lever that controls the footrest, and as he pulls, the footrest extends farther and farther, until there are hinged green rectangular sections of upholstered fabric as far as the eye can see, for he is not indoors anymore but outside, and the green fabric reaches the horizon, changing subtly in color and shape so as to form a facsimile of farm fields as viewed from an airplane window. And at this point sleep ought naturally to come, except that inexplicably it doesn't; instead the endless footrest retracts with a terrible bang and he is awake suddenly to find that there has been no companion noise in the real world to wake him: his father is merely brushing his teeth.

Well, it's good to know, anyway, that his father can remember to brush his teeth. Mailman rubs his face. What a clatter in his head! It's as if some rebellious part of him doesn't want him to fall asleep. Once Gillian banged her head on a rock in the yard, concussing herself mildly; far into the night the three of them strove to keep her awake. Their mother made her drink coffee, which she hated; their father slapped her cheeks. Mailman pinched her legs. Come to think of it, he twisted them too, Indian-rope-burn-style, and dug his fingernails into them, reaching fairly far up her dress to do so. How is it that their mother didn't notice? He is reminded briefly of his visit to Gillian yesterday and dreads calling her, as he has been instructed to do.

"What— you said— excuse me?"

"Nothing," Mailman says, getting up, and it's not hard to get up at all, the pain reliever is really doing the job. "I was talking to myself."

His father, of all people, ought to understand what that's all about, but he frowns a little (forehead only: mouth is still smiling, eyes are uncertain) as if this is something only a crazy person would do. Then they're off.

It takes a good five-ten minutes to get out the door and down the steps and into Mailman's car. Mailman pulls out, careful not to clip the mailbox on the way (and how in the hell does his mother manage this trick day in and day out?), and points himself toward the main road. "So, Dad," he says, "where to?"

"Oh, I don't— we can go wherever— that is, go. Where you want."

They are at the stop sign. Another car, a (yes) white (yes) SUV, has pulled up behind them. "Dad, I don't know where there is to go."

"Well— you're our— I mean, you're visiting, how about. And then we—"

The SUV is honking. Mailman peers into the rearview but the SUV's windshield is deeply tinted. All he can make out is a hairy arm, blotched with liver spots and encircled by an enormous gold wristwatch.

"The bird sanctuary," Mailman says suddenly, "let's go there."

"Oh! Well! Now, is that— or is it— I've never actually—"

More honking. Mailman sticks his arm out and waves the SUV past, but the driver doesn't seem to understand. Or understands but doesn't approve. He really leans on it now.

"Dad. Left or right?"

"Ah! L–l–l–l–right!"

So they turn right and the SUV races off left without pausing at the stop sign, its tires squealing on the hot asphalt. "Cripes!" Mailman says. "Do you know that guy?"

"Not— no."

"So how far do I go?"

"We have— you'd better— I got it wrong. Get, go, turn, around."

There is no one else about. Mailman executes a U-ey in the middle of the wide road. Ah, the turning radius on this wonderful car! Amazing!, he thinks as they lean right, pulled by centrifugal force. These morons in their SUVs couldn't possibly do this: if they were actually off-roading say in the jungle and they drove six miles down a one-lane dirt road that ended in quicksand, there's no way they could turn the thing around; they would have to back up for six miles. Not so with the Escort. Turn complete, Mailman straightens out and suddenly feels woozy. His vision doubles. The road seems to branch off into two, and then each of the two seem to fade in with the trees, the buildings, the sky. Two roads to heaven! He blinks, expecting the landscape to resolve, but it doesn't, and his wooziness progresses to outright nausea, and he says "Ah, shit" and pulls onto the shoulder, failing to crash into a mailbox only by the grace of God, or whomever. "Jussec," he says and gets out, and pukes copiously into the trees.

Pukes what, he doesn't exactly know, since he hasn't eaten in a while. Tea. Highway food. Stuff from New York that he somehow failed to digest in a day. He wipes his lips with a leaf from a nearby shrub (poison ivy?!? Nah, just some bush). He stands. His vision remains unsteady, but at least there's only one of everything; one quivering, lurching Ford, his father's pink-and-gray head framed by the hatchback window; one road, one sky. He looks at his hands. Two of them, but of course there are supposed to be two, and they are shaking. Mildly.

Can he walk back to the car? Yes, he's doing it now, one step then the other. His shoes flap loudly, disconsolately on the sandy pavement. He gets back in.

"So—" says his father.

"Yes, so, I got sick there, sorry," Mailman tells him. "All the traveling, I guess it's made me, you know."

"Yes."

He turns the key and hears a little click but the car doesn't start. Must have left the thing in drive. He looks down at the automatic transmission and finds that it's in park. He turns the key again, nothing. Remembers his aborted driving lessons, his silent father presiding over his mistakes: and here's Dad, right where he's supposed to be. Tries starting it from neutral. Nope. Back into park. He yanks the wheel back and forth—sometimes this has done the job. But the car refuses to start.

He ought to know how to fix cars. Really, he ought. He could fix his photocopier, he fixed a washing machine once, but he never did learn how to fix his car. Why not? Couldn't be all that complicated, he could have taken a class: but the truth is that he feared being the only intelligent person there, and feared even more deeply that despite this presumed advantage he would be the worst student, thus calling into question the most-intelligent status he so feared in the first place. His car hasn't broken down often, and never where help wasn't right around the corner, never in a desperate or time-sensitive situation, never when the weather was bitter cold or burning hot. This is no exception; they are sitting on the shoulder of the main road directly across from the entrance to Misty Cove Lane. Wait a minute. Lane? There are two signs, one right in front of their car, one across the street. The one nearest them says MISTY COVE LANE and the other one says MISTY COVE ROAD. "So what is it," Mailman says, "Misty Cove Road or Misty Cove Lane?"

"Road," says his father.

"So why this sign?"

He sighs, perhaps because he's explained so many times to so many people, perhaps because he really wants to ask about the car, perhaps because of the effort he knows it will take to respond. He says, "There was— that is, they planned— the road was going to go— and then the money ran out. Or no. Money something else. No, ah, a buyer, rich, wanted, and then, backed out. So no extension. But around then— new signs. And, and, and, and, put one up." He coughs. "So." He pants.

"It looks like we'll have to just go home, Dad," Mailman says.

"Broken?"

"Yes."

Mailman gets out, walks around, opens his father's door, helps his father out. The old man's arms are skinny, same as the guy on the beach. When he grabs one of them he feels a new wave of revulsion, the sinew and bone are right there under his fingers. How old is his father? Born when exactly? 1920. He's eighty. Or rather he's about to be eighty. When's his birthday? Now Mailman has gotten his dad out and he shuts the door of the car. When the road is clear they begin to cross: but both of them are shuffling now—Mailman's father with greater effort than Mailman, thank God—and by the time they're halfway across, several cars have arrived from both directions; they stop and wait for the two of them to finish. When they arrive on the other side, Mailman's father is sweating, large dark patches have appeared at his underarms and on his back, and Mailman realizes that he too is sweating, it's dripping down into his eyes and making him blink, and his vision is growing dimmer. Now—the old man's birthday. He hasn't called him on his birthday in years. What is it? Sometime in summer, he thinks, because they had picnics once or twice to celebrate, so it's got to be—wait a minute—June? June what?

"Dad?"

"Hmm."

"You're eighty. You're turning eighty?"

"Mm-hmm."

"When?"

"June ninth," he says perfectly clearly.

"You mean today? Today's your birthday?"

"Mm-hmm."

"You're turning eighty today?"

"Yah."

It's hard to know for sure—he's so damned tired and worn out and dizzy from the codeine, and it's so frigging hot, and Jesus Christ, this sweat!—but quite possibly tears are forming in Mailman's eyes. As if to confirm this theory, his voice breaks as he says, "Happy birthday, Dad."

"Mm-hmm."

"What are you— do you have something planned? Some kind of party?"

"Goin' out. Friends. Goin'— there's a good— we're— Italian. Restaurant."

"Tonight?"

"Hope you— if you want— come."

"Of course I'll be there."

They don't say much as they walk. Mailman can remember his father's birthdays better than he remembers his own. He and Gillian never got cakes, "All that cake for one kid?" their mother used to ask. Instead they got ice cream after dinner and a present. No parties. "If I wanted a house full of kids I wouldn't have quit breeding," said their mother. But Dad: he got the cake, he got the song, he got the forest fire of candles. He made a wish as he blew them out. It meant something to him: he was moved by the passage of time. Their walk is taking a long while, something like half an hour. When they get back, the house is quiet and comparatively cool, and Mailman's father says "Can't— too— a nap" and makes his way down the hall to the bedroom and closes the door. Mailman is left alone in the living room, where he also lies down, propping his feet once again on the duffel, and he closes his eyes and tries to sleep.

Nothing doing—his mind, his heart, his pores are all going at full speed; his head is filled with images alternately disturbing, banal and amusing: his lump exploding, splashing blood and greenish gore all over the room; toast popping out of a toaster; a cartoon frog eating the toast; the frog and toast being crushed by a giant rock; a dragonfly alighting on the rock; the dragonfly dancing; the dancing dragonfly stinging the lump; the lump exploding. Where is all this shit coming from?

He gets up. It's hard but he does it with the approximate speed and agility he would have employed were it still easy: in this way he will keep up appearances, until he can recover from this thing, whatever it is. His father is eighty—that's a lot of years!—but he never ate right or did a healthy thing in his life; whereas Mailman has been conscientiously healthy in both his diet and personal habits for decades. His good health, in fact, was a reaction to his father, who could not be bothered to take regular meals, who would fortify himself during his tinkering binges with gigantic bowls of off-brand ice cream and plastic sacks full of stale maple leaf cookies. There was none of that for Mailman, but if there is a reward for his responsible behavior he'll be damned if he can see it from here.

He is standing. The living room is arrayed about him, inertly awaiting his next move. It is eleven in the morning. Time to do something, time to get moving again. A job: that's what he promised himself he would get here in Florida, and so that's what he'll look for. He heads for the kitchen, where there is a newspaper folded unread on a corner of the table. It's a big table, it seems to fill the entire room, but only the portion nearest the sink and oven is clean. That's where they eat. Clearly they do not have people over for meals. The clean part is set off from the filthy, cluttered part by an arrangement of artificial flowers in a wicker basket; a tag attached to the basket reads *Happy Hanukkah Janet and Irv!* Who? He sits, unfolds the newspaper, begins searching through the want ads. He looks under PROFESSIONAL first, figuring that's what he is, a lifelong professional with a significant science background. The listings, however, are intimidating. Oncologist wanted, must make home visits. Dental technician. Regional manager. Chef needed immediately. Experienced mechanic, must have up-to-date training on Lexus, Infiniti, Mercedes, BMW, Volvo. Licensed dog groomer. Acupuncturist. Wildlife manager. There is nothing, of course, for the Postal Service, but even if there was he couldn't do it, so never mind that. He moves on to the unskilled ads. Hospital orderly. Maid. Maid. Orderly. Maid. Housecleaning technician. Driver. Fry cook. Maid.

Where are the good jobs, the jobs he'd be willing to do? Where's . . . ah, he doesn't know, *Efficiency consultant?* He'd visit some company, some factory or assembly warehouse, and stand around for a week holding a clipboard and taking notes on what people do. And then a few days later he'd report back: Sorry, you're terribly inefficient, you'll have to trim here and cut this corner, you'll have to lay off him and him and her, and then hire this guy to do this. Now *that* he could

do. Or how about *Traffic analyst*? That'd be a plum assignment, standing at intersections counting cars with a little clicker (or rather having
temps do that part), then feeding all the data into some elaborate civic
engineering computer, which would offer possible solutions to snags,
delays, jams, and imbalances. "You'll have to add a traffic light here,"
he'd tell them. "A new bridge is advisable." "Have you considered
diverting this river?" Where in the newspaper are these excellent
jobs? Maybe they're in another section—he rifles the pages looking
for supplemental classifieds until he comes across a headline that
reads SENATE JUDICIARY COMMITTEE CONDEMNS CLINTON and realizes
that the paper he's reading is two years old.

Two years! This table hasn't been cleaned for two years! This is
exactly the kind of detail he would love to share with Gillian—and
then he realizes that he can, and he is supposed to call her anyway,
she apparently wants him to.

He is given to wonder if everything about his visit to New York
was truly as *extreme* as he remembers. Did she actually *recoil in horror*
when she touched his lump? Was she really, ah, *coming on* to him?
Surely he is misremembering the scale of her anger, his shame, their
fear. It was late at night, after all; he was tired, she was depressed. And
she's his sister, for crying out loud, they've been through so much,
and this couldn't be more than a little bump in the road for them, a bit
of a stumble, that's all. So he picks up the phone, a cheap black thing,
which hangs dirtily on the wall like a giant dead beetle. For Chrissake,
they could get a new goddam phone! He examines the keypad, discovers that the thing has got speed dial. This is a heartening discovery,
suggesting as it does that his parents are not completely cut off from
the ebb and flow of American life: heartening at least until he notices
that there are only two numbers programmed in, his and his sister's.
Jesus Christ! Don't they call anyone else?

He employs his sister's speed dial key and is informed that the
number has been changed. At first he thinks she's changed it because
of him—because she doesn't ever want to talk to him again, and feels

this distaste so powerfully that she would hugely inconvenience herself vis-à-vis her other telephone-based relationships simply to prevent him from contacting her—but then it occurs to him that this might be an older number which his parents have failed to change. He tries the current number, the one he knows by heart (he has to start over halfway through due to a sort of swoon, a passing dizziness, that clears up immediately), and is rewarded with a normal-sounding, mellifluous ring, as opposed to the chunky, overloud, third-world-sounding ring that delivered him to the recorded message. He's still thinking this over—why the rings he hears should be different—when his sister picks up. Her hello is so hopeful that he is loath to identify himself, at least accurately. He says, "It's me."

Silence.

"Well, I made it down here, to Mom and Dad's."

Silence mostly, perhaps a gentle sigh.

"So, get this, I was sitting at the kitchen table looking through the want ads, and I realized that the paper's from two years ago! They haven't cleaned off their kitchen table in two years! Was it this bad when you were here?"

Silence. Not good.

"Gillian?"

And now, in a whisper: "Albert, what is wrong with you?"

He takes his time replying. "I hope you're not angry with me for leaving so—"

"Albert."

"—abruptly, but I got the distinct impression you wanted me out, and also—"

"*Albert.*"

"—also I stole your Tylenol with codeine, which wasn't very good of me to—"

"Albert! What the *fuck* is the matter with you? What was *that* on your *chest*?"

"I have an injury."

Now a silence that is pregnant with rage. And then: "Injury, my *cunt*, Albert, that's more like a goddam *Siamese twin!*"

"It's from a couple weeks ago when I bumped myself getting into the car. Remember I was telling you about that hallucination I had, with the—"

"Albert, *listen* to me." He listens—her voice sounds different, most of the pretense gone from it. It is rather frightening to hear. "That is not a *bruise*. It's some kind of— it's a *growth*, Albert. It's a *tumor*. You have to get to a doctor immediately. You scared the crap out of me the other night with that fucking thing." She sighs. "I shouldn't have been where I was"—her hand in his, he remembers; his hand on her hip—"but that's my problem, not yours. Your problem is that *thing* on your *chest*, and believe me I'd rather have my problem than yours."

Neither of them says anything for a while. It's a tired silence, not an uncomfortable one, though Mailman is, in fact, uncomfortable, leaning against the kitchen wall, his legs trembling faintly from the effort of standing. He says, "Well, okay. I guess I see your point."

"Go see a doctor today."

"Okay."

"You have to promise me."

"Okay."

"Promise."

"I promise."

"Okay. You promised. Now go. Open up the phone book."

"I don't have any insurance, and I'm—"

"You have a credit card, use a credit card."

"All right."

"All right, then. I'm going to get off the phone now."

"All right."

"Goodbye. Remember you promised."

"All right."

They hang up. He heads to the kitchen drawers in search of a phone book. There is one here, surely; even his parents have to have one, they drop them off for free on the front stoop: and sure enough he finds one underneath a pile of old electric bill stubs and restaurant menus, again several years out of date, but that doesn't matter as much with the phone book as it does with the paper. He looks under DOCTORS and finds a note to turn to PHYSICIANS; this in turn yields a long list of specialists and subspecialists, from which Mailman has a lot of difficulty choosing. Endocrinologist? Heart-and-lung man? Oncologist? Osteopath? His lump could be anything, and he figures he ought to just go to a general practitioner, but he can't seem to find any listed.

And then he remembers—if he makes an appointment, if he manages somehow to get an appointment *today,* how is he going to get there? His mother is gone for the morning, and besides, he doesn't want to have to tell her he has a doctor's appointment; and his own car, the trusty Escort, is broken down on the shoulder at the end of Misty Cove Road. So what he needs first, logically, rationally, is a tow truck, followed by a mechanic. He turns to AUTOMOTIVE and feels an instant lifting of the spirits; here is a problem that nobody will have trouble diagnosing, whatever it is, because it is a problem with his *car,* not with his *him,* and maybe they'll even be able to get to it today (unlike any doctor he could call, most likely), and he can try to set up a doctor's appointment tomorrow. He's in Florida, after all, America's Vacationland, so what's the hurry? Even if what he's got is dangerous, it isn't going to progress the way it did back home, what with the hectic pace he was maintaining there; relaxation slows the metabolism, it slows the blood and perhaps time itself. People don't age here, they *season.* He'll just *season* for a few days, and his problem, such as it is, will season as well, rather than . . . metastasize. Overwhelm. Consume. Whatever.

First mechanic he calls says they can get him in right away. "Car like that, yeah, I could fix in my sleep," says the voice on the phone; the voice, if not the man it's emerging from, seems to have a bushy mustache: it's that sort of voice. "These Lexuses all run on computers, I gotta hook 'em up to a computer to figure out what in the hell's wrong." A suppressed chuckle, as if he is delighted at Mailman's misfortune: but Mailman won't dwell on that. The mechanic requires him to meet the wrecker out on the main road, and so it's out the door again and onto the sandy sidewalk for another trek down the length of Misty Cove. On the way out he sees his camera tucked forlornly half-under a couch pillow and slips it into his shorts pocket. Immediately he feels more confident, better grounded. Go figure.

While he walks, he reflects upon how quickly the temperature has risen today and how moist it continues to seem. If it felt like this in Nestor, he thinks, there'd be a thunderstorm by five in the afternoon. But not here apparently, for no rain is forecast and all daytime garden sprinkling remains illicit. He's tired; his feet drag like a movie character's, carving tracks across a desert. He arrives at the end of the road to find that the car is still there, unstripped by thieves, unspraypainted by vandals, unticketed by cops, and he walks to it (half the car is now in the shade of the palm-and-kudzu barrier it's parked beside) and leans against it.

For a moment there is silence—no cars pass; no birds, disturbed by his arrival, squawk and flutter off to some unpeopled spot—and in that silence he hears Gillian's voice, making him promise to go to the doctor's. *Okay, okay, I'll do it.* Ashamed, his eyes fall to the gravel. There lies . . . something, a disgusting thing, once alive and doubtless identifiable to any half-competent zoologist, but now formless, fur-less, featherless: in short, a small red mound of biomass, pulsing with the colony of tiny creatures it has attracted, its membranes and connective tissues gleaming faintly in the shade, surrounded by a puddle of brownblack blood, itself carpeted by flies; and now the silence lifts and the insects that surround the object take up their terrible hum, a sound far deeper than ought to be possible for such tiny organisms, a kind of electrical noise, a transformer's growl. And transformer is about right, because what Mailman is looking at is a transformation in progress, the boundary of death being crossed by the most rudimentary of life. The sound has a pulse, actually, a sick, synthetic rhythm, and the pulse of the feasting insects shifts and shudders, intensifies then recedes almost to vanishing, and Mailman feels (irrationally!, but nothing that's happened to him in the past week is very rational) that this is a message to him, a portent, though of what (excepting the obvious, which is that he is doomed) he cannot figure.

Is there a stink? There is not. Well, if he edged closer (he's four feet away) he could probably smell something, but from here it is all clinical, a science-fair project. He wonders what the thing was when it was alive (and how the insects animate it, in such a terrible parody of life!), whether it ran, flew, swam. Behind him cars disrupt (mercifully) his concentration, but he remains transfixed enough not to notice when the wrecker pulls up and backs into position in front of the Escort. It's the slam of the truck door that awakens him, and he turns to find himself approached by, not a mustachioed man, but a woman, a man-sized woman with hair clipped short, who throws out between them a callused but clean hand and says, "Pat Slack, Slack Service, you must be Albert." She is not unpretty, this thickset, generously hipped woman; her face has a youthful tautness that belies her name and her eyebrows arch over her large eyes like triumphal banners. He is reminded of Semma.

"Oh! Hi."

"Talked to me on the phone? Okay, this the machine? Let's get 'er hooked." She releases Mailman's hand, goes to the truck, lowers the towing mechanism.

"Let's have the keys." He gives her the keys. She leans into the car, releases the steering wheel, puts it in neutral. Then it's back to the truck to scoop up the front end, to raise the Escort off the earth. Of this Mailman takes a furtive photograph—yet Pat Slack notices the camera and flashes a crack ten-dollar smile, facile as a starlet or pol. She idles the wrecker and comes out to the side of the road to get Mailman's particulars. "You riding along or should I call you?"

"No, you can call me, I—"

"Jesus Christ, now there's a piece of roadkill for ya! Howd'ya like that on a hot summer day, ouch!"

"Yes, I was just—"

"So gimme your number and I'll call you soon as I get up under this old gal's skirts. Betcha it's electrical. Driving around in this heat? Don't get me started."

He gives her the number and she shakes his hand firmly. Violently.

"All right then!" she says. "We're in business!" And he watches as the Escort is dragged away, its sad behind bouncing.

Back at the house his father has not emerged from his room, so Mailman arranges himself on the sofa and again tries to find the thread of sleep. It's in there, somewhere, that thin, strong strand; but it is as if the needle has fallen free of it; the gleam that announces its presence is missing. Even if he found it—and after fifteen minutes or so, he realizes that he isn't going to—sleeping would still be like sewing without the needle, it would be like forcing the frayed end of a thread through a thick fabric. Well, there is always resting—resting, though hardly as efficient as sleep, is said to have restorative powers—and so Mailman tries to rest. He folds his hands over his chest, and then lays them down at his sides, and then shoves them into the pockets of his shorts; he crosses his legs and then uncrosses them, then crosses them again, the other way. Meanwhile he thinks about Pat Slack, mechanic—did she have to work to get that bushy mustache into her voice, or did it come naturally? He imagines her exerting herself beneath the open hood of the Escort, grunting as she tugs at a seized nut or snakes her short arm around a tricky corner. He imagines the sweat on her back and under her arms, imagines the stooped, acne'd teenage boy who is her assistant and the tee shirt he wears, a black heavy metal souvenir with cutoff sleeves and a silkscreen of large-breasted women lounging in a hot tub while the band surrounds them with their enormous guitars: a silkscreen of which Pat Slack enthusiastically approves.

Then again, it could be different. Maybe she has no assistant. Maybe she isn't even a lesbian. And why does that thought disappoint him? Why does he want a lesbian to be repairing his car? He sees her shoulders working, her hands strong, and black with oil; and when she lifts her head, it is Semma's: she smiles, he can see in her face the effort of her hands. And when he looks down at her hands, they are clean and white and are working at his, Mailman's own, shoulders: he is watching himself being massaged. "Betcha it's electrical," Semma coos.

Clearly he is falling asleep. At last! He is falling asleep . . . and then he is asleep.

Then he wakes up. He does not feel rested, and in fact is briefly convinced that he didn't really sleep, not longer than a moment or two anyhow, but then he notices that the light is different, it is midafternoon, and his mother is standing in the living room, holding a torn paper shopping bag with clothes dangling out of it. "You look," she says, once Mailman has recovered his alertness and rubbed his eyes with his fists, "like you are about nine years old."

"Mmm," he manages to say.

"You're coming to dinner?"

"Mmm? Ah, Italian, right? Um, yes."

"Do you have any other clothes?"

"Ah, I dunno."

"You're dirty. I'd give you your father's clothes but they're too small and there are piss stains on all the shorts anyway. Here," she says, "look at what I got."

She sits down, rudely shoving his knees aside with her hipbone, and whips some dresses out of her bag. "This green thing, isn't it just like something Nina Simone would wear? And here, I'll have the tits of a thirty-year-old in this number. Sequins make everything look terrific. And this kimono, I'm thinking of giving this to your father, he'll look like an old gigolo in it, that would be a hoot. It'll be covered with solder burns in a week. And here—this sweatshirt—second-grade teacher chic. Don't you love how the dog's leash is a real chain?" Mailman has got himself propped up on his elbows while he nods and mumbles his appreciation, and waves of pain are swirling around the growth, and dulling into nausea. His breath is going shallow and he's beginning to sweat. He remembers his parents' visit to him in the psych ward, how she resented him for being sick and weak. He says, "Mom?"

"Christ, I can't believe I got these panties," she says.

"I have to get up."

"I just sat down."

"I have to . . . perform a . . . function."

She looks at him, eyebrows raised. She is at the top of her game. She says, "Perform a function? Do you want me to get you a chalkboard? A calculator?"

"Mom, please, it's urgent."

"Oh, get yourself off the damned sofa, you don't need me to move."

And so he is forced to bend his knees, to fetalize, removing his intestines briefly from the protection of his bowels, and he almost loses it right there on the sofa, beside his mother and her sack of booty. But he keeps it together. He shuffles bent over into the bathroom and shucks off his shorts and falls onto the toilet with a house-shaking thud, and then lets himself go.

Relieving himself, he thinks that there has got to be something wrong with this. It is not supposed to be so bad. He is not supposed to whine in shock and pain. He is not supposed to want to close his eyes as he tidies himself, for fear of what he'll see. When he's through he washes his hands before the mirror, and though he tries to avoid looking into it, he can't help it; his face is right there, and after all it is his face, the most familiar thing in the world, the thing that ought to give him comfort now that everything else has gone to pieces. But it doesn't. The wrinkles around the eyes and mouth, the hollowing of the cheeks. The past week has left its mark. He needs to shave, for one thing, but he hasn't brought his razor. Scabs are appearing where he didn't even know he had cut himself. He looks familiar, all right, but not in the right way. He looks like someone, but not himself. His father. It isn't simply that he looks older, it's that he is now, like his father, lost in his own life.

In the hall he can hear shuffling from his parents' room; his father must be waking up. But when he goes to the kitchen, there his father stands, blurred, sleep-rumpled, wearily talking into the telephone. He is holding a credit card. His stammer has been pruned. He says: "Sequins, yes, no that one's fine . . . a kimono? How— that is— what's the— Really? That's a lot . . . No, it's okay, I'll— we'll— that's fine. What's the total? All right. All right."

He hangs up. Mailman says, "Dad."

"Ssh." He dials. Waits. "Yes, hello, Edgar Lippincott. Hello, hi, I'm just— I'm wondering what she— if she— thank you." He pauses.

"Dad, what are you doing?" Sudden shooting pain in the side.

His father holds up a finger, impatient. "Yes? Okay. Panties? Really? Okay. Okay. Okay. That's all? All right, I'll— then we can just . . . Okay, great. Thank you!" Hangs up. Says to Mailman (now hunched in response to the pain in his side, rendering him a near-perfect replica of his father), "Just taking— that is, I'm settling up— because your mother— got to pay the shops where— that's all I'm doing."

"Mom what? Where she what?"

For a moment his father is weirdly purposeful and lucid. He leans forward, puts his finger to his lips. "Sssh. She'll hear."

"Hear what?" Mailman whispers.

"She . . . what she does is . . . she shoplifts."

"What!"

"All the stores— she does it all the time. So I call— pay them— they keep track of— that is, they monitor— paying attention to what she steals. And then I call— my credit card."

"She's *shoplifting*?" He remembers, suddenly, Gillian: fourteen years old, too tall, her breasts too large, her voice too deep: *Albert, look at the stuff I stole!*

"Sssh. No problem. Sssh."

"But *why?*"

Now his father looks angry. It is strange, because his father never looks angry. He says, quite clearly, "*Fun.*"

In twenty minutes they are ready to go to the restaurant, though it is only four-thirty. Mailman washes his face and daubs with a wet tissue at a grease stain on his ankle. He does find a fresh shirt in his duffel bag, though it is long-sleeved and monogrammed (MVD, whoever the hell that is); the shirt is a little too small so he rolls up the sleeves and the resulting look is not bad: Gulf-Coast-casual, you could call it. But the monogram is irredeemable. What is it with the American middle class, he thinks, that they have to have their *names* on everything? Always on the middle manager's desk, a little plastic nameplate; always on the wallets, the *cell-phone holders,* the pens, the neckties, their *initials.* This is a service for which they pay extra, this infantilization, like the name laundry-markered onto the buttocks of the stuffed animal brought to the first day of nursery school. He wishes he had a pair of sunglasses to hang on the pocket, to obscure the initials. But nobody will notice or care.

Mailman drives (the big leased sedan; he is forced to explain to his mother where his own car has got to, and she says, "Well, that's what happens . . ." followed by any or all of the silent but implied phrases: ". . . when you're a cheapskate," ". . . when you run away from home," ". . . when you never get a tune-up," ". . . when you are willing to settle for a crappy job in the public sector"). It is like driving a storm cloud: a dense, damp thunderhead, complete with little bolts of lightning that stand for his mother's imaginary comments. She looks like lightning, herself, in the sequined dress she stole this afternoon.

The restaurant, like all restaurants here, is part of a strip mall. Granted, it is a nicer-than-average strip mall, with palm trees carefully arrayed in rows in the parking lot and flowering shrubs forming borders, instead of the usual sculpted yews Mailman hates so much. The restaurant is called Sole-Mare, and it shares a roof with businesses called Nails 'n' Stuf, Yoga Depot, Marnie's House of Dog Beauty, and CompuCorner, which is not on any kind of corner. Inside, the air is cool and alive with conversation and clinking dishes, and Mailman has got to admit that this is a vast improvement over every other minute he's spent in Florida so far. It's a big room, carpeted but not uglily, the tables along the walls all enclosed by white wooden trellises carefully threaded with plastic ivy. His parents' friends are already here. They are annoyed by the lateness of the Lippincott party. Their *Happy Birthday!'s* are grudging.

Introductions are made. Leonard is tightly packed into his bright red skin; his hair is dyed black and hugs his scalp like a squid. Neat, elfin Paul is a doctor—he is introduced that way by Leonard, "This is Paul, he's a doctor"—and when Mailman shakes his hand the doctor grips hard; he looks into Mailman's eyes and scowls and continues looking and scowling for some seconds. These men have wives: Bea is married to Leonard. She is tiny and gray and says "Oh!" before she speaks, as if surprised that she's being allowed into the conversation. And Anna, Paul's wife, is bound to a wheelchair—literally bound, with straps around her ankles and waist and right wrist, leaving only the left hand free—where she trembles uncontrollably, clearly wracked by Parkinson's and not long for Slip Key. Her flowered dress is almost completely covered by a giant plastic bib, a constantly crackling thing with a large crumbcatching pocket on the front. Mailman shakes everyone's hand, even Anna's, an act that seems to silence the others, though he believes he sees some kind of gratitude in her face. He sits. It does not hurt so much to do so; he took three more painkillers before they left. There are only ten pills left now.

A conversation is in progress which they have interrupted. Leonard returns to it, eager to include them. "So get a load of what Bea was saying."

"Oh! Maybe I heard it wrong," Bea says.

"No, listen to this. Listen to this. She says she saw a commercial—"

"Really, I don't know if I really saw it, it might have been—"

"—a *commercial* about a *convertible Lexus.* And I said the hell you did, and she said it's true, she saw it."

"But I could be wrong."

Leonard throws up his hands. "But she *could* be *wrong.* Just listen to her. 'Hey honey, there's a lion in the bedroom, but I *could be wrong.*'"

"Oh, well, if it was a lion in the bedroom, I wouldn't get *that* wrong . . ."

"No," says Leonard, "she'd say, 'Ooh, ooh, I think maybe I saw a man-eating beast in the bedroom, ooh, ooh, or maybe it was a spider.'" He dangles his hands in the air, makes a kissy face, bugs out his already-bugging-out eyes.

"Oh, Leonard," says Mailman's mother, "quit being such an ass."

Leonard smiles, points at her. "Ya hear that? Ya hear *that*? Now *that's* a woman who won't take any shit! *There's* a woman for you!"

Mailman is trying to look at the menu, but all the entrées—elaborately described pastas, *carne, pesce*—seem disgusting to him, composed of too many ingredients, covered with too many sauces, cheeses, dressings. He could go for a piece of bread, or some kind of grilled piece of meat. A small one, without seasonings. He peers up over the edge of the menu at Paul, the doctor, who is giving him the eye. Mailman smiles. Paul looks away.

"What she said," Leonard is saying now, "is, 'They said there's a Lexus with no top.' 'A Lexus with no top?' I said. 'It's a coupe, it's got no top, is what they said.' So I said, 'What's this coupe called, then?' And so she says, 'Oh, I don't know, the XJ-niner.'"

"Oh, well, that's not what I said exactly."

"So I said, 'XJ-niner? XJ-*niner*?' I mean, if there's a new Lexus convertible called the XJ-niner, I swear on my mother's grave I'll go to bed with Clara here." He points to Mailman's mother. "I swear to God, if there's an XJ-niner, I'll make love to Clara!"

Bea is saying, "That isn't exactly what I said, I don't think."

"In your dreams, Lenny," says Mailman's mother.

"Every night, baby," is the reply.

Bea says, "Oh, Leonard."

Mailman's father chuckles steadily, quietly, like a pigeon.

The waitress comes and they begin to order, respectfully repeating the elongated titles, *the fettuccine with rosemary-infused alfredo sauce; the garlic-rubbed pounded veal cutlet*. There is a general hubbub about whether senior discounts can be combined with coupons (they cannot); whether they're early enough for the Early Bird prices (they are, having sat down before 5, even if it is now 5:12), whether the drinks come with refills (they do, excepting alcoholic drinks). Mailman gets spaghettini and meatballs bolognese, because why not? It doesn't matter what he gets because he isn't going to eat it, not much of it anyway. He asks if there's going to be bread and the waitress promises to bring them bread. She's pale, with glasses, both unusual in this place of contact lenses and deep tans; she reminds him, a little bit, of Marsha. Unconscious of her image, in command of her dignity. Hardly any body, though. As she takes his order Leonard aims a line of patter at her. "Hey, spectacles! Hey, don't go making a spectacle of yourself! Hey there, paleface, can we get some wine? Hey, red man wantum heap firewater, ha ha!" Doctor Paul quickly orders for himself and his wife; she is to get a chicken cutlet. "We only have breaded," says the waitress, glad to be away from Leonard, who continues to mutter his routine to himself. "Breaded will be fine," says the doctor. Mailman's parents go for the extra-virgin-olive-oil-brushed Argentine steaks in a sauce of peppered porcini mushrooms. Bea takes a long time to order, asking detailed questions about several of the entrées and then biting her nails while perusing the menu one more time. "Do you want me to come back?" "No!" say the doctor, Mailman's mother, and Leonard, all at once. At last she decides (ziti), and the waitress speed-walks away with obvious relief.

Leonard begins one of his stories. Mailman has never met him but it is clear this is "one of his stories." "So this girl wants a Le Sabre, no frills. And as you know, frills are my business—in more ways in one, right, Clara, heh heh—" "Go screw yourself, Lenny," says Mailman's mother. "—heh heh, I love it, I love it! Anyways she says no frills, no frills, if you don't have a plain one on the lot I want you to order one from the factory. Probably she's seen something about the car factory on the TV so now she's an expert. But anyway, I tell her, well, I could order it from the factory for you but there'll be the factory fees, which when you add 'em up are something like three grand, which is more than you'd pay for this Le Sabre I got right here, which is basically loaded. Y'know, I'm making all this up on the spot. I say, so if you want you can buy this baby and have it today and when you go home you can take all the extras out with a hammer. This girl says, hmm, factory fees, really? I go in the back and I actually get her the hammer, I say, here, I'll throw this in so you can get rid of those extras you don't want. Half an hour later she's driving that goddam Le Sabre off the lot, listening to the surround-sound, blowing the AC, switching on the cruise control. People don't know what in the hell they want! I mean, that's my job—I gotta tell people what in the hell they want!" He laughs. Bea laughs. Mailman's father laughs. The bread and wine come and for a while they are quiet.

Paul, the doctor, is looking at Mailman again. His narrow-headedness is emphasized by his gray hair, cut close on the sides, curly gray at the top. With his green shirt, his white face, his trim gray head, he looks like a cigarette. Right now he is smoldering. He takes slow bites of bread, sips his wine, and stares at Mailman, leaning a little to each side to get the full view, checking out his neck, his shoulders, his chest. Only Mailman's mother seems to notice this is happening. She gazes at Mailman, then at the doctor, her face full of wonderment. She puts her fork down.

"Albert, sit up straight."

Leonard, who has been telling a story to Mailman's father, interrupts himself to say, "You tell 'im, Clara!"

"Shut up, Leonard," she says, and to Mailman: "Seriously, Albert, you look like a gorilla."

"Sorry." He straightens himself.

"It's your father's birthday."

"I'm tired."

The doctor looks from mother to son, his mouth distastefully pursed. Both of them look back at him. And then, embarrassed, all three stare at their plates.

"This place stinks of fish," says Leonard.

"It's a goddam seafood restaurant," mutters Mailman's mother.

During this exchange Anna has been trying to eat her bread. Paul has torn it into tiny pieces, to make her chewing easier, but the pieces appear to Mailman to be too tiny, so that she is unable to get her shaking fingers around any of them. The old woman is completely focused on this task; perspiration has broken out on her forehead. Mailman leans over and says, "Would you like larger pieces?" He expects some kind of nod, but instead she lays her shuddering arm down on the placemat—Paul has removed her plate out of reach—and sweeps all the crumbs toward Mailman, covering his lap with them. Several are dampened by saliva; they must have fallen out of her mouth. She turns to him with great effort and looks into his eyes and emits something, a sound, a word:

"*Rikkkk!*"

Prick!

"I— I'm sorry, I— I was only thinking you . . ."

"Albert," says the doctor, "why don't you just let me take care of that, all right? Here, Anna," he says and breaks another piece of bread into tiny pieces and spreads them out before her.

And now the food has arrived, the salads with their heavy mantle of dressings, and not-quite-ripe vegetables, and the entrées, steaming, their meaty entrées with wetly mounded pastas and red puddled sauces ringed with grease, and soon their water and wine glasses are oily with the oil from the salads and their hands, and the tomato sauce on their lips is transferred to the glasses where it sticks and dries. Mailman is not feeling at all well. He is, in fact, sick, but the problem is that moving from his seat may make him vomit. But he may also vomit if he stays in his seat. He does not have time to figure the exact odds; there is only time to hear Bea say "I saw this show where there was a fellow who got lost in the Himalanias," and Leonard say "Himalayas, *Himalayas*, what are you, stupid?," before Mailman pushes his chair back, leaps to his feet, heads in the general direction where he figures the restroom must be. He finds it exactly where he pictured it (down a hall and behind a beaded curtain), pushes open the door and discovers the only stall occupied. So he throws up in the sink.

Could have been worse!, he thinks as his stomach turns itself inside out. He might have puked on the floor, the wall, the mirror, on another person! He gags until he can gag no more and then, without looking (well, barely looking, through squinted eyes), he runs the faucet and splashes the water around the sink. It's a small sink, quite lovely actually, painted porcelain in a Sicilian-pottery pattern, lots of red and blue; he rinses until he figures it's clean and then rinses his face. He hears the man in the stall mutter, "Fucking drunk." He opens his eyes.

A few splashes he's missed. He wets a paper towel and wipes the mirror and wall and the sides of the sink and the floor under the sink.

"Drunk, I wish," he says, and hears the man shifting on his seat. "I wish drunk was all I am." There are no further comments from the toilet stall.

When he emerges from the bathroom he discovers that the others have finished their meals and are waiting for coffee. Their place settings are empty, the silhouettes of their plates ringed by crumbs. His spaghetti, untouched, is the only meal still on the table. He stands a few feet behind his chair, staring at the heap of food. His mother says, "We ordered you a coffee, Albert."

"Thank you."

"Are we to assume you don't want to eat that? What with your big exit?"

Leonard says, "You had a look on your face like you were gonna blow."

"Yes," says Mailman. "Ah, yes." He remains standing and after a while they forget him and begin to talk about the drought. Eventually the waitress comes ("Hey, thanks a lot there, Poindexter, heh heh," says Leonard) and takes the food away. She says to Mailman "Was there something wrong with your food?" and he says "No, it's me" and she rolls her eyes.

They drink coffee.

"I dunno what the goddam problem is, we got plenty of water, we got a whole ocean of it out there, for Chrissake."

"That's salt water."

"So take the salt out!"

"You can't just take the salt out."

"I once put too much salt in Leonard's stew—"

"Ah, Christ, didya have to bring that up? I'm gonna ralph, whoops, sorry, Albert."

"—and I couldn't take it out again, even by putting in potatoes."

"I shoulda hired a cook decades ago."

"I think we get the point, Lenny."

"Some young thing, nice to look at, whaddya think, Bea?"

"Oh! I don't know about that . . ."

"You know what you need, Lenny? What's the opposite of Viagra?"

"Opposite of Viagra? Bea's the opposite of Viagra, heh heh!"

A sort of rhythmic rustle captures their attention; it is Anna, laughing.

"That's right, Anna, yuk it up, old girl!"

"Leave her alone, please."

"Ah, cool your jets, Doc."

"I don't see what's funny. How am I the opposite—"

"Bea, just ignore him."

"If only she'd done that forty-seven years ago!"

The coffee is gone now. Mailman figures it is time to leave, and that's when they bring in the cake, the whole waitstaff, all smiling large fake smiles, singing "Happy Birthday to You," mumbling in unison when they get to Mailman's father's name.

Edgar Lippincott grins as the cake is placed before him, and he blows out the candles (six or seven of them, not eighty), and cake is distributed and picked at unenthusiastically by all. Mailman, desperate for something to do besides eat, takes a few pictures. At last the evening has exhausted itself. Leonard insists on paying the entire bill—"It's Eddie's birthday, fer Chrissake!"—and then appears shocked and irritated when nobody tries to talk him out of it. Everyone but Anna gets up. As he rises from his chair Mailman feels a part of him linger, a part that doesn't want to exit into the world, because in a restaurant you know what to do, there is a traditional order, transitions are clearly signaled, and no decisions must be made that demand more than casual attention to one's hankerings. But outside, on the glittering sidewalk, in the blacktopped lot, in the car, it will be time to choose a direction. There are not many directions that seem appealing right now. For a moment Mailman doesn't move, and in that moment Doctor Paul comes around the table and grabs his left arm. As he does, Mailman feels the tough knuckles brush his lump, and he twitches. The doctor's face is close, just behind Mailman's, his mouth at Mailman's ear, and he says, "You'll come to my office in the morning."

"Sorry?"

"Don't be an idiot," he mutters, his hand still tight around Mailman's arm. "Here." Mailman feels a card pressed into his hand. "Come in the morning, come at six."

"Six?"

"Or earlier. I like to get out of the house."

"I thought you were retired."

"I am. I see a few patients. Show up."

"I don't—"

"Don't be an idiot," he says, and releases Mailman's arm. The doctor turns away, wheels his wife toward the clot of people at the door.

Mailman looks down at his palm where the card is nestled. It is cream-colored, rough-textured. It is printed in red, shinily embossed.

> PAUL MASSEY
>
> ONCOLOGY
>
> 2529 OSPREY ROAD, SLIP KEY
>
> 445-1812

NINE

On the Beach

——

Outside, unexpectedly, there is light. The sidewalk in front of the strip mall, studded with crushed glass, spangles orange and pink with the evening sun; the air is as thick and salty as a hollandaise. It's as if no time has passed, as if he is suspended in an endless ancient moment, like a dragonfly in amber: but then he remembers: it's June, and they ate early. It's barely seven.

"Outta the way, junior," grumbles Leonard, emerging behind him with a crumpled receipt in his fist and Bea tottering close behind. Mailman obliges, his joints cracking. The two move off toward whichever large car is theirs, Leonard bearishly lumbering, Bea turning several times to wave. The doctor and Anna are already gone. So where are his parents?

"Hey!" his mother shouts. There they are, parked beside the drive-up bank window. He walks across the parking lot, feeling its heat radiate through the soles of his shoes.

The meal has galvanized his mother; she wants to go for a drive, a birthday drive, before they turn in for the night, and she wants to be behind the wheel, which is better than all right with Mailman, as he slumps in back, behind his father, the doctor's business card curling in the damp heat of his palm. "So," she says, "did Paul detain you for the usual reason?"

"I don't know."

"To tell you you don't have any respect for your elders? Ever since Anna started shaking, that's his thing. Respect your elders! As if he ever gave a shit when he was young!"

"It was something like that, I guess."

"He used to be my GP. He's seen me stark naked. Never again! Talk about lack of respect. He's got the bedside manner of Frankenstein."

"Igor," says Mailman's father unexpectedly, with a dry chuckle. "Because— short."

"Ha! Right."

They cruise the domain of strip malls along straight wide roads, blinkered, neon'd, ashimmer in an envelope of music and shouts. Teenagers suck face leaning against their cars, the shirtless boys wearing giant shorts and sneakers, like clowns in an erotic circus; the girls filling cutoffs and bikini tops, which the boys casually, clinically run their hands over and under. "Look at that!" Mailman's mother says. "It's barely seven in the evening! They haven't even had dinner yet! If they're already that close to screwing at this time of day, what are they going to do for the next eight hours?"

"Drugs," says Mailman's father, on a roll. "Drugs."

They drive on. The strip malls become sparser; sometimes there is only one per block, or none, only an empty lot or overgrown orange grove (the fruit, untended, littering the ground), or there is a warehouse or nursing home. Passing one of these they can see residents sitting in the yard in their wheelchairs, watching cars go by. Mailman's mother waves and honks. "There we are in ten years," she says to Mailman's father.

"Five," he replies, laughing.

"Two."

"We should— really ought to— go ahead— tomorrow!"

"Think of it! Nothing but bridge and television all day long. Bland food. Hour upon hour of Albert and Gillian not visiting."

"Drugs!" They giggle like a couple of leprechauns.

"Wait a minute," Mailman says, seizing upon what his mother has said, or rather the gleeful insouciance with which she has said it—and then the pain in his side flares up, but only from the plateau it's already at. He crushes the business card harder into his hand. "That's not— of course we would come and—"

"Oh, shush," says his mother.

At last they have come to what Mailman's mother seems to have wanted to see, a low dark building from which the sound of slow music is leaking. Its gravel lot is filled with cars. She pulls in without parking and leaves the engine running. The windows are down and sung words reach them.

> *Please stay*
> *Please, go away*
> *Don't make me say*
> *That I love you . . .*

"Jesus Christ," Mailman's mother is saying, "she sounds like a duck in heat."

"I don't think— or rather I wonder if— do ducks actually—?"

"Stuff it, Edgar."

They sit still for a time, listening, and then Mailman's mother turns the car around, nearly grazing a stand of motorcycles. Mailman sucks in breath, because he is the one, not his parents, who would be beaten up.

He sleeps in the car. There are no dreams. There is only what happens when they arrive home, stranger than a dream: his parents help him out of the car, they swing his arms over their shoulders and half-carry him to the house, his father keeping his side up quite well despite his apparent frailty. They lead him up the stairs and through the door and living room and lay him down on the sofa. They have done this before, dozens of times, after every childhood trip; one or the other of them has carried him to bed and pulled the blankets up to his neck, and then, as now, he let them, even though he was really awake and could have walked, because he wanted their assistance, he wanted their attention, even if he could only get it when he was sleeping. And now, as he drifts back to sleep—so powerful, its pull—his mother leans close and looks into his sticky eyes and sees that something is wrong, if not exactly what, and she kisses him good night: but his eyes are closed before her lips reach his cheek. Wait, he wants to tell them, my appointment—the card is still in his hand—but he knows there will be no problem getting up early enough.

Still no dreams. Or if there are dreams, they are forgotten. They aren't important. Mailman does not need them to tell him what he should be afraid of. He knows what to be afraid of, and he is afraid of it. When he wakes (not in Nestor, not on his cot, but here, in Slip Key, Florida, on the day of his doctor's appointment) he senses that it is early, too early: and when he gets up (but it isn't like that: he doesn't just "get up": he is lying on his back on the sofa with his right arm and leg dangling over the side, and when he tries to right himself he is nearly knocked back into unconsciousness by a wave of pain and nausea, and so to get up he must sort of slide onto his knees, bending the right leg as he falls, then swinging the left down after it, kind of arching his back as far as it can go, and when he is on his knees he is able to pause, to catch his breath, and then to use his right arm to bring himself to his feet, because his left arm, for the moment, is almost incapacitated) and makes his way to the kitchen, he finds it is three-ten in the morning. Sleep is over. There is nothing for him to do for the next two and a half hours.

So he decides to go early. He takes his codeine pills (doesn't check to see how many: most, he supposes). He digs out the phone book, finds a map, figures out where Osprey Road is. He plots his route. Then he takes the car keys from the hook in the kitchen cabinet and lets himself out.

It's a chilly night, clammy and stale. The weather is changing: maybe the much-hoped-for rain is coming after all. Crickets chirp, but distantly, it seems, and without enthusiasm. He considers going back in for a jacket, but he didn't bring one of his own, and searching for one in the closet will wake his parents: so it's to the car, then, which also chirps, and pings when the door is opened. He shuts himself in quickly and shivers against the cool leather seats. When he starts the engine the lights come on automatically, illuminating his parents' bedroom window; he shuts them off quick. But there's no point; his mother is already awake, has perhaps been awake for hours. Maybe she doesn't sleep at all. The headlights revealed her face in the window, watching him. It looked so beautiful there, so like a marble statue, and for a moment the coolness of the car seems a comforting coolness, rather than an irritating one, and he raises his hand to her. But the lights are off now, and he can't see her very well, and he himself is in the dark. And so this wave, which might well have meant a great deal to Mailman's mother, may or may not have reached her through the car window, subtly glazed with moonglare.

By now Mailman is out of the driveway, he is in the street and the headlights are on again. He puts the car in drive and moves forward, leaving his parents behind. Houses, sidewalks dissolve in his wake. He follows the map he's made in his head of how to get to Osprey Road. He finds it—this does not take long—but there don't seem to be any numbers on the buildings, and the street signs don't reveal whether the numbers are rising or falling, so he drives almost a mile in the wrong direction before he realizes his mistake and turns around and goes back. In time he finds it, the oncology lab. It is square, it is gray, like the Nestor Post Office. The windows are also square and also gray: smaller squares, darker gray. He parks near the entrance—there are no other cars here that he can see, other than one, which he assumes is a night watchman's—and goes to the door, expecting a desk, manned by said watchman. Sure enough: the watchman is skinny, bug-eyed, cleanly shaved even at this hour. He sees Mailman, gets up. Unlocks. "Yeah?"

"I have an appointment with Doctor Massey, but it's later, I'm early, I was just killing time. I'll sit in my car, I just wanted to—"

"Jussec," says the guard, and he locks the door and goes to the desk and talks into a telephone. Then he comes back and unlocks again.

"Go on up," he says.

"He's here?"

"All the time, man."

"Why?"

"None of my business. He says go on up. So go on up."

He goes on up. The elevator is already open and waiting. Inside, the walls are mirrored, a terrible prank: must patients gaze upon their own wan, cachectic bodies, their blotched and scissored skin, their sunken cheeks, as they report to their doctors? It's that or close their eyes, which Mailman does. Rising, he feels unmoored from the earth, like he's being lifted into heaven to be judged. Ha!

The doors open onto a dark hallway. He steps out into it and the doors close behind him, shutting out most of the light. There is only streetlight, shining obliquely through the tinted square window at the end of the hall. He walks, feeling his way along the walls. "Doctor? It's me, Albert Lippincott." The words vanish into the carpet, into the nubbled paneling. He hears a doorknob turn and there, up ahead, a crack of light appears, and widens, and admits the shadow of a man. His lab coat, in silhouette, has the appearance of a duster: the doctor looks like a cowboy, a cancer cowboy. "Here," comes a voice, and the form recedes, leaving the crack of light to navigate by.

Mailman reaches the office and peers inside. It is an undistinguished room. White. An examination table, some black machines, a desk, a couple of framed diplomas. The doctor is at the desk, seated in his swivel chair, his shorn head visible over its leather back, the sagittal crest as prominent as a handle. Mailman closes the door behind him.

"I'm early," he says.

The doctor turns. His eyes are underslung with purple, but he does not otherwise look tired. "I'm here," he says quietly. He isn't keeping his voice down, it's just the way he talks. The cancer cowboy. He says, "Sit on the table."

Mailman sits on the table. The plastic is cold. There are retractable metal footrests, but they are presently retracted, so his feet dangle like a child's. He bumps his heels rhythmically on the table's side.

"Thanks for seeing me on such sh—"

"Just take your shirt off, Albert."

Mailman does not hesitate. If he does, he'll stop completely, he'll flee. He realizes that he would never have come to the doctor, to any doctor, if this one had not insisted. He would have had to fall down unconscious in public and be brought to one by the cops. He doesn't like doctors, doesn't like their attitude, hates the way they can't just *help* you, they have to make sure you're *grateful* that they've helped you, and then they have to *ignore* your gratitude, or worse act annoyed by it, so that you are fully aware *everyone* feels that way about doctors and there's nothing particularly *special* about you or your garden-variety gratitude. *You should see the stuff people thank me for,* their dismissive nods seem to say, *what I did for you is nothing.* But he's here now, and the doctor is telling him what to do, so he does it. He unbuttons his shirt and lets it fall off his arms, behind him.

The lump is large and pink and uneven. Especially here, where everything is white and at right angles, the lump seems impossibly large, for a bodily growth; it is grapefruit-sized. *Half*-grapefruit-sized. It hurts to look at it. He is embarrassed, as if he were the one who put it there. The doctor looks at it. He does this for a while, without getting up from his chair. There's an ambient sound here, the air conditioner sound, the decayed echo of every vague motion the two of them make, the muffled traffic outside, of which there is little. Mailman listens to this sound. He doesn't watch the doctor.

"When did this start?"

"Last week."

"No," says the doctor.

"Yes, last week. I bumped myself getting into my car. It was a bruise, and then a lump."

The doctor is shaking his head. "No," he says again, and gets up. He walks toward Mailman. He leans in close, his nose centimeters from the lump. He says, "I'm going to touch it." He touches it. He says, "Does that hurt?"

"Yeah."

"Where?"

"On it. Under."

"On or under?"

"Under. It hurts under."

The doctor stands up straight and peers into Mailman's eyes. Mailman watches him lean from side to side. The doctor says, "Don't follow me with your eyes. Stare straight ahead." Mailman stares straight ahead. There is a poster on the wall of a beautiful woman lying on a beach. Her body is slim and smooth and tan; a bikini barely covers her. She wears sunglasses and the sun is shining brightly on her skin. Underneath her are the words TAN NOW, PAY LATER, and beneath those, in smaller type, SKIN CANCER KILLS. The doctor moves into Mailman's field of vision, obscuring the poster, but Mailman continues to stare at it through the doctor's head. In a moment the doctor ducks down again and begins to palpate the lump. His fingers press, ever so gently. There is something both disgusting and erotic about his touch.

The doctor stands. "No," he says, "not a week. Can you remember any other pain, any other discomfort before that?"

"I wasn't paying attention."

"Unwise."

"I was healthy."

"I think you have a cancer."

There it is! Cancer! He said it! It's real! But wait a minute: is this guy listening to anything he, Mailman, is saying? Did he hear him say he bumped his side, he bruised it, that there was no previous indication of— that he had been in perfect— that he'd been— that he— that—

"Wait a minute—aren't you supposed to do some tests, take a chunk of it and—"

"A biopsy, yes, we'll do it, I could be wrong. But I don't think so. You're sick. Have you had any other problems?"

"No."

"No?"

"They aren't related."

"Then what are they related to?"

"All this Tylenol with codeine I've been taking."

"What are the problems, Albert?"

"Dizziness, vomiting, diarrhea."

"Your appetite?"

"Can't eat."

"How many Tylenol with codeine do you take?"

"Lots. Four or five at once."

"Look, you have to check into the hospital. We have to remove that." He gestures at the lump. The *tumor*, is what Mailman's being asked to believe. "And even then, I have to tell you, you should be ready for bad news. Even if it's grown a tenth as fast as you're saying, you'd have a problem. It may have metastasized. It could kill you." The expression on his face—a mixture of pity, irritation, and superiority—reminds Mailman of Ronk, and he is suddenly angry.

"I want a second opinion."

"Of course."

"I bumped myself. I bumped myself getting into my car."

"I suspect that the bump simply called this tumor to your attention."

"Stop that. I want another opinion." *That is not a bruise,* Gillan said. *It's a tumor.*

The doctor nods. "Yes."

What is that supposed to mean, *Yes?* What's with this fucking *agreeing?* "And what are you doing here in the middle of the night, anyway? What kind of doctor are you, sneaking around the office at three-four in the morning? What kind of operation is this, anyway?"

"I don't sleep."

"What?"

"I don't sleep." He does not appear to be expecting any particular reaction from Mailman. He is just answering the question, it seems.

"Why the hell not?"

"Anna used to keep me up. She shakes. I came to like being awake. I don't need much sleep. I use my body efficiently."

Mailman says, "Well, *good for you.*"

The two stare at each other for a moment. The moment stretches into a few moments, into long seconds. The doctor hangs his head, slightly, as if he is studying the lump. But he isn't. He says, "I don't like being retired. I want to work. I retired to take care of Anna. But at night—I come in and read up on the literature. I see patients early. They don't sleep much, either."

Mailman sighs. The sigh bounces off the bare walls like a bullet. He says, "Hand me my shirt." It is the oxford, the one with the monogram. He feels like a goddam idiot.

The doctor picks up the shirt and crushes it, ever so briefly, in his fist before handing it to Mailman.

"Thank you."

"You're welcome."

Mailman puts the shirt on. He buttons it. Meanwhile the doctor goes to his desk and sits down. He looks through some papers on the desk. Mailman slides off the table and stands there, in the room, breathing the recirculated air, getting ready to leave. He says, "You can send the bill to my parents."

"Albert," says the doctor.

Mailman waits. The doctor looks up.

"Don't waste time. I want you to get a biopsy. I'm going to schedule you for one."

"I have to think."

"Please," the doctor says, and they gaze at one another for a moment. Yes, probably, Mailman will listen to him. Within a few days Mailman will be in the hospital, and surgeons will be cutting into him. Another small sad room to suffer in: another padded cell, another mail truck to Syracuse, another doctor's lair. And afterward the radiation will begin, the chemo: toxic chemicals in his blood, more nausea, color leached from his skin, exhaustion, hair loss, bad smell. Worse smell, rather, because he already smells bad, and it isn't just because it is hot here and he's sweating, and it isn't just because of his inactivity or his reluctance to shower or having no real change of clothes. It's sickness, he smells sick. It's death. It's the smell of death, on him, a living person.

There's nothing he or the doctor can say that will satisfy the other. There is no secret code. Words simply do not have that kind of power. This seems to him an obvious revelation, one he should have had a long time ago, one that most people have early in life. Why did it take him so long? *There's nothing I can say that will make it better.* He turns and leaves.

The moment he does, his mood improves. It was those eyes: those horrible doctor's eyes, glittering with the knowledge of his, Mailman's, demise: the last thing he needs, some doctor's clinical pity. What he needs is a good night's—or maybe a third of a night's—sleep, and a bottle of some kind of painkiller, it isn't going to be Tylenol with codeine, of course, but maybe he'll be able to find something just as good. And then tomorrow—or rather later today—he'll get up, schedule something with another doctor, a couple more doctors, and they'll check him out and get him going on whatever is needed. And maybe—now, as he gets into the elevator, this suddenly seems like a possibility—the lump isn't cancer after all. Bigger mistakes have been made, and by younger men, men who actually sleep at night instead of coming to the office to read medical journals. (A diagnosis, like a letter, can be misdelivered.) The growth is probably benign, a lot of these things are, they'll just cut it out, plop it into a pan, burn it with all the other medical waste, and he'll be cured. He'll get his appetite back, his sense of balance, his continence. He'll sleep the sleep of the healthy, the living, the strong. (The diagnosis will be returned unopened.) He'll go back to Nestor, demand his job back; he'll fight the charges, because where's the evidence? Can they prove anything? Can they fire him, fine him, jail him, because of a few complaints from crackpots on his route? No goddam way. He got his job back once, he can get it back again. Pretty soon he'll be working again, punching in at seven with the herd, sorting and banding, cruising along the lake, pounding the pavement. "Morning, Albert!" Crows, squirrels parting before him. The hot coffee. The rolling cart. The dappled sun. Maybe there will be another contest on the radio, and he'll win that too. Another free breakfast. One for him, one for the Gray Fox. Anything's possible.

Then he strides out of the elevator (ouch—not so fast) and past the reception desk and promptly smashes his face against the locked glass door. Shit! "Hey, pal, let me unlock that for you there," says the guard, and he comes around the desk and jingles his keys, trying to find the right one. Mailman reaches up to wipe the saliva and nose grease off the glass, but only succeeds in smearing them around a little. The door is open now. "Thanks, sorry, you'll need a little Windex there." "Hey, no problem, you got more important things to worry about." And he's out.

He cruises around, looking for an all-night pharmacy. It isn't hard to find one, they're practically on every corner, giant freestanding Eckerds and Rite Aids and CVSes, gloaming castles of the American night, always open for the insomniac/walking dead crowd. Well, good for them, the poor suckers, give them something to do, let 'em buy heart pills at four in the morning. He picks a place, pulls over, parks, strides in (this time the glass doors part automatically: now that's more like it) and finds the pain reliever aisle.

They have it all, of course. Everything under the sun. No time to think about it, just buy: but money: he's almost out of it. Well, hell, he'll use his credit card, who cares if the inspectors catch up to him now, because he's going to beat them, that's what's important. He grabs up one of everything marked Extra Strength, and cradling them in his arms heads for the cash registers.

But wait: what's this? Lunex. NyTime. RestEase. Nocturna. Doz. It's the sleep aids: and God knows he's going to need them to go to sleep tonight, if not every night for a long time. He is too agitated. And so he piles them on, one of each, and manages to get this teetering mass to the counter, where there is no one in line, and a girl reads a magazine.

"Zat it?" she says, tucking her gum into her cheek, and he says "Yep" and she says "Cashercharge?" and he says, "Charge." So she adds it all up and runs the charge and while the machine calls the credit computer she stuffs it all in a bag. She shifts the gum, chews it. She waits, watching the little gray box on the wall, ready to tear off the yellow and white receipts as they come chattering out.

But it doesn't happen. She leans closer, she says, "Huh!"

"What?"

"'Call center.'"

Mailman reaches out, oh-so-carefully, and slips his fingers through the handles of the plastic sack. "Really?" he says. "What does that mean?"

"I dunno? I guess I call this number?" She is reaching for the phone.

"Wait—maybe I have cash." His credit card is just out of reach, it's sitting in front of the register.

"Yeah, uh," she says, "but I put it through as credit, I gotta get the manager to—"

"Oh, you don't need to do that, I'll just give you the cash . . ." He is digging in his wallet, counting out the bills, it's going to be close.

"Well, uh, hold on, 'cause I think I have to call this number."

"No, no need, here," and he is tossing little wadded-up dollars onto the counter, "really, here, it's okay, just take these and I'll take my card back."

Now the girl looks worried. Signs of intelligence—a focusing of the eyes, a wrinkling of the brow—blossom on her small tan face. She removes the gum and stashes it somewhere south of the counter. "Holdonasec."

"Here," he says, "I'll just take—" And he is reaching for his card, he is leaning over the counter and reaching and the counter is pressing into his lump. His *tumor*. No! His lump! His unproperly-diagnosed lump!

But her slim fingers, their nails meticulously painted like birds of paradise, press his card to the counter and slide it away, beyond his grabbing hands. And her voice: it has aged years. "Why don't you just wait there while I call the manager, sir."

"No! Here! Cash! Take it!"

She pushes the filthy pile back toward him. "Now, you hold on to that," she says. But he has the pills. She eyes the bag. "How about you leave your purchases here for a moment," she says now, patting the counter.

He bolts.

He hasn't shoplifted, not precisely. He even paid, although the amount may not be exactly right. As for his credit card, what happened? Has the P.O. got a lock on him? As he pulls away in his parents' car, the clerk and a fat guy with a mustache appear on the lot; the fat guy has got a little notebook and is writing down the license number. Great! Now he'll call the cops! An image comes to mind, of Shut-up speaking into a telephone: "Thank you, Officer, that's real helpful." Hangs up. Mephistophelean laughter.

After that, he drives. It remains very dark, the trees and buildings cloaked in it as if morning is nowhere near; but it seems to him that morning is all too close, waiting just beyond the horizon, like a mugger. His bag of pills joggles on the passenger seat as the car shudders over bumps, and a few of the boxes tumble onto the floor.

The question, of course, is where to go, now that his name is known to the drugstore, now that they have his credit card, now that a bulletin will go out on his parents' car. The answer is nowhere, really. Away from the car, he supposes. He is driving south on Osprey, and though he can make out the lights of the next town off in the distance, this length of road is largely undeveloped. The land here is swampy, undesirable to builders and bathers alike. A carpet of cattails stretches west into darkness; cypress trees are arrayed skeletally against the clouds. For it really is cloudy, isn't it: no stars are visible and the air has an incipient quality. Rain *is* coming. People will be relieved.

Mailman slows. He pulls to the shoulder. *Think, think,* he thinks: Can't stop now, got to get out of sight. If he looks in the rearview he can still make out the crenellated roofline of the drugstore he ripped off. Okay: take the first right turn, hide in the weeds. He puts the car back in gear and putts along the roadside, lights off (he never did turn them on), searching for a street, a path, a track, anything he can pull into until the coast is clear. Or at least until other drivers are out on the road.

It takes a while. When he finds it, it does not at first appear promising. A dirt road, no more than a couple of ruts, weeds growing up out of the gray fill. But there is a gate of rusted metal pipe, and the gate is chained, and a sign reads NO TRESPASSING BY ORDER OF THE STATE OF FLORIDA. He considers just parking the car here—it might be possible to miss it, driving by—when he notices that the chain is attached to no visible lock, it's just wrapped casually around the post, so he gets out and unwraps it, and the gate swings open. He gets in the car and drives through and stops and gets out and closes the gate and rewraps the chain, and it looks exactly the way it did when he pulled up. He drives as far as he can, and then the road turns to mud and the car gets stuck. It is like a dream: the engine whines, the Buick lurches, but nothing doing. He thinks of Pat Slack, of her cheerful wrecker, of his poor Escort. He is glad his father isn't with him.

At least he and the car are out of sight. As for the future, well, that can be worked out later. For now, everything is fine. He leans down, stuffs the fallen pill boxes back into the bag, picks the bag up. He should have gotten—stolen!—a bottle of water, but it won't be hard to swallow the pain relievers, they all have that coating these days. He gets out. There is just room, a thin strip of gluey road between the car and swamp, to accommodate him. When he clears the car he takes hesitant steps along the mudded ruts, toward the Gulf. His shoes suck and smack in the mud. There is sufficient light to see by, filtering through the clouds and trees from the road and the impending sun, and he can hear waves lapping on a shore. He walks for a long time, or what seems like one; there is so little context here, now, to judge.

In time the trees part. A grayness is revealed, a space in the murk. His steps have grown quiet, the ground firm. He has arrived at a rough beach, a crescent of coarse sand and soggy dead leaves, about large enough for a Boy Scout troop to camp upon. The lightest object in sight, it glows faintly. What is there for him to do? He sits down.

Instantly his shorts are soaked through: this is the edge of a swamp, after all. As his eyes adjust he can make out beer bottles, candy wrappers, a bra twisted in a strand of seaweed. It is not an attractive place, but it is a private place (provided no topless beer-swilling candy-chompers arrive), a place where he can think.

He pops open a bottle of aspirin. Plain old aspirin, better for you than the other stuff, he should have relied on it from day one. The codeine hooked him, he should never have taken it. He swallows one, two, three—ah, hell, a handful—of aspirin, washes them down with his own spit, what little of it he's got. Ahh. Better.

All things considered, he doesn't feel too bad. There's (1) pain in side, (2) hunger/nausea, (3) fear of death, (4) fear of imprisonment, (5) wet butt. Only five items, carefully typed (in his mind) on his father's Smith-Corona, and three-hole-punched. But then again, he could add (6) exhaustion/insomnia. (Pencil that one in.) But then again *again*, (6) can probably be eliminated, just as (1) will be, with drugs, if he's willing to pop a few of the sleeping pills and take a little nap right here, while the sun comes up. In fact, this seems like an excellent idea: romantic even, the kind of thing people sitting in front of computers in offices in Minneapolis in January fantasize about.

He takes the sleeping pills out of his bag. Lunex. NyTime. RestEase. Nocturna. Doz. Which to try? They all come in largish boxes containing smaller bottles that don't actually hold many pills; they tell you take two but no more than four in eight hours. After some consideration he chooses Lunex, in honor of the fingernail-clipping of moon that is probably directly in front of him, judging by the lambent clouds. And so he opens the bottle and takes two out (little blue caplets—cute actually, plump, smurfy) and swallows them. And then, because he's really sick and really tired and really, really having trouble sleeping, he takes two more. There's his four. That ought to hold him for eight hours. He crosses out (6) on the list in his mind, and scribbles *cured* underneath it, for good measure.

He waits to get tired. The slate sky seems to have lightened into shale, but that might be his imagination, it's still awfully late, or rather early; anyone in his right mind would still call it night. He wonders what the next land would be, if he were able to walk straight ahead, on the water, as far as he wanted. New Orleans? Texas? Or is he pointed southwest, so that he'd miss the U.S. entirely and land somewhere in Central America? How long would it take him? A long time, and it'd be boring as hell, even given the novelty of getting to walk on water. And presumably he wouldn't get to kick through the waves like water-walkers do in movies; he'd have to tread on the surface, that is *right on* the waves, and they'd slip out from under him and he'd lose his footing. And if there were a storm, forget about it. He'd be bounced all over the place, he'd be crushed. He wouldn't make it ten miles, actually, even in good weather; the first big breaker would snap his ankles.

Dispiriting, really, how little seems to be possible. Or, if possible, not in the way that you want. He's spent his life desiring specific things, things that don't exist, in fact that never will, not because they are impossible or too difficult to accomplish, but because the world doesn't care to make them. Things that he is the only person on earth to want. For instance the rubber pad he spent three days looking for ten years ago, the one he was going to set his photocopier on, so that its vibrations didn't rattle the pictures hanging on the walls or cause the machine to imperceptibly migrate east while copying, banging it into the hard metal edge of the folding buffet table it stood beside. He went to every office supply store in Nestor asking for a rubber pad, a thick one, half-inch thick, size of a doormat. Why don't you use an actual doormat? they asked him. Because I don't want a doormat, I want this: a smooth sheet of half-inch-thick rubber. Why? He couldn't explain: it was what he pictured, that's why, it was the perfect thing, rather than just an effective thing: he could imagine its unblemished matte blackness, its sharp smooth-grained edges, the little indentations the legs of the copier would make in it; he could imagine half-standing on it while he copied, the balls of his feet pressing against the taut, springy surface, and he could imagine the brown prints his shoes would leave, in a slightly different place each day, until two smudgy half-ellipses marked his entire history of photocopy sessions. And then, when all footprint definition was lost, he would wipe the smudges off, and the rubber would be restored to its pure clean blackness. No one would have understood why he needed to re-create this vision, they would have told him that any old hunk of rubber would do the job, and so he didn't bother telling them why, he simply sighed and shook his head and left the store. Until one clerk of above-average intelligence suggested he try automotive stores, one of which directed him to Onteo Supply, a fabricator of machine parts and accessories, where he was told to visit Allied Products in Auburn, which was supposed to have what he was looking for. And they did: they had giant sheets of half-inch thick rubber, ordinarily used as shockpads for huge industrial machines, that were exactly the correct color and weight and possessed the precise springiness he had imagined under his feet. The problem was that you had to buy an entire giant sheet, they wouldn't cut it to size for you, and one giant sheet (sixteen-by-sixteen feet) cost three hundred dollars.

Naturally, he paid it. This was what he wanted, and so what if he was only going to slice a three-by-four-foot chunk out of it? It was *exactly what he wanted.* So he paid. He couldn't bring the thing home, of course, not in the Escort, so Allied Products agreed to drop it off at his place the next time they brought something down to Onteo Supply. And they did: they dumped it in his yard while he was out delivering mail. The following week he would pay a man to come and haul away the excess rubber, for which he had no use, but on that day he was delighted, and set to work cutting out the perfect slab. He did it—he used his doormat (ironically) as a template, carefully boxcuttering out the precise corners and straight edges he'd envisioned—but it was not any fun. He realized this as he heaved the copier up onto the thing (breaking it, he would discover later, and necessitating a three-hour repair job): it was no fun, having to go through all that; clearly none of it was really worth it, in terms of money or time or anything else. He was a fool for caring. He could have put his own doormat under there, since it would have solved the original problem, and nobody visited him anyway. But instead he pursued his stupid vision. A perfect world—no, not even, a *half-decent* world!—would have provided it for him. He could have walked into a store and bought what he wanted, shrink-wrapped and labeled (PERFECT FOR COPIERS! it would read), and brought it home immediately. But the world didn't work that way. The world was flawed.

He is not tired. It's been—what—ten minutes? But there is a feeling of calm, of mental softness, unfurling inside him like a flag of surrender, and he figures a couple more of the sleeping pills can't hurt, and so he takes them, and he leaves the bottle open. Because you never know. It's a bit lighter now, and he can see the open bottle where he's wedged it into the sand, and he can see the bag filled with boxes of pills, and he thinks that if he came upon a guy who looked like him, at this time of day, in a place like this, with all those pills beside him, he would think that that guy was planning to off himself. It's the natural thing to think, of course; it makes sense: but this is not what Mailman wants. Mailman does not want to die, neither by tumor nor pill. (*Holdonasec,* says the drugstore clerk.) What he wants to do is exit, just for a while, to check out and be missing for a time, and to return. And he'd like to return different, not just in different circumstances but as a different person: not completely different, mind you, but subtly different. Maybe a good sleep will change him. Maybe that's what he's been lacking all these years, good sleep. He reaches into the little bottle and drags out another pill with his finger. On it the letter L is printed:

A nice touch, that script. Elegant. It's a good tactic, drugs-as-elegance: brings to mind a four-poster bed, lace everywhere, a satin nightgown (because it's women these things are aimed at, correct? Women who might otherwise be up all night worrying about their children's schedules and their husbands' affairs and their sisters' heroin habits and their parents' chronic illnesses?): luxury. No responsibilities. The servants take care of all that. All in the plump blue pill, plump like a pillow, like a breast (Semma's?), like a buttock (Marsha's?), and the scripted L. He turns it between his fingers and pops it into his mouth. Luxury! Leisure! (Lugubriousness! Licentiousness!) Bring it on!

It's definitely lighter now, the sun is rising behind him; and the waves before him (gentle, lapping) are foamy at their tips. He wonders if the fishing's good out here. He's never fished. Fishing would not be relaxing to him, he hasn't the patience for it, he'd be thinking about *fishing* the whole time, and that would ruin the experience. Behind him, on the road, cars are audible; he can't see them from here, of course, or even his own car. His parents' car. He wonders if his mother is still awake, if the cops have called their house yet. Ah, hell: no point in worrying about that. And so he stops.

He what? He stops worrying? It's true: he isn't worried about his parents, or their car, or their worries. Those things can work themselves out! He reaches into the bottle again and takes a few more Lunex, and while he's at it he takes some more aspirin as well. It's supposed to thin his blood. Could he thin it enough to make it a gas? If so, would he float away?

For a long time he sits, watching the water, taking pills. *Sittin' on the dock of the bay, takin' pih-hi-ih-ihls*. Light continues to gather, insects and birds begin to call, thunder discreetly rumbles. And then he hears, at last, footsteps behind him.

He's been anticipating it, of course; he's been waiting all night, all week. All his *life*! He feels . . . relief. Thank God, he mumbles. Now he can get it all over with: the arrest, the trial, the sentence, the surgery. *Sir, you'll have to come with us*, the cops, the bailiff, the nurses will say. *By all means*, he will reply. He will put himself, once and for all, in their hands. There is nothing like this feeling, of giving yourself over to trust: of crossing the street when the sign says WALK; of stepping into the elevator, the airplane; of eating the food you're served. It is the feeling of climbing into Gillian's bed during the night, or as their mother raged. But it isn't the feeling of being married. Always he withheld something from Lenore; she was his lover but also his competitor, and (as with Semma) never could he hand himself over completely. Why not? She wouldn't have appreciated it. She wouldn't have seen it as a gesture of generosity or trust; she would have seen it as weakness. Well, now he'll go willingly. He'll tell the doctors, the lawyers, the police, to do with him whatever they must. Given his condition, he probably won't even go to jail. The footsteps are closer now, they've combined the whisk of brushed grass with the slap of shoes in muck, and he figures he might as well just stand up and meet them with dignity. But he seems to be sort of immobilized.

"Albert!"

It's possible to turn his head a little to see who's here. He sees feet first, ratty mudsplashed sandals actually, and thin hairy legs and the bottoms of a pair of cutoff chinos. His visitor's knees crack as they bend, and as the full figure comes into view he wonders where exactly he's seen this guy before, under what circumstances. A glimmer of anxiety squeezes around the thick curtain of self-medication. Narrow face, thick beard. And the tee shirt, he's seen that before, too; it's got a phrenology head on it. It's— it's—

"Jared Sprain? Remember me? You used to deliver my mail. I was always getting packages? We used to hang around the door and chat. This was in Nestor. It's this beard, I bet, I didn't used to wear a beard."

"Right," Mailman manages to say. He remembers Sprain's desperate letters. *On days like today, with the wind beating against my windows, I feel that the all of man and nature are against me.* But Sprain does not look bad. That is, he looks the same, save for the beard: scruffy, undernourished, sweaty, unwashed. Except that now these same qualities have rendered him . . . *pure* somehow. *Integral.* Instead of scruffy he's . . . comfortable. Instead of undernourished, wiry. Instead of sweaty: aglow. Instead of unwashed? Natural! Mailman can't help staring. His medicated scrim is being blown aside by a wind, and his glimmer of anxiety is brightening into fear.

Sprain senses that something is amiss. He sits. "Hey, dude, it's all right. I'm not here to get back at you."

"Get back . . ."

"For stealing that letter. Look, man, I would've done myself in irregardless. Regardless? Whatever. Christ, that guy, Hopper—believe me, a letter from him is not life-affirming."

"So," Mailman says. "You are dead."

Sprain smiles. "I am dead."

Oh, Mailman thinks, okay, he's *dead*. Well, this is okay, then. He glances down at the pile of empty bottles and lids and scattered ungobbled caplets, and somewhere in the back of his mind he feels a bit alarmed, but not for long. After all, look!—it's Jared Sprain! I'll be damned! He says, "So . . . how is it?"

Sprain shrugs. "Pretty good, man."

"So you went to Heaven?"

"Yeah."

"So where are your wings?"

Sprain laughs, waves the question off. "Ah, that old saw. You know, it was a product of the times. They figured if Heaven was in the sky then everybody had to have wings, they couldn't think of any other way to work it. You can have them if you want, but believe me, there's no need. Actually, dude, they're pretentious. 'Oh, look at me, I'm an angel in Heaven!,' you know, that sort of thing."

"Sure," says Mailman. "So it's real? Heaven?"

"Hell, yeah. And Hell, too."

"Uh-oh."

Again Sprain laughs. "Don't worry about it, man. It doesn't matter."

Going to Hell, not matter? But he says: "So what's it like? Heaven?"

A low moan of cogitation. "Mmm . . . hard to describe. Like life, but, you know, not really. It's like the seventies meets the fifties. It's like a picnic that's not too exciting but really beautiful. And you're the picnickers but you're also the ants, get it?"

"Is there coffee? Sex? Do they have newspapers?"

"Sorta, kinda, and yeah."

"Yes? Newspapers?"

"Here." A newspaper has appeared in Sprain's hands. Mailman is having a bit of trouble reaching for it—his scrawny arms can only move very slowly, as if he is trapped in a gigantic ball of dough—so Sprain hands it over, placing it into Mailman's open fingers. It's a hell of a nice-looking newspaper. Smooth, strong ragstock; small, clear type; long columns. No pictures. The headlines do not make sense: GORMAL CLIPS MASTER PATHWAYS. SEVEN TO TWELVE MAKE REACH. PLATEAU MASK PROMISES DRENCH.

"Pretty nice, huh?" says Sprain. "Totally golden-age."

"None of it makes any sense." He tries reading an article, the one about the plateau mask. *Farther prints mechanize drench other bank. Spread matter plateau mask feeble came, several slab pressing . . .*

"Oh, yeah, don't worry about that. It's a kind of pidgin." Sprain grabs the newspaper away from Mailman and it vanishes from his hands. He wipes his palms together and a white dust rises from them. "So," he says. "Heaven. It's cool. Not everybody likes it, but I do."

"You're kidding."

"You can please some of the people some of the time, et cetera. It's not like it's a vacation, where you don't have to do anything. I mean, there's a reason you only go on vacations for a week or two, right? You get bored."

"Uh-huh." He remembers his last trip to Nantucket. It was dull after only a couple of days. Everybody there was on vacation, after all, and a vacation only feels good if other people are still working. Sprain used to go to the desert, he recalls. Always he remembered to have his mail held. Conscientious, but suicidal, a surprising combination. He says, "You said not to worry about Hell."

"Well, I don't mean *don't worry*. You might end up there. It's just . . ."

"What!" He's getting nervous.

"They're pretty much the same. Pleasure-and-pain-wise. Heaven is organized, Hell is a mess. You still have to find things to do."

"There aren't pools of fire? Devils with pitchforks?"

Sprain laughs long and hard over this one. "You mean 'Hell' Hell. Nah. Same with the wings."

"Pretentious."

"Right."

They sit, watching the water. It is the same water. Mailman says, "Can I tell you what worries me? About Hell?"

"Dude, I told you not to worry about Hell."

"But I worry. I worry that Hell is, that it . . . I worry that it's of your own making. That you get the Hell you deserve. You know, whatever you hate the most, forever."

Sprain doesn't respond, so Mailman keeps going. "You know, I've thought about it from time to time, what my Hell would be like. And I think for me, I would just never get there. I'd have to get on a bus, and then transfer to another bus, and then another one." He is thinking of Kazakhstan. "And every bus would be more crowded, and smell worse, and the road would get rougher, and the landscape would get uglier, and every leg of the trip would be longer. And I could never sleep, people would be stabbing me or crapping on me, and I would just sit there wishing I was still on the last bus. And everybody would be talking about the tortures of Hell—were they going to turn into lizards, or have their heads spun around, or what—but we'd never get there. It would just be wishing for the past and being afraid of the future, forever."

Again, silence.

"Which I guess is kind of how my life was."

"Is," says Jared Sprain.

"I'm dead, right?"

"Naw, you're alive."

Mailman turns to him, with effort, for his neck is terribly stiff. Sprain looks alive enough, aliver than Mailman feels. "I figured, the sleeping pills."

Sprain shrugs. "They're just antihistamines," he says. "Don't get me wrong, man—they might do the trick. All's I'm saying is you ain't dead yet. You could ralph it up."

The information surprises him. At first he's pleased, excited—none of what he's done is permanent. He could still come back, be cured, fight for his job, tell Ronk where he could stick his disciplinary action! But then a familiar despair settles over him: there will be decisions to make if he survives, there will be the future to imagine. He doesn't feel up to it. Heaven, he thinks, is knowing. Hell is hoping.

"Look," Sprain says, standing. "A lot can go on in your head between now and the moment you either wake up or croak. I'd think things over pretty carefully, if I were you. You might not want to check out, is what I'm saying. Heaven is not what it's cracked up to be. In fact, it's not any better than life."

"But you were so depressed in life." . . . *worthless, a faker, a cheat . . . life's end would only be a mercy . . .*

"Yeah, but there's things I miss. You know, I should have lived different. I should have taken my meds or moved out into the desert or something." He sighs. "Or at least killed myself better. Letting my buddies find me like that—I thought it would be the landlord." He brushes off his butt and then his hands. Amazing: in the afterlife, you still have to brush sand off your butt. "I'll leave you to your own devices, man," says Sprain, and he begins to walk away.

"Where are you going?" Mailman asks him, suddenly afraid of his own devices.

"I'll be back. Chill, Alberto." And with a wink and a shot from the gun of his hand, Sprain vanishes into the brush.

So here he is, alone. There's no getting around it now, he is nearly paralyzed, sitting straight up with his arms wrapped around his knees. The saving grace is that he can't feel his body, only the wind on his face; and any discomfort he ought to be experiencing is missing. He is a head on a pedestal. The light is here now, in the gray clouds, casting a brilliant dullness over everything, the bright greens and blues smoldering. Everything is very real, he thinks, and beside him he hears the voice of Gary Garrity saying, "Yes, Albert, but what do we mean by 'real'?"

"You!" It takes him some time to turn his head and scowl at his shrink; meanwhile Garrity continues talking. He is dressed in a short-sleeved oxford shirt and a pair of khaki shorts. The shirt is tucked into the shorts and the shorts are belted. His feet, at least, are bare. They are shapely, narrow, like a woman's.

"That which we call 'real' is a construct, Albert, a set of assumptions and interpretations we ourselves make. The only 'reality' is in the mind. Freud suggests that—"

"I'm not an idiot," Mailman says, and then: "I didn't know you were dead."

"I'm not *dead*," he says, touching his chest, as if this is a personal insult.

"How am I seeing you, then?"

Garrity smugly grins. "Maybe you *are* an idiot after all! What were we just saying about the nature of reality, Albert?"

"It's all in your head."

The grin widens. "Exactly! Albert, whether I am objectively 'real' or not—as if such a thing as 'objectivity' even exists—I am real *to you*, and that is what's important, for our purposes."

"Ha! That's very shrinky of you! If reality's all in the head, then every problem is a psychological problem, right? And that makes you the expert on all existence, right? Well, this is not going to be one of your 'sessions,' okay? It's my fantasy, and I'll run it how I like."

"Whatever you say, Albert. But you do owe me fifteen minutes."

"All right," Mailman says, "time!" And he looks at his wrist, where he wears no watch. And yet . . . there *is* a watch, a tiny clock actually: the clock from Garrity's office, the very one he stole the fifteen minutes from, its oaken semicircle rendered in miniature and strapped around Mailman's petrified forearm. It reads 5:12.

"Nice touch!" Garrity says.

"Fourteen minutes, forty-six seconds."

"Albert, do you remember Hoffmann?"

Hoffmann. Hoffmann. The old guy with the pit bull on Truman? No, that's Hellman. "Don't know him," he says.

Garrity emits a self-satisfied chuckle. "I should think not! He died in 1822!"

"Get on with it," Mailman sighs.

"Hoffmann was a writer, Albert, a German. He influenced Hawthorne and Poe, Freud and Jung. Offenbach made his stories into an opera. I told you about all this during our sessions."

"Sorry, your wife must have drowned it out."

"Touché! Very good, Albert! Now, the opera in question is called *Tales of Hoffmann*. Offenbach made the author a central character in it. At the beginning, Hoffmann enters a tavern—'goes into a bar,' if you will—and tells the patrons there about his three great loves. There is Olympia, a mechanical doll whom he breathes to life, but who falls apart; there is Giulietta, the whore, with whom he falls in love, but who sells him out for a richer man; and then there is Antonia, whose beautiful singing expresses her love, but also brings on consumption, which kills her."

Mailman cannot help but think of Semma, picking wildflowers for him in the dark. Of Lenore, of Marsha. But to Garrity he says, "Big whoop."

"At the end of the opera," Garrity goes on, tapping his wrist to indicate the dwindling of his fifteen minutes, "Hoffmann drinks himself to death—"

"What a terrific story."

"—and is transported by his muse, Stella, into writerly immortality. This is your life, Albert: betrayed, disappointed, unrequited, yes: but a hero, a tragic hero! The very brilliance that might have brought you greatness, laid you low. The love that might have saved you, destroyed you."

The words give way to the rustling of the trees, the lapping of water.

"As usual," says Mailman, "you have failed to make me feel better."

Garrity stretches his legs, cracks his feminine toes. "I admit it's small comfort. But look at what I have to work with, Albert. You defined your life by love, or the lack of it. You left little time for anything else. There were plenty of muses, but you didn't listen to what they had to say."

"I don't like your past tense."

"Face it, Albert, you were a mailman with women problems. There are worse things to be. So, rather than punish yourself for your failures, why not embrace your honest aims? To love, to be loved; to understand, to be understood. You cracked the bones of life and sucked out their marrow! Like Hoffmann, doomed, but driven by passion!" He shakes his head. "Would that I could say the same about myself, at the end of my life! Of course, I probably have a lot of years left in me."

There is silence again. The sky before them flickers with cloud-cloaked lightning; thunder cracks and rolls. Mailman turns, with effort, to his ex-shrink and mutters, "*Girl feet.*"

"What's that?"

"You have *girl feet*, you . . . you *Sigmund Fraud.*"

Gary Garrity holds one foot, then the other, up in the air. "You never saw my actual feet, did you. You had to make some up, not to mention these awful clothes, which by the way I would never wear. Believe me, I'd untuck this shirt if I could. But the feet, yes, they're girl feet. Big whoop, to borrow a phrase."

Silence, again.

"In fact, I think they're Lenore's feet, aren't they? That's whose they look like. Or perhaps your mother's. Your mother and Lenore have similar feet, how about that!"

In the minutes that follow, the sky does not clear. Lightning again fires, and this time the thunder is loud and startling. The gray light that day brought is again beginning to vanish. "We'll be wet soon," says Garrity.

But Mailman is already wet; it appears that he has begun to cry. He would like to cover his face with his hands, he would like to wipe his nose, but he can't. Garrity's right. He is, was, a failure. Heroic or not, he blew it.

"You could look at it that way, Albert," Garrity says. "But it won't do you much good." He stands, brushes himself off, crouches down in front of Mailman. He produces a handkerchief and uses it to dry Mailman's eyes; he holds it in front of Mailman's nose so that Mailman can blow.

"Thank you."

"You're welcome. I ask you to consider this, Albert: what is success, actually? What is a successful life? You are one person among many—a bacterium, say, in a petri dish."

"Great."

"Let's say that success, so to speak, is fame and admiration: in other words, one bacterium being held in high regard by the rest of the bacteria. But they are still in a petri dish, Albert, they are still merely bacteria. They are still just sitting in the dish on a laboratory counter, being bacteria. And so success, in these terms, is not very meaningful. A successful life, I think, should be self-defined, defined by happiness. Or, rather, satisfaction. Your life is successful if each day is fully lived. But that begs the question—"

"It begs a lot of questions."

"Yes, well, the one I'm thinking of is: What is it, then, to live fully? How fully can you live? Can you, say, climb a mountain and write a string quartet, *and* cure a disease, *and* have hot sex, all in one day? What can be expected of a single person anyway? You did what you were capable of doing, and then some. You lived as fully as it was possible for you to live. You loved badly, but you loved intensely. You left no emotional stone unturned."

"I suppose."

"There are people who are broken by the absence of love. You were broken by an excess of it. You shielded your heart from nothing."

He looks at Garrity as best he can. His neck creaks. He says, "Am I broken, then?"

"Well," Garrity says, "you aren't unbroken."

The rain has begun, too heavy to discern individual drops, and soon Mailman's face and clothes and hair are entirely wet. Beside him, the water splashes off Gary Garrity without apparent effect. "Here," says Garrity, and he reaches into his pocket for the handkerchief. He uses it to wipe the water from Mailman's face.

"Stop! I blew my nose in that!"

"It's a fresh one."

Lightning snaps the sky in two; the earth trembles. Garrity's sympathetic daubings are ineffectual, and soon they stop. Rain crashes into Mailman from all directions, it stings as it hits, like a rain of sand. Gary Garrity says, "This is good weather for soul-searching. You never know what will wash up."

The storm continues at full throttle for ten minutes. Behind it a brilliance can be discerned, lurking behind the clouds like a good idea. When the rain begins to taper, small patches of blue become visible. Rays of sun navigate along the swells of the Gulf. One of them illuminates an object, bobbing on the waves; as the object draws nearer it enlarges and clarifies into a rowboat. The rowboat, it seems, is filled with women.

"You see?" says Gary Garrity. "What did I tell you?"

Gillian stands at the prow, like Washington on the Delaware, though she endures rougher waters. Behind her Marsha and Lenore bear one oar apiece. Semma lounges in the back, with her boarder, Lily Gallagher. He is astonished, of course, and appalled. What have they been saying about him as they sailed? Indeed, when they hit land it becomes clear that they've been laughing, having a good time. (Telling jokes? About him?) Even Gillian, usually so impatient with other women, seems relaxed, confident. Certainly, it is a male fantasy, this idea—erotic, of course, but also a boon to the ego—that all the women he's gone to bed with would get together and have a good time comparing notes. But it is also a nightmare. He has been reduced to what they have in common, which is his desire, which is an embarrassment. And he didn't go to bed with Gillian! Or rather, he went to bed, her bed, but they didn't— that is, they would never have— ah, never mind. The women are all wearing red robes. This seems a vulgar touch.

Gillian hops off, youthful lightness restored, and pulls the boat up onto the sand; Lily clambers, skinny and quick, to assist. The remaining women climb out (Marsha with squinting tentativeness, like a toddler; Lenore with ungraceful alacrity; and Semma, dear Semma, robust as a lumberjack), their ray of sun following; they move up onto the drier sand and sit. A gathering of Mailman's failures. They do not appear to have noticed him slumped nearby, nor his girl-footed shrink. A glance at Garrity reveals that his girl-feet have been transformed into man-feet. They look familiar. They are, in fact, Mailman's. Garrity is amused.

"Not very imaginative. As for the ladies, Albert, they can't see you."

"Why not?"

"Do we have to go through all this again? You don't want them to."

"Oh."

The women are brightly lit. Their patch of light shifts in size and dimension with the movement of the clouds, but never leaves them. They chatter, gesturing with their hands: literally chatter, for there are no recognizable words coming from their mouths, only a rill of meaningless speech that seems to conceal some sense. It is extraordinary to watch them: Marsha, over thirty now, has got shorter hair and a new pair of glasses; she bows, hiding her face, when she smiles. Semma bears no sign of her encounter with the station wagon; she is balanced, poised; she offers her upturned palms as she talks, as if to indicate she means no harm. Mailman wants to touch her: to get up and go to her across the weedy sand. But he doesn't dare, and can't. Lily gestures jerkily, her nervousness transformed into excitement; she nods at what the others are saying, proffering quick crooked grins like aperitifs. Lenore is Lenore, restrained as always, her face austere and calm and white, a dictionary to Semma's sonnet; the poor woman wouldn't wear red if it were the last color on earth.

And Gillian is, of course, magnificent. It's the part she was born to play, leader of women. Her arms scissor the air as she tells a story; her laugh rings out the loudest. He misses her, of course; he misses them all.

"What's going on?" he whispers to Garrity.

"Shh," Garrity replies, for Semma is standing, as if to address the group. She smiles as they applaud her. Her shadow is cast across the laps of Marsha and Gillian as she places one hand on her breast and says:

> Albert was among a rash of failed romances.
> I feared sensation and deep emotion. My ex
> Had told me sex was too important and intense
> For me; I baffled Albert with my pleasure act.
> In the last years of my life, I turned to animals
> For companionship and love. The needs of cats
> Were simple; forest creatures ran away from me.
> I died before I could restore my faith in man.

The women applaud, nodding, wiping away tears. Mailman feels a stirring, a loosening; he resists it. "What the hell was that?" he mutters.

"Iambic hexameter," Garrity says. "Didn't you listen to a thing your Jim Gorman was saying? Anyway, it's the *content* that's important, Albert. Shh."

"Quit shushing me."

Lily rises, exchanges places with Semma, carefully fitting her feet into the prints the other woman has left. She bows, raises her head, begins to speak:

> At the time of Semma's death, I hadn't gotten
> Laid in seven years. On the way to Albert's
> House with Semma's cats, I resolved to nail him.

There is laughter, applause. Lily holds her hands in the air and quiet descends.

> He surprised me with his lust. I surprised
> Myself with tears. I was moved. Leaving
> Nestor, I discovered I had been restored
> To life. I suppose I used poor Albert, but
> There are far crueler ways to use a man.

There is more laughter, there are cheers. Lily seems embarrassed; she shrugs and returns to her place. Marsha stands up beside her.

For his part, Mailman is lost somewhere between dismay and relief: vaguely insulted at his extraneousness to the women's emotions; validated by the fact that they are bringing him up at all. Could it be that their feelings for him were as complicated, as conflicted, as his for them? Could it be that his doubt, his fear, are common things, bristling crows in the heart's backyard? His lower lip is growing sore from his gnawing upon it. Now Marsha has taken the stage; the circle of sunlight whitens her eyeglasses, which she adjusts on her face.

> Making Albert happy was terrific pleasure.
> Circumstances made attraction possible;
> I missed my dad. I was afraid that he would die.
> As it happens, I was right: the cancer took him
> While I was away. Even today I'm wracked
> With guilt. I cannot see Albert again. I was

> Naive. I didn't know that he could love me.
> My heart keeps its distance from men. I am lonely.

She is welcomed back into the group, hugged and touched by each. Even if Mailman could move, he would be stunned into stillness—is it really possible that he is making all this up?

"Of course it's possible," says Gary Garrity.

"I don't know these things about these women," Mailman whispers.

Garrity shifts in the sand, bracing himself for some major point. "You know more about people than you think. You're the mailman."

Lenore is standing now; the others applaud her quietly as she moves to the speaking place. "What Marsha said, that she didn't know I could love her," Mailman whispers. "What was that all about?"

"Listen to your wife," says Gary Garrity.

Lenore says:

> With Albert, I knew what I was getting, and I got it.
> I'm to blame for our divorce—he was my patient
> Until the end. I should have had respect for what
> He was, not what I might make him. Of course I never
> Cured him of his personality. That failure
> Killed my love for him. My present husband's much
> Like me, a cold perfectionist. To us, the world's
> A place to fix. I wish I could just live in it.

"It's not true!" Mailman whispers to Garrity, and then shouts it at Lenore. "It isn't true! It wasn't your fault!" The women don't hear. He turns to Garrity: "How can she say that, it isn't the way it happened, I was a jerk! How can she talk about herself like that?"

"To her," says Garrity, "that's the truth. To her, your flaws were manifestations of an emotional disorder. In her view, those flaws came of age during your breakdown, and it was then that you were under her care."

"But I was a jerk before she ever met me!"

"You told her that. But she couldn't have believed you."

Lenore is back in place in the group; the women have closed ranks and are holding hands, as if in prayer. Only Gillian is left now, and as Mailman watches she rises, seeming to float into the air, to glide over to Lenore's footprints and occupy them.

> Albert was in diapers when our mother left him
> In my charge. I feared responsibility,
> And so, to feel secure, I held and dressed him like
> A doll. In later years we touched like lovers, though
> We didn't know it at the time. Later still
> I touched my lovers as I touched my brother, and they
> Begged for more. To please them was to please poor Albert,
> But Albert, of course, was impossible to please.

Gillian does not sit down; instead, the others rise, hands still clasped, and return to the boat. Lily helps Gillian push the boat into the water, and the women climb in, laughing when they nearly capsize. They begin to drift, and the sun follows; soon they are paddling out to sea. Mailman wants to call them back, but there would be no point. He and Garrity watch until the boat is out of sight. Its ray of sun, still visible lighting the horizon, splits, and its pieces widen, and the pieces split, and soon the sky to the west is filled with light. The light comes toward shore and up onto the sand, and Mailman and Gary Garrity are washed in it. They squint. Mailman's eyes spill over.

"It's true," says Mailman.

"What is?"

"I am impossible to please. Or I was."

"But there's dignity in that, Albert. Always wanting more. The greatest among us are never satisfied, neither with the life of the mind, nor the life of the heart."

Mailman sniffs, wipes his tear-streaked cheeks on his knees. "The worst among us aren't satisfied either."

"Touché."

"And anyway, the greatest make something of it. They're not satisfied, so they do something. I didn't do anything."

"You had moments of great happiness, and they were priceless, because not much made you happy. You lived your life and never thought of ending it. Until now, I mean." He reaches into the pocket of his shorts. "Here," he says, "look at these."

Garrity places an envelope in his hands. Inside it are photos. "Hey, wait," Mailman says, "there are from my camera."

"I had them developed for you."

"But the camera's still in my—" he says, and then: "Oh, never mind." He thumbs through the pictures. Most of them are blurry and dark: the camera store clerk, the birthday party, a murky smudge that must be Gillian lying in her bed. But here is the Chapin-Caldwell fire, the majorette's baton gleaming in the park, the running feet of Kelly Vireo. Here are the developmentally disabled adults cleaning up the streets of Nestor. The drunken bus drivers. Pat Slack. He sighs.

"You see?" says Garrity. "You appreciated the world. You tried to understand it. You wanted to know how it worked."

"But I never found out."

"Who does?"

Mailman looks down at the empty bottles in the sand, at the crumpled bag with its worthless abundance of pills. "I didn't mean to take all those," he says.

"It's all right."

"The doctor told me I was dying."

"Yes. It's all right."

Garrity stands up, puts his hands on his hips. His clothes have changed: he's wearing a knit shirt now, and cutoffs. Sandals too. "Hey, thanks," he says, "this is much better. More my style."

"Where are you going?" Mailman says, suddenly nervous.

Garrity shrugs. "Wherever you happen to stash me, I suppose. But I'm going to walk that way." He points east, toward the road.

Mailman is overwhelmed by a certain heaviness. "I never meant to be a burden to anyone."

"No, nobody ever does."

"And everyone was a burden to me. I don't see why it had to be that way."

"You were a mailman, Albert," Garrity says, over his shoulder, for he has begun to walk away. "Your burden was great. Nothing sent— no idea, no object—is worth anything unless it gets where it's going." And he waves goodbye, his sandals snapping against his heels.

Nothing sent is worth anything unless it gets where it's going. Damn straight it isn't! He is reminded of his car, his poor broken car, its innards exposed in Pat Slack's garage, a device of almost boundless utility, rendered worthless—worse than worthless—by its inability to reach its destination. And what caused the breakdown? A failure of delivery: of coolant through a hose, or fuel through a fuel line, or power to a fan. A breach in a pressurized vessel, resulting in a misde-livery, the fluids releasing their energy in a diffuse blast, out into the air, instead of in a focused flow toward their intended destination, like a mailbag dropped, split, its contents scattered by a gust to whirl and flutter in the street. And the electricity that pumps the lubricant, cre-ates the spark, conveys the brake pedal's action: those agreeable elec-trons, bucket-brigading themselves down the line at lightning speed, shouting Charge!, setting things into motion. He can see Pat Slack (here, in his hand, her beaming photo), her strong body exerting itself over and under his car, her small fingers probing, her arms lifting, moving, and she herself delivers: herself to the roadside, his car to the garage, her body to the car. Her nerves deliver signals to the scabbed and callused digits, her blood delivers heat to the surface, her pores deliver sweat to the skin to cool it. Inside her, her lunch is breaking apart; the digestive juices rush to dissolve it, the constituent parts are probed, scanned, whisked away to the blood cells; the blood cells bring the food to the organs (and then it's off to the lungs for oxygen!, let's keep this thing moving!). And in her mind the neurons fire, impulses following the familiar roads, closing off ones disused, bull-dozing new ones to see where they lead: is this the problem, or this?, or could it be this?: the stray neuron firing wild, exciting its neigh-bors, setting off a grapevine of whispers, a chain letter, the burst hose reminding her: of a summer day in childhood spent overwatering the garden, her thumb pressed to the hose's end, the water fanning across the roses; of her father's heart attack, that ruptured vessel gasp-ing for blood, his white face drained; of the clarinet, her breath flow-ing over the reed; of the whistling breaths of her lover; of the incapacity of love to be expressed through the channels nature pro-vides: the love here, inside her; its object before her, mere inches from the source, yet it cannot be delivered through words, through lips and hands (these hands, grease-blackened, now tugging the ruined hose from the Escort's grip), through scent or gesture, none of it is enough. The love is here, it must be delivered, otherwise it will die (the way phone bills ripen and rot; the way catalogs shrivel, their offerings dis-continued; the way letters grow more distant from the emotions they record); yet it cannot be delivered, not all of it, not ever. But attempts must be made. There is no nobler endeavor. The face must be cupped between open palms, the eyes must be gazed into. The body must be caressed, the words whispered. It is the occupation of all existence, to ferry things from place to place, for the universe is filled with matter, and if it stays where it is, it is dead; and if it moves, it is alive. And since life exists, and since the aim of life is to continue living, and since the essence of living is to move, then movement is done. It is all—isn't it?—mail. Every particle, every force, every emotion; every thought, every object, every impulse, has its destination. Every datum is addressed with the name of its beloved: the pheromone finds its receptor, the dog roots out its bone, the sentence seeks the period at its end: and it is all mail. The love is in the molecule that tongue conveys to tongue, it is in the jolt that moves from tongue to brain; it is in the great forces, the hunger of planets for moons, of stars for planets; it is in the scented letter on pink paper, it is in the outstretched hand, it is in the blackberry pie. All of it is the mail. All of it is the mailman.

When he comes to—for he has been knocked quite flat by this train of thought, and he can feel a jagged piece of musselshell digging into his shoulderblade—the day is bright and new, the sun has filled the sky, the trees and grasses around him are dripping with rain and a silence has fallen over this glade, lagoon, what have you, and Gary Garrity is gone. There is silence, save for a low humming: a sort of thrum is more like it, with a kind of whine overlaying it, and Mailman wants to sit up to see what is making the sound and is surprised to find himself doing exactly that, sitting up without any difficulty whatsoever, and then (using his left hand pressed into the sand to support him) standing. He looks down at the hand and the arm attached to it. The hand and arm feel fine. Beneath the arm there is no lump. He peers into his shirt to make sure this is so, and there is only his chest and its attendant hairs, rising and falling in a half-panic of excitement and pleasure. He bends over to pick up his envelope of photos and wipes the sand off the paper.

A car horn honks. He spins around. Nothing; the mudded track is empty. A second honk turns him again, to face the Gulf, its waters blueing under clearing sky, and there, fifty yards or so from shore, suspended about eight inches above the water, is the largest and whitest Lexus sport utility vehicle he has ever seen, coming slowly toward him, gentle waves lapping at its underside. The windows are tinted but he can make out, behind the wheel, a figure hooded in white, its face dark inside the folds of fabric.

Mailman is not surprised. This too seems to fit. He waits for the SUV. As it approaches the beach, the figure inside raises its arm and waves to Mailman: not in a friendly way but to indicate that he should move aside. Mailman obliges, and the SUV floats into the space he has vacated and lowers itself onto the sand. Its engine (that was the thrumming) turns off and the driver's side door opens with that satisfying muffled click new car doors produce.

"You son of a bitch," says the figure as it hops out of the SUV and pushes back its hood, "you stole my shtick."

"Oh!" says Mailman. "Hello!"

"Forgot my name, didn'tcha? It's Ron, remember? Terminal leukemia? Vodka on the beach? You never told me your name but I know it now. Albert Lippincott."

"How do you know?"

"'Cause we're dead. You just know things when you're dead."

"Oh, right," says Mailman, "I guess I noticed that."

"Remember, Albert, I was gonna walk into the surf. You ripped off my beach-death routine. Anyway, I ended up firing a slug into my noggin. I didn't have the guts to drown."

"I'm sorry."

"Ah, gimme a break," says Ron—Ron Perkins, actually, the name has just come to Mailman. "*I'm* not. I was sick to death of being sick to death. Thought I might go to Hell but figured I'd take my chances."

"How'd you get the car?"

He shrugs. "Beats me. All I know's I woke up in it and I'm supposed to go around picking up people for the big ride. Wanna hop in?"

Ron Perkins climbs back into the SUV while Mailman walks around to the other side. He tries the passenger door. It is locked. He has to knock on the window to get Ron's attention. He watches a moment while Ron searches for the door lock control, and at last there is the telltale thunk. Mailman climbs in, shuts the door behind him, buckles up. He has to admit, it's a nice car: leather interior, CD and cassette, climate control. He hasn't been so comfortable in—well, years, probably.

"Albert!" comes a voice from the back seat.

It is Jared Sprain. "Hi there," says Mailman. "You're coming too?"

"Figured I'd get a ride back. Hey, can I see those snaps?" Mailman hands him the photos and he shuffles through them. "Ah, good old Nestor," Sprain says. "I'll miss it."

"Me too," says Mailman, and it's true: but he misses Nestor the way he misses a thing that was never supposed to last, like a good meal, or a movie. Like his life, behind him now, as lovely with distance as a battlefield.

Ron presses a glowing button on the dash which depicts a floating car. The car begins to rise. "Gotta go get some people who were in a boat crash. Can you look in the glovebox for my shades?"

Mailman opens the glovebox and takes out a leather eyeglass case. He slides out the sunglasses and hands them to Ron.

"Thanks. Ready?"

"Ready."

The SUV slowly rotates—no need for a K-turn when you're floating eight inches above the ground—and sets out over the Gulf, wide as any ocean, calm as a cup of tea. They drive in silence until the shaggy land is gone behind them, and there is nothing but water on all sides, its ripples still and bright. The sky is blue and dotted with clouds, and Mailman thinks that it is fine to be dead, it is fine indeed for all your problems to be behind you, forever. It does not occur to him—it will not—that he could be found on the beach and brought to the hospital. It doesn't occur to him that he might be operated on, his tumor removed, that he might lie unconscious in a pale green room with chemicals flowing through plastic tubes and into his body, a body that, against all reason (for reason has nothing whatsoever to do with it), clings filthily to life. He does not entertain the notion that nobody has been chasing him, not the postal inspectors, nor the drugstore owner, nor the police. Mailman does not consider that there might be more of life to live, more pain, more uncertainty: but even if it were so, it wouldn't crush him, really. He would not object. Despite everything fifty-seven years has taught him, he would not object to a little bit more life.

THE AUTHOR WISHES TO THANK THE FOLLOWING

PEOPLE FOR THEIR HELP WITH THIS NOVEL:

David Agruss, Lisa Bankoff, Jason Baskin, Dave Cole,

Rhian Ellis, Ed Gatch, Paul Gereffi, Brian Hall,

Margaret Halton, Katy Hope, Jack Macrae, Erica McCauley,

Mike Oates, Patrick Price, Megan Shay, Ed Skoog,

Rob Sullivan, Jim Spitznagel, Bob Turgeon, Bob Weil.

Portions of this novel have previously appeared, sometimes in

a drastically different form, in *Epoch, Granta, LitRag,* and *Tin House*.

Also by J. Robert Lennon and available from Granta Books
www.granta.com

THE FUNNIES

In his weekly comic strip, Carl Mix immortalized his family as a loving group of wisecracking imps. When he dies, his estate is divided between four of his children – in reality a dysfunctional, semi-estranged brood. The fifth, Tim, a struggling artist, is given three months to draw the strip. If he succeeds (giving up his own work) he will have inherited a gold mine; if he fails, he will get nothing.

'A poignant, wry novel, with laugh-out-loud moments' *Independent*

'A brilliant book' *Marie Claire*

ON THE NIGHT PLAIN

A beautifully written story about a man who reluctantly accepts his birthright in a sheep-ranching family riven by tragedy.

'Lennon's writing is wonderful: restrained but vivid, elegant but edgy. His is a dynamic new voice, with prose that can mesmerise'
Ann Beattie

'Lennon offers a vivid and acutely tender study of the arbitrariness of loss and the prolonged, impenetrable limbo of grief' *The Times*

THE LIGHT OF
FALLING STARS

A plane falls from the sky as a couple argue in their backyard; the whine of its engines drowning out their voices, part of the aircraft shearing through the roof of their house. A few miles away in the airport a young man anxiously awaits the arrival of his girlfriend, while in a long-empty house an old woman nervously anticipates the reappearance of a husband who left her many years before.